Praise for *Shivering World* from two
Christy Award-winning authors:

"*Shivering World* is an engrossing, thought-provoking tale, full of
intrigue and suspense, set on a world so believable and so fully
realized I felt like I was there. Good job!"

> Karen Hancock, author of
> *Arena* and *The Light of Eidon*

"*Shivering World* has it all—a strange new world, complex and believable characters, and a multi-threaded storyline. In short, exactly what
you'd expect from the incredibly talented Kathy Tyers. Top flight
science fiction that is a joy to read."

> Randall Ingermanson, author of
> *Oxygen* and *Premonition*

BY KATHY TYERS

THE FIREBIRD TRILOGY
Firebird
Fusion Fire
Crown of Fire

Shivering World

KATHY TYERS

Shivering World

BETHANYHOUSE
Minneapolis, Minnesota

Published by Bethany House Publishers
11400 Hampshire Avenue South
Bloomington, Minnesota 55438
www.bethanyhouse.com

Bethany House Publishers is a Division of
Baker Book House Company, Grand Rapids, Michigan.

Printed in the United States of America

Library of Congress Cataloging-in-Publication Data

Tyers, Kathy.
    Shivering world / by Kathy Tyers.
        p.   cm.
    ISBN 0-7642-2676-2 (pbk.)
    1. Women scientists—Fiction. 2. Mothers and daughters—Fiction. 3. Space colonies—Fiction. 4. Terminally ill—Fiction. 5. Immortalism—Fiction. I. Title.
    PS3570.Y4S54   2004
    813'.54—dc22   2003022940

To

Len and Cindy
Benj
Josh and Candace
Cheree
PT and Panya

I will not forget your grace and kindness.

KATHY TYERS is the bestselling author of *Balance Point, The Truce at Bakura,* and the FIREBIRD series. She has degrees in microbiology and education and lives in Bozeman, Montana, where she plays flute in the Bozeman Symphony Orchestra.

ACKNOWLEDGMENTS

Writing this book, I leaned on the medical expertise of Bob Flaherty, the terraforming wisdom of Steve Gillett, and the physiological and psychological work of Donald M. Joy. It took Steve Laube's persistence to keep me on track, Karen Schurrer's insight to focus and refine the project, and the Bethany House team to give it life.

Karen Hancock, thank you again for suggestions and encouragement, for setting an example of excellence and reliance on the Lord.

Len and Cindy and the clan, Bruce and Rebecca, Sam and Cindy, John and Susanna; Dave and Carolyn, Dwight and Marla, Sam and Priscilla; Mona, Matthew, Natalia, Tana, Sharon, Martha and Chris; Brett and Roberta and the girls, Cheryl, Poppa and Joyce; Ben and Jerolyn; Gayla and Basia . . . thank you for reflecting light along the way. He really does shine brightest in the darkest times.

God is Light, and in Him there is no darkness at all.
I John 1:5b, NASB

1. GRAVITY FROM BELOW

The ten-passenger landing craft's hatchway admitted a swirl of foul, frigid air. Wrinkling her nose, Graysha Brady-Phillips gripped her seat's armrests and stared out a tiny viewport. Yellowish-tan crater walls curved upward close by, like the monstrous rib cavity of some prehistoric beast that had swallowed the lander whole.

So this was Goddard, humanity's newest habitable world.

Habitable being a relative term, of course.

A tall figure stepped on board—a woman, Graysha decided after comparing shoulder and hip widths. Swathed in a belted brown coat that hung almost to her knees, the woman dangled a second hooded coat by its shoulders.

In that instant, everything Graysha had heard about planetary surfaces became real. There was no climate control out there. The very thought made her head pound . . . or was it just due to hunger?

Under the stranger's quilted parka hood, brown eyes gleamed over a proud, firm nose. "I assume you're Dr. Brady-Phillips." She had a throaty feminine voice. "I'm Ari MaiJidda, with a capital *J*. Colonial Vice-Chair." Raising her arm, she let the extra coat slide onto Graysha's lap.

Startled by the woman's abruptness and chilled by the blast of outdoor air, Graysha stood up and eased into the parka. She took special care to settle it gently on her shoulders. Her legs trembled, which she attributed partly to the mandatory three-day landing fast to prevent acceleration/

deceleration sickness. That made it especially hazardous to someone in her medical condition. But even more than the fasting, she attributed her trembling to sheer dread. Panic gripped her when she thought about standing on an unenclosed planet.

This was 2134. Born in a comfortable, enclosed space-city habitat, Graysha had never visited open air.

No wonder Gaea Terraforming Consortium offered triple frontier-duty pay to scientists and technical experts. Orbital habs provided greater opportunities and better air than any of the three established planets—dying Earth, sulfurous Venera, or not-quite-terraformed Mars.

And now Goddard....

"Are you feeling all right?" MaiJidda broke into her thoughts. "We heard you're terminally ill."

Annoyed, Graysha looked up from fastening her parka. All travelers arrived hungry! "All I need is to break my landing fast, Vice-Chair MaiJidda. Spending three days without solids leaves everyone looking a little peaked. And my complexion is fair, even under normal conditions." She had tied back her blond hair. Rare among the increasingly interracial settlers of space, it usually attracted compliments.

MaiJidda pushed back her parka hood, exposing a firm mouth and chin, and black hair cut close in a smooth dark cap. The effect was elegantly Near Eastern. "This isn't a habitat," she said. "A world that's being terraformed is only for the hardy. Unstable conditions are normal here. It is dangerous work."

"Why else would Gaea offer triple pay?" Graysha retorted. "I'm aware of the dangers. How could I not be? I'm replacing a man who was killed by the weather." She had been informed when she applied for the position that Goddard's previous soils-microbiology specialist died in a sandstorm.

Still, most of Graysha's doctors assured her she could adjust to life on Goddard if she could handle the repeated fasts of space travel. Elderly Dr. Bell differed, of course. Over and over, he warned her not to even try it.

She belted her parka. "I signed a contract," she said. "I intend to fulfill it."

MaiJidda glanced toward the hatchway. "On your head be it, then. We have made arrangements for you to see the lay of the land. I assume you've never been on a planet?"

Graysha gathered personal items from her seat's fingertip compartments. "Never."

"Ah. Then you'll enjoy this. You'll have to hurry, though. In a few hours, surface winds will make air travel hazardous. I'll have your things taken to your apartment. Here's your—" Vice-Chair MaiJidda reached deep into a pocket. "Hmm. Where is it?" As she searched pockets, her poise slipped. "I brought you a can of protein-fiber meal. You'd better not go far without it."

Graysha's flapping-empty stomach protested with an odd little noise. "You arranged an overflight?" she asked, torn between physical need and scientific curiosity. "If I'm going to be sitting down, I'll probably be all right." How *did* Ari MaiJidda know so much about Flaherty's syndrome?

MaiJidda raised an elegant eyebrow. "Are you certain?"

"I'll be all right." Five minutes into life on Goddard, already she had to prove she wasn't an invalid. Though every cell in her body clamored for nutrients—it felt like a dull general ache—she was determined not to show her weakness. Pushing up a sleeve of her brown parka and lavender pullover, she checked her forearm. Camouflaged at the center of a tiny floral tattoo, a liquid crystal tissue-oxygen button's pale green color showed all was well—enough—with her vasculature.

You can do this, she told herself. *Just don't look up.* She glanced over her seatback. The other passengers looked busy back there, so she stepped out into the aisle. A uniformed shuttle attendant pulled down her large carryon bag and strode toward the companionway. MaiJidda followed, and Graysha came behind, carrying her small duffel and trying to ignore the suffocating chemical odor drifting in from outdoors.

Beyond railed metal steps, a hovercopter stood waiting. Its white vanes, trimmed with weather-eroded red paint, hung limp. Vice-Chair MaiJidda stood down on the rock-strewn ground, arms crossed as if her time were being wasted.

Graysha wobbled down the steps, staring forward. The yellow-tan crater walls seemed taller from this angle, surrounding—as she'd been told—a roughly twenty-kilometer circle. During terraforming's first phase, icy comet remnants had been splattered onto Goddard's surface to expand its oceans, add volatile resources, and create city sites, including this crater.

A cold wind tore through her clothes, blowing in from some unimaginable distance. It was too *big* out here. And it stank: the wind, the pocket of still air she made when she turned sideways at the foot of the steps, everything.

She glanced upward—and was caught. That gray-blue dusty overhead arc consisted of pungent air and nothing more, nothing to hold the planet's air but unseen gravity, nothing to keep her inside. By daylight that firmament appeared comfortingly solid, but she'd flown down through it. One sight lingered in her memory: an unmistakable fold belt of ancient mountains, little weathered since Goddard's original atmosphere vanished into vacuum and ice. On the range's near and far sides, shadow gray craters splotched the hazy distances where the horizon curved perilously downward . . . and vanished.

She shuddered away the memory and shifted her stare. Cloud wisps trailed the sky over one edge of this crater wall, upswept like the tails of enormous ghostly horses. She might fly upward at any second. She wanted to scream. She opened her mouth. . . .

No! I won't! After one wistful glance back at the lander, she broke into a run, determined to catch up with the tall hooded woman. It felt good to stretch her legs. MaiJidda stopped to look back at her, smiling at last, nodding as if to encourage her on.

Elated, Graysha picked up her pace. Her duffel bounced against her hip. *You see, Mother? See, Dr. Bell? I can do this!*

Five meters into her dash, a tearing muscle cramp wrenched up her left thigh. With a cry she dropped her bags and fell onto glittering gravel. Rock shards ground into both hands.

No, no, not this, not now! As she moaned, her lips brushed the gravel.

Rapid footsteps crunched toward her. "Dr. Brady-Phillips?" A man skidded into view. "What happened? Are you all right?"

The cramps spread down her right leg and up her belly. Biting her lip, Graysha pressed open the torn left cuff of her lavender pullover. The tissue-oxygen implant on her forearm had gone baleful yellow. "Please," she whispered, "get me to an infirmary, if you have one. I think I know what's wrong, but—"

Before she could finish, the stranger dashed off. Graysha's legs throbbed. Ari MaiJidda strode back into sight, shaking her head as she bent down. "Oh, Dr. Brady-Phillips, this is just what I feared. We'll have a stretcher for you right away and get you on your way to . . . to a good facility." She hurried off. Moments later, Graysha heard muffled muttering, like that of a subdued argument.

The excruciating pain made it hard to concentrate on anything but her cramping legs and thighs, and now her torso. She was now cramping steadily toward her neck. Still, it seemed to Graysha that she'd been maneuvered into this attack. No food, sudden exercise—

Surely not. Why would MaiJidda deliberately do such a thing?

Please. No, she begged silently, reverting to the childhood ritual of prayer. Pungent air made a bitter taste in her mouth.

Half a minute later, two men in gray ExPress Shuttle uniforms rolled her onto a fabric litter and loaded her into a track-truck's rear compartment. Graysha clutched the stretcher's edge while the truck lumbered along. It felt good to tug one leg straight with her free hand.

The truck lurched and stopped. Then came a stretcher-carry down concrete stairs and a concrete corridor. A pigtailed woman in a drab shirt and floppy pants stopped hurrying to stare. Graysha concentrated on inhaling and exhaling.

Just past three hundred breaths, her bearers turned left and took her through a broad door. A woman's curt voice directed her transfer onto a metal gurney, and the men hurried away.

"Can you talk?" The woman rolled Graysha to slip her out of parka and pullover.

"Wait," Graysha croaked. "Emmer—my gribien . . ."

"Where?" asked the woman.

"Shirt collar."

The pigtailed stranger uncoiled the elderly pet, who had ridden this far curled tensely around Graysha's neck like half a blown tire. Emmer's limbs, clenched beneath downy black fur, almost vanished. "You keep a lab animal for a pet?" The woman laid Emmer on Graysha's exposed stomach, removed Graysha's black stretch tights, and prodded her legs.

Stifling a protest, Graysha cupped one hand over Emmer. "Muscle cramps. It's . . . Flaherty's syndrome." Flaherty's was supposed to kill her slowly and painlessly over the next twenty terrannums.

But without adequate medical care, she could go into shock and never recover.

The woman draped a white cloth over Graysha's torso, gribien and all. Peering past her, Graysha spotted a diploma that identified her as Yael GurEshel, M.D. At least Axis Plantation's medical facility included one fully trained physician.

Dr. GurEshel sat down on a stool, swiveled it away, and raised both arms to a countertop. Her long pigtail swayed down her broad back. "We have a complete med-op database, including your personal records from the shuttle's memory bank. They beat you by ten minutes."

Graysha shut her eyes, wondering if Yael GurEshel worked for Gaea Consortium or was a Lwuite colonist. "I need sugars, and an antispasmodic would help. But please hurry. I—"

"I said we have your records."

Gripping the metal railing that edged her gurney, Graysha pushed both legs away as hard as she could. They wouldn't straighten.

Something clattered beside the doctor's station. Startled, Graysha curled into a tight ball. Emmer dug in, too, pinching her stomach with strong claws. Graysha uncurled to give Emmer breathing room.

Dr. GurEshel pulled something from the cubicle, then moved toward Graysha's left arm with an alcoholic-smelling swab. "This is a muscle relaxant and a mild short-term sedative." She threaded a needle into a vein, injected fluid, then lifted one of Graysha's hands.

Slowly the cramps let go, reversing from torso down to her toes, though her palms and forearms stung as if scalded. With a trembling breath, Graysha gathered enough control to look around.

She lay at one end of a tiny room, under glowing overhead panels. At the gurney's head, GurEshel's computer sat on a countertop made of— could it be? Yes, it was—concrete! But the computer looked as modern as any at the high-school micro department she had left behind.

GurEshel looked about forty, and her pigtail dangled over well-padded shoulders. Flinging the pigtail aside, she slid her hand up Graysha's arm and fingered the tissue-oxygen implant. "We'll start a drip-pak as soon as we're sure you're not reacting to the first injection. Breathe normally, please."

A sharp medical scent of ethanol and phenol permeated the room. Her legs continued to release while Dr. GurEshel passed a handheld diagnostic imager back and forth across her forearm and hand. The physician's brown smock fit a little too snugly, and it was wrinkled across one side as if she just leaned against something.

"Might I have something to eat?" Graysha asked.

The physician turned her head, showing a generously rounded nose. "There will be sugars in the drip-pak," she said. "You've just broken a landing fast, and that's work enough for your stomach right now."

"I haven't broken my fast." Words slurred over Graysha's thickening tongue.

"Vice-Chair MaiJidda brought you a can of protein-fiber meal."

Graysha shut her eyes and exhaled. "She forgot it, or so she said."

Yael GurEshel tightened her lips. "Oh? All right, I'll start the drip-pak now." Another needle bit. GurEshel taped the fluid-filled pressure bag to Graysha's arm, and then the cubicle clattered again. GurEshel extracted a tray and took a grip on Graysha's left forearm. More pain followed, but Graysha was turning too wobble-jointed to react. After a minute, the pig-tailed woman displayed forceps that held a five-centimeter stone shard. "Impact glass—or plain, sharp lava. I'd guess that hurt."

"There's more in my hands." Graysha tried to smile, tried to lift her other palm.

The physician seized it. "Just relax."

Graysha tipped back her head and stared at a pale brown concrete wall. There would be time to worry about Ari MaiJidda once this sweet sleepy dizziness wore off. "No problem."

"It *is* rather disconcerting about your predecessor, isn't it?" GurEshel murmured, digging for an elusive shard.

"Dr. Mahera?" Graysha asked dreamily. "Sandstorm. Yes."

Yael GurEshel set down her probe and leaned close. "Dr. Brady-Phillips, try to concentrate. MaiJidda told you nothing more?"

"Sandstorm," Graysha insisted, fighting the sedative in an attempt to focus. The unblinking stare of Yael GurEshel's dark brown eyes probably would have unnerved her another time. "Frontier pay?" she asked.

"It will wait." The physician's face blurred as her voice faded out. "But before you check out of the Health Maintenance Facility, someone must speak with you. . . . "

"This is Vice-Chair MaiJidda," said the deep voice on Dr. Yael GurEshel's audi line. "We can only hold that shuttle lander twenty minutes longer or we'll miss the launch window. Dr. Brady-Phillips is sick enough to warrant sending her away, isn't she?"

Yael GurEshel frowned at her bare yellow-tan office wall. "Too sick," she answered. "She won't be able to travel for at least a month. You had no business holding back food—"

"A month?" The Vice-Chair's voice rose. "Cancel that, Doctor. Do you realize whose daughter she is?"

Yael GurEshel rocked her chair away from the desktop console. "I might not realize?"

"Listen," MaiJidda said softly. "I had only two hours to find out what would bring on that attack. The idiot lander captain insisted on sending her to you instead of putting her back on board. Scared of his legal liability. If there's no food in her stomach, we could still put her back on that shuttle. Or . . . Yes—we'll put her back on board, regardless. Acceleration sickness is messy, but it isn't dangerous."

Irritated, Yael drummed her fingers. "You aren't listening, Ari. In her condition, the stress of takeoff and acceleration could be fatal. The Hippocratic oath does not permit me to deliberately endanger her life, to say nothing of what we would stir up if Novia Brady-Phillips's daughter died through our malpractice. She must remain here for at least a month."

After several seconds, MaiJidda sighed heavily onto her own pickup, making Yael's desk speaker roar. "All right. I'll release the lander."

The line went dead. Yael GurEshel gripped her desk's edge with both hands, wishing this long Goddarday had never dawned. She would not knowingly endanger her newly arrived patient, but neither would she become emotionally involved.

Ari MaiJidda was absolutely correct: Novia Brady-Phillips's daughter must not remain on Goddard.

2. VARBERG

An hour later, Grasha rested with both hands bandaged and a fresh drip-pak taped to one arm. Emmer slept next to her shoulder, a warm spot alongside her neck. The clinic smelled of phenol and ethanol: sharp, clean, sterile. Natural daylight shone through a window that attendants had adjusted to minimal polarization at her request.

Outside, a yellowish plain blotched with vegetative browns and greens stretched out under the red-orange sun. She recognized two metal hulks, slowly chomping their way toward the crater wall, as mechanical crop tenders. What grew out there, unsheltered in the cold? About fifteen kilometers in the distance, a highway switchbacked up a sheer stony wall to escape her range of vision. Goddard's towns were all built deep below the highland surface, inside impact craters, where air collected thickest and the winds didn't blow so hard.

Graysha took a leisurely sip of water from her bedside glass, gagged, and set the glass back down. It tasted like dead algae and processing chemicals, just like the outside air. Concrete walls, grim and dismal, closed her in.

What was she doing here? She was a teacher with financial difficulties, not a soils specialist. It had been luck beyond her fervent prayers when Gaea accepted her application—or maybe not. Maybe Dr. Bell was right after all. Goddard was no place for a person in imperfect health.

She needed the money, though, and according to her Gaea contract, this position would be mostly lab work, not physically demanding. With what she intended to save over three terrannums at frontier triple wages, she might pay for ... Well, first she needed to settle debts created by a messy lawsuit-entangled divorce, but she had additional plans for the money.

She'd heard rumors about Goddard—stories that flew in the face of everything her mother preached, rumors that they practiced gene-healing. If she could find a geneticist willing to try to help her despite her mother's notoriety, then someday she might have normal noncarrier children. In Flaherty's syndrome—a mutation that first appeared at Newton Habitat— a protein-production function did not shut down at the end of capillary growth. Fifteen to twenty Earth-referent terrannums from now, nutrients and oxygen would no longer pass out of her bloodstream through micropores in the thickened capillary walls. No matter how much she ate, she would starve to death at the cellular level. There was no cure, no real hope for herself. . . . But at twenty-four, married only once and still childless, she could at least live productively and well—and hope to give her next husband children who might outlive them both.

She had to find medical help, legal or illegal. Now. Her mother, a high-ranking investigator for the United Sovereignties and Space Colonies' Eugenics Board, was starting to drop pointed hints about surgical sterilization—and she had the legal authority to see it done.

Graysha reached up to stroke Emmer, whose smooth black pelt parted under her fingertips. A fuzzy-haired stowaway caught on board the ExPress shuttle had been ferried down with her. Did he, too, come seeking the mysterious people they called Lwuites?

Openly, Goddard's colonists—a medico-religious sect claiming fifteen thousand adherents—had started fetal work back when they lived in Einstein Habitat, trying to decrease violently aggressive tendencies in the human race. Hearsay was far more interesting. It hinted that the Lwuites fled Einstein—the second largest hab in the Alpha Centauri complex— hoping to find a place where they might repair the genetic mutations that plagued space dwellers.

If Goddard's colonists were illegal homogenegineers, they would almost certainly question her intentions, especially since her mother and the Eugenics Board would pose them a genuine threat.

Graysha's door swung open, and another stranger appeared. A huge man, without the defined look of muscle, he held his left hand behind his back. Brown hair grayed at his temples and around the back of his head. "Dr. Brady-Phillips?" he asked, drawing out her name in almost a drawl. "Oh, I'm sorry. Did I wake you?"

"No," she said warily. Who was this? "Hello."

"Will Varberg." He thrust forward his right hand to clasp hers, saw the bandages, and drew back. "You really took a nasty spill, didn't you? I'm head of the Micro floor, your new supervisor. Welcome to Goddard. I hope things go better for you from here on out." He swung forward his left hand to present a nosegay of yellow and orange flowers. His thumb ring, which looked like a three-carat synthetic emerald, sparkled under brilliant room lights.

She smiled. "Thank you. Here, stick them in my water. It isn't fit to drink." She waved a stiff hand toward the bedside stand.

He reached for the tumbler. "It tastes vile, all right. I've learned not to notice."

"I'm looking forward to that."

"When do you get the mummy wrappings off?"

That sounded rude, but she played along, displaying her bandaged palms. "My fingers are free, so I could use a computer already. What is that smell in the air and water? Is it ether?"

"By-products of first generation bacteria, mostly. I assure you, within a day you'll barely notice it."

Graysha doubted his assurance. She'd made a hobby of scents. She even brought her perfuming kit to Goddard. "What's your specialty, Dr. Varberg?"

He tipped back his head and looked down at her. "Microbial genetics. Say," he said a little too casually, "are you related to the Brady-Phillips who—"

"Yes," she said, "the Eugenics Commissioner is my mother." *Novia's daughter,* she thought bitterly. *All my life, I'll be Novia's daughter.* Novia Brady-Phillips's Eugenics Board was responsible for enforcing the ban on human gene tampering, and geneticists tended not to like her. The Eugenics Board watched and regulated and harassed them constantly.

Varberg tossed off a shrug. "I've had a report on your condition. They think they found the problem."

"Oh?" Graysha smoothed a thin scratchy blanket over her flimsy gown.

"Repeated fasting from all the shuttle transfers," he explained, "plus weeks at low shuttle-gravity. Then you tried to run before your fast-breaking meal."

Obviously. But until she knew Will Varberg better, she wouldn't voice her suspicion of the colonial officer. One group or the other—terraformers or colonists—might help her.

Varberg continued, "Very little research has been done on Flaherty's sufferers, but it looks as if you've provided new data."

"I'm ecstatic." Graysha laughed quietly. "I just hope they'll give me researcher's pay and won't feed me gribby chow." Trying to speak through the cotton mouth of muscle relaxants was tricky. "I'm pumped so full of blood sugar I'm a vampire's holiday dessert."

Dr. Varberg wheeled the room's single chair toward Graysha's bedside. "How are you feeling?" He sat down and scooted the chair even closer, leaning one beefy arm on her bedside table and the other against the railing of her bed.

Intimidated by his proximity, Graysha pushed away from him, toward the wall and the other railing. "I'm only tired. And ve-ry relaxed. My legs think they ran a 10K race. Have you . . ." She hesitated, embarrassed again. She hated thinking of herself as an invalid. "Have you asked the doctors when I'll be well enough to go to work?"

"They want you to spend one night under observation. I've had your things sent to Gaea employee housing." From an inside pocket, he pulled a magnetic key strip. "Someone will escort you to your apartment when you're ready."

Graysha glanced at the laminated strip. "Dr. Varberg, I'm sorry about this. If I'd guessed—"

Varberg laid the key on the concrete bedside table and waved away Graysha's objection. "Don't skip any meals and they say you'll be fine." He scooted the bouquet closer to her, deftly plucking a petal out of one yellow lilium. "They don't smell good, but they look nice, don't they?" he asked in that deep, oddly lazy voice.

The powdery odor was a pleasant change from ethanol, phenol, and medicines. "I can't believe picking flowers is allowed."

"I grow them myself. Do save the wilted heads for me, if you would." He lounged in her bedside chair. "So you've put in a bit of soils work, besides your university credits?"

Of course he would wonder why Gaea had recruited a high-school teacher. She did, too. Once, briefly, she even suspected her mother had something to do with it.

But that couldn't be. Novia always kept her close, watchable, shielded from risks. It felt good to have so much distance between them. "Here and there," she answered. "One can't actively pursue all one's interests."

"True. I particularly liked your thesis work with nitrifying bacteria. We've set up a terrarium series in the main lab, hoping you'll want to continue that course of study."

Distracted, she stared at his broad hand. He pulled out a second petal and dropped it beside the other one. Did he even realize he was doing it?

She had another thought. If Will Varberg specialized in genetics, what would it take to convince him to repair her damaged twelfth chromosomes—how much money, how much reassurance that she wouldn't report him back to Novia?

No. That was layman's thinking. A microbial geneticist wouldn't be equipped to deal with human problems.

Another petal dropped on the bedside table as Varberg talked on about his own educational history. She wouldn't risk asking him, she decided. The Eugenics Board's policy was to defrock a convicted homogenegineer all the way down to the BS level. As for the genegineered subjects, they were punished with sterilization—no reversible tubal lig, but a whole-body irradiation that rendered every cell unusable for cloning, sentencing the victim to slow death by all kinds of cancers. The 2030 Troubles, a dark time in human history, anathematized human genetic tampering forever. Except for a few patients legally cured of specific diseases, genetically altered individuals no longer had human rights. By USSC definition, they weren't even human.

There went another petal. Varberg looked her way, then pulled back his hand.

"I'd be pleased to work with nitrifiers again," she said, pushing one thumb against her palm. The pain medication had to be wearing off, because it hurt.

"We do need you primarily on soils. No problem with that?"

"I get along well with soils. So long as I don't fall in them."

He smacked his hands together. "Perfect. It will be good to have Jon Mahera's lab filled again and to get back to full efficiency." He gave Graysha an exaggerated wink. "You might as well go back to sleep. If they let you out tomorrow, I'll see you then."

She glanced back down at the table. Beside her bouquet lay five ruffled yellow and orange petals. They cast peculiar shadows on dull gray metaltopped concrete. "The flowers are wonderful, Dr. Varberg."

Her physician, Yael GurEshel, visited again before dinnertime. After examining her hands, she replaced the dressings with small bandages. "You're healing more rapidly than we anticipated, given your condition," she said, folding her hands across her broad waist.

"Really, Doctor, I'm not an invalid."

"Mmm. Well, you may report to work at the Gaea station tomorrow. You should be fine, so long as you don't fast again."

Graysha flexed her hands. "This attack doesn't bar me from space travel, does it?"

GurEshel raised an eyebrow. "You should remain on Goddard for at least a month, though of course I cannot force you to stay. I doubt ExPress would even board you. Another three-day fast before your metabolism stabilizes would likely bring on a repeat attack. When you leave Goddard, I recommend that you remain a month at Copernicus Hab before traveling on and at every transfer point thereafter."

"A month at each transfer point?"

"Exactly." The stout physician nodded. "We would also like you to keep careful symptomatic records. For research, you understand."

Reminded again that she was not just a Ph.D. but a lab subject, too, she sympathized with Emmer and all her furry kin. People who considered her an invalid—slowly dying instead of rising in her field—would not respect her as a professional or as a woman.

But keeping her own research records sounded reasonable. They might help someone else some day. "I'll do that, of course."

"Now," said GurEshel, "about Jon Mahera."

Graysha shifted under the scratchy blanket. "What about him, Doctor?"

GurEshel's round eyes had a direct, honest intensity. "You ought to know we're in the middle of a murder investigation."

Stunned, Graysha crossed her arms across her chest. "Murder? I thought he'd gone out in a—"

"Sandstorm. Yes. After he was expressly told the weather would be safe for a trip upside."

False information was potentially as deadly as hard radiation. She struggled to put down her fears and retain professional poise. "Don't they know who told him so?"

Yael GurEshel shook her head. "Vice-Chair MaiJidda says current leads point to one of his colleagues. Professional jealousy can be a frightening thing."

"Oh," Graysha said quietly, seeing Will Varberg's nervous petal pulling in an ominous new light. Perhaps her new boss was a murderer, or maybe he feared he might be targeted next.

Or maybe Jon Mahera discovered something the new soils specialist also might learn, something the Lwuite people didn't want him to know, and they killed him for it. If members of this sect were mercy criminals, some of them might silence anyone they considered a threat.

In that case, Graysha could be their next victim. A final thought knocked the wind out of her: just like Ari MaiJidda, Dr. GurEshel was trying to scare her away—and was just about succeeding.

Graysha had a sudden urge to ask GurEshel to send her back to Einstein Hab via the next supply shuttle, regardless of medical risk.

Atop the crater wall, something flashed a slow rhythm. A navigational beacon for robot crop tenders, maybe, or for colonial air travel. The slow, steady pulse reminded Graysha that as time slipped away, her capillary walls thickened.

She needed the Lwuites' help. She had to stay on.

Smiling weakly up at GurEshel, she said, "Thank you for the information."

GurEshel stepped toward the open door. "Be careful, Dr. Brady-Phillips."

"I will," she answered, stroking Emmer's warm fur. *God help me, I will.*

3. STOWAWAY

Trevarre Chase-Frisson LZalle had hoped to make a break for it as soon as the ten-passenger lander touched down. Instead, ExPress Shuttle crewmen held him until the legitimate passengers had disembarked and then handed him over to three hooded characters who forced him into a waiting track-truck. Alone in the back, he hunched down on the uncomfortable seat, clenching both hands beneath his arms to keep them warm as the truck bounced across the crater bottom. *Looks like you've got yourself another planet, Trev. And another trip without a view.*

Oh, shut up. He'd been told that talking to himself—worse, answering back—was a sign of instability, but he didn't care anymore. This frigid planet smelled worse than his father's crimping fluid.

One more place where he *can take out his temper. . . .*

Hating the thought, Trev exhaled through his mouth and made frosty dragon breath. By the time his father finished with this place, a dragon might as well have passed through. The last time Trev ran away . . .

No, he mustn't sympathize with the people here. They could take care of themselves. He needed to save his own ugly hide. His three escorts didn't speak during the ten-minute ride, and if they couldn't be decent to a homely eighteener, he didn't have to put on manners.

They marched him down into a broad, bright tunnel sheltered from the wind and almost warm. His stiff, chilled legs hurt. "Left," said the smallest escort. Trev took the corner, saw a rough-walled stairwell going up, and ascended with them. He ran a finger along one wall, shuddering at the sharp pebbles sticking out through concrete. He was getting used to a furtive lifestyle, had even befriended a softhearted recycling tender aboard the last ship. After its stop at Copernicus, here in the Eps Eri system, the shuttle had been scheduled to head back for Barnard's Star and Halley Hab, making only one "local" stop.

But before that stopover, Corporation snoops caught him. So primitive or not, Goddard had to take him.

They'd regret it.

He stomped on upward. At the third landing, his escorts took him across a secretarial room into a smaller office. With the temperature in the metric twenties up here—or were they primitive enough to be using Fahrenheit degrees?—they peeled off their coats. The smallest man sat down on the desk chair. He wasn't all that short. Trev probably had only five centimeters on him. Small, strong features, look-at-me-I'm-in-control posture. Trev's father had looked a bit like this, back when Blase LZalle did classical and wanted to be "pretty" to do the "pretty music," as little Trev had called it.

The man muttered at a pocket memo, then motioned Trev to a chair. A bleak, bumpy horizon much like Venus's, with something that looked like a pipeline running toward it, extended outside the office window.

One tall goon stayed at the open door. Workers in the adjoining office seemed quiet, listening.

You're dead meat, you dimbrains, Trev thought, *and you haven't got a clue.*

The man behind the desk finally spoke up. "I'm Lindon DalLierx," he said, elbows resting on the— Oh chips, the desk was *concrete.* "Chairman of Colonial Affairs. The shuttle company contacted us by relay. We know you stowed away shipboard, wouldn't give a name or other identification, and they're working on tissue typing. I'm not affiliated with Gaea nor ExPress Shuttles. I'm a colonist. In case you don't realize what that means, this is our world. We've contracted Gaea Consortium to terraform it; we've set up shuttle service. We'd appreciate some straight answers."

Trev crossed one leg over the other knee and laced his fingers on one thigh, letting the man stare at his grotesquely blotched brown skin, widely spaced eyes, and uncontrollable hair, worn long in defiance of style and his famous father. His doughy body wasn't yet fat, but it was definitely smelly after three months living the ship-rat's life.

And he sure could use something to eat. "Do you suppose we could make some kind of a deal?" he asked. Maybe this time, things would turn out different.

"Deal?" The man frowned. "What did you have in mind?"

DalLierx didn't look old enough to act so stuffy. For one instant, Trev was glad the guy had gotten in Blase LZalle's way.

But not really. There must be some way out—for them both. "I'll tell you about myself if you'll let me, um ... I think the phrase is *give me sanctuary*. Don't tell anyone I'm here, and don't send me back." *Please,* he added mentally as the specter of cosmetic reconstruction brandished a scalpel against his mind's eye. Blase wanted his son's defective face fixed. Wanted him pretty. Even if it hurt—hurt him and everybody who helped him try to escape. Trev had grown to like the way he looked.

DalLierx glanced over Trev's shoulder, probably at the goon by his door. "Maybe you don't know what the fuel to ship a hundred-kilo human body as far as the nearest habitat costs. You'd have to earn passage up out of the gravity well. But if you'd like to live out of confinement, you'll need to answer some questions."

"And then maybe you'll let me stay? Call me X, then. I could give you any name I wanted, you know."

"Ex. First name or last?" DalLierx asked, straight-faced.

Trev gritted his teeth, then let his chin relax. "Actually, I'm traveling under the name George Smith."

"I know. I don't think I'll bother asking where you live. Are you of legal age, Ex?"

If only! "In some places."

"Here on Goddard, the voting and marriage ages are twenty and sixteen."

Sixteen? "Yipe. I'm not wife shopping. No, then."

DalLierx worked his keyboard. "Not yet twenty. Teeners work eight-hour circadays. What can you do?"

"Do? What do you mean, do?"

"Work experience?"

Trev frowned. "I don't work. I've been in school."

"What level?"

This was awkward. "It, uh, varies. I had a tutor."

As DalLierx swiveled back to face him, Trev spotted a row of small, primitive clay sculptures at one end of his desk, near some fat hardbound books.

Another proud father. Oh, joy.

"No work experience while in school," DalLierx observed. "Your family has money."

Trev scratched one arm through his black pullover. This interview was getting more irritating by the moment.

DalLierx raised an eyebrow. "Do I need to phrase that as a question for you to answer it?"

"No. I didn't have to work."

"And you dislike authority."

Trev rocked forward and started to stand up. "I dislike all these questions."

"Sit" came a voice behind him. DalLierx didn't flinch but picked up something that looked like a pen and twirled it between the fingers of one hand.

Trev sat back down. On his left, a window revealed some sort of crop fields. Back home, the only exterior views were of scummy lakes under sulfurous clouds.

He couldn't go back. He had to convince DalLierx to let him stay. Hide him, give him a bed. Surely they needed more colonists. "I don't eat much," he offered. His stomach growled as he said it.

DalLierx rubbed his face. As he lowered his hand, Trev decided the man was even prettier than Blase's classical look. Unlike Blase, he probably was born that way.

Did he have a sympathetic streak to match that face? "Really," Trev added.

DalLierx shook his head. "Obviously, you don't understand. We don't grow food to share out. Our margin of survival is too slim to support freeloaders. If you don't want to be locked up on survival rations until your family sends money for your fare home, you'll work." He made a sweeping gesture with one hand. "So give me some kind of information on your background."

The knots tightened in Trev's stomach, and his hope for sympathy dissipated like so much smoke. If these people were cash poor, they might try for ransom money. That would ruin them all—Trev, along with DalLierx and his goons. "I'll . . . be glad to work." He tightened his arm muscles to make them bulge. "I'm pretty strong." Looking out the window, he added, "There's probably something I can do for you."

"You'll work, on trial. I don't know what you're running from, and"— he raised one hand as if he hoped Trev might start explaining—"maybe I don't have to know. You don't act criminal, just spoiled. That's likely enough, since there's plainly enough money in the picture that you're afraid someone will come this far to get you."

If he only knew how much money! Trev relaxed the fists in his lap. He had to stop giving information away. DalLierx was no dimbrain. Maybe he knew the signs from experience. Maybe he grew up rich, too.

"The shuttle company will try to extract fare from your family,"

DalLierx said. "I'm sorry, but that simple fact means your people will find out where you are eventually."

You think you're sorry now? In that case, the countdown to disaster had already started. There had to be some way of warning them—

No. He could only hope to save himself. This looked like a big enough planet. All he'd need was a place to hide. "All right," he said, meekly ducking his head.

"Have you spent any time with animals?" DalLierx asked.

"Animals?" Gruesome thoughts sliced through his brain. "Don't tell me you don't clone your meat."

DalLierx laughed softly. "If our power went down, tissue tanks would die. You can't hitch a tissue tank to pull a plow, either. And halfers breed themselves. Happily."

Trev's mouth twitched. He tried not to smile.

"So. Have you worked with animals?"

"'Fraid not."

"No pets? Anything?"

"Animals"—Trev echoed the nanno who raised him—"are dirty."

DalLierx shot a glance at the door goon again. "If dirt's a problem, you chose the wrong world to stow away to."

He hadn't chosen it. He didn't dare insult DalLierx by saying so, though. He folded both hands in his lap and tried to look appealing. Fat chance, with a face like his.

"Ex—or George, or whatever your name really is—you remind me of my brother." DalLierx leaned back in his tall chair. "He wanted to stay at Einstein Hab when the rest of us moved out to Goddard."

This looked like his own chance to get information. "What about him?"

"He was tired of the family line," DalLierx said. "Chafing to be anything other than what he was, but he was underage, so he had to come with us."

Okay, so there was a family story. There might be money. "What's your point?"

"Why here? Why not the bright lights?"

This man's guesses—or conclusions—were downright uncanny. Trev exhaled slowly. "I don't like bright lights."

DalLierx's mouth crinkled as he said, "This gets more interesting all the time."

Trev blew out another breath. At least this room was warm enough not to give him a condensation cloud.

"You've had enough bright lights to dislike them?" DalLierx pressed.

Trev stared out the window.

"All right." DalLierx's voice hardened. "Frankly, I don't want you in with my people. They have to get dirty to survive, and that's a fact of colonization." He made a few jabs at his pocket memo. "Three days' confinement, disciplinary, just because it's USSC law. Then I'm assigning you to the Gaea building. They can probably use untrained help. It may be dirty," he added, mocking the word by accenting both syllables, "but it will be indoor dirt. It's time you learned how people live without money to waste or bright lights to hide from."

That stung. "You don't want my family mad at you, DalLierx."

The man laid down his pen, or whatever it was, and glared up from under those narrow, dark eyebrows and long eyelashes. "Is that a threat?"

"I didn't choose to come here," Trev said. "Maybe if you send me away, you'll—" DalLierx's scowl made him change course. "Never mind," he muttered.

"Listen," said the other man. "I'd love to send you back where you came from. We don't need bodies that aren't our own. We're barely storing reserves as it is. I've been honest with you, even if you've weaseled your way around the truth. You're an imposition, but it would be expensive to send you back. You're lucky to be alive, *George*."

No one had ever spoken that way to Trevarre Chase-Frisson LZalle. "So are you, DalLierx."

DalLierx beckoned to the door goon. "You probably haven't heard," he said, "but shuttle crews used to jettison stowaways. Into space."

Appalled by the image, Trev followed two tall goons to a bare little underground room, where they left him an amazing fast-breaking meal: half a tureen of bean soup, three shades of cheese, and a chunk of fresh brown bread. After stuffing himself, he felt hope seep back into his brain. It helped him think again. He pushed up off the floor and grasped the door handle. When it didn't shock him, he applied pressure. It stayed stuck. Locked.

Okay, scratch that possibility. A quick escape would've been hard to trust anyway.

He sank down on the thin mattress, thinking things through. He needed information, and he couldn't wait three days to get it. He had to find someplace to hide. Goddard had to be better than Venus—or Earth, where his father's cosmetic surgeon waited.

Venus had cooled enough to support human life under domes, but to call it beautiful, a person would have to love poisonous seas and roiling, boiling clouds. Dome lights suited his father. They could be darkened at any hour.

Trev preferred natural light. He'd run to Mars the first time. Terraforming made it marginally habitable, but it proved too close. Blase found him only two weeks later. He'd hired agricultural and financial experts and wiped the small community that had harbored his runaway son right off the maps.

Could he take on Gaea Terraforming Consortium?

Trev clenched his hands in his lap and considered the magnitude of that vast commercial enterprise. In 120 terrannums, Gaea Consortium had run up its own problems. Terraforming was harder than building space habitats—and didn't pay off as quickly. It was also dangerous. The Messier project, a planet Gaea terraformed and abandoned in the Barnard's system, had been a disaster. And rumor said Goddard's temperature, which ought to be rising, was going back down.

If there's a way to make Gaea abandon one more Mars-type world, he reflected bleakly, *Blase LZalle will find it. Any corporation can be leveraged from inside. Even clear out here in Eps Eri's neighborhood.*

Oh chips. Gripping his head with both hands, Trev wracked his brains for a plan.

4. DALLIERX

After Graysha put down a huge breakfast, an uncommunicative pig-tailed woman led her from the Health Maintenance Facility out through a wide tunnel into a broad parklike area with a domed roof. Graysha paused and looked up. "What's this place?" she called.

The woman, already several paces ahead, spoke over her shoulder. "We refer to it as the hub."

It was easy to see why. Several paved routes crossed it like concrete spokes, edged on both sides by strips of closely clipped grass. Heavy benches hunched here and there on the lawns, looking like solid citizens tending the trees and flower beds, separating routes. She took a deep, appreciative breath. The cool air smelled of sweet, fertile soil: *Nocardia asteroides,* she guessed from its odor.

Why, on this world where soil-building was such a critical issue, would someone kill a soils specialist? Professional jealousy, or fear of discovery?

Graysha's escort led out again, following one paved route into a nearly cylindrical corridor. Their footsteps echoed off pale, unattractive yellow-tan concrete. Heavy machines stood parked to one side, some with joints leaking thick black lubricant. A scorched-metal smell hung in the air around them.

Not a leisure settlement, she observed, no matter how pretty a hub they built it around.

Another stairway took her back into her own element. Site Supervisor

Melantha Lee, a fiftyish woman with Asian eyes, took over escort duty and walked her into an open laboratory. Graysha looked around momentarily and then leaned against a wall in relief, still clutching her drinking glass of marigolds. "No concrete."

"Only the walls and floor."

Glancing past Lee's iron-gray curls, Graysha saw *Jon Mahera* still posted disconcertingly on her door.

"Gaea Consortium does not believe in slighting frontier employees," Dr. Lee went on. She pushed a gray panel on one side of the lab, and it rippled. "Nonflammable fabric. You can—"

"I hear voices," boomed a familiar basso from beyond Lee. "Hello in there."

Will Varberg sauntered in to stand beside the site supervisor. He stood head and shoulders taller than Dr. Lee and probably outweighed her twice. Browncloth trousers like the nurses wore showed under Dr. Lee's lab coat, but Varberg dressed like a well-off habitant in fine gray woolens, and he smelled of scented soap. Eyeing his thumb ring, Graysha fingered a naked spot on her own knuckle. She'd left jewelry behind. Too heavy, both with mass and with memory.

Varberg tipped back his head to peer down his nose, and Graysha wondered if he needed new lens grafts. "Good morning," he drawled, and she clasped his hammy hand. "Are you sure you're feeling better?"

"I'm fine, thank you, Dr. Varberg."

From the startled look on Lee's and Varberg's faces, Graysha guessed Emmer had finally raised her ears. "Emmer is my family," she explained. "Just a lab gribien."

"It doesn't do anything." Varberg wrinkled his nose.

"She's warm, clean, soft, and omnivorous. Don't worry," Graysha added. "Most of the time, Emmer lives curled up on my bed pillow. I won't bring her to work very often once I have an apartment to leave her in."

"We'll check you into Gaea housing during lunch break." Dr. Lee took one step toward the door. "Chairman DalLierx wants to show you a reconnaissance vidi this morning at nine, so you'll have to head out almost immediately. I'm sorry we had to cancel your overflight. Have a pleasant day." Lee picked up a notebook from the lab's countertop island and walked out.

Varberg sat down where the notebook had lain and rotated the marigolds a quarter turn. "It sounds like this will have to be the quick tour, then."

Graysha bent to examine a glass-walled incubator between Varberg and the window.

"You should wear your hair down," Varberg said abruptly. "Backlight through blond hair is beautiful."

Hearing that kind of talk from a stranger made her uncomfortable. She lifted a hand to snug her hair tie. "It flops into my face when I work."

Varberg hopped down from the countertop and motioned her into a concrete cubicle at one end of the lab. A smaller polarized window broke the office's outer wall, and up a side wall nestled a composite-top desk. On its right end near the window, a keyboard and display were built into the desk itself, a conformation Graysha thought she recognized. "Is this computer a microfluidic?"

Will Varberg tipped his head back and smiled. "As Lee said, Gaea believes in taking care of its employees."

Graysha touched one key. The screen lit briefly, then blanked. She shook her head. Even on triple-pay frontier duty, MF computers cost two terrannums' wages.

Wait. Varberg hadn't been in the lab when Dr. Lee said that about the Consortium. He must have eavesdropped from the hall. She eyed him with distaste.

"You'll need a five-character password to access the Gaea net." He pulled out her chair and typed +BLOND+. "How's that?"

She didn't like the password, and she especially didn't like his knowing what access word she'd use, but this didn't seem like the time to object. "Fine," she said, making a mental note to change it later.

He touched a few more pads, and the word vanished. "That will get you onto Gaea net and the colony's general system. The Lwuites have their own net, but ours works like any university system within USSC jurisdiction."

Just like home. "Who monitors?"

"No one, supposedly."

She didn't believe that for a moment.

"It's automated," he continued. "But be careful around those colonists, Graysha. Particularly Chairman DalLierx. I have suspicions about him." He glanced at Mahera's nameplate on the door, reinforcing the hint. "I'll leave you and your computer to get acquainted." Stepping back toward the doorway, the big man paused. "Suleiman and Ilizarov are both working today, so introduce yourself when you get a chance. Oh, and cover up if you go outside. The high last night was fifteen below, and it's dropping fast."

"What?" she asked. "Wait a minute. The high—last night?"

"While we were asleep," he said in a faintly condescending tone, "the sun passed overhead. The maximum temp, Celsius, for the four-workday period generally falls just before we get up on Cday."

"Okay. Okay," she said, concentrating. "I did study this. We get four working days out of a planetary rotation, right? Aday through Dday equals one so-called Goddard day?"

"One word. Goddarday. Our short little workweek." He blocked her view out into the lab when he passed through the door.

She moved to the window, glad he was gone. Now she could take a look around. From up here, on the fifth floor, she stared out over a cluster of tiny row houses to an arc of larger constructs that looked like barns or equipment sheds, ringed by open fields. The fields reminded her of farmland in winter fallow. Her grad course in soils development included day trips into Newton's production area.

She never dreamed she'd end up working this specialty.

Outside, the distant fields were predominantly brown—ash brown, russet, or yellow-tan. That reminded her to push up her sleeve. The t-o button on her forearm still was green. If she wanted to stay at her peak, she ought to pick up a roll of mints or dried berries, or whatever was available here, and keep them in a pocket.

Later. Working quickly, she signed in on the Gaea database to learn what she could about these Lwuites before she met their Chairman. He could be a critical contact, in several ways.

She'd heard a little about them back at the school where she taught in Einstein Hab. A researcher in the subtle sexual dimorphism of the human brain—in other words, how men's cerebral structure differed from women's—Dr. Henri Lwu had hypothesized that most of human warfare resulted from overaggressiveness in both sexes, but primarily in the male. He chose the corpus callosum, the brain structure connecting the two hemispheres, for his specialized field of study, and he found something interesting. Between the eighth month of pregnancy and the second month after birth, male infants developed a differently shaped corpus callosum. After a massive brain-cell die-off, fewer neurons crossed the cerebral midline.

That, he speculated, left male children less gifted at wholistic thinking, which used both hemispheres at the same time. Lwu found ways to alter the corpus callosum's shape and thickness without using illegal gene manipulation. In test after test, the change made a quantifiable difference in his male patients' aggressive tendencies. Those infants grew up to carry on normal lives, including fathering children, but rarely—if ever—exhibited belligerent behavior.

So the literature claimed.

United Sovereignties and Space Colonies policy blamed violent aggressiveness for much of humankind's misery. Consequently, for nearly a hundred years, women had dominated human leadership. Henri Lwu found no shortage of Einsteinians willing to take part in his experiment for the sake of humanity's future.

This information was common knowledge. Now Graysha hoped to learn more, but here, as at Einstein, specific medical data was lock-coded, sheltered by a label that cited the Religious Liberties Act of 2085. Many sects kept their ceremonial and doctrinal practices private. The RL Act, passed to protect the masses from obnoxious proselytizers, worked both ways.

The only new information she now found concerned Lwuite surnames and explained MaiJidda's pride in her capital J. The first Lwuites chose to be called by the first syllable or so of their mother's surname, then a significant syllable or two from their father's name (or husband's, after marriage). Graysha nodded understanding. She'd inherited her mother's hyphenated surname, which proved more of a handicap than a help in her life.

Emmer clicked and grunted. Graysha scratched her, took a few of her remaining minutes to look over microbial inventories, then shut off her computer and hurried to the elevator. Down on the first floor, Dr. Lee's harried-looking secretary issued directions to the Lwuites' Colonial Affairs office.

Graysha eyed passing colonists on her way across the cool hub and up a long northbound tunnel. They walked purposefully, most women wearing their hair long and plaited like the physician's, while the men's was cut short. All wore shirts and pants of heavy, coarse brown cloth.

DalLierx: Mother, then, was Dal-something. Father, something-Lierx. If she could win this man's approval, it might be a start toward seeking out a gene healer from among the Lwuites . . . still assuming they were capable of doing such a thing. Her name, pointing back like a signpost toward her infamous mother, would work against her.

Colonial Affairs was painted in black on concrete over a stairwell arch. Graysha started up. On the fourth-floor landing, she hesitated a moment, catching her breath—mentally and physically—then strode in. Off the stairwell, desks were scattered toward all points of the compass. Along opposite walls, pairs of black doors watched her like the pupils of disapproving eyes.

It took her a moment to realize there was hardly a scrap of paper anywhere. Desktops, waste cans, and shelves were bare of paper products. Composite film she saw in abundance, and a few framed sheets of what looked like linen parchment hung from the walls.

Tree shortage, she guessed. Maybe they relied on composite film and taught their children to memorize.

A pigtailed woman at the closest desk directed her to the last door on the left. Graysha rapped on it, then walked in.

The man standing beside the desk, not much taller than her and looking her in the eye, had to be Lindon DalLierx. Wavy black hair cut short and small ears framed his boyish face. He had narrow black eyebrows that drooped toward the bridge of his straight nose, giving him a Peter Pan never-grew-up look. His serious stare hinted at disapproval, and she assumed yesterday's sudden sickness did little to advance her chance at squirming into this man's good graces.

A pity. Irrelevant as it was, she liked his looks. She stuck out a hand. "Good morning, Chairman."

His long-sleeved shirt was muslin, his hand as rough as a field mechanic's. "Sit down," he said. "I have a reconnaissance vidi cued up. I would like you to see our world."

Graysha took the seat beside DalLierx's desk. Though his desk had a concrete frame, the desktop and chairs wore smooth brown leather covers. On the desktop, several childish clay figures surrounded a treasure: three leather-covered antique books. "Thank you, Chairman. This long sun cycle is intriguing." She spoke casually, wanting to sound nonthreatening. "When will the sun set?"

He sat down on a high-backed chair that curled forward around his shoulders. "At about midnight of this working-day cycle. Officially, this is Cday, the third circadian period of four in a Goddarday. The schedule requires some mental adjustment." His delicate features made him appear no older than twenty. He pressed palms together under his straight chin. "I am surprised to find someone so closely allied with USSC's Eugenics Board at Goddard, Dr. Brady-Phillips."

She gave him full credit for directness. "My EB stint was a long time ago. I've been with Gaea Consortium for three months. Before that, I taught at a public high school at Einstein."

"Yes, but you did promotional work for the Eugenics Board until recently."

Plainly, he knew more of her history than she expected. "That was only part time, while I was teaching." She'd been an idiot to try working for her mother. Ellard's unsubtle pressure to leave the EB for good was the single honest debt she still owed her ex-husband. "I quit in '31."

"I know."

Was she digging this hole wider with every attempt to climb out? "There are thousands of us—genefective people—living under USSC jurisdiction. I could no longer act as an EB spokesperson."

Instead of asking what triggered her decision, he rocked forward and eyed her silently. She stared back, wondering what combination of genes produced such a delicate though unmistakably masculine face . . . and what other effects Henri Lwu's treatments wreaked on his brain, body, and psyche.

"Are you feeling better?" he asked, leaning back.

Oh, she was sick of this! "Thank you, I'm not an invalid. Flaherty's syndrome is a microvascular capillary disease."

"Yes—"

"I must stay a month," she interrupted, then explained the Lwuite physician's directive. She added, "I was relieved to have stayed calm under open sky." Maybe she might draw him out with what had to be a shared experience. "I couldn't escape the sensation that . . . that the wind up there meant a meteor puncture."

He clenched one hand, and for an instant, his eyes widened. "You'll have to get over it. I did," he said, hollow-voiced. Before she could ask what terrible memory haunted him, he spoke again. "This vidi was made by a hovercopter pilot taking off here at Axis Plantation." He reached for a keyboard and dimmed the room.

Emmer tensed, curling closer to Graysha's throat. She stroked the flat-bodied gribien. Soft, warm fur gave way under her touch, a welcome relief from this prickly conversation.

DalLierx had only a small screen mounted on his desktop, but its resolution was excellent. Closest to Axis—filmed in summer, she guessed—were wedges and patches of soft-looking green crop fields. Dull, sandy flats beyond the croplands led to distant haze. Dusty gray-blue sky hung close and intimidating. The only clouds in camera range were thin and extremely high. As the copter flew low out of the crater, Graysha found herself fascinated instead of frightened to see how the haze vanished around the outside of the planetary sphere.

DalLierx leaned up to his keyboard and did something to interrupt the vidi. Two more keystrokes brought up a map. He pointed to a dot near the irregular continent's center. "You're here, at Axis Plantation." Surrounding the continent, a blue-gray sea held unknowable threats of its own. His finger slid northwest. "Hannes." Then eastward, almost to the coast. "Port Arbor, and . . . Center." The fourth settlement lay due west of Axis.

She wondered if all the settlements smelled bad and if all that water came in as cometary ice. "What's the scale?"

"We're about 500K from Center." He restarted the vidi, which panned a counterclockwise circle. Beyond the crater, a moving cloud of black dust came into view.

"What's that?"

"Ore truck. At Hannes, we're refining metals. Track-trucks in this area mostly bring in crushed stone for carbonate processing. We're always short of the carbon necessary to manufacture CFCs, and all our organic waste that isn't recycled as crop nutrient goes into CFC production. Here at Axis, we specialize in agriculture and atmospheric alteration."

She nodded. CFCs—chlorofluorocarbons—were greenhouse gases that slowly warmed the planet.

"And we have the Gaea station here, of course," he added without enthusiasm, "monitoring all planetary sciences."

Hostile but well mannered, she observed. She wished she'd had time to find out more about his interests, his history, anything that might serve as conversational currency and put him at ease.

Between camera eye and high mountains, northerly gray-black lava flows lightened to pale rose. Black sand drifted over coarse pink gravel, blown southwest from its parent material. She found the effect stunningly beautiful until she recalled Goddard's sandstorms killed Jon Mahera.

Will Varberg's warning filtered back up through her memory. Was Chairman DalLierx party to a murder?

He leaned away from the vidi when she did and brought the lights back up, then raised one dark eyebrow. "What do you think?"

She reminded herself that he'd dedicated the rest of his life to developing this world. "It's actually rather pretty, in an eerie, savage sort of way."

"I agree." At last, a smile.

"Thank you for the . . . tour."

He rested one hand on the leather desktop. "Why did you decide to pursue terraforming when you left your teaching position?"

Back in the habs, the second part of that question generally was "Otherwise, you seem like a sensible person." Many habitants saw no justification for the time and resources necessary for planetary-scale development. Space colonies, built outside the gravity wells that surrounded planets, made trade and travel so much easier. Graysha steepled her fingers. "I went into Ecosystems Development more as a field of study than out of any practical onsite intention. I'm a teacher, both by training and preference."

"Ah. So you hope to go back and teach terraforming with the added qualification of three terrannums' experience?"

"Yes, and I believe that within the next few generations, we'll solve the problems of transport down into gravity wells."

"I heartily hope so."

One more empathy point scored. She hoped. "When that time comes, people might choose to resettle planetside. They'll need habitable worlds to live on."

"And frontier wages did nothing to dissuade you." His darkly serious expression reminded her of a dear old friend. During the happy years—pre-Ellard.

Thinking of Ellard irked her. She rubbed a bandage on her tender right palm. "That's true," she said flatly. "I can use the money."

"You're not averse to working with Lwuites?"

She laughed, hoping to convey an image of friendly professionalism. "I have no prejudices, Chairman DalLierx."

She expected him to ask if she had religious beliefs and whether she followed all the Church of the Universal Father's teachings. What he said instead was, "Prejudices aren't necessarily bad. There are people I'd rather not work with. There is a time for cooperation and a time for separation."

Startled, she did not answer. The silence stretched over several uncomfortable seconds, until she changed the subject. "What happened to that . . . Was he a stowaway?" The youth caught on board her shuttle was so homely she had pitied him, like a runt puppy.

"We have him in disciplinary confinement. I'll assign him to the Gaea station to work off his shuttle fare home."

An opening! She dove in. "I used to teach his age group. If it would help, I'll take him under my wing."

DalLierx stroked his chin, then said, "That might work. Thank you."

She acknowledged his thanks with a nod.

"Other questions, Dr. Brady-Phillips?"

It sounded like he was starting to wind down the conversation, but she still needed to know if her hopes were completely futile. "Tell me, Chairman. Why didn't you simply have me watch this vidi from the Gaea building?"

He frowned, but smile lines gathered under his eyes. "I wanted to see for myself if you were adjusting to the notion of an open-air planet."

"I seem to be." She rubbed her left thumbnail, a nervous habit her ex despised. "The colony must depend heavily on transgenic mammals," she said, cautiously pressing on. "Are they gene-tailored or cloned here as conditions change?"

"Neither," he answered without hesitating. "For the present, we're working with standard crosses. At least that's my understanding. Your Dr. Lee provides breeding stock. She'd know better than I."

Had she seen a flicker of guilt? "All right," she said, "I'll ask Dr. Lee. One more question, though. I caught a rumor that Goddard may be recooling." Also, her computer inventory showed odd gaps in cold-tolerant microbial populations. "Any truth to it?"

DalLierx uncrossed his legs and sat up straight. "There could be. Where did you hear that?"

Finally, a reaction. "Back on Einstein."

He shook his head. "I was hoping you might've heard it confirmed here. I've spent hours trying to convince Dr. Lee that this cooling trend is serious. She keeps telling me, 'Field data are ambiguous.' Evidently you're not yet infected by local Consortium policy."

"Policy?" Graysha repeated, wondering what sort of compost she was stirring. "Surely the Consortium works as closely with your people as humanly possible."

"That is why the Consortium decided the late Dr. Mahera had to be replaced, though meeting your salary meant doing without a secondary fusion generator we could've bought used from Copernicus Hab."

It was an opening she couldn't resist. "Dr. Mahera's death. What has the investigation brought to light?"

"We've known for some time that a message was left in his personal mail on the morning of his death, assurance the approaching sandstorm had dissipated. The difficulty has been in tracing that message through the system. Gaea's first reaction was to cast aspersions on possible Lwuite malcontents. That's ridiculous. I'll grant you some of us forget the Gaea people are our protectors. But I've seen men and women crack under the strain of field labor. These people held office positions before they came to Goddard. You must understand the changes they've been through."

"Unless some of your people suspected Dr. Mahera was somehow responsible for this Gaea policy of nonresponse."

Lindon DalLierx shook his head. "Sooner or later, the data will convince everyone. Goddard is meteorologically unstable. It could fall either direction, into permanent glaciation or permanent habitability."

"But they've found nothing new?"

"Dr. Brady-Phillips, if they have, I have not been told."

Nor, plainly, would he tell her anything he knew. Especially if he was guilty, or if he ordered Mahera eliminated. For that matter, if Mahera was killed for the colonists' security and the colonists were investigating, they might pretend to solve the case. Who might they accuse?

"I don't understand why Lee hasn't asked the Gaea station to act on the recooling evidence," he added, "but I'm not a scientist."

"I'd guess Dr. Lee is reluctant to respond to data she sees as ambiguous, assuming all the simulations still give go-ahead readings. We do place higher value on computer projections than on raw data. I am personally willing to take the concept of recooling quite seriously." Graysha drew a deep breath. "And what would have been the advantage of buying another fusion generator?"

"Direct, aren't you?" He raised his head.

"I try to be honest, Chairman."

"Good," he said. "Think about cooling, then. If it continues, extra generator capacity would ensure my people's survival a little longer. Since you are frank, I shall be, too. I will continue to petition Gaea Consortium to review the decision to hire you, particularly in light of your illness."

"I am not an invalid." How many times would she have to repeat that sentence? "Wait a week or two before you petition for my dismissal, since I have to stay a month anyway. I hope to surprise you."

DalLierx shut off his little monitor. "Well, I hope you enjoy your time on Goddard. Do you have any other questions?"

"No." She stood up. "Thank you, Chairman."

He stood, too. "It was pleasant meeting you, Dr. Brady-Phillips, and I wish you all success in your career, wherever you . . . and your pet . . . eventually settle."

Maybe he disapproved of non-useful animals. For herself, she relished Emmer's velvet fur and fond noises. "Would you tell me if any more information turns up on Dr. Mahera's death?"

"Certainly." He walked her to his office door.

She found her way back down to the concrete corry without trouble. Maybe it was her imagination, but many of the colonists in this building looked like young people rapidly turning old, aged by long hours and hard, wearing labor.

She headed south, back toward the hub and her own work, feeling burdened by too much new information and plagued by the sensation of having heard something terribly important without recognizing it.

5. NOVIA

"I heard Graysha ended up on Goddard, of all places."

Novia Brady-Phillips set down her mug of black coffee and eyed Hannah Weil over the student union cafeteria table. Light streamed through an open ceiling, mingling with breezes from Newton University's rooftop ventilators. The largest hubitat in the Alpha Centauri complex, Newton housed a sprawling campus complex that included USSC's regional offices.

As a matter of fact, Novia did know about Graysha's new posting. She'd waited two terrannums to find that vacancy. "Her proposed teaching position at Halley Habitat was converted to on-site terraforming," she said.

"Is Gaea Consortium having organizational problems," Hannah asked, "or is Novia Brady-Phillips investigating something again?"

Novia frowned. She'd just returned from Einstein Habitat, another great space city in the Alpha Centauri Complex, to her old home in Newton Hab, near this university—and she was quietly reopening the inactive posthumous surveillance of Henri and Palila Lwu. Fifteen thousand followers survived them, and Henri Lwu's work in callosal equalization was well known.

"Whatever you heard," she said, "I would appreciate your keeping it to yourself."

"Your own daughter." Hannah's tone reproached Novia.

"She is doing on-site terraforming," Novia said firmly. "She went over to Halley to pick up a few more credits, and she was going to lecture undergrads at Gaea's new high school. It was beneath her." Novia's connections at Gaea Consortium snared Graysha the second, more lucrative job offer. Acceptance had been up to Gray . . . nudged by those terrible debts.

Novia knew how to use debts.

Hannah Weil folded her hands. "Your own daughter," she repeated. "Novia, if you are using her in an investigation, she has the right to know."

Novia raised her chin. "Graysha makes her own decisions." And to reach this important goal, Novia didn't feel guilty about nudging Graysha in a risky direction.

Gray had so little life left. It should count for something important.

Hannah picked up the lunch tab. Half an hour later, back in the stuffy dorm room she'd rented, Novia keyed on to the headquarters' EB net. Its Goddard file still was small, for Gaea Terraforming Consortium had only declared Goddard open for settlement five terrannums ago. Out there in the Epsilon Eridani system, only Copernicus Hab was up and running. After two terrannums' search, they had enlisted the Einsteinian Lwuites. *L-wu,* she pronounced carefully to herself, giving the name its two distinct syllables.

Novia scratched her chin. Less public than Henri Lwu's brain work was the fact that his wife, Palila, was related to one of the last surviving offspring of the Strobel Coterie. Those legally transgened so-called humans were responsible for the 2030 Troubles. During the twenty-first century, when humankind lived only on planetary surfaces, young Coterites tapped the UN's information and control nets with the intention of eliminating third-world populations. They believed that those poverty-stricken millions were decreasingly useful to technological civilization.

The genocide wouldn't have been violent, of course. Coterites would have diverted aid and laced charity foodstuffs with slow but virulent poisons and abortifacients—that, at least, had been their plan, as pieced together by investigators.

What actually came to pass was a series of uprisings that threatened all human survival.

Novia's Eugenics Board traced its beginnings to the mop-up decades. UN officials gave the EB unprecedented rights over cloned and transgened individuals. They were hunted down, forcibly hospitalized, and rendered incapable of reproduction or cloning.

As a crowning touch, UN and EB publicity engines blamed the entire post-human race of "laboratory creatures" for the catastrophic Troubles.

Novia had long suspected that the late Lwu partners' so-called religion was an excuse to conduct genetic manipulation. Why did Henri Lwu find so many individuals willing to impose fetal brain work on their own helpless offspring? Until the Lwuites quietly shipped out, not even the EB suspected there were so many of them.

Fifteen thousand!

Keying quickly, Novia used her security pass to access the Henri/Palila Lwu inquiry file. This one was larger. Though the original case had been tabled for lack of evidence, all information was saved by EB surveillance at Einstein Hab.

Novia pushed back from the desk, glancing out her window at a forest preserve that arched upward from the vast campus's edge. Space habitats did not have horizons—not inside, where people lived.

So what sent the Lwuites so far out? To get Graysha healed, and the Lwuites convicted—if they were guilty, of course—would take more maneuvering than even Novia normally put in to a case.

Poor little Gray was one of a tiny minority truly victimized by anti-homogenengineering laws. Illegal supergening was too dangerous—to everyone—to allow even the smallest transgening clinics. As the human race spread into space, it would get harder for the Eugenics Board to police and protect everyone.

So be it. Novia rubbed her pre-arthritic left knee. Conceived with the ill luck to inherit recessive Flaherty genes from both parents, Gray was the sweet, ordinary-looking kind of girl that people tended to pity . . . as her roach ex-husband, Ellard, found out. If the Lwuites were illegal practitioners, they might approach Graysha. That could give Novia's EB a string of rapid convictions.

She couldn't move too quickly, though. She must wait until Graysha could realistically hope to be gene-healed, because for Graysha, the alternative prognosis was too sad . . . too brief. Novia's excellent connections would ensure Graysha immunity from prosecution or irradiation. She'd only need to serve as key witness against the Lwuites.

Novia knew she had passed the deadly gene herself. She'd love to atone for the act and get normal grandchildren in one step. Now that she'd reopened the investigation, her next logical step was to search out any surviving Lwu employees.

If Henri Lwu had set illegal operations in motion, tampering with the human genome behind the Lwuites' peaceful front, Novia Brady-Phillips would find out.

Recognizing pride in that conclusion, she hastily asked forgiveness. If the prayer felt mechanical, she could plead repetition as her excuse. Talented people often had to confess their pride. The Universal Father would understand. One of His first and greatest spirit-scions fell under that very sin, and personally, she found Lucifer a sympathetic character.

As she reached for her computer, a sparrow perched on a structural brace outside the open window and sang noisily. Novia touched a button on the desk's rim. Her window slid shut, silencing the distraction, and then she darkened it to maximum polarization.

Across Axis Plantation's hub from the Colonial Affairs corridor, near the broad Gaea hall, Graysha located Gaea employees' housing. This tunnel was narrower, with low walls that rose straight up from the floor. Cooking scents drifted from her left.

Since she had not seen her apartment yet, it was easy to picture herself lying down, orphaned once again, in the Health Maintenance Facility tonight. Emmer's warmth around her shoulders felt comforting and companionable, though it would be nice not to have to explain the gribien to everyone she met.

Graysha found the Gaea cafeteria easily. Inside its fan-fold doors, she joined the shortest of four food lines, accepted a pre-filled tray, and then found a familiar face—Dr. Varberg—at a table near the big noisy room's center. "Feeling all right?" he asked in a solicitous voice.

"Absolutely." She sat down across from him, unwrapped the large sandwich she found on her plate, and twisted for comfort on the concrete bench.

On the other side of Varberg sat an extremely tall black woman. "Jirina," Varberg said, "this is our new soils person, Graysha Brady-Phillips. Graysha, Dr. Jirina Suleiman looks down upon us all. She's Virology."

"Born and schooled on Mars, so I'm used to planets." The black woman had a voice as deep as her rich dark skin, while her high-bridged nose and strong cheekbones suggested complex racial blending. "You just had an interview with the CCA, I understand. How hard did he bite?"

"Not half as hard as he could have," Graysha answered. "Is he really as young as he looks?"

"No. Midthirties, with two daughters."

Married. Too bad, she observed lightly.

"And they're as pretty as he is," Varberg said.

Graysha bit into her sandwich. The filling was bean paste and cheese, and it tasted better than she would have expected. The bread was whole grain and chewy, as fragrant and fresh as something from a fine hab restaurant. She saved Emmer a crust wrapped in a cloth napkin, enough for a full day. To her relief, the gribien slept peacefully, keeping her ears down.

Varberg and Jirina continued a conversation she'd obviously interrupted, something about immune reactions and viral sheaths. When it lulled, she asked Varberg about the shortage of cold-tolerant microorganisms she'd noted when reviewing the microbial inventories.

"We're getting warmer, not cooler," he answered around a mouthful of something green, "so you don't need cold viability." He nodded across at Graysha and aside at Jirina.

This must be part of the "local Consortium policy" DalLierx had alluded to. Graysha looked at the tall woman, who winked and inclined her head toward Varberg.

Graysha pursed her lips. "Supervisor Clayton on Halley gave me the impression there was a problem with the temp cycle."

Varberg stirred cream-colored pudding with his fork. "Offworlder. Too busy with equations to deal with real weather patterns. They fluctuate, Graysha. You can't rig a solar sail to tow an air mass."

When he looked away, Graysha raised a questioning eyebrow toward Dr. Jirina Suleiman.

Later, the woman mouthed, and the conversation moved to other topics as Graysha worked on her sandwich. Ten minutes later, Jirina walked her up the corry to her apartment. "Thanks for that cue over lunch," Graysha said. "Doesn't Dr. Varberg like to explain simple things to new people?"

Jirina laughed so shortly it sounded like a cough. "Varberg can be a pomposity. Particularly in a group, for some reason."

Wanting to like her boss, Graysha frowned. "What's the story, Jirina? Was Jon Mahera murdered?"

"We honestly don't know. For a week, it looked accidental. Then one of Vice-Chair MaiJidda's brownclothers started asking questions, and before long no one was certain."

"MaiJidda?"

"You met her. Vice for Police."

Graysha blinked. The Vice-Chair for *Police* met her at the shuttle? What were they so afraid of?

Mother, she guessed.

Jirina went on. "I'd be inclined to believe MaiJidda just wanted us nervous if it weren't for . . . well, the day after it was first called murder, everyone on the floor found a cupful of sand on their computer station. Took half an hour to clean up. Someone here is not quite right."

Jirina slowed to a stop. "What number are you?"

Graysha thought of Will Varberg plucking petals from her marigolds. She pulled out the mag strip Melantha Lee gave her and read, "Unit seventeen."

Jirina led her to the door. Graysha passed her key across a reader, walked through and glanced around, then gaped. At the center of the room, between her three flexcases and her long, soft duffel, stood a bare cement pad. Tired as she was, she couldn't sleep on that. "No, Jirina, no. Concrete beds?"

"Don't worry, Blondie." Jirina tapped a hollow at the bed's foot. "With the roll and covers in here, it'll be comfortable. Hope they gave you enough closet space."

"And a pillow?" Graysha asked, reaching up to her shoulder. Emmer hung limp as she lifted her off.

"I wondered if that might be a gribby." Jirina stroked Emmer with a ruddy palm. "Friend of mine kept one for a pet. Handy, I thought. Almost no work."

"All I need is a pillow for her to sleep on. She's getting old."

Jirina raised the hollow's lid and pulled out a plump cushion. "There, gribien. Home—" Jirina halted.

Graysha followed the black woman's stare. Squarely centered on a shelf behind the bare concrete pad was a rounded pile of fine-grained brown sand.

"Well," Jirina said lightly, "I guess you're really one of us. Welcome to Goddard."

Graysha uneasily curled Emmer onto the pillow around the crust she'd saved. Emmer raised her head, looked all around with gleaming black eyes, nibbled briefly, and then fell back asleep.

Jirina swept the shelf clean with one hand. "How old is she?"

"Five terrannums." Determined to ignore the sandy pile and the questions it raised, Graysha rubbed her creature's back. "She was the cull of her litter." Curious, she stepped around a corner. To her dismay, odor-free clean room facilities of the habs were here replaced by a small sink and hollow stool, with one storage hatch beyond the antique facility.

The bedroom, at least, felt cozy. From a flexcase, she pulled her perfuming box, wrapped carefully with stockings.

"What's that?" Jirina asked.

Graysha unclasped the styroplast box's catch and flattened it on her desktop. Fifty rows of tiny vials lay tucked into foam-padded slots. "Scent art. Something I picked up on Newton. These are esters I didn't think I'd find in Halley Habitat."

"Interesting hobby for a micro person. Especially if your specialty is soils."

Graysha closed it up, grinning. "The fact the job literally stinks makes subtle scent work especially satisfying. Thanks for your help, Dr.—"

"Don't 'doctor' me. I go by Jirina, in and out of the lab." She unfolded her impressive height off the bed.

Graysha nodded. "Then I'm Graysha, please. My mother calls me Gray."

"You look white to me. Or maybe pale pink."

Concerned, Graysha glanced down at her fingertips. They looked rosy, as they should after lunch. Then she realized the remark referred to her race, not her health.

Jirina pivoted on one foot. "You don't mind me calling you Blondie, do you? It's fun to tease the other minorities, but only if they're willing."

"Always glad to be teased," Graysha answered. "It's a sign of friendship."

"You understand." Jirina winked. "Good."

Several minutes later, as they strolled back through the hub and into the warmer Gaea tunnel, Chairman DalLierx's words came back to her. She asked Jirina, "Do *you* think Goddard is cooling?"

"Doesn't matter what I think. The charts say it is."

"I don't just mean seasonally—"

"This winter," Jirina interrupted, "is already two degrees colder than the last, which was one degree off the predicted average. But we can handle it, I think. Varberg was right about one thing—you'll find it frustrating to deal with a physical world when your computer will simulate a ten-terrannum weather pattern change in six minutes flat."

"Why do you think this is happening?"

"I like albedo." Jirina stared up the corry as she walked. "We're getting more reflection of light and heat back into space from ice caps that are freezing purer and brighter than we simulated. We have another carbonaceous asteroid under tow right now. Next G-year, we'll blow it up over the north pole and give that ice a nice dark dusting. That should warm us up."

"So you don't think it's anything to worry about."

"Dr. Lee doesn't seem to think so, and she has the entire project's overview at her fingertips."

"But DalLierx thinks so." Why wouldn't the colonists worry? They hoped to pass this planet to their children. "Could our green plants be taking up too much carbon dioxide, as well, thinning the greenhouse layer?"

Jirina shrugged. "You want to talk greenhouse layer, talk CFCs. They're supposed to play a much bigger role than the CO_2."

They climbed a short, broad flight of stairs to the Gaea building's first level, then boarded the elevator. "CFCs," Graysha echoed. DalLierx also mentioned the chlorofluorocarbons. "But CFCs linger in an atmosphere for a century after we put them there. Otherwise, why would we bother using them for temp raising?"

"Correct, Blondie. On Mars, they stayed, but could they be getting away here?"

Graysha thought about all she'd learned concerning terraforming. "Why should they? Goddard has more gravity than Mars. It ought to hold green-house gases perfectly well."

"You explain it, then," said Jirina.

"I intend to."

The black woman tilted her head and asked, "Why?"

Because I want this to be a habitable world some day. Graysha gripped the elevator rail. "Call it a hunch." Why should she care? She had an ulterior motive for being on Goddard, but she also loved the idea of making a world live. "Just a hunch."

Graysha waved good-bye to Jirina when they reached her own lab. She'd just opened one roll-side cupboard beneath the countertop, intending to inventory her glassware, when movement at the far edge of vision caught her attention. A young woman—sixteen, perhaps seventeen—peered in through the lab's hall door. One brown pigtail dangled over her shoulder.

"Oh, hello," said Graysha. "I don't think we've met."

"Hello. I was just curious. I work for Dr. Paul."

"You're a tech?" Someone so young had to be a colonist.

"Uh-huh. I've got to go. Bye." Her head whipped back and out of sight.

Goodness, the Lwuites were skittish. Graysha stepped to the door and looked out into the hallway. High-ceilinged, it reminded her of a habitat dock, except for the strange angles at which floors met walls. Abruptly she realized she'd learned to see almost-right angles from a slanted perspective. These corners, truly ninety degrees, looked odd.

Without warning, the ground shook and trembled. Graysha grabbed for a large flask she'd brought out onto the counter. Exactingly fitted into slots on the shelves, her array of graduated cylinders rattled but didn't creep.

"Hoo," Jirina's voice called out from the office next door. "Shall we dance?"

"What was that?" Graysha asked, willing her hands to stop trembling.

"Microseism. We have them all the time. Goddard's adjusting to weight in new places, especially out under the ocean. Geology injects lubricants down into the subduction zones every now and then. Little quakes now are better than big ones later—so they say."

"I hope Geology knows what it's doing."

"Oh, we've got the best," Jirina answered. "They've even located sub-crustal magma northeast of Axis. We might restart continental drift in this century."

Then the planet *really* would live. Subcrustal magma sounded danger-ous, though.

On the other hand, Jirina didn't sound concerned.

Graysha decided not to worry about it.

Lindon DalLierx stepped up to the edge of Colonial Affairs' broad rectangular roof and shaded his eyes to stare northeast toward Axis Plantation's spacefield. Beyond the Axis cluster of stone-and-concrete domes and cubes—and the fields, gray and brown, touched with hopeful green—was a small, blackened crater. That scorched landing scar was his visual memory link with the home and lifestyle he'd left behind. It was the colony's tenuous tie with the supply trade it needed to survive.

He adjusted gray-green UV goggles to keep them from pinching his temples, then turned back around. To the south, beyond greenhouse Quonsets, stretched a barn-dotted animal production range of twenty square kilometers. Past the production range, a battery of wind-powered generators whirled like the pinwheels he once gave his daughters.

Vice-Chair for Records Taidje FreeLand waited close by on the roof, warming his hands in parka pockets. "None of us wants to go," FreeLand said. "We don't have to give up yet. We'll weather this." A wisp of white hair fluttered from beneath FreeLand's browncloth hood. One of Henri Lwu's three surviving research assistants, Taidje FreeLand never lost his air of calm self-assurance.

Lindon pushed his own parka hood back to let the wind cool his head. "We should have had at least a G-year before they found someone qualified to fill that position. And now this. At the last minute we find out the woman Gaea found is N—"

"Novia Brady-Phillips's daughter," FreeLand interrupted. "We all know it, as of six-thirty yesterday morning. Calm down. Think about something else. Pray, if you can keep your mind on it."

"Calm down," Lindon muttered, pivoting to face the building's other edge. Though the sky still gleamed, he imagined he could pick out a flicker low in the sky that might be the colony's near neighbor, Copernicus.

The planet Goddard was desirable. True, one had to fly outside this crater scar to see its eerie geologic beauty, but even down here, as dusk gathered over the east rim and the turquoise sky dimmed to gray, he felt a sense of promise, of freedom, and a link to one noncorporate Creator whose Buyout already was paid.

Back on Earth, billions of people scurried to build shelter domes, huddling away from its rancid air and the deadly UV that now poured down a vast ozone hole. Many of Earth's wealthy and educated people had moved to habitats, but hab life was ruled by the dangers of depressurization and radiation. That took a heavy toll on freedom.

On broader worlds like this—he squinted toward the red sun his people had once called Eps Eridani—a wiser humanity might start again, cautious of its resources, knowing what treasures they really were.

Goddard is ours, Lindon insisted. *Ours. We've worked so hard for it.* Within two of his people's generations, there should be a temperate, habitable band along Goddard's equator. His great-grandchildren would build up the population, spread out, and start new settlements. One generation more, and they could start buying out Gaea's investment—billions of maxims that the consortium spent on resource-rich asteroids, surface microorganisms, and infrastructure . . . plus interest.

Increasing the colony's numbers, committing more people to lives of hard work, would bring buyout sooner. Some day, maybe, they would send a representative to the United Sovereignties and Space Colonies.

First, they had to protect themselves and their children. They could not go back.

His thoughts shifted back to the new arrival. Dr. Brady-Phillips had asked specifically about mammalian genengineering.

And she brought a pet. A *pet!* He'd given up Valentina, his daughters' adored champion Samoyed, when they emigrated. Pets simply couldn't be tolerated under stringent colonial conditions. She—

"This isn't working," he muttered.

Gravel crunched under Taidje FreeLand's shoe. "We might bring the woman in, befriend her. Undoubtedly she could provide key information about Eugenics Board policies and standard procedures."

Lindon laughed shortly at the older man, trying to shake off a sense of impending doom. "It's looking likely that whoever killed Dr. Mahera was a co-professional. Suppose Graysha Brady-Phillips were killed next. What are the odds Commissioner Brady-Phillips would decide *that* needed investigating? Suppose—"

Taidje FreeLand raised a silencing finger. "You're not yourself, Lindon. I called you up here to talk sense into you before you frighten your staff. Now calm down."

Truly, he wasn't himself. Hardship, even tragedy, had steadied him in the past, stripping away all defenses but his faith. That foundation held. Always.

"That's better," FreeLand said. "How much production will it take to outweigh the funds she'll cost us? Calmly, now."

Lindon took a deep breath of the late afternoon's pure, chilled air. "Thank you, Taidje. I apologize for behaving that way."

FreeLand straightened his goggles. His goggle strap made a long, straight dent around his puffy parka hood. "We could send her away, escorting that stowaway to Copernicus. I'd rather see him tried there, anyway."

"Possible," Lindon answered, sniffing the frigid wind. Had he caught a breath of pine from the infant forest?

"Offer her a bonus if she would accept transfer. Could we do that without seeming to incriminate ourselves?"

"That stowaway could be an EB agent, too." Lindon calculated quickly. "Fare for two to Copernicus would drain our reserves."

"Yes, but if we could find the boy's relatives, perhaps we could convince them to pay both fares."

"I got the feeling, talking to him, that contacting his family might not be our wisest choice. But you're agreeing with me, aren't you?" Lindon stared eastward into a darkening sky, where two star-dots had appeared since the last time he looked up. "Even Ari is backing me on this, and we haven't matched goals twice since the crossing." And FreeLand knew nothing about all that happened between them en route to Goddard. "We agree then—Dr. Brady-Phillips must leave."

"Yes," FreeLand admitted. "It will be better if she does."

6. WASTEWATER

After a hasty shopping trip for local clothing and a slow, satisfying dinner, Graysha foot-dragged back to her room, so full she could scarcely move. She untied and brushed her hair, pulled off her clothes, and slid between sheets on a genuine concrete bed. She'd unrolled a thin fabric-covered foam mattress to cover it, and it felt wonderful. Yellow-brown walls made her feel like she was burrowing in a cave.

Emmer grunted beside Graysha. Thirty centimeters long when she stretched out, she waved her stubby forelimbs. Graysha batted one paw from behind, avoiding claws. The aging gribien never had been active, and these days she rarely wanted to play. Tonight she seemed tender and kittenish, but after half a dozen swipes, her paws curled up and her eyes fell shut.

Graysha yawned. It was Cday, and Eps Eridani wouldn't set until late "tonight," but down here she could shut off the light and go to sleep in total, comfortable darkness.

She was more than ready. The covers felt deliciously warm, though the chilly room air made her uncovered nose tingle. Turning carefully so not to jostle Emmer, she clutched a feather-stuffed pillow. Weird prickles, probably feather shafts, poked her through its case.

Sand, she remembered as consciousness faded. Sand on her shelf had to be a threat, or a warning. Who had known this apartment would be assigned to her? Was someone afraid of what she might find here? The questions faded as she drifted off to sleep.

An unsettling image floated on her mind when she woke the next morning: after hefting trays full of concrete-encased bacterial cultures into stone incubators, she watched heavy-hearted as carefully inoculated dishes sank under icy water.

Only a dream, she observed as her mind focused. *Get up and get moving. It'll fade.*

She bathed at the sink, then pulled on one of her new shirts and a new pair of pants. Colony-woven fabric scratched her shoulders and legs. What was it made from? she wondered. Wool, linen? She fingered the organic weave roughened by slubs of brown thread.

Well, she decided, *when in Rome, wear what the Romans wear.*

Roman togas probably itched, too.

She was pleased by how easily she made it to her lab. Two sharp left turns took her to the Gaea building, just southeast of the housing wing along a wider hall. To her surprise, a message waited on her computer. Colonial Affairs was offering her seven thousand maxims as a severance gift if she would escort the stowaway back to Copernicus Hab. Dr. Yael Gur-Eshel would provide medical assistance for the trip if she needed it.

Graysha smiled as she finished the message. She wanted to find out the secrets of this new world before she went anywhere. The cooling "nonissue" presented a fascinating puzzle. After sending a firm but polite refusal, she checked Dr. Varberg's list of catch-up duties and pulled a rack of banked soil samples out of her refrigerator.

Will Varberg brought in a younger man about an hour later. "Did you meet Dr. Paul Ilizarov, our oceanic microbiologist?"

Graysha turned away from the glassware racks beside her ion sterilizer. This must be the tech's "Dr. Paul." Such blue eyes on a brown-haired man were probably cosmetic transplants, but they glimmered convincingly. With his cleft chin, muscular shoulders, and slim hips and waist, he looked more like a vidi actor than a scientist. She clasped his hand, feeling self-conscious about the small bandages still spotting her own.

"Very glad to meet you," he said. She heard Russia in the lingering trace of his accent. "I've covered some of Mahera's non-oceanographic water-related duties. I am pleased to hand them back to you."

"Wastewater?" she asked.

"One guess—very good. Wherever did you get such beautiful hair?"

Graysha's cheeks warmed. There undoubtedly was a shortage of new women in the Gaea building, since shuttle trips were so expensive and rare. "From my mother, I suppose. It's the Newton Hab blond-dominant gene."

Dr. Varberg cleared his throat. "Dr. Ilizarov makes Goddard's isolation a little easier for Gaea's women, as I understand." His mouth smiled. His eyes did not.

"When does the wastewater need to be checked next?" she asked.

Paul Ilizarov turned his head so Varberg would not see him wink. "Yesterday. Shall I show you around?"

"Thank you." Even if he treated all Gaea women like this, his manner charmed her.

"One moment. Let me shut down Jirina's differential filter." He pivoted smoothly and strode off up the hall.

Graysha stared after him. She'd always enjoyed dealing with Russians, so strangely self-assured and wonderfully self-deprecating. Though their lead in space colonization ended decades ago, the best astronomers, and most top scientists in any discipline, still carried Slavic surnames.

"He's a heartbreaker," Varberg said quietly, almost growling the words. "I hope you're not easily victimized by that kind."

Surely Varberg was too old to be jealous. Anyway, it'd taken no heartbreaker to victimize her before. Ellard was as homely as a hog. "I don't think so," she murmured.

"It's quite an amazing place." Paul Ilizarov paused in front of the underground wastewater treatment facility's door.

Feeling dubious, Graysha adjusted the shoulder strap of a black sampling pack. Paul had draped her ceremoniously with the pack, calling it Jon Mahera's personal property.

That was almost as bad as having Mahera's nameplate still on her door. Later today, she'd pry it off. By morning starlight, the threat of sand on her shelf seemed preposterous, even funny.

Paul pushed open the treatment facility's door, and she braced for ten minutes of choking chlorine fumes.

Instead, the first warm puff of breath smelled of damp jungle. Trickling and bubbling sounds played along with humming unseen pumps and heaters. On her left, along the building's southerly wall under banks of lamps separated by broad skylights, fat glass cylinders stood three meters tall. Three were black with sludge, six were intense with the green of dense algal growth, and three were water clear. Everywhere else lay mats of greenery. On both sides of a concrete path, plants floated on small fluorofoam rafts—willows and watercress, ruffled lettuce, and other species she didn't know. She'd grown up with greenhouse technology, for her father was a pharmaceutical botanist. But this was wild, spacious, lush, and more enchanting than any greenhouse she'd ever seen.

"This is one of the best kept secrets on Goddard," Paul murmured. "Be so good as to not tell others. Too much visitation would compromise our drinking water's purity."

"I understand." She knelt on a pebbly concrete walkway and lifted a half-meter raft of red lettuce off the water. Dripping roots dangled through a mat of transparent eggs. There had to be fish, or maybe amphibians, breeding along this raceway.

She slipped the raft back down into its berth. "So the system's like hydroponics?" she asked.

"Lwuites have adopted self-sustaining systems wherever possible."

"If it's *their* priority, why do we go along?" Not that she objected. She would've gladly moved her office right here onto the path.

Crouching, Paul pressed lightly against her arm. "Technically speaking, we work for them. Only until they're capable of taking over, or so says the fine print."

She set Mahera's sampling kit down and eyed the greenery. "All right. What do I do?"

He pointed at one corner of the kit and answered, "Your nutrient tubes are marked, one for each sampling spot. I'll show you where the first raceway begins."

She made the circuit, mindful of her audience and her sampling technique. Finally, he paused beside a black, foreboding aeration tank and grasped a petcock. "Be ready to move quickly. This one smells as you expect."

He didn't exactly roll his *r*'s and *l*'s, she decided. He *rubbed* them. She drew a pipette and fitted it with the clickdraw. "Ready," she announced. One-handed, he screwed open a sampling port. Graysha plunged in the pipette, holding her breath. He closed the port as she inoculated the tube. "Phew!" she exclaimed.

"Even a small whiff is pretty awful." He offered a beautiful smile.

Realizing she was about to ask if he'd ever found sand on his computer station, she raised her guard again. She mustn't confide in him. In her experience, unbelievably handsome men—and women—weren't particularly trustworthy. "It's no worse than I expected. Dr. Varberg says I'll be sampling compost, too, and topsoil aging beds." She closed the kit.

Stretching out one hand, he touched a wisp of her hair that had escaped its tie. "Plenty of good smells. If you find anything missing from the biologic inventory, come back in two days with necessary cultures and inoculate. Somehow I always found something missing."

"I'll bet," she murmured, smiling.

He smiled back. "The inoculating is particularly good on B- and Cdays, when the sun shines." He looked down at her lab coat in a way that warmed her cheeks again. "It's a good place to sunbathe, and very private."

Following standard procedure for corporate employees, Paul brought her back from Wastewater right at morning breaktime. Graysha left Jon Mahera's sampling bag in her office and joined the rest of the micro floor in the break room.

Actually a long lab, its accoutrements suggested it served as coffee bar (ceramic water heater on an end table), confessional (deep chair and several stools), first-aid station (crimson kit mounted on the near wall), and experimental-animal quarters (shelves full of opaque cages with metal grate tops). Graysha wrinkled her nose at the combined scent of coffee, alfalfa tea, and rodent droppings.

The floor's Lwuite techs—Graysha had met another young woman before leaving the floor with Paul—shared their break separately, in the hall. Detached sibilant *s*'s were all Graysha could hear of their conversation.

She swung her legs beneath her stool and sipped a cup of slightly bitter alfalfa tea, brewed from plants "pharmed" with a caffeine-producing gene from tea camellias. Grown as green manure throughout the crater, a smaller dwarfalfa cultivar survived on minimal water, fed the livestock, and furnished several local delicacies, or so Dr. Varberg claimed.

She mentioned Mahera to Will Varberg.

"Couldn't remember his place," Varberg drawled, stirring coffee crystals into his cup, "both literally and figuratively. Never knew where he was. Had a hard time remembering he wasn't in charge, too."

Paul Ilizarov swiveled in a seat two meters to her right. "Clumsy fellow. We wash these floors daily, and every day Jon slipped."

"A wonder we didn't lose him earlier." Jirina swung through the door and bent to dose her own cup from the decaf jar. "You know how it is when you're thinking hard."

"Exactly," said Varberg from the depths of a stuffed chair. "Didn't know where he was. Couldn't keep his place."

And so it was easy to claim he'd wandered off? How would death come in a sandstorm? she wondered. Had he suffocated, or was the flesh slowly scoured from his bones?

And if the Lwuites didn't do it, whom did they suspect? "I suppose the colonists are pretty amateurish when it comes to conducting an investigation," she said, watching the others for reactions.

"What else would you expect?" Jirina asked, rolling her dark eyes. Ilizarov nodded. Varberg merely sipped his coffee. "They hauled us in one by one," Jirina explained, "everyone in the building clear up to Dr. Lee, but they've got no po-lice equipment. They're a joke."

Thanks to her mother's investigative work, Graysha knew more about "po-lice equipment" than she liked. "Did Mahera have children?" she asked the gathering in general.

"No, thank goodness." Paul leaned against a counter. "Most of us are single and enjoying the hunt, an odd group by hab standards." He blinked slowly, catlike.

She found his presence electrifying. "Did he have trouble with this Chairman DalLierx?" she asked, crossing her ankles on a rung of the stool and willing herself not to scratch her legs. "Was there any suspicion of foul play committed by the colonists?"

"DalLierx suspects us," Ilizarov commented. "Maybe we should suspect him."

Clasping long fingers like a bracelet around her upper arm, Jirina grinned across at Graysha. "DalLierx has one thing on his mind, that's all. He's the great leader. He is determined to breed his Lwuites, seed them around Goddard, and keep them doctrinally pure. Like the way he called you in already."

"What do I have to do with—"

"Wanted to check you out, make sure you're no threat," Jirina said. "Maybe see if you could be bullied into leaving. I don't think he's capable of murder. The rest of them? Who knows?"

Digging noises erupted from an opaque cage. "How could I threaten the Lwuites?" She knew, of course, but she wondered if it had occurred to her co-workers. "Surely they're not so short on food that they can't support one more specialist."

"All very mysterious." Ilizarov winked, smiling blandly. "They're hiding something. They take their babies early. Did you know that?"

Graysha nodded. "But only the males."

"No, all of them. They do a second treatment at puberty," Jirina added. "Some kind of hormonal soup, injected right through the forehead. Supposed to encourage little axons to connect speech centers with spatial centers or something. Very secret."

"Very weird." Varberg slid his cup toward the sink and let his head loll to one side. "Come to Goddard, join the Lwuites. Lobotomies are our specialty!"

Graysha discreetly pushed her stool backward, wanting to get more distance from Varberg. Up until this moment, he hadn't actually been offensive. This callous disdain for others' beliefs was worse than petal pulling.

Paul and Jirina added their cups to Varberg's in the sink. Out of habit, Graysha reached for the washing sponge. Her fingers almost touched Paul's, about to clasp the same sponge.

"Yours. This time," Paul said. "Perhaps dinner some night soon?"

His attention was balm to her spirit. "Definitely," she said, glad to turn her back on Varberg. "Thank you."

He strolled back out into the hall.

"Hey."

At the sound of Jirina's stage whisper, Graysha glanced up.

Jirina stood near Graysha's shoulder. "Send those pants through the laundry about ten times and they'll lose their bite," Jirina said. "Sorry I forgot to tell you yesterday. And be sure your shots are current before getting too close to Paul."

"What?"

"Social diseases." Jirina's long body swayed as she walked out of the break room.

"Oh," Graysha said as Jirina's back receded. The diseases Jirina implied would have been eliminated before immigrants arrived on this world, but her meaning was clear. Perhaps she ought not to be quite so friendly with Paul if—as Jirina hinted—he simply wanted to score with the new woman on the team.

Graysha carried her refilled tea mug back to her office and depolarized her small window. Orion hung overhead, strangely positioned but reassuringly familiar. Galactically speaking, Eps Eri wasn't all that far from the Alpha triple system she had always called home. Not that she'd spent much time stargazing. Stars meant vacuum, the ever-present danger she had dreaded ever since she was old enough to understand that depressurization was the potential apocalypse stalking all habitants.

The winking light of a communication relay passed slowly overhead. She thought of the necklace of geosynchronous mirrors that also lay in a high orbit. Small beacons, they focused patches of sunlight onto seas and over poles, onto black-sand areas and the continental snowpack—slowly warming the world, helping drive Goddard's weather. Other satellites focused light onto solar generators, providing electrical power as inexpensively as in a hab.

Graysha now had an inkling of why Gaea's task would take generations to accomplish here and why the importation of raw materials was so vital. For one thing, the planet was open to the sky, with heat lost to space every night.

Knowing her ancestors spent all their lives shackled to planetary surfaces like this had been one thing. It seemed distant, romantic, long ago and far away. It was all too close now, and she couldn't forget that she lived out here by choice. For the moment.

She dimmed the window and raised the office light's intensity. Nights masquerading as working days would not lower her productivity if she could help it. Sinking into her office chair, she touched on the computer. On her duty roster she found an apparently endless list of undone tasks created by Jon Mahera's death. She must familiarize herself with bacterial, algal, and fungal populations. She touched up a map, then sipped her cooling tea.

Evidently Mahera kept excellent records of Axis's microbes. Her first task, then, was to take a complete biological inventory from agricultural sites. Changes might have occurred while her position was vacant. She would need plates and tubes of growth media for the nodulators and their group, the sulfur-cycle group, soil streps . . .

Footsteps approached in the hallway. She heard a soft voice, then a rap at her outer door.

"Come," she called.

A woman she guessed at close to her own age, with chestnut pigtails pinned up over the top of her head, shuffled into the office. "Good morning, Dr. Brady-Phillips. My name is Liberty JenChee. I have an undergraduate degree in General Sci and two G-years experience at Port Arbor Clinic. When I asked about employment this morning, Dr. Lee sent me to you. Will you be needing technical help?"

"Certainly." Graysha pushed a wisp of hair off her forehead. "Just a minute, Miss JenChee. Sit down, if you'd like."

She typed a query to Melantha Lee's secretary. Gaea did pay technical staff. She was, in fact, allotted two techs.

A good thing, since she'd offered DalLierx—

Yes. She might be able to employ the stowaway. That would give her one educated assistant and a "grunt," like most field researchers. It was likely that Liberty JenChee had been sent by the Chairman of Colonial Affairs to keep an eye on her.

Fair enough.

She swiveled her chair. The woman had stepped out into the lab. "Miss JenChee?" Graysha called.

When Liberty returned to the office doorway, Graysha took a moment to look her over. Ethnically mixed and long-waisted, she wore browncloth softened with wear. She seemed unable to look long at Graysha's face, darting her glances aside and then trying again to maintain eye contact.

"I'd be happy to offer you employment," Graysha plunged on, "but at the moment I'm still settling in myself. What I'd like to do is have you come in, say, about every third day until I know where I'll need you. If that will be all right, I'll see you tomorrow morning—no, come the next day, at about eight." Graysha stood up and offered Liberty a handshake.

After the young Lwuite woman left, Graysha spent the better part of an hour selecting abstracts at the basic level, then filing them in a new index for Liberty to read. It occurred to her to wonder what happened to Jon Mahera's assistants. Had they left the work force, departed Axis Plantation for other settlements, or found better employment during the job's brief vacancy?

Abruptly she realized that a low-pitched rumble had started somewhere off to her right, like an army of approaching track-trucks. That couldn't be. Those solar vehicles would be shut away in garages during today's darkness. The floor didn't move, so this was no microseism.

Sandstorm?

She sprang to the small office window, depolarized its dimmer, and peered out. Stars winked on and off with those queer atmospheric disturbances. That looked right—until before her very eyes they faded and vanished. Barn lights disappeared next. The rumbling developed a whistle.

She spun toward the hall door. Jirina intercepted her there. "It's snowing," Jirina exclaimed, "and, sister, I've seen it snow sideways here. It's blowing due south. Catch that wind?"

Graysha nodded. Her window, she'd learned, faced south by southeast. "It scared the pants off me. We're supposed to have stars this time of day."

"Right. Come around to the other side of the building. We've got a few outdoor lights close enough for you to see what's happening."

Standing in the break room, Graysha watched a flood of white pellets wash past. A few tiny eddies around the window's frame slowed the onslaught, letting it swirl. She hoped the window glass was good and thick.

"Our third snow this G-year," Jirina said, standing at Graysha's shoulder. "It means we're getting enough water into the ecosystem to saturate the atmosphere—what air there is, and at this temp..." She touched a keyboard. "Twenty below freezing, and it's dropping."

Graysha stared. What a violent atmosphere. What a waste of water and energy. "The poor animals," she murmured.

Jirina picked up a spare cup from under the water heater, and Graysha noticed the black woman wore no more jewelry than she did. Evidently Jirina preferred not to flaunt hab wealth when living close to colonists. "Meteorology's on top of things," Jirina said. "The AnProd people will have had warning, and all the babes will be warm in their barns. But aren't you glad we're going home by tunnel?"

"What about the colonists in their new little houses?" Graysha tried to imagine how isolated they must feel, waiting out the storm, unable to go anywhere.

Filling her cup with double-distilled hot water, Jirina stirred in a spoonful of decaf. "Those that live upside are stuck at work, or school, or wherever. But that's okay, too. They have to learn to watch the forecasts. It's part of their new life."

Graysha shook her head, thinking of Jon Mahera, sent outdoors into a sandstorm as powerful and deadly as this blizzard. Maybe worse. "There goes the collecting trip I planned for next Bday," she mused.

"Maybe not." Jirina shrugged. "Read the forecast. This will probably break by planetary morning. When we finally get really long storms, that'll mean Goddard is coming alive."

Graysha rubbed the chilly window, marveling at the clear trail her finger left in a fog of condensation. Sooner or later, she'd have to go out under that untamed sky again. "Is it safe outdoors right after a storm?"

"If you dress for it. People do it all the time."

Like the ancients, they consistently wore extra clothing to control their warmth. "Incredible." Graysha stared, steadying her legs against vertigo as unending whiteness whipped past in the dark. Her triannum would be six swings through the local seasons, including six uncontrolled winters. If solar batteries flickered out or hydroelectric lines broke during this kind of blast, only wind-generated power would keep the chill outdoors.

"Jirina," she mused, "on days like this I'm going to miss living in a hab."

The storm howled over Axis Plantation all twenty-four hours of Aday, ending sometime during the late planetary night. By Bday light, right after lunch, Graysha layered culture-growing dishes and a case of enriched soy-broth swab tubes into Jon Mahera's collecting briefcase.

Will Varberg stepped into her lab as she set the case beside her sink and washed her hands. "Your trip day," he observed.

"Yes, finally." She reached for a yellowed homespun towel. "It's about time, don't you think? I've been here four circadays."

"I'll go with you—show you around."

Warning bells clanged in her mind as she turned to hang up the towel. If Varberg was the murderer, she might put herself in danger if she let him come along. Was she already asking too many questions?

But he was her supervisor and likely the wrong suspect, and she could think of no good reason to beg off. "I'm about ready to head out," she said. "How soon can you conveniently leave?"

"Give me ten."

"Thank you." She swung around and managed a smile. "I'm still not too secure about that sky up there."

He took longer than ten minutes, and when at last he rapped on her door, he offered no explanation. Supervisory privilege, she guessed. She maintained silence while they boarded the elevator.

It opened across from Dr. Lee's office. "Just a moment, Graysha. I think

I should let Administration know where we're going."

"That's fine." She followed Varberg's massive silhouette through glass doors and past the jittery secretary, who flicked one hand at him in greeting. Vivid yellow and orange marigolds crammed a waist-high planter along one wall, and the outer office smelled faintly of jasmine over sandalwood, as if Melantha Lee occasionally burned incense. Beige and gray floor tiles formed a random patchwork underfoot.

Inside Lee's private office, Graysha stared at the side wall. On a smoothed concrete slab, someone had painted a glossy life-sized mural of tall reeds root-drowned in water. Two stately white cranes framed the reeds, cocking their heads, watching for fish with bright black eyes.

Sitting behind her desk, Dr. Lee tracked Graysha's stare back over her shoulder. "With so little paper to spare, I've taken to ornamenting walls. I see you like it."

"You painted it?" Graysha exclaimed. "Dr. Lee, it's almost alive."

"The adjustment to living underground is difficult for many," Lee said, "even for some habitants. This is one reason the newer constructs are no longer dug underground—and it's easier to build upside."

"I hope you're teaching some of their children to paint." Graysha spotted a small brown fish hiding in painted ripples.

"We're going sampling this afternoon," Varberg said. "Tour of the plantation."

Dr. Lee swiveled her chair. "An excellent idea, Dr. Brady-Phillips. Small changes occur every day, particularly after a storm."

"It's curiosity as much as anything," said Graysha. "I'd like to see how your greenhouses compare to those at Newton or Einstein, or even Halley."

"Our under-glass crops come along as quickly as in any habitat." Dr. Lee stared over Graysha's shoulder as she spoke. "The colonists' chief goals are to pay for our service and make the colony self-supporting. As soils expert, you are a particularly valuable person to them."

Except for one small problem—my mother. She would have said it out loud, but Varberg was speaking. "Gaea's goal, on the other hand, is to make the planet live. Neither is going to be easy."

Lee's audi line buzzed. "Excuse me one moment." The supervisor turned aside.

As Dr. Lee spoke toward the pickup on her desk, Graysha murmured, "It sounds like you and Dr. Lee have a long-standing friendly disagreement."

"We've heard rumbles," Varberg answered softly, "of reorganization from Gaea's Copernicus office. The home office back on Earth isn't impressed with regional management. It has nothing to do with long-term

Goddard policy, though. Shouldn't affect us."

Graysha distrusted *shouldn't* on principle, whenever she heard it. "What kind of reorganization?" she asked. Could corporate greed offer another clue to Jon Mahera's murder?

"The same kind of stories I've been hearing since I was hired twenty years ago." Casually, Varberg reached down to the glass of marigolds on Melantha Lee's desk. Graysha watched, fascinated. He plucked a petal, then another. "Consortium money about to run out, maybe," he said, "or too many projects too far separated to manage them all efficiently. Surely you've heard them."

She had. If Gaea pulled out of Goddard, her triple pay—and her best and perhaps final chance at finding a homogenegineer—would vanish like Mars's polar ice caps. She tried not to stare at his hand. "Well, yes," she said, "I've heard lots of stories." Switching her web-handled carry case from one side to the other, she stepped away from Dr. Lee's desk. On a low table near a window, a large woody seed hung suspended by thin wooden picks over a drinking glass. A broad-leafed sapling, half a meter high, sprouted from its rounded top. Someday, if Goddard warmed enough to support tropical flora, one avocado tree would be ready for transplant.

Lee turned aside from her soft conversation. "Oh, excuse me. I didn't mean to delay you. Have a pleasant afternoon."

Graysha strolled beside Varberg toward the plantation's central hub. She sniffed the indoor air, catching a faint tang of curing concrete. Most of the heavy machinery she'd seen parked along this corry was gone today. Axis Plantation must have mammoth elevators.

Headed due north, they passed a stairwell marked Textiles. She worked up the courage to ask, "Tell me more about your genetics work, Dr. Varberg. What's your specialty?"

He smiled faintly. "Whatever's needed. Agriculture says, 'Let there be acid-tolerant cyanobacteria,' and I provide. Our gene bank is one of the best, and it's rare when I don't have the right organisms to start with."

"That's excellent."

He squinted across at her. "You're not opposed to gene-jockeying on principle?" he asked. One eye narrowed as one side of his mouth smiled.

"Should I be?"

"Just thinking of your mother."

Mother, mother, mother. Stop following me! She adjusted the parka she'd slung over one arm. "My mother and I," she said, "don't see eye to eye on some things."

He laughed. "Such a nice normal family."

Not exactly, but she didn't care to explain any further.

Beyond the textile mill, another broad stair bore the label Farm Complex IV. "That's closest," he said. "We'll take it." He paused to pull on his coat. Graysha copied him, feeling fettered head to waist by the bulky parka. She left her goggles atop her head, wanting a first look at the upside farms with unfiltered vision.

At the top of the stairs hung a thermometer that read twelve below freezing. Graysha cringed and walked out into the wind—not the mild breeze of an air-conditioning unit but a gale that tugged hairs loose from her band and whipped them into her face. It blew steady and cold, slanting out of the north. She fastened the jacket snugly and raised its hood.

As wild as it seemed, this site wasn't truly exposed. A transparent shelter tent flapped overhead, dimming her view of the blue, blue sky. She still felt awed—buffeted physically and emotionally—by Goddard's untamed atmosphere. Human determination and human helplessness had to go hand in hand in a frontier environment like this, even when the frontier was being shaped by human intelligence.

She hugged her chest for warmth. Wilted stubs of harvested plants drooped over plowed soil, making rows of long brown humps. Several meters west down the nearest row, men worked in a line, pushing some kind of wheeled machines. Out of the windward distance came chomping sounds from a heavy cultivator.

Varberg bumped her shoulder. "It's heating over the equator," he shouted, "so we get northers most of Bday."

Graysha faced windward and tried to let her shoulders hang loose. If she tried, she still could smell dust, algae, and odd gases. "How far to the crater wall?" she asked. By early-angle light, the wall looked more rugged and jagged than ever, spattered with snowcapped boulders that had to be huge.

"Twelve K north is the closest point."

Mentally upgrading those *huge* boulders to *gigantic,* she eyed the row of broken plant stubs. "I want a soil sample from each field."

"Fortunately, it's not frozen too hard to sample. Too little water in it."

Frozen crop soil . . . She balked at the notion and then finally, fully comprehended. There was no way to protect it from freezing in this environment. "Ah," she said.

"I'll dig. You inoculate." Varberg flipped up his coring shovel, took a two-handed grip, and stomped on its foot peg as naturally as if he'd been born holding one of the implements.

"What about that rumor," she asked, crouching downwind of him and clenching her hands for warmth, "that the Lwuites were running from something back on Einstein?"

He grunted as a small cylinder of dirt dropped out of his shovel's blade. "Oh, you've heard that one, too. Where, from your mother?"

"I don't remember." Graysha scooped part of his core with a spatula. The wind blew the soil away. Turning against the gale to shelter the next sample, she trickled soil into a tube, then placed it in the case. Varberg still hadn't answered her question. "Did you get your start in soils?" she asked, brushing the dirt from her browncloth pants.

"Potatoes, check. The next field up has sugar beets." He stood and said shortly, "Six terrannums on Messier."

"Oh, no." Instantly, she felt that she understood him better. "I'm sorry," she added. Messier, a stony world orbiting Barnard's Star, was the first planet terraformed outside the home solar system. Tragically, a two-degree rise in atmospheric temp, compounded by the loss of jet stream stability, melted a tenth of the world's newly introduced water onto one continental plain—the plain where all its colonists lived.

As Varberg followed Graysha up the crushed-rock path, he added, "Messier was my first and last attempt at settling a planet for good. Goddard gets three terrannums of my life and no more, and then Edie and I are gone. Gone," he repeated. "Take my advice, Graysha. We're all here for the money. Just leave as soon as you can. Planets are good for mining, field studies, and killing settlers."

"I think . . . I understand how you must feel." Maybe this explained his nervous petal pulling. He'd doubtless gone confidently into the field only to have naïve academic ideals stripped away, but he had been unable to make a career change.

"You couldn't understand," he said through gritted teeth. "Gaea employees who were heads of families drew lots for places on the last shuttle away. I won a place, but if it weren't for Edie, I'd wish I hadn't. I knew every man, woman, and child at the Gaea installation. Every one." He kicked at a clod on the path. It vaporized into a small, dusty cloud. "I should have seen it coming, done something. Seventeen terrannums later, I still have nightmares. Edie has to take pills to sleep at all."

Chilled by the images, she stepped backward against the wind. "By all rights, it never should have happened."

"Bimonthly supply flights might have allowed more staff to evacuate, but they couldn't land during that season," he said. "It was tragic."

By all established theories, the Messier disaster shouldn't have happened. Projections for runaway flood conditions weren't even in the right ballpark. Too much energy was supposed to be required, too long a time period, or too small a world.

But try explaining that to the old folks whose colonizing sons and daughters died there.

And don't remind Dr. Varberg again, she decided, not if it gave him nightmares. She looked north across a stretch of blinding white toward the crater wall. Its jagged silhouette clawed the blue sky. She, too, would be glad to return to a habitat, where the horizon curved the right direction and the weather was servant instead of deadly enemy. With a mental sigh of sympathy, she dismissed Varberg from her list of murder suspects.

He trudged west toward the last field. Heaps of stone and sand lay here and there. A huge orange vehicle with some kind of scoop attached to its front bumper sat on the road's edge. Knobby ice stems connected its wheel wells with the ground.

At that point, the shelter tent ended. She plodded behind Varberg up a ramp onto the half-buried pipeline. Her pulse beat faster. Rounded white hillocks extended toward the crater wall, forming an eerie pattern of rippled C-shaped drifts in a wild symmetry, like ocean waves. Sparkling wisps of white crystal blew off the near drifts. She pulled her UV goggles down, covering forehead and eyes, then stomped both feet to reconfirm that this world's gravity would hold her and she wouldn't blow away like newly fallen snow.

"Storm's buried everything out there. Grain, dwarfalfa." Clenching fists on his hips, Varberg stamped out a circle in drifted snow atop the long, snakelike rise. Footprint by footprint, he flattened a standing space along its summit. "And I think that's flax over there on the right—"

"Flax. That's what they weave the browncloth from?" Under the parka, her shirt still itched.

"That, and wool from their halfers and goats. Snow won't reduce production of any of those critters. Out beyond the crater, we've got experimental fields. Cold-kudzu, increasingly modified dwarfalfa strains."

"They actually survive out there." The notion awed her.

"Yep. There'll be trees soon, hardy softwoods. Talk to someone up at Hort if you want to know species. Plants don't exactly thrive under UV, but if we plant enough of them, we're bound to get some adaptive-favorable mutations. Eventually."

A spray of snow seeped off the nearest mound, glittering like spun sugar on a huge icy cake. She raised her eyes to the craggy rim. "If it's blowing like this down here, what's it like up top, outside the crater?"

"Pretty wild at true dawn. I wouldn't want to be there."

"I'll bet," she murmured.

"Late Bday, early Cday, closest to planetary noon, is our tropical calm. *Tropical* being a relative term, of course."

She tried again to imagine this world warming enough for someone to plant Dr. Lee's small avocado tree.

"Cday evenings," he continued, "if the clouds are heavy enough, that's when it rains. The wind shifts around from Storm Sea, and in she comes."

She couldn't fault them for naming Goddard's ocean Storm Sea. "And if wet weather blows in on Dday, it snows," she murmured. "Fascinating."

"But deadly."

"Right." She stared southwest again, past the colonial buildings. A cylindrical concrete stack rose behind the hub's low dome. Chlorofluorocarbon production, she guessed. Thousands of tons of freons, formerly used in refrigerating units, were splattered on Goddard's frigid surface during the cometary impact decades. This plant spewed more. Carbon came from crushed regolith, as did the fluorine, and chloride was extracted from Storm Sea.

Graysha stamped her feet and realized that her body felt good, standing there with her leg muscles warm and tingly tight. "They have genegineered animals, I take it."

"Halfers. Lots of halfers."

The standard post-bovine strain of meat and wool producers. "All the EB's work aside, it certainly would be simpler to gene-tailor us, too, for a particular planet. Don't you think?" She held her breath, waiting for his answer. If only—

"Hmm."

Exasperated, she clenched her sampling bag's strap. If she really wanted answers, she might try changing her name. She faced him on the path. "Just for my curiosity's sake, Dr. Varberg, do the colonists practice homogenegineering?"

"Blast, you're persistent." He scowled. "Like a fly. I don't know. Don't ask me again."

"It's me asking, Dr. Varberg. Not my mother."

He shook his head.

Mother! Where have you ever been when I actually needed you? If legalistic Novia Brady-Phillips had had the courage to locate her own homogenegineer, Graysha wouldn't be wondering where to find one now.

"Had enough?" he asked tersely. "It's almost quitting time."

"I'm fine. The parka is very warm."

"I don't want to lose another soils person, Graysha. Dr. Mahera was sampling a duricrust *Streptomyces* seeding up on the wild when he . . ." Varberg fell silent. Graysha looked back over her shoulder. Three hooded figures had turned aside from the main road and were trudging toward them. The wind whistled, flapping a torn edge of the shelter tent.

Varberg walked down the ramp to meet them. Once the parka-swathed colonists stood in hailing distance, one stopped while the other two marched forward. "Dr. Varberg?" asked one of the approaching pair. "Colonial police. Please come with us. You have the legal right not to speak, but I must arrest you on suspicion of causing the death of Dr. Jon Mahera."

Graysha backed several steps into soft, deep snow. The next instant froze in her memory: Will Varberg dropping his sampling gear to reach for the nearby policewoman; the second colonist poised to fight or flee; the colonist who hung back leveling a medical trank gun at Will Varberg's midsection.

Evidently Varberg spotted the trank gun, too, because he let his hands fall limp without touching either officer. "This is a mistake," he drawled, "and you are legally bound to let me prove it."

"Yes, Dr. Varberg," said the taller man. "Walk ahead of us, please."

Graysha stood with legs buried to her shins in snow, scarcely able to believe she was watching an arrest. Her emotions seemed even number than her chilly toes. Will Varberg led the taller guard and the gun wielder toward the nearest blockhouse, and then the other officer—the woman— approached. "You're Dr. Brady-Phillips?"

"Yes," she said warily. "I am."

Raising one hand to display a recorder button nestled in her palm, the officer asked, "Has Dr. Varberg said anything in your presence that might give you cause to wonder if there were ill feelings between him and the late Dr. Mahera?"

Graysha groaned softly. She'd heard so much new information during the past four days. How could she hope to remember anything that specific?

And if the colonists were responsible for Mahera's death, Will Varberg might be their choice of scapegoat.

"No," she admitted, staring down at the sandy path. "That is, I don't remember hearing him say anything like that."

"Did he express ill will toward anyone, Dr. Brady-Phillips?"

Another wind gust flapped the shelter tent. "He did give me the impression that he doesn't like or trust colonial government."

The colonist shot her a glance that could have frozen exposed flesh.

Ari MaiJidda frowned, disappointed, as Yael GurEshel injected an antidote into Will Varberg's beefy arm. Using a law enforcement drug that made a subject relaxed, talkative, and almost unable to lie, Ari had confronted Varberg with evidence: the fateful message that the sandstorm was over originated at a terminal he frequently used. With bright eyes and softly slurred speech, he admitted sending it. She exulted.

Then he maintained it was accidental, not intentional. He'd decided not to come forward "to spare Edie the embarrassment."

DalLierx stood over the Gaea employee's chair, finishing follow-up questions that would determine the degree of Varberg's actual crime. Manslaughter, probably. "Recommendation?" she asked DalLierx when he finished.

DalLierx hooked both thumbs into his pockets, looking natural in a boyish stance. "Half a G-year's recompense work on behalf of Mahera's parents. On planet."

Varberg glared up at him, rocking back and forth on his chair. His resentment showed so plainly that Ari guessed it'd be a while before he regained full control. She had time to ask one or two more questions. "Was there any other reason, besides sparing your wife embarrassment, that you didn't come forward?"

DalLierx frowned, but she wasn't about to retract the question. Law enforcement fell under her jurisdiction.

"After Messier," Varberg said, sounding thick-tongued, "do you think either one of us wanted to try another planetary assignment? You people make me laugh. You're all going to die on Goddard."

"Sooner or later," Ari murmured, spearing DalLierx with another glare. He turned away.

She focused on Varberg. The weirdly bright gleam in his eyes faded out. Yes, it was safe to ask this question . . . now. "What about those notorious sandpiles, Dr. Varberg? What was the point in leaving those on so many of your co-workers' desks?"

Sitting perfectly straight in the office chair, he glowered at DalLierx's back. "Find another suspect, Madam Vice-Chair. I'm not guilty of that one."

DalLierx spun back around.

"Hmm," she observed, catching Lindon's eye. "Too late."

"I didn't do it," Varberg repeated.

"You may go, Dr. Varberg," she said. The escorts took him back to the stairs, and she gave Lindon another somber look as she closed down her file.

He walked out, too, and then she smiled. She knew perfectly well Varberg didn't leave those sandpiles. If Gaea employees suspected one another, so much the better. She didn't want them making themselves at home on her world.

Sand was one of Goddard's cheaper law-enforcement resources.

Novia Brady-Phillips raised a hand, gesturing welcome across her desktop. This was a happy moment; she'd tracked down another one of Henri Lwu's surviving employees. "Sit down, Mr. Witt. Thank you for coming."

"Your invitation mentioned incentive money." Lon Witt sank into the chair across from her desk. High-backed, striped in tan and brown, it sloped comfortably.

Novia swiveled her own chair. Her office had good lighting and ventilation, always desirable in habitat living. Along the left wall, mirrored shelves displayed tasteful ethnic artifacts from the Jordan-Euphrates region of Earth, where three major human faiths had originated—faiths reconciled one hundred years ago within the doctrinal embrace of her own denomination, the Church of the Universal Father. She glanced at the framed three-star emblem she'd been given for special service to the Church. CUF honored and defended humanity, the sanctified multimind of the one true god—who did, after all, visit Earth as a genetically unmodified human. The Eugenics Board preserved and protected that god-endorsed genome. Novia was privileged to give her life to work that had such eternal significance.

At the far left corner of her desk, a curved cup hid a glossy black ball that was visible only from the other side. She eyed Lon Witt across the desk's expanse.

Witt, retired two terrannums, had the soft chin and expanding waistline of someone who ate well, but he claimed he had money problems. "A nice incentive," she answered, "payable monthly over ten terrannums. I know about retirement," she added, raising a sympathetic eyebrow. "My grandfather complains constantly. I help him on the side, when I can."

Lon Witt nodded curtly. He appeared to share her pride problem.

All the better. "What exactly did you do for Henri Lwu?" She knew the answer from EB files, but she always started with easy questions.

"I wrote grants, looked for funding."

Money focus, a root of evil. Perhaps he had a guilty conscience. "And you remember some things that might be worth our attention." She lifted a smooth green tigereye marble from a cradle beside her antique fountain pen and cupped it in her right hand.

"As a grant-writing specialist, I learned to notice patterns," he said. "Lwu's funding came in oddly."

Quietly elated, Novia squeezed the marble, applying pressure and rotating it leftward. On the desk's far corner, the mirrored cup copied that rotation in subtle slow motion. She released the marble. "That could be significant."

"Particularly since most of it wasn't from companies at all but from wealthy families in Einstein Hab."

"Oh?" Witt's shoulders reached the second tan stripe on the chair's back. She raised the mirrored cup slightly and asked, "Do you remember which families?"

"Some were in local politics. Jensen, Dalquist, Morikone. I began to wonder if campaign donations were being diverted to Henri Lwu's office."

"It seems unlikely that any politician would sacrifice his own campaign money for fetal research," she said. "Wouldn't do him much good." She replaced the marble in its cradle and pressed her right knee—the good one—against a flexing desk panel. In five minutes, Witt would be immobilized below the neck. The chair would cradle his body. He would not fall; the experience was no more embarrassing than was absolutely necessary. "What about the nonpolitical families?"

"Lwu's research benefited heavily from Marc Lierx's estate, back in 2122."

"Ah. Him, I remember." Founder of a pharmaceutical empire, Lierx supported several fringe denominations as well as social work among humankind's less desirable factions. "What do you know about the experimentation itself?"

"Fetal work," he said. "Trying to improve cross-hemispheric connections in the male brain. That much was public. But—" Witt raised his head—"that wife of his—"

"Palila?"

"She was a geriatric specialist."

"Yes." Novia already thought the fetal-geriatric marriage an odd one. "Maybe that would explain the politicians' interest. We all grow old." Truly, merciful euthanasia was better than letting invalids gasp out their last breaths in pointless pain.

Witt fingered the crease in his double chin. "She published several papers stating that over time, the body develops borderline immunities to itself, causing gerontological breakdown. Aging."

And Palila Lwu's aunt was a lab child, one of the few whose full-body irradiation didn't kill her right away. Novia tapped her pencil against the desktop. "Was she having any success? With the research, I mean. We'll discuss funding presently."

Witt swung his chair left and right. "Her primary research grew out of cancer work that took a left turn back at the end of the twenty-first century. She managed to find a group of families without any history of chromosomal fragile sites." He paused, looking her in the eye, obviously wondering if she knew what he was talking about.

She nodded. Others had talked, persuaded by EB funds. "Fragile sites," as well as "programmed cell death," had been mentioned several times.

He continued. "We know she isolated several genes those families carried, transferred them into gribien populations, then started stress work. I think she might've been looking for key gene complexes, hoping to help the immune system stave off aging."

Novia repressed a shudder. Supergening created abominations, and every attempt to alter humankind resulted in tragedy—such as the Strobel children's aggressiveness, which caused the catastrophic Troubles. Any supergened group that seized resource-rich Earth or a productive orbiting habitat might subjugate humankind in short order.

No wonder the Church of the Universal Father, founded just over a century ago, grew quickly. The desire for self-protection proved stronger than any other spiritual concern. A few Hebrew scholars claimed humans once lived for centuries, before the Flood mentioned in many cultural myths. Contemporary science claimed it still was possible to live that long. She shuddered to think what supergened creatures might achieve if they lived three or four hundred years. Each couple might have two or three hundred offspring, like insects or amphibians.

"Gene complexes," she said mildly. "Ah. No wonder you felt it your duty to come to us. Well done."

He nodded stiffly.

"She—or her husband, Henri—mentioned no significant success in the aging research while you were there, though?"

"I'm afraid not. Does that mean I don't qualify for money?"

"It doesn't mean that at all." *Just one less thing to ask about today.* "Already you have been most helpful. Perhaps you left Henri Lwu's employment because you guessed his wife meant to involve herself once again in homogenegineering?" Convicted practitioners were professionally defrocked. Witt must have feared for his own career.

"That was part of it," he said, "yes."

"Then, naturally, you are innocent of criminal intent."

She had been trained to notice the tiniest glance or other sign of evasion. His irises flicked sideways now. Perhaps he was beginning to notice the lethargy field's effect.

"Mr. Witt, if you will commit yourself as a Board witness, no charges will be brought against you."

"What? Are you hinting—" She recognized his next gesture, an abortive jerking back of elbows as he tried to grip his armrests and pull himself upright. The lethargy field hadn't yet immobilized him, but sluggishness was enough if he would cooperate.

"To qualify you for the reward money," she said calmly, pulling open a desk drawer, "I must confirm your testimony using a cerebral monitor. I will then be able to erase your name from all EB records except payroll. It's big fish we want, Mr. Witt, not fingerlings."

He scowled when she said *fingerlings.* Here, definitely, was a pride problem.

She could use that weakness to help him cooperate. From the drawer she drew out a rotary depilator. "Only the temples need to be shaved."

Many witnesses balked at this point. One injured her badly enough to necessitate hospitalization. An assistant stood ready in the hall, but she didn't want to call him unless absolutely necessary. Jambling made people uneasy.

"I haven't done anything," Witt insisted.

Novia pressed the knee panel again, deactivating the black ball. "That's good," she said, "and think of the incentive money. Turn your head left, please."

To her relief, he cooperated. She cleared one pale temple. From among the artifacts on the mirrored shelves, she drew out a small box and applied an electrode patch it held. "To the right now. Thank you."

Prepped, he sat nervously with his double chin twitching. Novia slid a larger box off the shelf and touched its power panel. "Were you involved in homogenegineering research, Mr. Witt?"

His eyes stayed wide. "No."

On the green screen inside the box's hinged lid, she read numbers off a chart. Shunting of impulses from speech and reason to fear centers would challenge Witt's truthfulness. That didn't happen, though. So far, he spoke truth. "To your knowledge, was either Henri or Palila Lwu?"

"I don't know for certain."

Again, verity. He was, indeed, a fingerling.

"But Palila mentioned it to be among her interests," she suggested.

"She did. I already said that, I think."

"Explain," she ordered, "the connection between her research and the aging process. Take your time, giving as many details as possible."

As Witt rambled, she watched the instrument's screen. In some places he remembered less than he thought he did, but at one point, he paused. "Six," he said. "They celebrated one night, something about having found the sixth one of something. They felt it was a critical number. Another fragile site, maybe."

Novia gave him a bland smile. By itself, that wasn't grounds to convict anyone—but puzzle pieces were falling together. She could almost taste another round of USSC funding.

"Can you move your hand, Mr. Witt?" she asked, guessing she'd learned all he knew. All that mattered, anyway.

He flinched, plainly startled, when it lifted easily off the armrest.

"It's really a temporary, harmless procedure." Deftly she plucked the patches from his temples. "I'll need one more thing—your signature on a release form stating that this information was furnished without duress."

She knew it for hypocrisy, and when his eyes narrowed, she knew he recognized it, too. This was another critical moment. If he signed, the information was "obtained conscious, legally," and OCL data would stand up in any court under USSC jurisdiction. Otherwise, she would need a second witness's testimony to the same bit of information.

He hesitated. Novia drummed two fingers on her stiff left knee. She could, if necessary, offer a 10 percent bonus on his blood money. She wanted that OCL signature.

Witt stared down at the floor, plainly comparing his options. She waited. If Lwu's heirs had to be investigated out in the field, she alone might carry the responsibilities of inquiry, prosecution, and punishment. Cautious groundwork could turn a potential botched case into a USSC-net auto-convict. How satisfying it might be to execute God's judgment on site, in person.

Every terrannum or so, EB operatives caught one or two renegades who bilked payment out of some ambitious parent who wanted supergened children. So far, those arrested were just frauds and charlatans.

Novia had to believe that the smart ones, the real supergeners, were still out there. They were the true idol-worshipers of this century. The creatures they bred spread violence, warfare, and death.

Witt wrinkled his nose. "I'll sign," he said stiffly. "It's for a good cause."

"Well done," she said, giving her knee a pat. She comforted Witt with small talk while his muscle tone returned, then walked him up a wide bright hall to the exit. He departed with a credit chit in his pocket. The disbursement secretary said nothing about shaved spots on his temples.

Graysha dumped her breakfast dishes in the housing cafeteria and hurried to work, swinging her arms as she made the hard left turns into the Gaea corridor. The outside temp had crept back up, and topside, snow was melting. She'd just reached her lab when Dr. Varberg hailed her from the break room. "Graysha. In here a minute, please."

She'd been greatly relieved to read in the Bday evening bulletin that Varberg's murder charges were converted to manslaughter and the case was declared shut. Anyone could "commit" an accident. Anyone might hope not to be caught in it. Now she could stop worrying about a schizic running loose.

Inside the long break room, that weird mixture of coffee, soil, and rodent smells made her feel at home. Varberg stood beside a tall shelf, and with him hunched the stowaway. The youth managed to appear both sullen and frightened, dipping his chin to glower up from under his eyebrows. He no longer smelled like a goat barn, and now he wore baggy browncloth pants and a shirt.

"Dr. Graysha Brady-Phillips," Varberg said with an uncharacteristic sigh, "this is Mr. Ex, aka George Smith. Chairman DalLierx assigned him to us as laboratory help. *'He who will not work,'* and all that. The Chairman suggested since you're new on our deck, you show him around and ask questions for two. Any objections?" He laid a hand on the boy's shoulder. "Ex" wriggled it off.

Graysha straightened her spine. "No objections. I asked for him, in fact. I'd like to train him as my second tech."

Varberg brushed imaginary dirt from his hand onto one pant leg. "Oh. Well, that's fine with me. Mr. Ex, you'll touch out on your time card in my office at five-oh." He strode out, leaving Graysha alone with the animal noises, her unanswered questions about Jon Mahera, and Ex, aka George Smith.

He twisted full pink-brown lips to one side of his face, amazing her: he could make himself look homelier. Scraggly eyebrows and sunken cheeks accentuated the shortest, broadest nose she'd ever seen. One earlobe was noticeably higher than the other, just as she remembered from the shuttle lander. "You *asked* for me?" he demanded, sneering.

"I came in by shuttle when you did." She studied the pouting set of his lips, hoping she hadn't made a judgment error. "We new people ought to stick together. I have plenty of work to keep a tech busy. Laboratory technician—translation, drudge. It's not such bad work, really. I mucked animal cages for my first annum of college."

He wrinkled his mouth, sticking his lip out farther. She fought the temptation to laugh.

"I am Dr. Brady-Phillips," she offered, "but I prefer Graysha. The tall woman who works up here goes by first name, too. Jirina. Maybe you've met her."

He shook his head rapidly, about one centimeter each direction.

What a ham. At least he responded.

"Do you want me to call you Ex?" she asked. "I'd rather not. I have an ex back at Einstein. Ex-husband."

He rolled his eyes. "Your problem, not mine."

"I'll bet George isn't your name, either," she said evenly. She guessed him to be seventeen or so. She'd worked with that age, teaching the usual mixture of achievers and reluctant learners. Some stayed in school only because it kept them off lab-drudge jobs. Habitant teeners were required by law to train or produce. Ex, she guessed, was used to getting his own way.

She waited. Something made digging noises in a cage nearby.

"You can call me Trev," he said, barely opening his mouth.

Hoping he'd decided to trust her, she smiled. "Thanks, Trev. Want a look around the floor?"

Trev showed little interest when she led him past the automated media kitchen and when she raised the lid on a steaming, smelly incubator, but he gave off flickers of attentive disgust as she explained the soil-layering terraria back in the break room. "You people make this?" He pointed into a glass cubicle black with rich histic loam. "You can get a doctorate from brewing mud?"

"Some do. I didn't cook that up," Graysha admitted. "I just arrived. This is a biannum potting. My predecessor started it, and I work with the same kinds of bacteria."

"What's so great about dirt?" For the first time, he stared into her eyes. Beneath those scraggly eyebrows, she caught a glimpse of a teachable moment.

At what level did she start explaining, though? "The pulverized rock out there—regolith—has been seeded with bacteria that break it down, releasing nutrients for higher plants and animals. Nutrients such as oxygen." She paused.

"Bacteria?" he repeated. "Eating rocks?"

Not scientifically literate, she decided. Testing that guess, she started a detailed explanation of the nitrogen cycle. Within two sentences he was tuning her out, turning aside to the animal cages.

She fell silent.

"Trapped." He addressed a long rectangular pan covered by a metal grate and inhabited by a 30-centimeter female rodent. "What is it?" he demanded.

Graysha turned to the brown creature, which raised a whiskered nose to sniff the air. It probably expected to be fed whenever someone paused nearby. "Those are yabuts."

"Yabuts?"

"Some gene jockey's idea of a joke," she explained. " 'Rabbit? Ya, but . . .' " She winced.

Trev peered into the cage. "Stinking, filthy, and ugly as sin—" The yabut waddled closer, dragging several hairless pink progeny under her belly. "Ee-uch," Trev exclaimed. His lips twisted, first pursing and then frowning. He wheeled toward Graysha with fear-wide eyes. "You aren't going to cut her up, are you?"

"No," she said softly. "Yabuts are our primary upside herbivores. We test experimental feeds made from gene-engineered plant species on them."

His eyes looked more sad than defiant. She thought she understood. She'd spent more than a little time haranguing staff at Einstein University to take gentler care of lab animals.

"But yabuts are edible," she admitted. "So's their chow, for that matter, if food runs short. This is a frontier world."

He grunted.

Evidently she'd lectured long enough. "Our coffee's instant, but it's made from real beans. Want some?"

He raised his head. "Coffee? I mean . . . yeah. Uh, thanks."

Several minutes later, in the privacy of Graysha's office, they sat sipping.

"Did you hear the news, Graysha?" Jirina's deep voice called from the outer doorway.

Trev cringed. He twisted to peer out into the lab.

Standing in the office arch, Jirina looked like a black goddess compared to the cowering youth with his mottled cheeks. She peered down at him and asked, "What are you so afraid of, little brother?"

"Forget the 'brother,' " he muttered. "I'm not anybody's brother."

"Ooh," Jirina said with an exaggerated shrug.

Graysha beckoned her in. Jirina took her usual spot on the cold concrete floor, then said, "I'm sorry for you."

Amused, Graysha solemnly told Trev, "Jirina's my friend. I don't have many here yet." Turning her head, she added to Jirina, "This is Trev, and he's here, and he's frightened of something. Why else does a person stow away?"

"I paid passage." Trev vehemently accented each word.

"How far?" Graysha asked softly.

He took a long, slow drink of coffee.

Graysha recalled Jirina's question at the door and murmured, "What news?"

"That it was Varberg."

"But it was accidental," Graysha added, watching Trev for a reaction.

"Look," he said, "it's like this. But you've both got to swear to be quiet about it, at least until word gets out."

Was that all it took to draw a confession—a little show of sympathy? Graysha raised her eyebrows.

"Ever heard of Blase LZalle?" he asked.

Graysha pursed her lips, thinking. She hadn't spent much time studying history, nor did she pay much attention to politics. Jirina stared silently at Trev.

"Music," he prompted.

Jirina made wide eyes. "Had a guitar pick grafted on in place of one thumbnail, once."

"Him. Five complete surgical transformations in twenty-one terrannums, plus minor alterations. Sometimes he's Afro, sometimes Sino, sometimes Abo. Limbs made of rubber."

"I've heard of him," Jirina said.

Trev glanced at Graysha as he reached up into his wiry hair to scratch the lower ear.

She shrugged. "I'm sorry, Trev. Maybe he wasn't big in Einstein."

To her surprise, he smiled with real warmth. "Finally, someone with the good taste not to know the man. Anyway, he held a competition about nineteen terrannums ago to find the genetically perfect woman to bear his child. Married her and then hid her away on Venus, the world of love. Or Venera, as natives and Russians call it."

"Yes?" asked Graysha.

He touched his chest. "Trevarre Chase-Frisson LZalle, son of the Rebuilt Wonder and the Genetically Perfect Woman."

Jirina puffed out a breath. "Glad to meet you, Mr. Chase-Frisson LZalle. What brings you to our happy little rock ball?"

He twisted his features into a leer. "Do I *look* genetically perfect?"

"Oh," Graysha exclaimed. "Dear God. Your father wanted a perfect child. He rebuilt himself. Now he wants to rebuild you."

Trev's fingers, clenched on his knees, turned pale. "Exactly. Exactly. He doesn't care that I don't want to be beautiful. He knows even local anesthetics give me double-sick migraines. But he wants to debut me, his Mr. Perfect Son, at a music fest in two terrannums—it's already booked—and I can't even stand his music. I'm a failure, and he's used to million-maxim successes. He expects them. Nothing less."

"You're the only son?" Graysha asked.

"That's me."

"Well." She rocked back on her chair. "You couldn't hide much farther afield than Goddard."

"I wasn't heading for Goddard," he insisted. "I bought passage from Earth to Alpha under the Smith name. So far so good, only it wasn't far enough out. I spotted his name on a sales marquee. So I decided to stow for Galileo Hab, in the Barnard's system."

"It's supposed to be pretty there," Jirina said. "Experimental forests."

"So I heard. I like that stuff. Trees, bushes. But there were two shuttles leaving Halley's main loading dock at once, and I—"

"Got on the wrong one?" Jirina asked.

"I've been tissue typed." Now he looked really glum, lips twitching, arching his eyebrows. "ExPress Shuttle Service could have me ID'd within a week and have word to LZalle in two. He can afford to send a private shuttle out to get me. But," he added, dropping his voice, "I don't think it'd stop there."

Graysha shrugged off the threat. She'd hired a resourceful assistant, she guessed—if he would just learn to cooperate. "He can't force surgery on you," she said. She tapped the space bar on her computer.

"No, but he can start with psych therapy. In two months I'll be panting for them to cut."

"I'm sorry," said Graysha. "Really, I am. I don't have a lot of clout around here, but if you could make yourself indispensable to Gaea, I would think there'd be some chance they'd let you stay on."

"How do I do that?" He leaned into the question, looking a little too sincere.

What does he really want? Graysha wondered. *And what else is he afraid of?* "I'm sure you aren't interested in this kind of work," she said, "but Gaea is the only employer here, and I'll give you a chance to do some real research if you'll promise to give it your best." Abruptly she chuckled.

"What?" Jirina asked.

Graysha folded her hands over one knee. "I gave up a teaching job for this position, Trev. I miss it already, and I'm glad you're here. I'll show you what I can. I'll even lend you some text capsules tonight, and I'm sure Dr. Lee will check you out a viewer."

"Sounds all right," he said, staring at his feet.

"Are you a good student?"

"When I want to be."

In other words, normal. "First, then." She stood up. "Let me start on the glorified dishwasher we call a 'glassware processor.'"

"Sounds thrilling," he grumbled.

"Oh, it is." Graysha grinned.

Jirina snorted.

Graysha organized Liberty's and Trev's schedules, set up a soil-nutrient scan to run, then had twenty minutes of spare time. Inside her inner office, she kicked the heat up a notch, then signed on the Gaea net. Free-associating, she found one more open file on Henri Lwu. The abstract was from a postdoctoral thesis, buried among Gaea library headings.

Balance of Logical and Emotional Processes in the Human Male, she read. She glanced over her shoulder to make sure no techs were watching, then she read on.

According to Henri Lwu's abstract—the short summary at the head of his article—the problem was a lack of cross-hemispheric connections in the male brain. "Good thing a female didn't do this research," Graysha muttered. "She would've been ostracized for sexism."

Lwu's experimental research supported an old theory that the splenial region of the corpus callosum, a connective region between the brain's frontal hemispheres, shrank in a flood of hormones and serum fractions at about the eighth month of a male's gestation. In experimental groups, starting with rodents, he'd done cranial injections to protect the corpus callosum from cell die-off at this critical phase. It was one way to affect the brain without diminishing primary sexual development. An experimental summary gave details of how the procedure could be practiced among a general population.

Graysha scratched her head. He'd found volunteers for that? Mothers willing to let him experiment on their children for the sake of so slight a change? She knew how to read graphs. The results were measurable but marginal.

Finding the notion ugly, no matter how nobly inspired by Henri Lwu's devotion to peace and nonaggression, she shut down the computer and resumed work in her lab.

Ten minutes later, it struck her as odd that Gaea Terraforming Consortium posted that abstract in its own library.

Trev yanked a rattling rack of inverted culture tubes from the processor and started sorting them into drawers. "All right, it's your turn," he said. "I told you where I came from and why. Now that you know about me, tell me about these Lwuite colonists."

The faint off-odor of warm TSY growth medium drifted down the hall from the media kitchen. Blinking at her clock, Graysha pushed her stool back from her scanning scope and rested her eyes. It would've been nice if Trev asked about her own background first. Trev obviously didn't make "nice" a priority.

He was young. "They don't mix much with us outsiders," she said. "I don't know if they're secretive or if they feel awkward about being labeled a religious group by humanity at large." Graysha could understand that sentiment. All her life, people assumed that Novia Brady-Phillips, defender of God's unaltered creation, had raised her mutant daughter to be likewise religious. Variant faiths piqued her curiosity, but Graysha distrusted all religions, especially her mother's Church of the Universal Father. It just didn't seem logical that the God who inspired so many religious wars would suddenly announce that He really only meant to create perfection and watch it run down.

If He existed at all.

"So tell me what you know about them," Trev said.

Graysha sighed. "Supposedly, they were founded by a scientist who insisted the male mind didn't need to be as compartmentalized as it is."

"Try that in English."

"Men—allegedly, Trev; I'm not saying I buy into this—tend to have trouble balancing logical and emotional thought."

"Oh, that. What did this scientist do about it?"

Young people sometimes accepted such abrasive assertions! Amused, Graysha said, "Dr. Lwu theorized that this was part of what made men too aggressive. Too likely to start fights." Hedging the concept in vague scientific jargon, she told him what she'd learned from the computer. As she finished she rubbed her eyes and looked out the window, where stars sparkled.

"I heard that," said Paul Ilizarov's voice from the door.

She whirled around.

Paul lounged against the arch, making her wonder how long he had stood there. Pointing at Trev, he added, "Don't let him damage glassware. The colonists charge us five hundred percent of market value for glass."

Varberg or Jirina must have told Paul about Trev. "He's doing fine. What do *you* know about our colonial employers?"

The oceanographer moved languidly, as if he'd spent time on a seagoing ship. "Those rumors you mentioned? Rumors. I'd guess the truth is even stranger. Otherwise, why would they hide out here? Parsecs from civilization, living from provision ship to provision ship, dependent on us for everything, and meanwhile freezing their fingers to plant kudzu. At least they don't have to weed it."

"Not yet." Graysha returned Paul's smile, then saw that Trev looked blank-faced again. "No native plants to blow weed seeds into their croplands," she explained, then she turned again. "Paul, you have a Lwuite tech. Don't you know something about their faith?"

"I have two Lwuite techs. Twins. I think you've only seen one at a time. They won't talk religion, and believe me, they've got the RL Act memorized."

Proselytizing, according to the Religious Liberties Act, was illegal without duly registered inquiry—and inquiries need not be answered. The Act had been pushed into USSC law by her mother's church, probably to keep splinter groups small. "But they are religious." Graysha pursed her lips. If Paul knew this little after two terrannums, the Lwuites certainly did not preach outside their own numbers. Maybe Liberty would tell . . .

No. Liberty JenChee was not what one would call talkative.

Paul rubbed one thumb against his elegant chin. "Trevarre, is your father really that much of a beast?"

Trev drew up tall next to the lab counter. "Who told the Russian?"

Graysha had no idea. "Trev," she said, "this is Dr. Paul Ilizarov."

Scowling wide-eyed, Trev turned back to Paul. "I don't think you want to know."

"He tours. You must not have to see him too often."

"If he ever gets to Goddard, you'll wish you never heard his name."

Graysha sympathized with Trev, despite his atrocious manners. What a thing to look forward to—a complete surgical reconstruction. Transgening would have been kinder.

Paul pulled a hand from his lab-coat pocket. Manicured but strong looking, it was the shapeliest man's hand she'd seen. A faint whiff of citrus made her guess either his hand soap or his lab lotion came from offworld. He gave Trevarre an ice-blue glare, then looked away from the youth. "My techs are on town-meeting crew today, and I need some filter plating done. Think he can handle it?"

"Trev, are you finished?" Graysha asked.

Trev pointedly dropped another handful of tubes into a drawer.

"Carefully," Graysha murmured. She'd better separate these two, even if it meant equivocating. "Yes, Paul, I've taught him how to plate. I'll send him over when he's finished with this."

Paul touched her shoulder, making her shiver. "Thank you," he said.

Flustered by the electric tension emanating from that man, she was glad to be alone with Trev again.

"Plate?" Trev demanded. "What's that?"

Graysha shook her head. "You need to try and get along with Dr. Ilizarov."

"Ha." He wiped his nose with a brusque backhand. "Come to Venus some day, Graysha. Spend time with the Novaya Muscovites and then tell me to get along with Russians. My father took me out of school after the third time they ganged up on me."

"Paul knows who and what he is, that's all. When you've got his kind of experience, you can accomplish all you want."

"Oh, save that stuff for your students." Trev shoved the tube rack back into the processor.

Exhaling, Graysha shut her eyes. "All right, *student,* let me show you how to prepare a filter plate so you won't have to embarrass yourself asking Dr. Ilizarov how to do it. Is that fair?"

Trev endured the demonstration, and she sent him to Paul's lab. As she was about to return to her own tasks, she heard a rap at her doorway, then a voice from out in the hall. "Dr. Brady-Phillips?"

"Good morning," she said to a petite woman in cuffed browncloth trousers. "Come in. Have we met?"

The woman smiled back, eyes sparkling below black bangs. Her braids were very short. "No. I'm Chenny HoNin, Chair of Hannes Prime. I really don't have time to talk, but I wanted to see you while I was visiting Axis. You seem to have acquired an instant reputation."

"The fall I took?"

"You're all right, aren't you?"

"Healing well, thank you." She appreciated the woman's cheerful disposition.

"I just think you should know Hannes Prime's Colonial Affairs Committee was unanimous about wanting to hire you."

Hannes? Mentally she reran part of DalLierx's vidi. *Hannes settlement . . . northerly mining community . . .* "Oh," she said. "That's kind. Thank you."

"Must go." The small woman extended a hand. "Hope you're settling in safely."

One more name to remember, one more colonial face. Could Hannes be a more sympathetic place?

Muddled by too much humanity and too many questions, Graysha returned to her scanning scope.

Early Sunday—Bday by the scientists' designation and not a Sab-
bath—was still too cold for much outside activity. Lindon sat in his office,
catching up on desk work. A soft tone hummed out of the speaker in his
chair's headrest. He fingered a desktop switch and spoke toward the audi
pickup. "DalLierx."

"Lindon, I'm glad I caught you." Chenny HoNin, Chair at Hannes
Prime, had a voice that radiated cheerful assurance. "But I wish I had better
news."

He darkened his monitor so he could give Chenny his full attention.
Like him, Chenny had been elected during their people's crossing from Einstein Habitat. Unlike him, she had voted with the majority to bring in a
new soils person. She couldn't have known how dangerous that decision
would prove.

"Whatever it is," he told her, "I'd rather hear it from you than be blind-
sided by someone else."

Chenny laughed softly. A born peacemaker, she even managed to stay
friendly with Ari MaiJidda.

Unfortunately, Ari had approached Lindon a little too directly during
the crossing. She didn't take gentle discouragement well.

"All right, then," Chenny said. "Ari wants your job. She's going to call
for a fresh election."

Lindon sucked in a breath.

"What, does that surprise you?"

Chenny was right. This shouldn't startle him at all. He glanced out his office window. Stars shimmered over the toothy horizon. "On what grounds? Did she say?"

"Lindon, you'll have to fight your own battles. I just didn't think it would be fair to let her shock you publicly during the next town meeting. But you didn't hear it from me."

Lindon polished the edge of his leather desk cover with one palm. "I appreciate knowing, Chenny. Thank you."

"Maybe she just thinks Axis Plantation would be better off if you got a fresh vote of confidence."

"Ari?" He didn't think so.

Again the soft laugh.

On the other hand, he reflected, between the Brady-Phillips threat and the worrisome cooling, a crisis could come soon. Axis Plantation probably could weather it better during the honeymoon phase after an election, with either a freshly elected or reelected leader. "How long will you be here at Axis?" he asked.

"I'm heading back north tomorrow, as soon as the track-trucks are running again."

That was one disadvantage of relying on solar energy. Limitless it might be, but battery power wouldn't carry heavy trucks far in darkness. "Stay warm." He switched off, reached for his monitor control, and then hesitated, laying his forearm on the smooth desk cover.

So he would be challenged. True humility, he'd been told, meant acknowledging his gifts and using them to serve others. He hoped he wouldn't cling to authority just because he liked being respected, but what life would he have chosen if he hadn't been drawn into leadership?

He would like more quiet time with his children. Really, he could learn to enjoy any work where he felt genuinely useful.

I'm ready, he told himself, *for any turn of events.* Still, it would feel good to talk this over—but not with Ari.

Kenn VandenNeill, Vice-Chair for Budget, was a church brother. Lindon made the call and explained Chenny's news. "The worst of it," he finished, "is that Ari really is entitled to disrupt everything at this point. Elections within the First Circle can be called by any committee member."

"I wouldn't worry." Kenn's voice filtered through the headrest speaker. "Ari MaiJidda hasn't got the public profile for office."

"Maybe not." On Goddard, homozygous Lwuites, those who had pure Lwuite genes on both sides of the family, had every advantage. Ari's extra-marital birth—her mother's indiscretion—also counted against Ari in subtle genetic ways. "The other reason I called," he said, "is that I have to speak with Melantha Lee again. I could use prayer."

"About the cooling?"

"Yes. I've had five people ask me about it this Goddarday. Five who speak probably means fifty more who say nothing. I was elected to represent them all."

Over the private audi line, Kenn VandenNeill exhaled onto his pickup. "Lindon, you went to Lee before. It didn't help."

True. Melantha Lee had retreated like a poked turtle. "I backed down too quickly."

"If Lee does know why the warming reversed," Kenn said, "and if she's refusing to tell us, things could get sticky between the CA and Gaea buildings. You know that."

There it was, out in the open: their suspicion that Gaea, or at least Melantha Lee, knew about or was even orchestrating the climatic change that endangered them all. "If something has gone wrong," Lindon said carefully, "and nothing is done about it, our lives are in jeopardy. Our children could be moved offworld, and then what would happen to them?" Kenn had children, too. "We depend on Gaea."

"So we can't antagonize them."

"But there's new evidence," he said sharply. "I spoke with one of our young people who works in their meteorology department. Did you know the records show two consecutive G-year drops in temperature?"

"Hmm. Lindon, if you botch a confrontation with Melantha Lee, and if Ari does call a challenge election, some people might vote against you just to pacify the Gaea people. They could say, 'Better a sincere atheist than a religious man who makes mistakes.'"

Lindon nodded, though Kenn couldn't see him. The alleged Lwuite religion was, after all, a sham. The circumstances of his birth forced him to live a lie, and he didn't like it. His faith was deep and real, and he could respond honestly to questions about religion—if he took them as referring to him, personally. Others might draw the inaccurate conclusion that all Lwuites shared his views.

Still, the Religious Liberties Act was their only legal protection. Goddard colony recognized all faiths—ancient and modern, logical and illogical. Fearing that their leaders might be questioned by Eugenics Board agents, they'd always elected believers who could honestly shelter behind the RL Act. Chenny was Noetic. Effi GurEshel of Port Arbor, like her sister Dr. Yael GurEshel, was an Orthodox Jew.

Henri and Palila Lwu's only faith had been universal peace and a certainty that people who hoped to live more than 150 years wouldn't risk that life-span by fighting one another.

"The EB isn't likely to question our leaders anymore," Kenn said. "Not here."

"No? What if we have a spy among us?"

Kenn didn't answer. Lindon fingered the desktop. He would live with the ramifications of every mistake for 120 terrannums. His daughters would endure them even longer. "If we hadn't been forced to fill that Gaea position so quickly, we wouldn't have a Brady-Phillips here."

"Do you suppose she knows her pay comes out of Goddard's production?" Kenn asked.

That was a sensible question, Lindon decided. "It's possible she doesn't."

"I'll mention it if I see her," Kenn said coolly.

"I doubt she would feel guilty about that. She claims she's cash-motivated."

"The Eugenics Board pays well."

"I know, though she claims she's no longer affiliated. And—now, this is something, Kenn—she is worried about the cooling. I sent Liberty JenChee to work with her, so we'll recoup Liberty's salary from Gaea, at least."

"Brady-Phillips came into Gaea at assistant professor's wages, didn't she?" Kenn, true to his position with Budget, seemed determined to ignore Lindon's diversion. "How much will her triannum cost the colony? Forgetting, for the moment, anything recouped by her hiring a tech."

"Associate professor." Lindon pulled the figures out of memory. "Four hundred thousand maxims, more or less."

Kenn's whistle made Lindon lean away from the audi pickup. "You're right," Kenn was saying when Lindon leaned close again. "That would make a good excuse to offer Melantha Lee."

"I'll be careful," he said, "but I do have to talk with her. If I . . . submit a proposal to send Dr. Brady-Phillips back offworld, may I count on you to support it?"

"If I can count on you," Kenn answered, "not to push Lee too far today. Put off calling her for at least an hour. Wait until you're perfectly calm. Then, if you still feel you must speak out, be careful anyway. It's my guess you'll decide the risk isn't worth it."

"You'll pray?" Lindon asked.

"Of course."

An hour later, Lindon's conscience clamored louder than ever. The cooling was Gaea Consortium's problem, and nothing was being done, and if everyone kept quiet out of fear for his own position, Goddard might freeze over.

Lindon did not dare let ambition make him too cautious. If Goddard were lost because he hunkered down for reelection, he'd never forgive himself.

Staring up at the tall white crane behind Dr. Melantha Lee's desk, he spoke carefully for ten minutes, accusing no one, addressing only his concerns. "In any organization," he concluded, "there are occasions when an employee either disregards or counteracts policy and then is afraid to admit it. We could announce a waiver of any penalty, professional or otherwise, to see if anyone admits knowing why the planetary greenhouse may be failing." Forgiveness—the universe's highest incentive—sometimes settled everything.

Melantha Lee rocked her chair, resting both hands on the armrests. When she raised one gray eyebrow, his stomach settled hard. She'd only been letting him dig his grave deeper. "Tell your concerned people," she said irritably, "that if they will continue to administer CFC production, domestic crops, and livestock, and settle personal and political differences between colonial factions, Gaea Consortium will take full responsibility for Goddard's ecosystem until it has been examined, adjusted, and declared self-sustaining."

He decided to speak plainly, since she obviously meant to send him away empty-handed. "We are two degrees colder than last winter, Dr. Lee. It took only two degrees of climatic change to spark the disaster on Messier."

Melantha Lee folded her fingers. "I shall convey your concern at the next weekly supervisor meeting. Thank you for coming, Chairman DalLierx."

"Thank you." *For what?* he wondered. He stood and strode back out across the Gaea building's grandiose marble-paved lobby. The Gaea offworlders made every effort in dress, eating habits, and building construction to remind his people that they would soon leave Goddard and return to a more opulent life.

Or was his difficulty the memory of a favored childhood, of having only to ask for gifts and they were his, of the comforts of Einstein Habitat and of the Lierx family money his daughters would not enjoy?

He sat in his office chair again, talking to the audi pickup, staring at patterns in the concrete wall. "I promised I'd call you back."

"How did it go?" Kenn's voice asked.

"I was told to mind my own business."

"Did she seem angry?"

"Not particularly."

"That's a relief. Maybe she—"

Kenn's next words were drowned out by a double explosion that burst through Lindon's office door. The larger projectile slowed to a walk when Lindon held a finger to his lips, but eight-year-old Sarai decelerated only when both her arms squeezed his neck. Her hair, freshly shampooed and damp near the scalp, smelled sweet and soapy.

"Kenn," he said into the pickup, "my girls are here. May I call you later, at home?"

"You'll have to. This won't wait."

Nothing ever would wait. He switched off the connection, reached over his shoulder, and pried thin arms from his throat. "Sarai, be gentle. That hurts."

Tiny black-haired Sarai slumped around in front of him, poking out her lower lip. The crèche mother, he observed, had to stop giving her special treatment. She wasn't so sickly that discipline would harm her.

Bee waited at the end of his desk, flicking one corner with her finger. She looked more than two terrannums older than her tiny sister. At ten, she was starting to question who and what she was. A fascinating child, she deserved a long, secure future. "Daddy, they gave me my own terminal this week."

"Congratulations." He extended a hand, and she threw back her head to laugh as she shook it. Bee's eyes showed the epicanthic fold, widest near the ridge of her nose, like her mother's. Lindon pulled her in, then seized Sarai and gathered both daughters into a communal hug, squeezing away hurtful memories.

Victim of a freak meteor puncture of Einstein Habitat when six months pregnant, Cassandra died in seconds, shaking two-year-old Bee loose from all security, leaving Sarai a fragile preemie and Lindon a stunned young widower.

"All right, then, is it the co-op tonight or does Daddy cook?"

"You cook!" Bee spun free and twirled on the office's slick flooring.

"Daddy cooks," Sarai insisted simultaneously, still clinging to him.

He squeezed her once, then pushed back his chair. "All right. I'll try."

Lindon used his small kitchen only once a G-week, for dinner with his daughters every Sunday. Bee and Sarai devoured the stir-fried shell peas and vat-grown shrimp all three had peeled together as if they knew nothing tastier. "You don't know how tired I am of co-op food," Bee declared as she carried a pile of dirty stoneware from the table.

"Me too." Sarai leaned back on her chair, closing her dark brown eyes and showing curly lashes.

Lindon slid along his concrete bench. "Help your sister, Me-Too. Daddy cooked."

Sarai stalked to the sink. *So thin,* he observed silently, watching his daughters. Bee, after two terrannums a master at minimizing usage of the precious supply of purified water, directed Sarai to the towel. In a few short terrannums, they'd be women. They would marry and bear children.

And what of their unborn sons, his grandsons?

Lindon knew his medical history. Delivered prematurely and immediately treated with temporary cerebral cohormones, he had central brain tissues that were richer in cross-hemispheric connections than those of an untreated man. He could think, he'd been told, like a man, but he understood holistically, like a woman. He truly wondered if the risks involved in such treatments were justified by the only slight changes in behavior even Henri Lwu's most faithful supporters had been able to document. His brother certainly showed no holistic tendencies.

It was his other heritage—the illegal genetic manipulation—that troubled him more. In his opinion, gene work was simply another medical tool humanity must subject to God's higher laws of righteousness and humility. For instance, God surely had reasons to limit the human life-span.

Yet his parents, also believers, had sought out the treatment. He'd listened to their explanations but never really understood.

One thing, however, he understood well. He had inherited not just a sin nature but illegally obtained chromosomes. He'd had no choice over either inheritance. His body was virally altered, his seed infected . . . but his mind was that of a habitant. His parents knew no other world view. They couldn't teach him to think in so long a term as 150 terrannums. Feeling his way along that path would be tricky. Teaching his girls to do so would be even harder.

Oddly, thinking about eternity came easier. His salvation rested not on what he'd been given or even on what he did with it but on faith alone. He hoped to prove, by his life, that people who were born "physically fallen" in Lwu as well as "spiritually fallen" in Adam had the same need—the same chance—for redemption.

He wanted to propose an end to the dangerous newborn treatments. But unless he stepped carefully, that revolutionary declaration could ruin his political career, and plainly, at least for the moment, God wanted him in office. Goddard's cooling was urgent, but all their work, from the Lwus' era right up to the present, could come to nothing if Graysha Brady-Phillips reported to her mother.

"Three hours until you have to go back." DalLierx stood up as Sarai delicately piled his stoneware dishes. "What would you like to do this week?"

"Climb the crater," Bee returned instantly. "Darrin got halfway up the wall yesterday, and I'm at least as strong as he is."

"No, Bee. We have to do something together." *Something Sarai can do,* he wanted to add, but he cherished the tiny girl's self-confidence.

"I'll climb," Sarai insisted. "I can do it."

She wanted to try? He considered, then decided that even failure had its pleasures and taught its lessons. He checked the outside temp. Six below freezing: not too bad. Whether or not they managed the climb, a walk through the sapling forest to Axis's crater rim would keep them from going stale underground. "We can try," he said. "Gloves, hats, and goggles. Boots, too."

Bee danced a small circle on the kitchen floor.

On a broad sandy ledge created by slumping of the crater's inner wall, Lindon settled into a nest between boulders. Little Sarai sat panting between his arms. Wearing her middleweight parka for the warm, late Sunday with Eps Eri high in the sky, Bee scrambled toward the next slumped ledge. Beneath her gray knit cap, brown braids dangled over her jacket.

"She's always doing that," Sarai whined. "It's not fair."

"You said you'd try." Lindon pressed her shoulders with both arms. "And look how far we got."

He gazed down over the plantation. Beyond the circular scars and short landing strips of the spacefield/airport complex, concrete buildings and white smokestacks were making Axis's original dome and bunkers hard to pick out. One new stack billowed a pale steam of greenhouse gases.

Water-settling beds and a shining shelter zone made the nearer ground look like a textured quilt, green on green on yellow-tan, under imported plastic that protected the ground from cold and ultraviolet in the beggarly atmosphere. Other greenhouses gleamed in game-board rows, rooftop solar panels tilted toward Eps Eri's face. Clusters of brown and black dots that were goats, sheep, and halfers fed at long concrete troughs.

We've done so much and come so far, he observed. Only a pioneer truly grasped this kind of beauty—that of accomplishment, of weeks and months invested by hundreds of hands in each halfer shelter and smokestack. Outside the shelter tents, in another season, he would see more shades of green, crops created specifically for this world. *One Person shaped all the ecosystems on the world we called home,* he reflected, freshly awed.

He huddled closer to his daughter, impressed by how little climbing it took to earn this view. On the northwestern rim, they sat sheltered from prevailing winds in an area where sunshine had melted off the recent storm's snow. He loosened his coat—not without a struggle, since Sarai would not lean away and his goggle strap kept sliding down the back of his head. To their left, a four-hundred-meter waterfall veiled its cut in the crater wall. Narrow, icy Peace Reservoir stretched eastward, ten kilometers into the distance, where a pumping station stood ready to send excess away through the crater's rim when rains and snowmelt brought in enough to call "excess." Today, thank heaven, the reservoir looked full, a banked account against need. At the end of the reservoir nearest Axis Plantation, five circular treatment pools reflected the sky in shades of blue that varied with their icy crusts' thickness.

He settled his back against hard stone, cherishing his daughter's weight against his chest. He hadn't been up here in almost a Goddard-year, not since new plantings of duradurum wheat sprouted inside the crater, along the highway to Center Settlement. Under a white blanket of snow such as hadn't fallen here in thousands of years, finger-long wheat stems waited for planetary spring. Within a few G-weeks they would shoot up, if all went well. Along a streak where howling wind had blown the snow away, he spotted the dark green of dwarfalfa and the even darker cold-tolerant kudzu, both struggling for root holds. They would be excellent forage some day.

A recently released bird declared its territory up over the ledge, singing short, strident chirps. They made perfect sense to Lindon. He had come to love this world, stark as it was. Its asymmetry, its potential, its very wildness touched his spirit.

"How's school?" he murmured, making a pillow of his parka hood and leaning his head against the rocks.

Sarai shifted against his chest. "We've finally reached Colonial Period in history. It's exciting."

"Do you like being a pioneer?" For years, he'd wondered whether they would thank or blame him for the life they would inherit.

"I like having you for Chair of Colonial Affairs."

"Oh." Lindon paused, surprised. Bee never mentioned any pride in his position. How interesting that Sarai would take notice.

"Mrs. DenChun said you were the youngest candidate."

So that was her reasoning. It looked as if she would always be his youngest child. These girls' lives, and those of their descendants, were pledged to Gaea Consortium, their work the indentured price of land and technical help. His own life he'd pledged willingly. Signing over two more generations sat poorly with him. Gaea had no idea how long those servants would live. Soon, Colonial Affairs would have to decide how best to falsify death certificates.

He hoped that by then he wouldn't be involved in making decisions for the colony. Telling or even implying untruth sat poorly with him.

"I was youngest," he agreed. When she was older, he could explain some of the more complex reasons why he'd been chosen: his great-grandfather Marc Lierx's money and name, the Dalquist family's leg up in politics, and the fact that he could honestly evade questions, quoting the RL Act—giving answers for himself that EB investigators might assume to hold true for all Lwuites. He'd been desperately glad to escape Einstein without enduring EB questioning.

"She also said it was a two-person job, at least. Is that why you always look tired, Daddy?"

Lindon coughed out a laugh. "I want my girls to grow up on their own world, a world that can support them, where they don't have to worry about crop failures or late supply shipments. So I work very hard—for you two, and for all of us—to make Goddard safe." Sheltering his eyes with one hand, he glanced toward the sun. Eps Eri shone jasper red even through goggles, the normally dusty sky washed azure by the storm.

"You'll make it safe," she declared.

He cherished the moment, locking it away in his memory. Such utter confidence in her father could not last. "Sarai, I have to work with the people at Gaea. Getting along with them makes me tired sometimes. They have the science to make this world come alive. We pay them to tell us how to do it."

"That's really not fair. We shouldn't have to pay them to order us around."

Lindon shifted his elbow against a rock's sharp edge. "But that's our agreement. I've wished we had colonists on the science staff, but until one of our people is the best in her or his field, I'd rather hire the best to direct us." He crossed her braids under her chin and pulled up both ends. "Does that make sense?"

"I'll grow up and be a terraformer for you, Daddy."

"I think you will." He tickled her nose with the ends of her braids.

They sat in a silence full of communion. Visually he traced the pale arcs of highways curving in from his right, from Center, to the crater's middle, and east again to Port Arbor. The squat solar track-trucks would be out today, charging their reserves, sparing the expensive auxiliary fuel. He spotted one crawling up the Axis notch. Straighter pipelines drew a giant 7 from Peace Reservoir to their point at another set of water purification beds beyond the settlement, then toward the crater's tall wall and through it, straight as light, for Storm Sea.

"Rock!" Bee sang down. Chipping and thwacking noises followed. Lindon scrambled to his feet, dragging Sarai along the ledge. A small scree avalanche settled near where they'd sat, flushing a winter-white ptarmigan three meters above them.

"Sorry!" came Bee's voice again. "I'm coming down."

"Good thing you warned us," Lindon called up the wall.

When Bee reached the ledge, she brushed sand off her clothes. Scrapes on one hand betrayed at least one slip, but they didn't look serious. There was little risk of infection on such a sterile world.

"Ready to head back?"

Bee leaned against a boulder, thrusting a finger into one boot. "I just hit a vertical I couldn't climb. Pure impact glass. It was beautiful, but it was impossible."

"Sorry, Bee, but we have to go. It's getting late."

"But I haven't spent any *time* with you."

Lindon shrugged. "It's never enough, Honeybee, that's certain. We can talk on the way back."

He let the girls descend first. Bee jumped like a goat, using gravity's pull to guide her from perch to perch, while Sarai held back, fighting for balance but just as determined. Lindon's knees ached by the time they stood on the crater floor again. A faint trail led between rows of shoulder-high lodgepole pines at the edge of the shelter zone. Sun-warmed pitch gave off a smoky smell. Neither girl stepped off the trail. They didn't need to be reminded of the undergrowth's value. At the "forest's" end, the wind hit. Sarai snatched his hand, while Bee thrust hers into her pockets. "It *is* colder than last year," Bee announced.

It had been good to forget Melantha Lee for two hours. Lindon gave Bee a dark look, and she broke into a trot.

While Bee and Sarai dressed for bed, Lindon lingered in the crèche's bright common room, talking with their crèche father and mother. Then he slipped into the girls' tiny private bedroom, one of five built in a cluster around the common room, to kiss them good-night. Childish graphite-pencil sketches, drawn on the school's washable paper-equivalent, were pinned in neat rows over the beds.

"I want you to listen to my prayers," Sarai said firmly. She clenched a fist on her pillow and covered it with her other hand.

He knelt, briefly wishing they still lived in Einstein. There, couples could afford the years spent raising children instead of using crèche efficiency. His great-grandfather had bequeathed Lindon's first-generation Lwuite parents enough for comfortable security right there at Einstein.

They sold nearly everything to come here. The weight of lost possessions, of all those other families' willing sacrifices, lives now looking to him for leadership, was too heavy to think about too often.

It baffled him that Ari MaiJidda wanted to take it upon herself.

From his apartment, Lindon called Kenn VandenNeill again and tentatively secured one more vote to petition Gaea for Novia Brady-Phillips's daughter's dismissal. She might not be a spy, but they couldn't afford the risk. If she wouldn't escort the stowaway to Copernicus, they must approach Site Supervisor Lee. They dared go no higher in the Gaea chain, or they might attract attention.

Four hundred thousand maxims saved would account for only half the funds to import that generator, let alone other colonial needs. Cradling his head between both hands over his desk, he pressed his eyes shut. A headache was starting behind them.

Colonial funding was his least favorite aspect of the Chair. Goddard's metal wealth was in high demand at Copernicus Hab, as was its delicate marble, but quantity transport of heavy items was costly. He looked forward to the day when they could offer the habs raw materials for composites: sodium soon to be percolated by rainfall into sea water, tungsten and other rare metals, if they ever were found, and maybe the rare lithophilic minerals used in stellar navigation, boron and beryllium.

Planetary and colonial demand for rare lithophiles was on the rise, particularly those responsive to the magnetic fields surrounding most stars. Since those elements weren't stable enough to be made in stellar reactions, they were found only on planets and in a few large asteroids. The Sol system's resources were playing out. The CA Committee had gambled on colonizing Goddard largely in the hope of finding such specialty minerals. They'd be allowed to keep seventy percent of profits from all minerals found before the Buyout of their indenture, including the prospector's bonus. After Buyout, they would have exclusive rights to market their own wealth wherever they chose.

A G-year ago, his brother had vanished onto Goddard's open wild. Lindon guessed he'd gone prospecting. The brothers were almost exact opposites; Kevan hated responsibility and despised working a schedule. He'd taken advanced basic survival training. He was still alive—Lindon had to believe that.

A shadow passed over his skylight, maybe from a worker cutting a bend on the road above ground. Lindon returned his attention to the list on his screen, which was keyed to the secure Colonial net, and entered another vote to send Graysha Brady-Phillips away.

He rubbed his chin, sanding rough skin off his fingertips with second-shift stubble. It would be terrible to be dying inside. A call yesterday to the HMF had given him more details than he wanted concerning Graysha Brady-Phillips's medical condition. She was 50 percent likely to die before reaching age forty and 95 percent before she was fifty. This in a civilization where seventy was vigorous middle age, and Lindon hoped to achieve a century and a half.

Living with the condition under normal circumstances sounded painless, but Yael GurEshel's write-up of the muscle cramps that dropped the woman made him ache in sympathy. Absently he rubbed his own forearm in the spot where her t-o button had been implanted. The HMF's insistence she wait a month for travel gave him a bad feeling about her chances.

He wanted her gone, but he still could pity her. Shutting his eyes, he offered a prayer for her comfort and health—and her immediate departure.

If she tumbled onto the truth, it might be possible to keep her from reporting. Perhaps her terminal could be monitored to ensure she sent no mail that might contain coded messages. Isolating her from supply shuttle crews would be wise, as well.

He left Ari MaiJidda a message to that effect, then swung his feet up onto the couch and stared through the skylight. Bee and Sarai would soon hear about Ari's call for a fresh election. It would be better if they heard the news from him—before the next town meeting.

It was too late, he decided, to speak with them today. He'd pay the crèche a visit before work tomorrow morning. The children were rising earlier and earlier on Windsdays, an adaptation their elders couldn't make. Over generations, maybe humans could adapt to effectively use Goddard's long days. He would not live to see it, but it was gratifying to think in the long term.

May we be granted the long term.

Novia stood at an onboard work station, screening a news burst. She was finally headed for Eps Eri, sharing a USSC shuttle with an outbound civic councilor and her family. To her relief, they kept to their stateroom. The governmental shuttle had picked up local broadcasts at Halley Habitat, then streaked back off across space. Other travelers depended on ExPress Shuttle Corporation, the only dependable commercial service. USSC shuttles ferried governmental employees at 133 percent of ExPress's top speed. At this point, the craft was well on its way to Copernicus Habitat, and that great new space city orbited Epsilon Eridani within seven light-minutes of Goddard.

It might've been nice to bring Lenard along, but he'd known he married a career woman. She often left for extended periods.

She keyed up the Copernicus news burst, searching for any word from Goddard. Timing would be everything in this case. She must not arrive before Graysha won the colonists' trust, went in for her operation, and started to recover. Guessing that Graysha would succeed easily and affairs on Copernicus would take several weeks to settle, Novia had planned what seemed a reasonable schedule.

Novia had been only a minor investigator when Graysha was diagnosed *in utero* with her awful condition. That diagnosis made Novia a spokesperson for genefective anti-homogenegineers overnight. It brought her to the Chief's attention, launching her rapid rise in the division—but it left her torn, half wishing she'd known she and Lenard both carried the Flaherty gene and that homogenegineering had been available. Should she have given up her career for an unborn baby's sake?

Of course not. She should have terminated the pregnancy and given Graysha a far better life, an instant entrée to eternity.

She last spoke to her daughter three months ago, when Novia stopped off at Halley on her way back to Newton University. Coffee after church on neutral ground had made it an amicable hour. Novia had reminded Graysha that true happiness came from obeying the laws that protected her descendants from exploitation. She wanted Gray's few terrannums to be good ones.

Ellard Huntsinger had taken advantage of Graysha's kindly nature. Novia tried to warn Gray not to marry the first man who showed an interest, but a mother had to let her grown daughter make mistakes. She still wondered whether marriage and divorce drove Graysha to despondency or strengthened her faith. Gray refused to admit either.

Novia sighed and tucked both feet deeper into holdfasts that kept her body close to keyboard and screen. Her left knee twinged. She'd replace it soon, when her pain patches had to be changed more than three times weekly.

Searching the roster of known adherents to Henri Lwu's "religion," she had found two odd facts. First, the expected history of known genefects didn't exist. Second, many very wealthy and very able people had been brought in, some at the last possible moment before crossing.

The wealthy and able feared death even more than struggling workers. The more she found out, the more she suspected Henri and Palila had achieved some kind of victory over aging.

That would not endear the colonists to short-lived Graysha.

Their numbers did imply secrets, though, which suggested criminality. On the screen she spotted something that looked significant: manslaughter, and accidental death, had been proved in the death of Gray's predecessor. *Excellent!* As long as the case remained unsolved, she had worried. Now no one on Goddard could blame EB nettechs—posing, as they sometimes did, as supply crewmen—for killing Jon Mahera to create a vacancy for Graysha. They hadn't, as far as Novia knew. Still, she needed to keep the settlers' suspicions quiet.

She would learn more, she hoped, when the shuttle reached Copernicus Hab.

" . . . and so water and other volatiles splashed onto Goddard's surface from those asteroids and comet nuclei will eventually evaporate, giving us more atmosphere."

"Volatiles," Trev echoed. He'd stuck one finger into a test tube and was tapping it against Graysha's desktop, staring through the metal grate into a cage that held a young black gribien. Ordinarily twenty centimeters from its pointed black nose to the end of its flat body, this one lay curled into a tight ball, desperately sick for no apparent reason. At Trev's pleading Graysha had given it a massive shot of antibiotics, but she was afraid all they could do was watch it die.

Emmer had been this small once. Graysha had been married to Ellard, craving gentle company. . . .

"Volatiles," she said softly, "are substances found primarily in ocean or atmosphere. They evaporate easily, so we say they're 'volatile.'" She studied Trev's face for signs of comprehension. Beneath blotches of darker pigmentation, one cheek twitched.

"No," he finally said. "Adding ice to a planet won't warm it up. I can't buy that."

She sighed and glanced at Libby JenChee. The chestnut-haired assistant shrugged but didn't seem to consider enlightening Trev to be part of her job. The little inner office, three meters by two and a half, was snug for three adults.

"Let's take it once more, from the top. There are five pillars of terraforming. Enough gravity to hold a new atmosphere." Graysha raised one finger. "If air gets away into space, you can't even start to make a world live. Then volatiles, the evaporable things we were talking about. Water, oh-two, nitrogen. The ocean and air themselves."

He nodded.

"Number three—energy sources. Something to burn or run generators so we can fuel modern civilization."

"I'll say."

"Four—physical and biological agents, to change the atmosphere and make it breathable. That's our actual work, plus setting up biological and biochemical cycles by introducing microbes, plants, and animals. And, finally," she said as she lifted a fifth finger, "time. Lots of that." She relaxed her hand beside her keyboard. "We're discussing number three right now—energy sources. The greenhouse gases we're producing or importing—carbon dioxide, CFCs, and methane—absorb the energy that flows in from the sun and reflects back up off the planetary surface. Okay so far?"

Perched on a lab stool with his back to the darkened window, Trev lifted the lid of the metal cage to stroke the gribien's feverish body. "Okay," he said, but he sounded like he'd lost interest.

Distracted herself, Graysha reminded herself that the gribien was only a lab animal, one of Varberg's breeding population. "Greenhouse gases let solar energy stream in," she explained, "but they don't let reflected infrared out. Infrared and heat are so closely related that some people think infrared *is* heat. Now, with a good planetary greenhouse layer, less energy will leave the planet than it receives. As a consequence, it will warm slowly and gradually."

"Too fast, at Messier," Trev said.

Libby frowned and put in, "Too slowly, in our case. Original predictions have this G-year's temp average 16 percent higher than we're measuring."

"Huh," Trev said in a gloomy voice. "All right, Teach, I've got that much. Can you really call it 'solar' energy in the Eps Eri system?"

This kid wasn't stupid. "Common usage," she answered.

"If Goddard's so small, it must be mighty heavy to have normal gravity."

"Not heavy, dense," Graysha said. "Wrong term, but the right concept. That's good. What was your area of study, Trev?"

"Aircraft. Pre-engineering." He set his chin. "And I had enough science to know that adding ice to a planet won't warm it up."

She sighed. Pushing away from the desk, she rotated her stool. It was Aday, dark again, and Trev couldn't hope to save every sick lab animal.

It was odd, though, to find a gribby that wouldn't respond to food or stroking. Pathogen free and raised under radiation shielding, the creatures were phenomenally tough. This one might have been poisoned, but for the life of her she couldn't guess why anyone would pull such a prank.

Trev leaned against the window, fingering stubble. He was trying to grow a mustache. "Huh," he said. "I almost wish I hadn't come here."

"Why?" Libby demanded.

"Well," he said, eyeing Graysha, "this is turning out to be an interesting place. And I'm going to be trouble for you."

Graysha shook her head. "Well, you're . . . no, you're no trouble. Not really. Teaching you makes me prove to myself I really understand this. Anything I can't explain in simple terms I probably don't know."

"I mean Blase." He pursed his lips. "He's going to be beyond fury when he finds out where I am. He's got enough backing to make really deep soup."

"Now, Trev—"

"Yanking me home is only where he'd start. You don't know what kind of trouble he could make for Gaea. There are ways to devalue a stock. If he managed to decapitalize your priceless consortium, Goddard could end up abandoned. We all know Gaea isn't much of a money-making proposition."

"Not in the short term," Graysha admitted. Libby glowered.

Graysha balled a fist and rested her chin on it. "Trev, you must have a terrible self-concept if you think your father is such a scoundrel. But you're smart, and you're cagey. You're a survivor, and when you find your niche, you're going to excel."

"My mother was the survivor." He huffed out the words. "And she's gone."

"Gone?" Graysha asked, alarmed. Surely Trev's father hadn't done away with her. No, he couldn't have. That fear of his father sometimes made Trev ugly. "She disappeared?" Graysha guessed.

He grimaced. "She and Blase had a falling-out terrannums ago. She was of age, so Blase couldn't have her psych-conditioned."

Graysha winced, understanding that Trev feared precisely that kind of conditioning.

"She made time for exactly one of me, then vaporized—for Galileo, I think. Yeah, for Galileo. Huh." He stared at the floor. "I wonder if she made it, if she's still there. I haven't thought about her in ages." He brought his head back up. "Anyway, I didn't have the option to go, and she was under contract to leave me with him. I'll give Blase credit for one thing—he didn't track her down."

"I'm sorry, Trev." Graysha folded her hands together. "I truly am. I hope it's a long time before he finds you. At the least, you'll have a few months. Time in transport and all."

"Great." He struck the desktop hard with his finger. The glass tube split off, and he jerked back his hand. Both halves fell to the concrete floor and shattered.

"I'll get a minvac," he muttered, then ducked out of the lab.

Libby, who had been staring out into space, came back all in an instant. "Excuse me, Dr. Brady-Phillips?" She held up her left wrist to show Graysha the time.

It was town meeting day, Graysha recalled. She nodded. Libby hurried out.

Graysha looked back down into the cage. The young gribien lay limp, slowly uncurling from its feverish ball shape. Groaning, Graysha lifted the lid and prodded its midsection.

It didn't respond.

11. TOWN MEETING

"What's a town meeting?" Trev asked in a sullen voice, vacuuming glass shards as Graysha quietly set aside the dead gribien's cage. Libby would see to recycling its body. Nothing could be wasted.

Paul, she recalled, had kept Trev working over the last meeting day. "On Aday," she explained, "it's too cold to do much outdoors, so people with petitions can take them before the Colonial Affairs Committee. The whole colony's entitled to watch, even Gaea people. I'm still trying to figure out the Lwuites, so I plan to watch the meeting when I can." So far, she'd caught it both times.

Working his jaw in anger and frustration over the little gribien's demise, Trev stalked beside her up the hall to the break room. Libby and the building's other Lwuite employees would be watching together in a lounge on the second floor.

Jirina sat near the big monitor on the south wall, swinging one leg and sipping at a cup that smelled of decaf. Greeting her, Graysha took the next stool. Trev sank into the deep cushioned chair. "Better not, Trevish," said Jirina.

"Trevish," he repeated scornfully. He didn't get up. Graysha shrugged. She would tell Jirina about the gribien later.

Jirina wrinkled her nose. "Find any critters to adjust on your wastewater check?" she asked. "Paul claimed Mahera had let it go desert."

"Mm-hmm." The facility was in perfect balance, but she intended to take warm green sanctuary, too. She might even find Paul there. "Bit of an overgrowth problem in tank four, possibly." It *was* possible. . . .

Will Varberg appeared at the doorway. "My chair." He gave Trev a jerky eviction gesture with the thumb wearing the emerald ring.

"I don't see why," Trev growled.

"My chair," Varberg repeated.

"I think you could afford another one." Trev took his time about rising. "Look, you just lost one of your animals. A young one, with its whole life ahead—for what *that* was worth, locked in a box. But if you'd taken decent care of the cages, it might not have happened."

"We've given work to a *tech*, Mr. Trevarre." Varberg made the noun into a sneer. "If you don't like the way things are done in laboratories, find yourself another job." Varberg sank down with his eyes flaring and his mouth narrow. The wall monitor lit up.

The colonists' town meeting room, across Axis in the CA building, had a monitored "live" audi zone flanked by two tables, all in pickup range. To the committee's left, several young men and women sat at operator stations to accept observers' reactions and comments or double-check electronic votes if called for. Other colonists walked back and forth, taking positions.

Ignoring Varberg and Trev to scan those tables, Graysha recognized Chairman DalLierx and Ari MaiJidda. Beside MaiJidda sat a thin white-haired man whose name she picked up four days ago, Taidje FreeLand.

She saw as many men as woman. The shift to femalism might be peaking out here in the colonies, where male muscle and fortitude were useful attributes. A few radical researchers like Henri Lwu, forbidden by (mostly female) lawmakers to tamper with human chromosomes, were working in other ways to swing the pendulum back toward equality. Graysha believed able men deserved equal opportunity. Certainly her father deserved it. Lenard Phillips was widely recognized in his field of pharmaceutical botany.

However, the basic plan of the mammalian organism was female. Graysha knew enough embryology to understand that a fertilized egg stayed female unless told to be otherwise by modifying hormones. Females had dominated hab-based society for almost a century, after millennia of male rulership and a twentieth-century golden age of near equality. It seemed almost inevitable that society would skew-flip once more.

She frowned, half seeing her mother on that screen. "*God knew what He was doing,*" she'd heard at least a hundred times, "*and we have no right to alter creation.*" Whispered voices argued, "*If He'd meant us to fly, we'd have wings,*" and, "*If you had enough faith, you'd never get sick.*"

She did believe that the human mind was God's finest creation.

And also that the human heart was desperately wicked. On that point, she agreed with her mother's favorite set of Scriptures. Maybe, by trying to make male and female brains more similar, the Lwuites weren't so much tampering with the organism as restoring part of it to its original embryonic status.

That, she realized, was a notion most nonscientists would dislike. Embryos probably were better left to take their natural course of development, no matter what marvels medical science achieved.

What, then, about fixing mutations? She fidgeted. She'd been ordered to report any such transgressions. EB reward money might pay off her divorce loan and make her a free woman. Her mother would like it, too.

It was useless to consider, though. She wanted other things worse than financial freedom: children of her own. Normal children, with a normal life-span.

To an extent, she could fulfill that hope simply by marrying a man whose ancestors never spent time at Newton Hab. She'd have normal-*looking* children. Still, every one would carry her recessive, mutated gene. And if one of them married another Flaherty's carrier, her grandchildren might face a bleak future she knew too well.

Marrying a noncarrier, she'd decided long ago, simply wasn't good enough.

She glanced at Varberg's chair. Only his arm was visible, relaxed on one armrest. He had killed Jon Mahera indirectly, and certainly by accident. Still, she wanted to inch her stool farther away. Maybe Trev was right and he neglected his animals, too. He destroyed homegrown flowers without thinking.

Chairman DalLierx called the meeting to order, and Graysha paid full attention to the monitor. The colonists' first argument concerned a petition to Gaea's Botany Division, to switch a tree planting near Axis Crater from alpine-hardy lodgepole pines to modified cold-tolerant apple trees. Melantha Lee had tentatively vetoed it. It wasn't Graysha's department, but Trev attended closely from his perch atop a counter. Maybe he liked trees, or apples. The proposal would eventually reappear on some Gaea supervisor's terminal.

Slender, black-haired Vice-Chair MaiJidda glided into the "live" zone. Her controlled grace reminded Graysha sharply of her older sister, Asta, a full professor of Doppler physics at Einstein U. Not as graceful as MaiJidda, Asta probably was twice as intelligent. Graysha had been her family's "slow" child, working hard for grades while the rest of the family stayed up late discussing unified field theory—when her father was home, anyway. She missed him.

After formal introductory remarks, which Graysha ignored, MaiJidda cleared her throat. "Preliminary documentation has been finished on the conversion of Axis's rudimentary police force to a defense group, and the CA Committee has allocated funding. We may now begin training and implementation."

Jirina raised both eyebrows and ducked her chin, looking mystified.

Ari MaiJidda faced more fully into the vidi pickup. "Positions are now offered. Training will be voluntary, unless we don't get enough volunteers. D-group service will be part time and will be paid in additional fractional colony shares."

On Ari MaiJidda's left, Taidje FreeLand pulled a small folding knife from his breast pocket and tapped it against the palm of one hand. Graysha had seen Melantha Lee do that.

"Those with experience in any kind of defense position will be commissioned as officers." MaiJidda gestured toward the operators. "We are available to take your calls, and a ten-minute break in new business will ensue."

"What's this about?" Trev asked loudly, voicing Graysha's unspoken question.

Varberg uncrossed his knees and made the heavy chair creak. "This MaiJidda policewoman has had it under her bonnet for a couple dozen Goddardays that Goddard might become so desirably terraformed that someone, someday, might want to take it away."

"It's an army they're talking about?" Graysha asked, swiveling her stool. "I thought these people had treatments for nonaggression. Can't they use USSC Marines if they need help?"

"Maybe they think the Marines would take too long to get here," Varberg answered, "and evidently Gaea's not going to stop them. I suppose we're convinced they're nonaggressive enough not to be a threat."

"There could be aliens out there," Trev said in a stage-spook voice.

Jirina hooted. "Nothing lives in the Eps Eri system but Earth humans and a pack of gene-tailored biologicals."

But it was a frontier world, and it made a kind of sense to maintain readiness. Out here, even imaginary dangers might prove concrete. "They aren't threatening us, are they?"

"Doubt it," said Jirina. "They're our employers. As long as they want to live here, they need us."

Graysha kicked at her stool with one heel. Here was a chance to meet the Lwuites in their own quarters and maybe figure out the best way to approach them. It was also a chance to lay herself at their mercy, which might win their trust . . . or leave her as dead as Jon Mahera.

Gathering courage, she said, "They didn't ask for Lwuites only, did they?

What if I volunteered? I enjoy picking up training in odd fields."

"And if they won't take you, then Gaea can start worrying." Jirina cocked an eyebrow. "Not bad, Blondie."

Youthful on-screen operators started fielding calls. A committee member Graysha didn't know left the table and fetched a water glass.

Graysha crossed the lab to an audi line pickup.

"Wait a minute." Varberg swung his chair. "Graysha, you'd better let Paul. Or Jirina. Jirina, you do it."

Graysha narrowed her eyes and stared lasers at the side of his head. *I am not an invalid,* she thought at him. Now she was determined to try it. "Any idea what number I punch?" she called across the room.

"Operator should know," answered Jirina. "Just switch on the line."

Graysha touched the button.

"Assistance," said a businesslike female voice.

"I'd like to be patched through to the town meeting, please."

"One moment."

The line went dead except for static. Varberg and Jirina watched the screen, but Trev focused on Graysha. She wondered what was passing through her student's mind, whether he wanted to join her or disliked her idea based on his dealings with parental bodyguards. In the nearest yabut cage, two chubby littermates pushed noisily at alfalfa-smelling chow piled atop their unit, gnawing fragments off the rolling pellets. If only human life were that simple. Food overhead, water handy . . .

Yes, life without freedom would be very simple. There'd been little real freedom on Earth as recently as the nineteenth century. Then uncontrolled industrial development started making hot-and-sour soup of the planet's atmosphere. Soon, maybe, there would be even less freedom there. Gaea's Earth-based sister corporation, Terra Two, now lay under USSC jurisdiction in an effort to control global processes. It would take desperate, possibly repressive measures to make Terra beautiful again.

Voices came on in her ear. The loudest said, "Meeting."

"Yes," Graysha answered. Jirina and Varberg turned to watch her. "You're accepting volunteers for the defense group?"

"We are," said the young voice. Graysha touched another control and put the Lwuite operator on a room speaker as the voice continued. "Have you any military or guard experience?"

Varberg smirked.

"None," Graysha said, "but I'm experienced with a number of computer types."

"Laser-radar is in need of volunteers."

"Very good. I volunteer."

"Name, please."

Graysha gave it. Knowing that her name set off alarms every time the Lwuites heard it, she watched the screen. One pigtailed girl glanced up from the audi bank and around the studio. "One moment" came over the speaker.

Graysha muted the pickup. "Look," she whispered loudly, and her co-workers swiveled. The girl hurried up to Vice-Chair MaiJidda, who sat at one end of the committee table. They conversed for maybe thirty seconds, during which the pigtailed girl positioned herself between MaiJidda and the monitor.

If they wouldn't take her, Graysha decided, that almost certainly meant they were hiding things.

For a fleeting moment she pictured herself gene-healed, working Goddard's thin soil alongside a Lwuite husband, discussing the health and quirks of their children.

According to Novia, healing mutations would open the door for further tampering with the human organism. Who had the right to judge where the line should be drawn?

They'd take her, all right. They didn't dare refuse her.

"Here she comes," Trev announced superfluously. The pigtailed operator walked back to her station.

"Thank you for holding" came the young voice. "We are pleased to welcome you for training. Please report to the D-group building when your relief week begins. When will that be?"

Graysha looked at Varberg.

"Dday," he mouthed.

"Next Dday," she echoed into the pickup.

"Very good, Dr. Brady-Phillips. We will expect you two days after tomorrow, on Dropoff. Thank you for concerning yourself with Goddard's future." The line went dead again, broadcasting static over the lab speaker. Graysha switched it off.

Jirina touched her forehead, chin, and chest in homage. "Welcome to God's little army."

"Dropoff?" Graysha asked.

"Well, after two terrannums you don't expect the colonists to go on calling days of their week by letter designations. Not all the time. Just when dealing with us oh-fishial types."

"Aday is Freezeout," said Varberg's voice from the deep chair, "Bday is Sunday, Cday is Windsday—it shifts around from Storm Sea, remember?— and Dropoff. All together, one Goddarday, or G-week. They haven't decided which one of those they're going to use consistently."

A minute later, the older man—Taidje FreeLand—rose and said something about the colonial covenant, one planetary month, and challenge elections.

"What?" Varberg barked.

Startled out of a daydream of what D-group training might entail and what precautions she ought to take, Graysha attended again.

"Declared candidates thus far," said FreeLand, "are sitting Chairman Lindon DalLierx and Defense Group Coordinator Ari MaiJidda. No other committee member has declared candidacy, but applicants feeling themselves qualified may register in person at the CA office this Sunday or Windsday."

Jirina whooped. "Election? DalLierx is being challenged, Graysha. Maybe you'll outlast him after all!"

Trev said, "Maybe this woman called the election to make sure Graysha stayed. I notice they aren't calling her Vice for Police anymore."

"She wouldn't have done this for my sake," Graysha told him. No one else knew Ari MaiJidda tried to expel her from day one, and she wasn't about to spread it around.

Up on the screen, Lindon DalLierx sat calmly watching FreeLand. Graysha waved at the image. "That's a mighty open government they've got."

"It's not a government," Varberg pronounced. "They're just playing games."

"Odd games." Jirina swiveled her stool. "You'll notice they're electing as many males as females to that committee."

"I noticed," Varberg answered blandly.

"So maybe this Dr. Lwu was a . . ." Graysha searched memory for an archaic term. "A masculist? Trying to restore men's right to govern by taking away some of their aggressiveness?"

Trev rubbed his hands together. "They're crazy. Playing God like that."

Did Trev care about God? Graysha wondered. "But what does all this have to do with calling fresh elections?" she asked everyone in general.

Jirina leaned back on her stool and flexed one leg. "The physical laws can't be trespassed. If you go outside at the wrong time, you die. Like in a hab, only worse . . . for now. Maybe they're politically casual to compensate. You know, make a hard life just a bit easier. Where they have a freedom, maybe they overuse it. Calling elections any old time."

Break the physical laws and die. At Jirina's sidelong reference to Jon Mahera's death, a nasty feeling crept up Graysha's spine. She glanced at Varberg without moving her head.

That's when she saw Paul standing in the doorway, wearing a lab coat tailored to accentuate the line of his shoulders. "Perhaps," he said, "that woman feels she's been held back long enough." He pointed toward the screen and Ari MaiJidda. "It's my experience she has more of an urge to dominate than *he* does."

Varberg spread his fingers over the arms of his padded chair. "An early colonial environment is like a time warp," he told Paul. "They have to cooperate utterly. Utterly. It creates an ultraconservative society. Messier's colonists were well on their way to creating a monarchy, or a dictatorship."

The pain in his voice when he mentioned Messier made Graysha cringe. Paul shrugged and walked away, light on his feet for a man so well muscled.

Back on the monitor, the committee was discussing a proposed river diversion to create a controlled flood as soon as thaw season arrived. Proponents claimed it would bring more dust and minerals to the potential croplands near Axis, creating new highland soil. Opponents voiced concerns regarding its controllability, citing Messier and then the possibility of bringing in too many soil salts.

Graysha half listened, more interested in the colonists' interplay than in flood engineering. Males, females; dominant, submissive; a complex dance. DalLierx's boyish face was attractive, much like the way a jewel or a star or a planetary sunset was attractive. And he was vulnerable now, challenged by Ari MaiJidda.

Why was such a young man placed in command of the settlement's affairs? He must have been elected by colonial vote. What qualifications had he claimed?

He could be overruled, too. Otherwise, Graysha wouldn't be here.

Melantha Lee followed the broadcast with less visual interest. On the near corner of her desk, her pocket memo blinked seven times, then repeated. Her day's agenda was far from cleared.

Goddard's colonial covenant did allow the Lwuites to establish a defense group. She'd discovered that ten minutes earlier when, stunned by MaiJidda's announcement, she examined the document line by line.

So they could train and maintain a small military force. Gaea people at Copernicus Hab, always monitoring, would have heard MaiJidda's announcement approximately three minutes ago, slightly delayed by the distance. With luck, they would suggest that she enact restrictions.

Employed as a theoretician during the Messier disaster, Melantha Lee had watched Gaea stock and Gaea's reputation plummet. It had been excruciatingly difficult to find families willing to risk the dangers of another project.

Next time, if her quiet little scheme bore fruit, colonists would enroll confidently.

She mustn't let the Lwuites slip Gaea control, though. DalLierx was getting to be a particular pest, and he made her suspicious. If Lwuite non-aggressiveness was fact and not fantasy, no one should've come complaining to Gaea about atmospheric imbalances until they nearly righted themselves. Terraforming probably could succeed beyond previous experience. But the equations still had too many variables. After Messier, it was plain that a planet must not become too warm too quickly.

Perhaps MaiJidda also thought DalLierx overstepped. He never should have come to Lee with veiled accusations. This call for elections could be MaiJidda's attempt to offer him to the Gaea station as a scapegoat.

She considered her office's blank wall. Like Goddard, it had potential. Like Goddard, when she selected and painted one mural, that would rule out all other possibilities.

Someone had to choose. She wasn't about to dance for MaiJidda, either. She reached for her keyboard and keyed in, +Varberg—call Lee.+

Several minutes later, he acknowledged.

By then she had a response from Copernicus, a wishy-washy wait-and-see message that left her fuming. The system supervisor, a Graham's Reach man, was long overdue for transfer. She'd already started typing a recommendation. She saved it to an active file, then answered Varberg. +You should know DalLierx has been here asking about cooling again. All but demanding investigation.+

+Isn't that interesting.+

+Let's wait,+ she typed, +and see if they toss him out. We might not need to do a thing.+

She was about to switch off when more words appeared. +Thought any more about bringing Graysha inside the group?+

A USSC official's daughter? Lee grimaced. +Not for a while,+ she typed, thinking, *and maybe not ever.*

Graysha rolled over and stretched, and warm covers rolled with her. Where was she? What day was it, what time...?

Answers floated up through her luminous, contented confusion: Goddard, Dropoff—the first circ after sunset—at six-thirty in the morning. Last Sunday, after the town meeting, she had watched her first supply shuttle land planetside, where a craft could splatter in full gravity. It was a frightening experience. The lander seemed to drop too fast, threatening to undershoot the landing crater—and then, like a bird sweeping out its wings at the last possible moment, it braked. Track-trucks rolled out to intercept it. That night, the Gaea cafeteria served a fresh vegetable mélange that reminded her of Thanksgiving feasts back at Newton.

She lay in bed, blinking her way back to the present. Her relief week started today, but she wouldn't have time to lie around. Today she started D-group training, a career in laser-radar, and her cautious informal investigation of Lwuite practices.

Her alarm wouldn't ring for a while. She stared up at yellow-brown concrete finished in a pattern of overlapping swirls, then looked aside at the gathered browncloth hanging she had bought Windsday at a craft fair in the hub. Loose blue embroidered arcs radiated out from its center, suggesting a magnificent tropical flower. She got up and mixed a few drops of scent onto a pile of precious wood shavings—her most extravagant purchase—on a plate underneath it. The room would smell like rain forest until the fragrance faded.

It was the first time she had scented a room since the happy time, her first two months with Ellard. They'd been close in those early weeks. His genius made conversation a delight, and every private touch was like opening a new door in a house full of secrets. At last she'd known what the love songs meant.

Or had she?

She reached for Emmer. The gribien contracted in alarm at her first touch, then relaxed again, arching to present her sleep-warmed belly for a rub.

Ellard, brilliant like the rest of her family and an inspired researcher in submolecular electronics, must have thought her a typical Brady-Phillips when they met. He courted her with poetry and synthetic jewels.

After a brief taste of intimacy, he became a mean-hearted, belittling dominator, gifted enough to be truly cruel. He contrived to make her believe every problem in their lives was her fault. He controlled his male aggressiveness in public but unleashed it privately. Her teaching suffered. His farewell letter, which she found clipped to the top of her jewelry box, said he'd rather live alone than with someone who did such imbecile things.

She sterilized the letter before dropping it in the flash box. She should've kept it. She never dreamed he would sue her for more than she possessed as part of the divorce settlement. It never occurred to her to countersue.

Stroking Emmer, she thought of how ignorant she'd been and for how long. Maybe she was starting to recover a sense of self-worth. Trev helped, allowing a relationship she dominated . . . gently, of course. Jirina demanded nothing, accepted everything, was amused by it all. Will Varberg . . . well, he gave her a challenge, as did blue-eyed Paul Ilizarov. Even Lindon DalLierx forced her to assert herself. She owed him for that.

This world had been good for her.

She rolled out of bed, fed Emmer a cracker and two grapes she'd saved from dinner, then sink-bathed. By then, she needed to head north for her morning commitment. Following directions she'd found in her message box, she dressed in loose, washable clothing and stuffed a change into the browncloth backpack she had also bought Windsday at the fair. She tucked in an HMF glucodermic, which she'd taken to carrying in a pocket— always. It might save her life if she had another Flaherty's attack. Finally, she loaded her pockets with hard sour candies, smiling as she remembered the Lwuite woman with snow-white braids and a free candy ball for every child who visited her sales table.

Graysha patted her pockets. This time, if Ari MaiJidda pushed her limits, she would be ready.

In the cafeteria, she put away two servings of syrupy pancakes. Then, whistling softly, she strolled up the hub and north almost to the co-op. Beyond Colonial Affairs, the next set of concrete stairs wore a newly painted Defense Group sign. She had no idea what it had been before—concrete storage, she guessed as she plodded upstairs. It smelled like old dust.

The room where she reported had padded metal chairs set up in rows, unpainted yellow-tan walls, and a high ceiling. She found a chair. By now accustomed to Axis's public rooms having concrete furnishings, she felt queerly transplanted as she sank onto the cushion.

A woman on her right turned toward her, a greeting dying visibly on her lips as she got a good look. *It's the hair,* Graysha moaned to herself. She'd braided it back, but to really fit in, she'd have to dye it. Surely among the Lwuites were a few ordinary two-recessive blondes, but she hadn't seen any.

Picking up the greeting where it dropped, Graysha extended a hand. "Graysha Brady-Phillips," she said, "and I've been cooped up in a laboratory for thirteen days."

Before her neighbor could answer, someone ahead of her swiveled around. "Good morning," the new woman said cordially. Refined features and expressive eyes countermatched her girlish, barely upturned nose. Loose braiding—most colonists started their pigtails close to the scalp—gave her face a haloed appearance. "Don't worry, you don't know me. I'm Crystal DalDidier. I've been hoping to make your acquaintance. Welcome to Goddard. They told me women would be coming in from the other settlements, but with you here from Gaea, this group will really represent all of Goddard. I'm glad."

Graysha clasped the young woman's hand, warmed by her welcome. She was opening her mouth to ask Crystal where she worked when Ari MaiJidda appeared up front and conversations ended.

"Thank you for contributing your time," MaiJidda said. "All of you."

Crystal turned back around, and Graysha settled into her chair for a lecture.

"We are Earth's newest beginning," MaiJidda intoned, standing close to a lectern near the wall's center. Against the yellow-tan concrete, her olive complexion looked almost ruddy. "We are humanity in a new milieu. Whatever you do today, do it for the common good and leave selfish notions in the corridors."

A woman on Crystal's left nodded.

"The first order of business with other D-group squads has been to blow out the vents, get rid of rumors."

Yes, Graysha thought, *good idea.*

"Every planet yet settled, every habitat constructed, has a small police force at the ready, watching the unknown for persons or conditions that could prove a threat." MaiJidda wore a one-piece suit, cut close to her slender hips and waist, loose through the shoulders. "Goddard is not under any threat of imminent invasion or forced evacuation. With our small population, maintaining a D-group of any efficacy will simply have to involve a higher-than-normal percentage of us."

The phrase *forced evacuation* snagged in Graysha's ear. *Evacuation,* yes. Every habitant dealt with that fear in childhood. Graysha had suffered through a spell of particularly vivid nightmares as a nine-year-old, but who—or what—were these people afraid of?

The Eugenics Board came to mind, with its threats of irradiation and imprisonment. *So far, so good,* she observed. If they would help her, she would protect them with every resource she could muster . . . though that wasn't much.

Vice-Chair MaiJidda curled her fingers around both edges of her lectern. "Some women in my previous training squad asked why we segregated the sexes. There are two reasons. Men and women working beside one another in combat situations tend to become distracted, protective— they put the safety of an opposite-sex comrade before the unit's goals. Therefore our D-group will operate in two sectors, male and female.

"Besides, aren't you all ready for a short vacation from *them*?"

Graysha rubbed her left thumbnail, vaguely bothered by MaiJidda's disdain. To her satisfaction, the room remained quiet. Some women she'd known might have giggled.

"Two reasons?" called a woman near the front.

Leaving the lectern, Vice-Chair MaiJidda walked slowly to one side in a sensual, swaying gait. *If she despises men,* Graysha observed, *she must not be above using her charms to control them.* "The other is for exercise purposes. In mixed physical-education situations, many of us don't work as hard as we're capable. Yes, philosophy has swung back and forth concerning that issue for centuries. Since the current swing is back toward integration and equality, you're going to call me reactionary."

This time there were giggles.

MaiJidda frowned. "But you're also going to call me 'Coordinator' for the duration of your training week."

Dr. Lee would want to hear this little speech repeated if she wanted to know her employers better. So would Jirina, for that matter . . . simply because she was curious.

After MaiJidda answered logistics questions and distributed cloth-tape

ID tags, Graysha followed the group into a larger adjoining room, where drag scars marred the concrete that wasn't covered by thin gray foam pads. This new gym obviously held stores until recently. Along one wall, huge metal crates were still piled six high. She crunched and swallowed two sour candy balls when no one was watching.

On a gray pad in formation, Graysha spent the most physically demanding half hour of her life, eventually growing concerned enough to check her t-o button without caring if Ari MaiJidda noticed. *If I survive this,* she huffed while walk-running her sixth lap of the room, *I'll prove to Ari MaiJidda—and to myself—that I'm stronger than anyone thought.* She popped another candy. Each foot felt heavier by the step, but it was pleasant not to be coddled. At Einstein, she'd exercised sporadically. She would keep up with these women, most of whom probably did physical work every day, or collapse trying. Most of them acted friendly, though a few glimpsed her name tag and turned stiffly polite.

Then came a gang shower that reminded her of school days, sweaty female bodies clustered under water-conserving thin sprays. She and her squad mates quickly changed into their other clothes in a long narrow room with concrete benches along its center. Their worn clothing reeked. Quicker dressers encouraged and chaffed the slower, despite an apparent average age of well over thirty.

"I never expected boot camp," commented a woman with white hairs threaded down her black pigtail. She sat sideways on the bench, lacing shoes woven from some heavy fabric. "I guess I should have. Why else would they tell us to bring a change of clothes?"

"It's just basic fitness." Crystal rolled up her worn clothes and tied a browncloth sleeve around them.

Graysha pulled her own shoelaces tight. "We're learning to follow orders, I suppose. We've been our own bosses for terrannums. Most of us, anyway." The older women smiled sidelong at a cluster of shoulder-punching teeners.

As Graysha left the shower room, she was shocked to be herded into line, issued a pair of ear protectors, and given a handgun.

Incredulous, she carried the square-angled metal pistol into a third echoing room that was also piled along one wall, ceiling to floor, with huge metal crates. Other women looked as uncomfortable as she felt. *They've been mining metals at Hannes Prime. Have they got an armament factory?*

Melantha Lee definitely should have joined up.

Who was in charge of this group, anyway? Ari MaiJidda alone, or had others taken part in the decision to arm?

Gaea would have learned about it eventually. With Graysha enlisted, they'd just hear sooner.

Ari MaiJidda wore a holster on her right hip now. Standing at a corner of the room, she clipped a button mike onto her collar. "All right," she called, "form a line along that back wall. You're wondering what you're doing with this in your hand."

I should say so. Graysha shuffled to the indicated area, trying but failing to get a spot near Crystal.

MaiJidda drew her weapon. "Remember, first of all, you're no longer in a habitat. Projectiles won't puncture bulkheads here." Graysha set her jaw, half expecting the woman to demonstrate. "The design may be antique, but they're cost-effective." She holstered it again, and Graysha breathed easier. "They're efficient for hunting and for personal defense. Yes, hunting," she continued. "Suppose we found it necessary to scatter our population across the planetary surface. There's edible plant life up there, and there's meat. It's sparse right now, but if we get this cooling trend turned around, there'll be more of both after a few seasons."

In MaiJidda's pause, murmurs broke out in several spots. Graysha scrambled to keep pace with her own speculations. *"Forced evacuation"* snaked through her mind again, followed by *"if we found it necessary to scatter our population."* These people—some of them, anyway—were definitely afraid. If she had meant to report to Novia, she would've had to warn her mother these people could fight back. From what she knew of Eugenics Board history, that would be a first.

But she meant to tell Novia nothing, especially now.

"Basic handling," MaiJidda said, pointing at her holster as the racket of women's voices faded. "Never, never aim a weapon at something you aren't willing to destroy. That means you. Right now. Where's it pointed?"

Up and down the line, women adjusted their stance. To Graysha's relief, she'd been holding hers two-handed, aimed at a crack in the concrete floor.

She lay on her belly a few minutes later, rotating to the right each time targets were set back up, then trying again to hit little pyramids of yellow-tan clay cubes. She found herself enjoying the game, and surreptitiously she celebrated each near-miss by slipping another hard candy into her mouth. The heavy pistol's firing chamber was fed by inserting coiled spirals of dart-shaped pellets against its side and by replacing two chemical charges up through its grip. Even after her arms started to shake, she had no trouble loading the thing, but evidently marksmanship would not be her forte.

Just before the watch on her wrist changed over to twelve noon, she lay next to the wall stacked ceiling-high with crates, beside Crystal.

Someone behind her shouted, "Hey! Look out—"

Graysha rolled sideways, glancing back and up. The near end of the pile tottered. The top crates tipped dangerously. Three squad leaders dashed for the wall.

Graysha sprang to her feet, shouting, "Crystal!" She seized Crystal's right elbow and dragged her half a meter.

From behind came a crash. All down the line, guns clattered to the floor and heads whipped to stare in her direction.

Crystal's weight pulled Graysha down. She crouched, waiting for the terrible cramping from sudden hard movement. One calf contracted in a painful charley horse, but that was all.

It had taken maybe five seconds. Panting, she spun around. Behind roiling dust, women scrambled to get away. Ari MaiJidda's voice rang out over the firing-range's speakers. "Clear the range, please. Clear the range while we make sure no one has been injured. Leave your pistol with a squadron leader at the door. Drill will resume in one hour. Get some lunch while we clear the room."

Graysha kneaded her painful calf and rejoiced that she didn't hurt all over. "Thanks," Crystal said softly. "I couldn't get my balance. Are you all right?"

"Give me a minute," she grunted. She hesitated, wanting to step on her sore leg but not wanting to put weight on it before the muscle relaxed. Thanks to all that candy, she hadn't—

Good Lord. As the dust cleared, she saw that a huge metal crate had spilled broken bags of concrete exactly where she'd lain seconds before. Her senses should have been dulled by the morning's exertion, her blood sugar at a pre-lunch low. She should have been . . . might have been killed, along with her new friend.

Beside the fallen crates, Ari MaiJidda straightened out of a crouch and covered a sneeze with both hands. She gazed out into the room, and Graysha guessed she knew who Ari was looking for.

A flush of anger warmed her cheeks, and she knew she'd better leave the scene. "Let's get lunch, Crystal," she muttered. "Give me a hand up, if you would."

Crystal pulled, and Graysha slowly straightened the aching leg. She couldn't guess how Ari MaiJidda got those crates to tip over, but any police investigation under MaiJidda's leadership would certainly declare it accidental.

Would MaiJidda have willingly sacrificed one of her own people to make sure nobody suspected the act was deliberate?

Leaning on Crystal's arm, Graysha limped out into the corridor. It didn't seem appropriate to mention her suspicions to the young Lwuite woman.

"Is the co-op all right for lunch?" Crystal asked. "It's close. It's bound to be noisy this time of day, but I'd like to visit my children. I'm a crèche mother when I'm not in the D-group."

"Fine," Graysha said shortly, conserving energy to hobble faster. She just wanted to get away. She didn't dare say any of the things she was thinking. She wanted to build bridges, not burn them.

Crystal shook her head. "If you hadn't grabbed me, I'd still be there. Thank you."

"I'm just glad that I . . . well . . ." Tempted to say too much, she bit back the urge. "You're welcome. I'm glad it worked out."

Besides, shared danger tended to bond people. She liked Crystal already. It would be nice to count her as a friend.

A careless cacophony of high-pitched voices filled a huge concrete room at the north end of the main corridor. Graysha hadn't seen the colonists' food co-op before. Unsmoothed concrete walls and matching yellow-tan tile flooring, beneath rows of long tables, made it plain no one had bothered to dress it up like the Gaea cafeteria. Still, warm smiles and animated conversations made it feel homey, and a long linear skylight—dark now— probably warmed it on Bdays and Cdays. Over a stew of mingled food smells, Graysha caught soapy astringency and the pervasive musty-wet concrete odor. In a few years, after these walls finished curing, that scent might remind settlers of their early days here.

"You're sure you don't mind eating in the sound chamber?" Crystal asked. She carried a loaded tray to a spot amid one table lined with giggling primaries. Two of them hugged her as she sat down, one circling her waist and the other clinging to her leg. Grinning, she shook them off. "I find it comforting, but I know lots of folks who don't."

Children. Sweet-faced or irritated, dirty or clean, pigtailed or barbered with a buzz-razor, they jostled and elbowed and shouted at one another. Graysha took a spot facing Crystal next to a black-haired boy, who reached up to stroke her blond pigtail before fishing his spoon out of a soup bowl where it had fallen, handle and all.

"I like noise." Graysha had to raise her own voice. "I like children." What safer person to admit that to? It wasn't as if she were coming right out and telling Crystal, "I'm risking everything here for the sake of having normal children of my own." Her leg no longer hurt. Maybe soon her hands would stop shaking. "Do they all live with you, or are you their teacher?"

"Both." Crystal reached out to remove another soup spoon from its spot of contention inside two grabbing chubby hands. "They're my crèche, all ten of them—bless every runny nose—and these three are my own." She bounced the flat of her hand along two pigtailed heads at her right side while indicating the boy next to Graysha with a quick nod. "Ages three through seven—we try to keep sibs together. It would've been nice to have left cold viruses behind on Einstein, but . . ." Shrugging, Crystal flipped a thick braid back over her shoulder.

Graysha agreed. It might've been nice if they'd left Ari MaiJidda behind, too. Maybe if she offered MaiJidda a pledge of secrecy—if she openly, bluntly gave the Vice-Chair power over her as token of her sincerity—she might be allowed to live unharmed inside the Lwuites' mysterious veil.

Maybe. But if thousands of lives had depended on *her* keeping secrets, she would tell no one, no matter how sincerely they appealed to her.

"So it was Will Varberg after all," Crystal observed aloud, out of the blue. "I'm awfully glad it wasn't one of us. Things have been tense enough."

Graysha pushed back her fears. She'd only been threatened. Jon Mahera had died. "I'm sorry the Gaea station hasn't made better efforts to get along, to join in your activities and so forth," she said. She tore off a chunk of coarse bread, dipped it in soup, and chewed the juicy mouthful. Something occurred to her, something utterly nonessential. Something that might make light, easy conversation. "May I ask a ridiculous question?"

"You think I don't get ridiculous questions all day, every day?" Crystal asked, grinning.

Graysha liked the young woman more every minute. "The Gaea people call your particular, um, lifestyle . . . occupation 'baby farming.' What do you call it?"

"Baby farming," Crystal answered promptly. "During our relief week, there's a pair of rovers who take care of our—oh," she exclaimed. A curly-haired man laid a hand on her shoulder, hoisted his leg over the bench, and slid into place next to her. "Duncan EnDidier," Crystal said firmly, "meet Dr. Brady-Phillips."

"It's Graysha," she insisted, shaking the man's hand. He had a broad, pleasant face. "You're Crystal's husband?"

A bowl hit the floor, creating crockery shards and bean islands in a lake of broth. Duncan and Crystal scooted off the bench, Duncan comforting the child while Crystal dashed for cleanup gear.

Graysha slid down to help them mop spilled soup, unreasonably delighted by events. Ari MaiJidda had accidentally done her more good than harm.

She definitely had a Lwuite friend.

After lunch, the group divided into specialties without reentering the firing range. Graysha and three other women followed a young black-haired man out into the tunnel and then up to a first-floor room arranged like a computer classroom.

"Each station is programmed for laser-radar, or 'lidar,' simulation," he announced. His name tag read *VanDam*, and he paced with a limp. "You have been selected for lidar training because of your familiarity with e-systems. Access your tutorial now, and begin. I am here if you have questions, but it's my advice to try all options yourself before asking for outside help. What you learn on your own, you'll remember longer."

Graysha called up the tute, relaxing. At last, here was something she felt comfortable with. This layout had controls she wasn't used to seeing, but by the end of a fast-paced hour, she knew which one keyed in tracking, which amplified signal strength, and which alerted other lidar trackers to a threat. The tutorial program indicated she would now be allowed her first simulation. She pressed the appropriate tab. To her surprise, the console beeped.

VanDam limped over. "On to phase two?"

"I think so. I'm enjoying this."

"Good. But you have to pass a little test before you go on." He pressed another tab, and the screen gave directions. The man stood at her shoulder, watching while she worked through them. Only one problem, concerning three-dimensional tracking, made her hesitate.

By then her instructor was leaning two-handed against her desktop and nodding. "Not bad, Brady-Phillips." He touched the board's *S* key, and the promised simulation appeared.

Another student's station beeped at that moment, and Graysha realized she'd just gone to the head of the class.

The second day's exercise and handgun sessions—this time, no one was assigned to lie closer than five meters from the restacked crates—left her quivering and weary, and tiny sore spots blossomed on her gums from chewing sour candy . . . but Ari MaiJidda appeared to have granted her a respite. As they showered, Graysha passed Crystal a slick chunk of sour-smelling soap. "I haven't felt this wobbly in ages."

"Nor me," Crystal admitted, "but you're doing better than I expected. Coordinator MaiJidda passed word to us about your condition before the first meeting. Did you know that? We were supposed to watch for anything like muscle cramps and report them right away."

Surprise, surprise. Graysha reached for her scratchy brown towel. "Don't tell me the Coordinator is paranoid."

Crystal laughed merrily. "Why else would she be in charge of this operation?"

That afternoon on the sim, she learned ground and air tracking. Lieutenant VanDam pulled her aside after midafternoon break, separating their conversation from others' eyes and ears behind a bend in the concrete wall. "Graysha, we're glad to train you, and you certainly seem to be getting along. I'm pleasantly surprised."

"Thanks," she murmured.

He leaned against the wall. "But in a crisis, can we count on you not to turn tail and hide in the Gaea building? If we call you up, will you come?"

"Of course I'll come," she said firmly. "I wouldn't have volunteered if I didn't mean to honor my commitment. If the attackers on these sims ever show up, you have my solemn word I'll be on Goddard's side."

He nodded and limped away. Graysha examined the room. Bare except for the ceramic-topped desks and computer installations, it did have the ambience she imagined for a wartime setup.

She couldn't beg healing from the Lwuites, then abandon them. If they were capable of helping her, then they had reason to fear the EB . . . and she would become her own mother's enemy.

Lindon DalLierx rested one elbow on his desk. His monthly policy meeting with Gaea's three bio-floor supervisors—Microbiology, Botany, and Zoology—had been little more than a waste of two hours. Nothing had changed, they claimed, nothing needed revising, and his hints about global cooling were unanimously ignored. Feeling weary, he asked, "Anything else, Dr. Varberg, gentlewomen?"

"I don't think so." Varberg reached over DalLierx's desk, scooting aside the glass of marigolds he'd brought, saying, "This building is too colorless, Chairman." He enfolded DalLierx's hand in a firm clasp that showed off the big man's emerald ring. The jewelry didn't impress Lindon. His father's sapphire thumb ring was larger, clearer, and better cut.

It was also a natural stone. Varberg's had the vague opacity of a synthetic. "I'll see you all in another month," DalLierx said blandly. *Either me or Ari MaiJidda.*

"Certainly," said Varberg. "By the way, be sure to save those seed heads for me."

Lindon escorted them to the CA building's stairwell, paused, then clumped down after them, resting his hands in his pockets. Antonia Fong of Botany had seemed sympathetic last month, but today she had apparently gone deaf. Evidently during the interim, Melantha Lee convinced her.

Did Lee have a blind spot—or a hidden agenda? he wondered.

It was time, he decided, to make an official visit to the Defense Group training session. He guessed Ari was using her defense position to improve her chances in the challenge election. She would see every woman she trained as a potential vote in her favor, someone who decided she liked looking to Ari for leadership.

He could not stop that; in fact, he had no right to try stopping it. They all had become possessive of their world, himself included. Sometimes he felt like Moses in the wilderness. With his people separated out of "Egypt" and relatively safe here in the wilderness, making a nation of them would take at least forty years.

And, like the Israelites in the wilderness, most of them would die before milk and honey ran freely.

He plodded downstairs, distracted by his thoughts. *I can live with that, Father,* he said silently. *I have known luxury, but it didn't bring contentment. I can be content anywhere you are.* His family's wealthy hab peers, in fact, had been some of the most discontented people he knew.

At the foot of the CA building's stairwell, he turned right. A group of men passed. One bade him good afternoon, and he responded, but he felt distracted. Did the notion of elections bother him? he wondered for the hundredth time. Ari played other people's emotions freely. People often followed a charismatic—even violent—leader in difficult times.

Violence might even be a survival factor here, and that contradiction of a concept he'd been raised to revere shocked him. Goddard had shocked them all with its survival demands. Their long life-spans had to be risked daily for one another's sake. All types of people had come to Henri and Palila Lwu wanting long life for their descendants. Some saw Goddard's harsh environment as a testing ground. Those families who survived would earn the right to pass down longevity genes—so said Ari and others whose parents and grandparents were recruited for ability, not money.

In other words, she hoped Lindon and the other sons of wealth would die out, and the sooner the better.

Goddard's colonists, he observed, were no different in nature from the Einsteinians they had been. Everyone tended, without guidance, toward depravity. Since there were unstable Lwuites, as in any other sample of humanity, one of his daughters might be attacked by a depraved person carrying a knife or a rock. Therefore, allowing handgun production on Goddard had been emotionally difficult but logical. The combined CA committees, only four months after making planetfall, overcame hab-ingrained fear of projectiles to make the vote unanimous. Producing weapons seemed a natural part of self-sufficiency.

He took another right into the new training building and walked straight into the underground firing range. The smell of gunpowder made his nose itch and reminded him of his first efforts to shoot straight. To his surprise, he proved steady-handed. Lwuites might not be aggressive, but if circumstances ever took him where he did not want to go, he might survive.

In a culture without bodyguards, this skill was imperative for someone in leadership.

About twenty women stood along the range, backs turned toward him, bright blue ear protectors squashing their pigtails. Pressing both hands over his ears, he peered through a gap in their backs at a line of clay cubes. A few were unscathed, but most lay in pieces. Some older crèche children, he'd been told, had been given new work creating those targets.

"Chairman DalLierx." A young man wearing a hip holster strode along the back wall, smiling. The women kept firing in their rotations. "Good of you to come by. What about conducting an inspection?"

Yes, he ought to make his presence known, if only to remind Ari he wasn't conceding authority just yet. "I'll wait here," he said, "until you're ready."

The man hustled back to the lineup, flicked off and on the range lights, then stood waiting for silence. Blasting noises died away, and women turned to look at the range instructor. "Holster your pistols," he directed, "and stand at attention for review by Chairman DalLierx."

Varied female figures pulled their feet together, straightened their clothing, and slicked hair into their braids. He smiled as he watched.

The instructor nodded. Lindon strode forward, wondering if he ever would feel completely comfortable wearing the mantle of authority. He had no militia experience except his own D-group training. Consequently, he said nothing about disarrayed clothes or unfastened holsters, though he suspected untucked blouses were inappropriate. Ari could handle that. He knew many trainees by name. ID tags helped him with the rest of their faces.

At the sight of one face—one very familiar face, staring straight forward with her chin tilted and a smirk on her lips—he stopped and grinned. "Well, hello, Crys."

His sister's salute included a wink. "If Mother could see us now," she said.

Their parents had chosen to live at another settlement. Lindon laughed softly and walked on, reassured. Crystal was an excellent judge of character, and she'd sense any bad feelings directed his way. She would also let him know if Ari MaiJidda mishandled the D-group.

Ari was nowhere in sight, he realized. Had she delegated responsibility for today's target practice? Looking around for her, he spotted a new long, pale gouge in the concrete floor. Huge crates were haphazardly piled low along the floor instead of high to the ceiling as he remembered them.

There'd been an accident, he concluded. At least he could assume no one was hurt. He'd have heard about that.

Almost at the far end of the line, he found himself staring at dark blond hair pulled back from a less familiar face.

"Dr. Brady Phillips," he exclaimed, trying to hide his shock. Why hadn't he been told she was involved in D-group? Surely Ari warned the other women not to talk openly about certain things in her presence. "You're . . ." *You're here* seemed like a stupid thing to say. "How goes the practice?"

"I've improved about 600 percent in three days." She stood erect with her shoulders back and a twinkle lighting her silver-blue eyes, looking much healthier than he remembered. "I'm pleased to be working with your people, Chairman DalLierx."

"Thank you," he said, making a mental note to speak with Ari. Dr. B.P. must not be put in any position where she would hear too much. Nor must she be harmed. At least she'd been able to keep up with this training squadron.

Crys. He already had a spy here, he realized. He would ask his sister to watch her.

Quickly he moved on, finished reviewing the line, then returned to his spot at the back wall. The instructor signaled his class to start again.

As the women resumed firing, Lindon eyed Graysha Brady-Phillips from the awkward angle, then stepped along the rough wall to watch her target. She wasn't doing poorly at all. Perhaps she'd trained with handguns before, at EB offices on Einstein. Maybe she was an EB nettech after all. The notion sent a spasm of fear up his spine.

He pulled a deep breath, reminding himself that no one should be declared guilty without proof. The sight of twenty women shooting, even at clay targets, disturbed another of his protective instincts. "Hand-eye coordination exercise, and a sense of unity, pride, and accomplishment" had been secondary objectives of the pistol training program. Those, too, made logical sense. But he still was a man, and a man noticed certain things.

With her back arched slightly, one arm barely dropped and the other held stiff, Graysha held her head cocked, concentrating down her sights. She had a wild beauty that her odd hair color enhanced. . . .

Astonished to find himself thinking that way, he left the firing range and jogged back up to his office. A road-building project needed attention this afternoon. Settling into his high-backed chair, he was struck by one more thought: Graysha Brady-Phillips was the only Gaea employee who bothered to join their rudimentary defense organization. She might have done so for purely innocent reasons—or as a spy. Not long ago, he'd hoped to send her away on the next shuttle.

Now he wondered if they dared let her leave.

13. DEVIATIONS

Sarai mentioned Dr. Brady-Phillips that night when Lindon visited their crèche. Seated on the other couch, Bee created eerie almost-music on a borrowed vidharp. The triangular lap instrument constructed from spare electronic parts belonged to the colony school and was available for anyone over ten to check out.

"I've seen her." Sarai's young voice sounded uncannily solemn. "Everybody in our crèche knew about her the day after she came. We saw her with the tall black lady. They looked like salt and pepper."

"She's not well." Lindon stretched out both legs on the central room's brown couch and watched Bee play.

As she gripped press points for chords along one edge, her right hand waved up and down the slick, clear central reading surface, where it broke a light path and set the pitch of melody notes. She seemed lost in her improvisation. The curve of her chin and her rapt stare at nothing visible reminded him sharply of watching Cassandra play.

Fourteen terrannums ago, when they furnished their first apartment, Cass brought home a commercially produced vidharp, engraved on all three sides with a swirling knotted ribbon design. She sang to him the night Bee was conceived.

From the floor beside him, Sarai leaned her head against his knee. "Then I like her even better," she said. "I know what that's like."

Graysha. Sarai was talking about another woman, not her own mother.

Galled by the thought, he caught himself up short. How long had Cass been gone? Sarai never even knew her. "No, Princess," he said, wishing the very thought of Cass didn't made his chest ache. "You're stronger than anybody thinks you are. Including you." He kissed the top of her head. "Dr. Brady-Phillips has a rare disease and shouldn't stay here. She should go back to the habs, where the very best doctors are."

"We have very good doctors," she said firmly.

"Not the same kinds of doctors," he answered.

He dreamed of Graysha that night. She stood spread-eagle in firing position, aiming one stiff finger for the horizon. Wind whipped her dark golden hair, and when she twitched her trigger finger, a broad green swath appeared on the ground, slowly fading to yellow.

Alone under the polarized skylight, he woke craving the dream woman's company. Hastily he sat up and waved on a lamp. He'd had night-mares about Graysha's mother, but he hadn't peaceably dreamed of another woman since Cass died eight terrannums ago. Why now, and why—of all people—Dr. Brady-Phillips? He stared at the thin fiber rug covering his apartment's concrete floor.

Because, he decided, Sarai mentioned her. He was also concerned for her health. His subconscious mind had to be trying to reconcile that with the need to send her home and the worry about her possible EB connection—compounded by his own stress over the impending election. He lay back down, pulling a softly woven sheet over his shoulders. Dreams were creations of the mind, mixing and juxtaposing inappropriate images.

He still felt vaguely guilty. Rolling over, he took the sheet with him and tried to push his face into a comfortable spot on his feather pillow.

When Goddard was established, and when he had free time again, he must consider remarriage. The population must increase, and it was not good for a man to live alone. He had that on the highest authority.

The following evening, Graysha's final night of training week, she joined Crystal and Duncan in the co-op for dinner. Twilight filtered down through the long skylight. The few older crèches present ate quietly, and most tables were lined with adults. Their backs presented an oddly regular pattern: short hair, pigtails, pigtails, short hair, up and down both benches.

She felt strangely content, comfortable enough to accept her dinner invite before going home to sink-bathe. Tonight the professional and cultural concerns she had shared with Jirina seemed downright superficial. How odd that physical exercise and one moment of crisis could link her so strongly to the Lwuite woman, when with Jirina there was a world to shape from bedrock up. Maybe humans, for all their cerebral posturing, were still more physically oriented than most cared to admit.

Or maybe the difference was Crystal herself. She had a warmth and depth that went beyond Jirina's playful intellectualism to a profound sense of contentment.

Struck by the number of couples who arrived together, she finished brown rice and cheddar—a sticky dish, but tasty—and asked Crystal about the entering pairs.

"It's our ethic to job share with your spouse. It seems to work." Crys glanced at Duncan, who was getting second cups of coffee from a glass-sided tank. "But Duncan and I don't have to spend all our time together. We'd both go crazy, I think."

"I've heard the same thing from retirees." Graysha shrugged.

"So have I. Anyway, there's a lot of organized recreation, which tends to be women only or men only. It's a chance to escape the person you work and sleep with. But working together keeps us in communication and almost doubles the work force."

"That's why baby farming is such an important part of your economy?"

"I guess so."

"How did you meet Duncan?" Obviously, Crystal had done a better job of spouse hunting than Graysha, with her chemistry-lab flirtation.

"Our parents thought we might get along, and if that isn't archaic, I don't know what is. I was sixteen when we married, almost eight terran-nums ago, and I still enjoy his company. It's a secret, but—" as she trailed off, her eyes flicked down through a net of sudden smile lines—"I'm two months along again."

"Congratulations," Graysha mumbled. How ironic. As one biological clock coated her capillary walls, a different clock molded life in Crystal's womb. There was a name for this ache: "Earth-womb fever" was a barb perennially leveled at unattached females in the life sciences.

"Were you ever married?" Crystal asked.

"Briefly," Graysha murmured. "He was extremely intelligent but very critical. Apparently I didn't meet his expectations. He left."

Crystal rubbed her upturned nose. "I'm sorry."

"It was for the best, I suppose." Graysha spooned thoughtfully into bread pudding studded with raisins. "I'd guess you're glad to be planetside, too, out of the radiation, if baby farming is so important to your colony. Fewer chances for new genetic problems."

Crystal's startled look seemed to confirm Graysha's hopes.

"Strange, though, isn't it?" Graysha pressed on. "Once, it was Earth's wrecked atmosphere that gave people cancers and chromosome breakage. Nowadays, genefects are the price we pay for living in space."

"Oh. Genefects." Crystal took a forkful of sweet-potato pie. "That's right. You're—"

"Yes," Graysha interrupted, but she kept her voice casual. "Back at Newton where I was born, we're starting to have quite a few show up. Was it that way with your people?"

Crystal tapped her fork against her plate and said, "Forgive me, I'd forgotten."

"There's nothing to forgive," Graysha insisted. There it was again, the willingness to discuss any question but the one she really asked. "You have no idea what it's like to work at terraforming a planet," she plunged ahead, "when it's illegal to fix your own broken chromosomes." If only Crystal would quietly say "Yes, I do."

Instead, she answered, "I guess I've never worried much about genetics." She flicked her bangs. "I mean, worrying won't change anything, will it?"

Graysha hesitated. That answer didn't fit the pattern she expected, not at all. If the Lwuites recruited settlers who needed gene-healing, Crystal surely would have feelings one way or the other. "You're lucky to have . . . what you have. I'm going to miss you, and the others in D-group."

Crystal's wide, wary eyes seemed to relax. "We'll run into each other," she said. "Axis Plantation isn't all that big, and I have a lot of freedom in this job. I can take my crèche on field trips."

Was that a hint? Graysha pictured a troop of primaries marching through the Gaea building's halls, and she declined to answer.

At least, she decided, she'd planted a seed in Crystal's mind. Or had she? Did Crys understand what she'd meant?

This could be her last chance. "Crys," she blurted as Duncan started back across the wide room, carrying two steaming cups, "is it true you people . . . help genefective individuals? Before you say anything, I want you to know this is not for the infamous Novia Brady-Phillips. I want to know for me. For me alone."

"No." Crystal's sympathetic expression faded to blank, and for one moment, her somber eyes darkened like Lindon DalLierx's. "No, we never have. I'm sorry, Graysha."

Graysha slumped on the bench, sensing she'd risked—and ruined—her chances, her hopes, even her budding friendship with Crystal DalDidier. "I'd heard a rumor, you see," she said quickly, then added, "I haven't mentioned even *that* to Novia, and I won't. You have my word." Graysha smiled up at Duncan, who stepped up to the table and set down his mugs. "Maybe I'll see you at the refresher session next Dropoff, Crys. Hope so." She stretched out her legs under the concrete table. They felt stronger than they'd felt a mere four circs ago. "I hope I can stay in shape."

"Lots of us jog the hub, evenings. Thanks, Dunc." Crystal sipped her coffee, then stood up. "They keep the hub cool, fifteen or so. Comfortable for running."

Duncan swatted a young boy whose offense Graysha hadn't seen, then touched Crystal's arm. "Wait a moment," he said. "Graysha, I've been meaning to ask something, and it's never come up. Before you leave us, tell me whatever you can about these recent deviations from our expected temp."

Goddard's cooling, rumor number two. Graysha exhaled sharply. "I've found out just about nothing, and that's despite the fact that I've made a real pest of myself asking. It's almost like there's a . . . " Did she dare use the word? Well, why not? It felt this way. "Like there's a conspiracy," she finished, then realized how lame it sounded.

Duncan cradled his mug two-handed. "Will you let us know if anything comes up?"

She looked from Crystal—vibrant, young, and too busy with her children to risk telling secrets—to Duncan, who, like Graysha, had dared to ask a potentially dangerous question. "Well, yes," she said. "I'll do anything I can, and I'll start by keeping a watch on the Gaea net."

Duncan nodded solemnly. "We'd owe you for that, Graysha."

Was he saying . . . did he mean. . . ?

As Graysha's head whirled with unanswered questions, Duncan and Crystal carried out their coffee mugs.

Twenty preadolescents arrived late at the door and stampeded for the food line. Graysha walked to the dump window and left her dishes with the short-haired teener inside.

Enough browncloth. It was time she got back to work and her own professional circle. It would be good to see Jirina again and to catch up with new developments in the lab.

And *that* reminded her she still hadn't reported back to Dr. Lee about the Lwuite philosophy that made them gun carriers. She whirled away from the dump window, almost bumping a tray-carrying woman behind her.

Could she speak frankly with Dr. Lee? Four days with the Lwuites had made a staggering shift in her perspective. She'd gone to D-group as a spy—not for Novia, but a spy nonetheless. Now her concern was chiefly for Goddard.

Maybe a few days with the Gaea people would restore her earlier perspective. As she plodded out into the green-smelling hub, she reminded herself that genetic healing wouldn't clear her capillary system anyway. It would merely let her have children who didn't carry the defective gene—

and what would that matter, since she had no husband?

Global cooling, though—that mattered. If the Goddard project might succeed through her efforts, she could leave a legacy to Crystal and Duncan and their people. She had a fighting chance at that.

Fighting . . . Yes, she decided as she marched past a bed of bright yellow flowers. She'd better report the handguns. If Dr. Lee heard about them later, from someone else, she'd want to know why Graysha didn't report.

Varberg probably had several new bacterial strains to farm out, too. A plague on geneticists—some of them certainly deserved one.

She passed south through the utilitarian concrete arch into the echoing Gaea tunnel, found her own door, and waved her key across the reader. Emmer uncurled on the pillow as if to greet her. Smiling, she stirred the potpourri under her browncloth hanging, laid her duffel beside her desk lamp, and then noticed a message light blinking on her console.

To her surprise, it was a personal letter carried by shipboard computer from Einstein, then sent on by laser pulse from Copernicus Hab.

17 October 2133
Gray—

How then is life at Halley? Are the students any more grown-up than the crowd at King Pre-Coll? How's the air? Our exalted supe got caught dipping into air-tax money. About time they threw him out the lock.

I miss you. Now that you're on Gaea salary, spend a few maxims and answer right away—at length.

Always,
Luce

Graysha shook her head at the screen. She and Lucile Coyote, languages teacher at the high school, had shared countless coffee breaks. She calculated backward on her fingers: a month transit Einstein to Halley, two more en route to Copernicus, roughly a week to cross the Eps Eri system. This letter had been chasing her for over three months, and Luce wouldn't hear back until Graysha's first G-year was half over.

She had a lot of explaining to do. First, though, she still felt grimy and sweaty. She headed for the clean room, dropping clothing on her bed as she walked. Emmer squeaked protest. Chuckling, she arranged her sweaty shirt around Emmer like a nest. The gribien clicked contentment.

Two minutes later, half finished with sink bathing and naked and chilly, Graysha gripped the basin's edge while the ground rattled and shook. Rumblings echoed off into the distance.

Back in Einstein, huge metal struts occasionally rearranged stress up and down their length, but those shakes always came down from overhead. No matter what Jirina said, shudders from below rattled her nerves. Not only was Goddard open to the sky, it had a core of molten metal. Magma seethed under crustal plates that hadn't moved for millennia. Maybe, by restarting continental drift, Gaea was asking for trouble.

And can you do anything about that, Graysha Brady-Phillips? she asked herself.

Of course not. She slipped into thick pajamas and covered them with a browncloth robe. Then, still wondering what to tell Luce Coyote, she pulled her perfuming box out of her clothes closet and opened its top and bottom. Something old style, green or floral, would make her feel rooted and grounded tonight. Hearing from Luce reminded her how alone she was.

Plucking six ester vials and the fixative from their slots, she lined them up, then took out the tiny micropipette with gradations along one side. Did any Gaea chemists in residence share her hobby? she wondered. Easing microliters from the ester vials through their sampling nipples, she added the tiniest draw of fix and shook the dropper.

She squeezed the resultant potion onto one wrist, then pressed both wrists together and sniffed.

Lilac. The bushes had grown outside her bedroom window at her parents' home in Newton.

Breathing deeply the scent of childhood, she turned her chair to face the desk and started typing.

2 February 2134
Dear Luce,

She paused and touched her left wrist to the skin under her nose. What to tell? That she was earning three times as much as Luce anticipated? That she was stuck on a bare, unstable rock with colonists who were somehow both kindly and militaristic? That she worked with an oceanographer who had to be the best-looking man she'd ever met?

Or—again she sniffed the fragrance of lilacs, organic and springlike on this stony, shivering world—maybe she should tell Luce she was homesick tonight for Einstein Habitat, where the ground arched comfortably overhead.

Graysha fingered the rough desktop, considering the Lwuites against all her mother's lectures. In her own opinion, genetic healing was like terraforming. Each was a use of intellect leveled against a potentially animate object. Either had potentially good uses. Either could be turned to evil.

Did human gene tampering fall into the same category? Should each case be considered on its own merits?

The thought made her stifle a bitter laugh. By the standards of her own upbringing, she was thinking treason—or even heresy.

Late that same evening, Ari studied a letter Graysha Brady-Phillips had placed in the outbound queue, headed for transmission to Copernicus Hab and thence outbound to Einstein Habitat. Luce Coyote might be a real person. The message might be what it appeared, a simple social letter. Ari's decoding program hadn't found any secret message.

Still, certain words might be prearranged signals, set up before Graysha left Einstein Hab—and its Eugenics office.

Ari's most recent gamble, rigging the firing-range crates to tumble by remote control, had seemed like a clear opportunity. Too bad she'd muffed it. She hadn't even brought on another attack of Graysha's infamous disease.

On the other hand—she rubbed her forehead—this small failure might've saved her from serious consequences. Axis Plantation could've tipped toward giving Lindon the sympathy vote if his sister Crystal had died down there. Sacrificing an innocent bystander was one thing. If she threw the election out of sheer stupidity, she never would forgive herself.

Her friend Chenny HoNin still spoke well of Lindon, but Ari was sure Chenny had never cared for someone, then had him treat her like such filth that her feelings slammed around 180 degrees. *"Unbeliever,"* he had called her. To her face!

Masiihi, pretty boy. Of course she believed. She just didn't buy into his patriarch-god.

Well. Flexing her fingers, she reached for the keyboard. She wouldn't waste time second-guessing Graysha Brady-Phillips. For now, the solution was simple. Nothing originating with that woman would go offplanet.

Using her own security override and adding DalLierx's authorization code to muddy her trail, she destroyed the outbound letter.

14. TELL UNCLE PAUL

Graysha reported to Melantha Lee promptly the following morning. From where she sat, one of the regal white cranes seemed to peer over Lee's shoulder, and a mug full of small round flowers bloomed beside Lee's keyboard. Though she would have preferred to cover for the colonists, she dutifully mentioned weapons training.

Dr. Lee rocked her chair, curling both hands around its armrests. "We would normally expect colonists to ask for USSC security at this stage," the supervisor observed. "They're supposed to be too busy planting crops and digging bunkers to build weapons. Since they already have operating pistols, plainly they've been at this for some time."

Graysha chose not to guess out loud where they might be manufacturing guns or what else the gunsmithing know-how implied.

Lee opened her small pocketknife and flipped it over and over. It was amazing what people would play with if they didn't have pencils handy. "You did well to speak with me," she said after a long silence.

She had to ask one more question. "Dr. Lee?"

The supervisor's head came up.

This wasn't easy. Confronting people went against her nature, so she'd rehearsed this request. Lee's answer, pro or con, should be revealing. "Some of these colonists are deeply concerned about the recent cooling trend. If I check a few figures for them, that won't create a problem, will it?"

Melantha Lee pressed her palms together. "You will find that you've enough to do over the next few days, settling back in after your relief week, without engaging in extraprofessional research."

"Very well." She mustn't argue, but that answer took her breath away.

"We should have dinner together sometime," Lee said. "I'd like to know you better, Graysha."

It sounded like a dismissal, so Graysha excused herself, but she also wondered if Lee were looking for leverage to use against her, to keep her in line. Disquieted, she rode the elevator back up to her lab and signed in on the Gaea net.

Her incoming line of reports didn't faze her, nor did Jirina's break-room gibes about "Private Brady-Phillips" an hour later. She brewed a cup of alfalfa tea, sniffing appreciatively while the dried leaves steeped. She'd developed a taste for that deep green scent. It smelled like morning. Libby wasn't due to come in today, so she wouldn't need to create tasks for anyone but Trev. Instead, she settled in at the computer to read what had developed outdoors while she took a Goddarday off.

Evidently, after the brief warm spell, winter was continuing to deepen. Several experimental soil organisms she'd seeded into her media collection were adapting less hardily than she'd hoped. It was a normal problem for gene-spliced bacteria, but she'd taken Varberg's claim of extra hardiness at face value. Should she suspect that claim, too?

With cooling—and Lee's caution—on her mind, a report from Botany caught her attention. An experimental fenced zone north of Axis—she'd never heard of Lower Infinity Crater—was losing its plant cover. After reading the brief report twice and considering the break-room intercom (which wasn't exactly private), she opted for the supposedly secure net and messaged the botanist who filed the report.

She took time to check on Trev, who was leaning over a scope counting spots on a culture strip, and took a long drink of her cooling tea, and then the computer called her back with two beeps. A. Fong, fourth floor, had come on: +Here.+

+G. Brady-Phillips, fifth floor,+ she identified herself. +Just got back from my relief week and read your report. What do you think the cause could be?+

+I only reported the botanical aspect. Problem's plainly overgrazing.+

Graysha knew of only one herbivore up on the wild. +By yabuts?+

+Our Van Dyk weasel-crossed lynxes have vanished, so yabuts are stripping greens it took us half a G-year to encourage into full foliation.+

She nodded. In a predator die-off, herbivores would multiply out of control. +Could lynxes be hibernating?+

+Dutch cats and yabuts both transgened not to hibernate unless average temp falls below −10 C. That's why we planted dwarfalfa. It's good to −12. Remaining dwarfalfa looks sickly, though. Theory, not yet published: plants went down first. If a few yabuts tunneled under the fence looking for more food, lynxes could've gone following them.+

Dutch cats—official designation, Van Dyk weasel-crossed lynxes. Earth's mid-North American Hollander community, a hardworking agricultural group, had fallen headlong into enthusiastic terraforming. She flexed her wrist, remembering the scent of lilacs on a potato farm she once visited. +All of them?+

+Why not? Cats love a chase, and those yabuts might be smarter than we think. Must try stable isotope tracing.+

+Ho,+ Graysha typed. +What made dwarfalfa sick? Cold damage?+

This time she waited several seconds before Antonia Fong came back. +Are you baiting me?+

Graysha tightened her lips, daring to hope. Maybe she'd found another Gaea person not infected by Consortium policy, someone with facts to support that stand. She typed quickly, +Not at all. I'm concerned about this cooling business.+

+Me too+ appeared instantly. +Will look you up sometime. We need to talk.+

+I'll expect you to call some evening.+

She keyed off the net, then sat and stared. It wouldn't take a hugely multiplied herbivore population to strip weakened vegetation. All these balances were incredibly delicate. She hated to precipitate a split among Gaea people, but disagreements often led to progress, and she must find out why the planet was recooling.

She flicked on the next report.

When break time arrived, she still felt unsettled. She got to the break room so late that Trev was already counting yabut progeny in the breeding cages. He'd developed a fascination for the creatures, though he still made faces whenever he dumped the smelly old cage litter.

"So how was your week with the colonists?" Will Varberg drawled as she walked in. Behind the massive supervisor, Paul smiled a quieter greeting. His cadet-blue lab coat seemed to light his blue eyes, making them shine more intensely than usual.

"I don't know." Graysha rinsed her cup, then filled it with fresh coffee that had a darker, smokier scent than the colonists' co-op brew. "They're incredibly good at not talking about their religion. I didn't even hear anything that sounded like in-group language."

"They are strange," Jirina said. She curled her fingers around her other arm. "Well, go ahead. What else?"

"It's hard to put my finger on this, but—" should she even mention it?—"well, it seems to me that the differences they're trying to overcome between sexes aren't any greater than standard differences among normal males or normal females. *We're* all different, aren't we?" She swept out a hand, indicating the group gathered in the break room.

"I would hope so." Varberg sank into his chair and glanced up at Ilizarov.

Emboldened, Graysha said, "For example, the woman in charge of the D-group, Coordinator MaiJidda, is extremely aggressive. Nothing's been done to 'fix' her."

Jirina grinned. "What did you do besides lidar?"

"Would you believe we had handgun training?"

Jirina's grin winked out. Varberg pulled up straighter in his chair. Only Paul Ilizarov's posture remained languid, with both thumbs tucked into his lab-coat pockets. His steady stare, interpreted in light of that stance, gave her goose bumps after a week spent mostly with women.

"Handguns? On Goddard?" Varberg asked.

"The real thing. They claim they might need them for hunting. Frontier survival and all that." She thought about mentioning "forced evacuation" and decided against it.

"You told Dr. Lee?" Varberg stroked his chin.

"Of course." Flexing her legs, Graysha sipped her coffee. Ari MaiJidda would push even harder the next time around, she guessed. She'd better be ready for stiff exercise—and she'd better change the subject. "Jirina, do you work out?"

"Twice a week. And not with handguns. Why?"

Involuntarily, she flicked a glance at Paul. "I'd just hate to lose the bit of body toning I've started."

He blinked slowly.

"Talk to you later about it," said Jirina.

"Just be careful," Varberg said. "Don't overdo."

"I did fine in training, and they didn't go easy on us." *I am not an invalid!* There was a brief silence perforated only by sipping noises. Trev rounded one end of the cage rack, removed a wire cover, and reached into a plastic cage.

"People," Graysha said at last, "did anyone else read Dr. Fong's report?"

"Yes." Varberg's huge hands looked as if they were steaming. There was a cup between them, somewhere.

Jirina nodded. Paul's shoulders rose and fell.

Graysha tapped a foot against one rung of her stool. "I really am concerned. A planet at this distance from its sun would become a stable ice ball if it froze, and Gaea's technology would take centuries to thaw it. Meanwhile Gaea goes leggy-up, and the Lwuites lose their chance for a—"

"No, no, no." Will Varberg crossed one leg over the other. "Graysha, you're too young to remember Messier."

She frowned, recalling his narrow escape.

"Messier started out warmer than this, it's true. Still, with the introduction of water, it needed a cold trap and greenhouse layer beneath to catch warmth, otherwise it would have done exactly what you're worrying about: It would've become an ice ball before we had enough of a planetary ecology to create the Gaea effect and make the planet live."

"I've heard all that," she said softly.

"Keep listening, then." He steepled his fingers. "If we hadn't been in such a rush to add atmosphere to Messier, if we'd done it more gradually, we might have kept it in balance. But!" He raised a finger. "It's safer to keep things on the cold side here than to run the slightest risk of jet-stream shift." He shook his head. "The slightest," he repeated. "Goddard's settlements are separated farther from each other, too. A local difficulty could still arise suddenly, but it wouldn't endanger our whole population."

First Lee, now Varberg—all this protest over supposedly insignificant cooling. Graysha set a palm on one hip. "If something is going awry here, now," she said, "the Messier disaster has nothing to do with it."

Paul reached out and touched her arm. "You've been with the colonists for a week. We all understand your concern, but there's simply no indication we're about to lose Goddard. You'll find just as much field data indicating solid warming as in alarmist reports like Fong's." His hand rested on her shoulder, warm and smelling of citrus.

"Okay." Graysha clenched her cup two-handed. "Different groups will interpret identical data differently, depending on their bias and what they're looking for. Time will tell whose interpretation of these seasonal fluctuations is correct. But will we know the truth before it's too late? We stand to lose less than the Lwuites do."

"We'll know. Easily." Varberg pushed up out of his chair and stood looking down at her, tipping his head back in a gesture she now recognized as "me-dominant, you-submissive." "And if there's too much cooling, we simply increase CFC production."

"With what carbon?" she asked. "Where do we get the base that quickly?"

"It's all around us." He squeezed the shoulder Paul wasn't touching.

Feeling surrounded, she asked, "Where?"

He shrugged. "Geology has prospectors out constantly. Ask them. It's not our department."

"All right," she mumbled. Of all the people on Goddard, she mustn't antagonize her supervisor. "Come talk to me later, Paul." Clutching her cup, she backed out into the hall. Several steps along, she heard someone behind her. To her surprise, Jirina followed on long legs.

"Talk with you a minute?" Jirina asked.

Graysha led into her office, where Jirina sat down on the floor. Graysha joined her down there. Hard cement chilled her hindquarters.

"So. Did you get to keep it?"

Graysha wriggled, trying to find a comfortable position and finding only a colder one. "The handgun? No, they were on temporary issue."

"That's a relief anyway."

"I have to go back for practice."

"Were you good?"

"I improved."

Jirina ran one finger along a tiny ridge in the concrete floor. "I wonder if I'm being paranoid."

"About the possibility of armed colonists?"

"Mm-hmm."

"It occurred to me, too," Graysha admitted.

"Anyway, that isn't why I came down. Paul was asking about you while you were gone. Thought you'd better be warned once more."

"You did mention social diseases."

"He's made the Gaea rounds once or twice. DalLierx is getting fed up with Paul romancing his little pigtailed girlies, too."

That didn't make a nice picture. "The famous Ilizarov charm."

"He does stick to single women, but that's most of us. Your Lwuites probably think we're all either irresponsible or undesirable."

Maybe we are. "Or genefective," she said lightly.

Jirina paused, staring at the floor. "Graysha, it's none of my business, and I mean nothing personal against your mother or anyone else. But seems to me, they ought to allow genetic manipulation in cases like yours. It's not like you'd be selfish, asking for a gene fix. It wouldn't help *you,* would it?"

"No." Stiffly, Graysha folded her hands on her lap. "My mother used me, as a young child, to make propaganda broadcasts—at least that's how I see them now. At the time, I thought I was helping other people do the right thing."

"I can't imagine your own mother taking advantage of you like that."

"I worked at her office during school for a while, too. It beat cage mucking and paid better. But I hated being their token staff genefective."

"I think I can see that."

Was there a chance Jirina, the virologist, knew enough about chromosomal manipulation to work on a human? Standard genengineering used harmless but infective viruses to insert or delete specific bits of DNA within host chromosomes. Highly illegal "Strobel Probes" could be implanted along a woman's fallopian tubes to ensure the infection of every ovum released.

"Jirina . . ."

The black woman arched an eyebrow.

Should she ask? Jirina definitely was sympathetic.

Still, something held her back. "I doubt they'd change the laws in this generation," Graysha said. "Whatever happens, it'll be too late for me."

To her relief, Jirina didn't demand to know what she'd meant to say. "That's what I heard."

"There are still too few of us for the Eugenics Board to bother making exceptions. Most genefects are correctable with transplants or prosthetics, after all. If all those thousands of people were as incurable as I am, as a group we'd have some political clout."

"But you can't blame them for going along with what's legal."

"Of course not." Graysha stretched out a leg. This floor was anything but comfortable.

"As a researcher," Jirina said, "I understand. But personally, I don't know why you stand for it. You would think if we can terraform a world, we could change a capillary system. And no," she added, giving Graysha a sharp glance, "since you're being too gracious to ask, I don't know any way to fix your problem. Unfortunately."

"Thank you anyway." Graysha meant it sincerely. "Do you enjoy terraforming, Jirina?"

The other woman shut her eyes, exhaled, then spoke. "I think all day, week after week, on a planetary scale. We're trying to duplicate hab technology here, but with uncontrolled temps and air masses. It's so much. So big.

"Then I notice some tiny detail on a table in front of me, the weave of a basket"—she shaped her long hands around an imaginary object—"or the design painted on a stoneware bowl, and I see the beauty of things on my own scale. That's when I feel truly insignificant." She opened her eyes, raising her head. "But yes, I enjoy terraforming. I've had to learn to think in the huge while living in the small."

"Yes," Graysha said, "yes. I see what you mean."

"Are you avoiding me, lovely woman?"

Graysha almost dropped a tiny Erlenmeyer flask. "Don't sneak up on me like that," she exclaimed. Across the counter, Libby smirked. "No, I'm not avoiding you."

Paul lounged against her countertop, pulling at one of his neatly top-stitched cuffs. "I'm still covering one of your predecessor's jobs, and I'd like to pass it on."

She touched the flash switch to denature any protein molecules on her loop dropper, then eyed the row of flat white phoresis gels she'd loaded. "Here, Libby." Handing them across to the Lwuite tech, Graysha took a deep breath. Then she turned to Paul. "Why didn't you tell me about it sooner? I didn't mean to—"

"Experimental greenhouses need sampling only every month or so. Can you take an hour this afternoon and get to them?"

"Yes, good," she said calmly. "We need to talk anyway."

Strolling up a path between sandy dirt and open starry sky—it scarcely bothered her anymore, if she didn't look straight up—Graysha recounted highlights of her Goddarday with the D-group. When she came to DalLierx's firing-line inspection, Paul laughed heartily. "Surprised him, did you? Good. He needs his tree shaken every now and then."

Remembering Jirina's comment about "romancing pigtailed girlies," Graysha bristled. Maybe DalLierx had reprimanded Paul for pestering Libby.

A long row of greenhouse Quonsets looked like pale gray humps under the starlight. Graysha glanced back and eyed the tall smokestack. Above its blinking beacon, stars seemed to shimmer and dance.

Paul squeezed the remote he carried and a row of lights came on, washing out the stars. Graysha read off the signs painted on Quonset doors. Greenhouse D-I, D-II, D-III . . . There. Greenhouse D-V, their destination. Paul lunged forward to open the door. She stepped through, enjoying the sensation despite her irritation with Paul and her determination not to become his latest conquest.

Once the door boomed shut, he peeled off his parka. "Here, look. Isn't this clever? Grain growing in racks, hybrid grains." He lifted a drooping green seed head to reveal its support system. "Stems run through layers of wire mesh so they don't flop over. One cubic meter of space can produce food for several people each G-year."

It was far too warm for coats in here. Graysha left hers beside Paul's on the floor. "Those are fiber-optic cables coming down that corner," she observed.

"Right. Focused at growth spots on the plants. Watch."

He touched a control box, and the lush grain-rimmed room instantly darkened. As Graysha's eyes adjusted, clustered pinpoints of green focused. "There must be an automation and sensor system," she guessed, "to make the fiber tips follow those growth spots."

"Very good" came his voice in the darkness.

Fainter light started gleaming near her hip level. "Is that luminous plankton in the nutrient tanks?"

Paul was a wide-shouldered shadow in front of the next container. "Either that's a good guess or you've been studying. Yes. Water's very cold, but plankton releases enough energy to make a difference. That's what you'll need to check."

She turned on one foot, making mental notes. How many growth tanks—

"Graysha."

The shadow moved closer.

"I don't mean to pry into matters that aren't mine, but you seem to be needing a man."

"Needing?" She backed away from the shadow, feeling behind her with one hand to make sure she didn't crush precious greenery. "What do you mean?"

"Jittery," he said gently. "And little things seem to upset you. I know the signs."

"I'm fine." She tried to sound firm.

"I only wanted you to know that if you had a need . . ."

"Paul," she began, but this time reasonable statements caught in her throat.

He stepped closer. He was taking her hesitation as an invitation. She should say something. She wanted to speak—

His arm slipped around her shoulders. The citrus scent that always surrounded him drew her into a warm cocoon. She let him kiss her, and her eyes fell closed.

He pulled his lips from hers, and she felt him tug at the hair tie at the nape of her neck. "Here?" he whispered, "or would you be more comfortable somewhere else?"

"Paul," she said, grappling deep inside her convictions for the strength to resist her own urges . . . let alone his. This pounding physical urge felt too much like fear. She did not want to be conquered . . . to become one more notch on Paul Ilizarov's belt. "Paul, let me go. Just for a minute. Let me get my breath."

He strolled back to the control panel, switched the greenhouse lamps on again, then sank cross-legged onto loose pebbles, patting a spot beside him. "Tell Uncle Paul."

She almost laughed, then realized the condescension was no joke. To him, women were toys to be enjoyed and discarded. She sat down, re-smoothed her hair, and picked up a smooth stone—where had river rock come from on this world?—to rub with one thumb. "Thank you, Paul. I have been needing a little attention. Forever, it seems. I was married once, did you know that?"

He pulled open his lab coat. Beneath it he wore a blue V-necked shirt, perfectly color-matched to his eyes. "Yes. I read your file on the Gaea net."

"I haven't read yours."

"You're not nosy enough."

Graysha laughed shortly, just starting to realize how narrowly she'd escaped. "So. Have you been married?"

"I don't believe in marriage."

She seized the opening. "I do," she said, staring at his eyes. She must convince him. "Please don't get me wrong." Friction from her thumb warmed one side of the rock. "You . . . do good things to me. Are you hearing me, Paul? This is neither a put-down nor a put-off."

"No, no." He rested both elbows on his knees, his chin on both thumbs. "I want to know how you feel. Go on."

By heaven, the condescension was real. As if she needed proof! Further armored by that realization, she drew a deep breath. "I don't want to do anything along the way that might endanger my . . . my chances, my future, with the right man." If Paul were the right man, he'd understand

"You don't want me today." He ducked his head and stared up at her, his eyes like blue coals. "But I'll be around. You're a beautiful woman, and you need a man, not one of those brain-warped Lwuites. I cannot fathom the fact that you're unmarried, if you wish to marry. Unless . . . is it the disease?"

"That's a factor," she said slowly. "I shouldn't pass on defective genes. Most men who want children don't want known genefects."

"I see your problem." He raised up on his knees, twisted his legs, and sat down closer, pressing his shoulder against hers. The blue shirt gleamed as if wet. "Promise you'll come to me if you're lonely. That's all I ask."

It wasn't all you asked earlier. But at least he offered an escape from the situation without obvious hard feelings. Ellard's ego had been too brittle to let him do that.

"I promise."

That evening at her apartment keyboard, she punched on to the Gaea net and ran concurrent searches on *cooling, temperature, Celsius,* and every other key word that might shed light on the atmospheric issue. The net gave her a five-page list of experimental references, coded by floor, researcher, and date. Too tired to bother checking them all, she saved the list to her personal file, sublabeled it *Cooling*, and signed off.

After a hot sink bath, she curled around Emmer. "What do you think, old lady?" she asked, rubbing under the creature's sharp little chin. Emmer made clicking grunts of contentment. "Do you care if it's cold up top?"

Probably, as Jirina intimated, the downturn was a random fluctuation in planetary equations, a tempest in a teapot. Still, if she'd learned anything from working with Novia, it was to beware the woman or man who steered you too hard in some other direction.

She fell asleep curled around Emmer and woke about four, fully rested. Might as well start skimming those references, she decided. Smoothing her wrinkled clothing, she sat down at the desk and called up her *Cooling* subfile.

Her keystroke brought up half a screen of gibberish.

She snatched her fingers away from the keyboard. Was this a malfunction or had someone trashed her file? Could it be a virus programmed onto the net to protect someone's secrets from nosy investigators?

Working quickly, she repeated the search, then saved it again, this time as *Ellard.* Guessing she might also find that file garbaged unless she camouflaged it, she wished fruitlessly for a hardcopy printer, then—inspired— she added a screenful of divorce data at its head. Then she recopied the list once more, onto the end of the reading file she'd made for Liberty JenChee.

After stretching, she punched up the first entry, *Methane, Ice, and Albedo.* Jirina had mentioned albedo, the reflection of energy back into space, as a possible factor in planetary energy loss.

She propped her elbows against the desk's rough edge and started to read.

Graysha was eating lunch alone the next Dday in the Gaea employees' cafeteria when someone tapped her shoulder.

Behind her stood a small thin woman and a man nearly as small, both carrying trays. Most of the woman's curly black hair was caught loosely in a tie like the one Graysha wore. "I'm Antonia Fong," she said, "and this is my husband, Benjamin Emerson, of Sociology. You responded to a report of mine."

Fong, Emerson. *Now* she remembered where she'd heard the name Fong. Jirina had claimed Fong and Emerson were considering re-upping to spend another triannum on Goddard. She swallowed a mouthful of green salad, then asked, "Would you join me, Dr. Fong, Dr. Emerson?"

Antonia took the spot on Graysha's left while Benjamin came around the table to face them. "I understand you spent a Goddarday with the colonists," Antonia said, then went to work on fragrant rice and vegetables.

"It seemed appropriate, particularly when I learned I was the only Gaea person volunteering. As new person on the Gaea team," she added, "I'll be here the longest, finishing out my triannum. That made another good reason to work myself in."

"I see. You must like them." Antonia tugged on a long, loose strand of curly hair and pushed it behind her ear.

"I do so far, as a group. They have their share of cranks and oddbods." Graysha finished the last bite of her salad and started on the grilled fish, wondering if it was raised in an algae-filled tank at Wastewater Management. That notion gave the old expression "trash fish" new meaning. "The colonists are certainly concerned about the cooling. What do you think of it?" she ventured when nothing remained of the fish but three fins and a pile of bones. She thought it better not to mention yesterday's lobotomization of her file.

Benjamin Emerson frowned, but Antonia answered. "Only a hunch. Call it intuition, if you will. Field data as a whole support Consortium policy, but I can't shake the feeling something's wrong. Have you gotten any new directives from Halley Hab?"

Graysha stirred the bone pile with her fork. "You don't have data, either, other than your paper on the Dutch cats? I have only a hunch, supported by contact with worried colonists."

Benjamin Emerson gave his wife a glance that hinted at "told you so."

"All I can offer is moral support," Antonia said, "and a promise to send you anything I find out for certain."

"I'll take it," said Graysha. "And you have the same promise from me."

The next day, Graysha brewed a second cup of caffeinated alfalfa tea and dawdled along the yabut-cage shelves as she waited for the town meeting to start. Several new batches of offspring, hairless and pink with grape-colored spots where their eyes would be, wriggled inside the middle row. Trevarre's tiny, almost illegible handwriting recorded breeding codes, birth dates, and litter sizes on the end of each cage. She'd caught him singing at his work earlier and stood dumbfounded by a rich, mellow baritone that made her own occasional warbles sound like distress calls from a sick bird. No wonder Blase LZalle wanted to exploit him.

She finished a circuit of the room, and still the town meeting didn't come on. Libby had joined her today, opting to remain on station and catch up on her reading. Jirina occupied a corner stool, and Trev sat in Varberg's chair pulling at one ear. She'd never noticed how far they protruded. He must've had his hair cut.

"Graysha?" Libby called. Her tone of voice made Graysha suspect the problem before she reached the screen. "Look."

At the end of her reading list was half a page of gibberish.

"I must've hit a wrong key," Graysha murmured. "Sorry. Delete it." This had to be a viral defense, possibly left on the net from Jon Mahera's last days. If she wanted to read abstracts, she'd have to search them down one at a time.

She could do that. It made her uneasy to remember that Dr. Varberg knew her password, and she'd never bothered to change it. Maybe surviving

Messier had left him mentally unstable, attempting to submerge a split personality while trying to maintain professional confidence.

Or something like that.

Her chest constricted. As farfetched as it seemed, that might explain the "accidental" miscue for which Jon Mahera died . . . and the fact he'd been able to cover for it. Half of Varberg's mind might truthfully answer that he didn't mean to send Mahera out to his death.

Those mysterious piles of sand remained unexplained, too.

She shook her head. The entire train of thought was too paranoid to carry weight. She would change her password, though. Immediately.

The screen lit. To her surprise, it showed not the meeting room but an office Graysha thought might be in the CA building, its concrete-block walls unpainted and undecorated. "We are sorry, but this week's meeting is postponed," said the eldest CA committee member, Taidje FreeLand. "Chairman DalLierx is seriously ill. Issues scheduled for today will be discussed as soon as an interim chair is chosen by the CA Committee."

The screen went blank.

Ill? What diseases were there to catch on Goddard?

Libby sat up rifle straight.

"He's sick?" Jirina asked aloud.

Graysha took a stool and repeated her mental question out loud. "We don't have diseases here, do we? I went through a thorough health screening." She raised an eyebrow at Libby.

"We do have cold viruses," muttered the Lwuite tech. "I know that from experience."

Graysha wrapped her ankles around the stool's legs, anchoring herself to what was real—not speculation. HMF physicians insisted they'd screened out major pathogens before allowing colonists to immigrate, and she'd sat out a short quarantine. Mutant bacteria, or viruses? she wondered, chilled. A mutant plague born of the ultraviolet bombardment might rip through Goddard's population too rapidly for evacuation. Maybe an ancient native virus lay dormant inside its sheath over the world's dry layers, only to be rehydrated by human meddlers.

Seriously ill, they'd said. Her well-stocked medical imagination furnished the boy-faced CCA with terrible disease symptoms before she squelched it, gripping the stool harder with both feet. The notion of one sick man didn't have to draw out all her frustrated maternal instincts. Particularly that man. To the mental image she added his pigtailed wife, waiting white-faced with two small daughters in an HMF hallway.

She turned abruptly to Trev. "We should get to work. I have a culture from Varberg you need to grow out. I'll give you a list of media we'll need."

She let him spread out the project there in the communal lab, close to the vidnet terminal.

About an hour later, as she was flicking a sedimentation tube, a sharp tone from the power box made her jump. FreeLand's face came on-screen again. "Please stand by for a priority announcement," he said, then vanished.

Graysha glanced around the lab and couldn't spot Libby or Trev. She pushed up her sleeve, feeling vaguely unwell. Her button said tissue oxygen wasn't the problem. "Trev?" she called. "Libby, did you hear that?"

Trev leaned out from behind racks of breeding cages, rubbing gloved hands together. "Libby punched out."

Why hadn't she told Graysha? "Do me a favor," she said. "Tell Paul and Jirina—and Dr. Varberg—that the station's going to run something important."

"I don't know why they'd care," he said, but he strode out through the door.

They clattered in together, as if they'd been talking. Graysha relayed Vice-Chair FreeLand's fanfare but said nothing about her darker fears. If Goddard did face an epidemic, the microbiology floor would start losing sleep soon enough.

Paul took a seat beside her and peeled off his transparent gloves. "Would you like dinner tonight?" he murmured.

Before she could answer, the screen went from black to full color. "Wait a minute," she whispered back.

This time, the screen showed a medical station and an HMF staff member leaning against a countertop. Graysha pursed her lips. Surely, if the HMF were preparing to announce a sudden death, its spokesperson would be more formal in posture and location.

"I have been asked to give an update on Chairman DalLierx's condition," he said. "The initial diagnosis of acute hypoglycemia has been proved false by pancreatic scan." The man gripped one hand with the other. "Chairman DalLierx, who has no history of hypoglycemia, remains unstable. Symptoms suggest insulin poisoning, but no insulin source has been identified. Further information will go out over the conventional net." The spokesman looked aside.

In his silence, Paul rested a hand on the edge of Graysha's stool, nearly touching her hip. Over a soft pounding in her ears, she heard someone off-camera say something unintelligible. A woman walked into vidi range, and from the strip of cloth tape over her shirt pocket, Graysha recognized her as a D-group squad leader. "Security forces," she said, "both colonial and Gaea, are being alerted. An investigation will begin immediately."

The screen went dim again.

Will Varberg threw back his head and laughed. "Now it's begun!"

"Someone was very stupid." Paul shook his head, and hair flopped over his ears. "There is nowhere on Goddard for a poisoner to hide. They'll watch every lift-off for weeks."

"Remains unstable," Varberg came back. "Did you catch that? It sounds like maybe they got him. Maybe we'll be watching elections sooner than we thought."

Trev looked from one Gaea man to the other, dangling his gloves from one hand. "What jumps you to the conclusion somebody poisoned him?"

"You have some reading to do, LZalle," called Varberg. "Look it up."

"Trevish, if his pancreas is normal, then the insulin that's got him in hypoglycemic shock came from some . . . where . . . else." Jirina drew out the last words, wagging a finger.

Graysha pulled away from Paul's hand. Had this kind of callous banter gone on behind her back, too, when she arrived and promptly fell sick? "So we don't have a mutant virus on our hands," she choked out in Jirina's direction.

"No," she answered. "No, thank the goddess. We figured these people were going to start cockfighting sooner or later. But insulin? We're talking pre-transplant era."

"Some people can't take a graft, just like some can't take a joke." Varberg's nose twitched.

Graysha didn't follow. "His poor wife," she murmured.

Jirina tapped one foot. "What have you heard that I haven't, Blondie?"

"Didn't someone tell me he had two daughters?"

"Wife's dead," said Varberg. "The daughters are baby-farmed."

"Simple solution," Paul said, slipping off the stool. Either he'd forgotten dinner or he realized Graysha's appetite had gone south.

Before she could ask him to explain that statement, Trev yanked his gloves back on and stalked toward the animal cages. "This is crazy," he said. "It's inhuman, the whole business. I'll spend my time with the yabuts."

"They suit you," Varberg called.

Trev spun around. "What was that?"

Varberg heaved up out of his big deep chair. "They suit you, LZalle."

Trev lunged before Graysha could react. Jirina caught Trev just short of contact, one arm back, his lips pulled wide in a grimace. "Easy, Trevish," she said. "Watch your temper. Varberg, back off. He's just a kid."

Trev struggled to pull lose, losing one glove. Jirina held him with no visible effort, but Paul seized his other arm.

Nothing, Graysha decided, was going to go right today. They might as well all go back to the housing wing for naps.

Varberg took one step closer to Trev. Without so much as a backswing, he brought up a fist. It contacted jawbone with a soft thump. Trev crumpled jelly-legged.

Graysha squeaked surprise and ran to kneel beside the youth. A trickle of blood started from his chin. He shook his head.

Jirina stood above them with her arms stiffly extended. When Varberg sidled closer, she kicked toward his thigh but pulled back centimeters from striking. "All right, Varberg, we all know he's been asking for discipline," she said in a knife-bladed voice. "But next time, don't take him when I'm holding him for you." Graysha felt the wind when Jirina turned and strode out. Varberg rolled his eyes, then followed her.

Paul snatched a towel off the clean pile, bent down, and pressed it against Trev's bloody chin. "It's just a cut from Varberg's ring," Paul said softly. "Let me take care of him. I don't think he's going to want mothering."

He had a point. Graysha used a countertop to pull herself back up. Biting her upper lip, she reached toward a coffee cup, then changed her mind. Pouring coffee into her churning stomach could give her an ulcer. Out one corner of her eye, she saw Paul help Trev to his feet and guide him out of the lab.

If Varberg had a submerged personality, that agonized specter had just surfaced to breathe.

Half an hour later in the solitude of her office, she dimmed the window so she would not see the dark sky, then sat down on her desk chair, curled her body forward, and stayed there. *God, if you exist, don't let that man die.* She'd expected hazardous duty. She hadn't expected to land in the middle of a war zone.

She shut down her computer, hung her lab coat on the inside of the door, and strode to the elevator. Crossing the chilly hub's corner toward Gaea housing, she eyed the bright red Health Maintenance Facility door. On impulse, she walked in.

Ethanol and phenol—she wouldn't forget that smell.

A man at the front desk looked up.

"I'm Dr. Brady-Phillips," she said, not quite sure how to do this. "I'd . . . like to leave a message for Chairman DalLierx, if I might."

"He's not allowed visitors." The man looked professionally emotionless, from his firmly folded hands to his blank stare.

"I'm sure he's not." Graysha tugged an itchy side seam of her pants. "Can you say . . . is he any better?"

The man unbent enough to purse his lips. "Hard to tell, Dr. Brady-Phillips."

Staff not allowed to give information except to family members: standard procedure.

Those poor little girls. Mother dead, father . . .

She mustn't think *dying*. No one had said that.

Still, insulin poisoning sounded serious. "May I leave a goodwill message?"

"By all means." The receptionist gestured toward a concrete desk along the nearest wall.

Graysha took the hard seat, stared at the keyboard, and wondered what she wanted to say. That she would pray for him? She didn't want to affront his mysterious Lwuite religion by using an inappropriate term. She stood again. The man glanced in her direction.

"I'll send something on the net," she said.

From her rooms, she gave it a try. Her first attempt to compose a note sounded condescending, the second, cold. The third filled her screen twice but showed only ineptitude at communicating with strangers.

Then be brief, she thought.

She shook out her hands and tried again.

Chairman DalLierx:
My prayers for your health.
Illegitimati non carborundum.
Get 'em.

Sincerely,
Graysha Brady-Phillips

She hoped he would know the old Latin joke. At least she might make him understand she didn't wish him ill. Deciding she was unlikely to do better, she touched the Send button. With the deed done and the HMF holding the message until he was able to read, she had the rest of the afternoon with nothing to do.

She curled around Emmer on the bed, stroked her long enough to wake her up, then fed her a crumb of cheese. The little creature delicately lipped the crumb, then wrapped a pink tongue around it and sucked it down, clicking the whole time.

Graysha sighed. She had no desire to return to work, not until the men settled their differences. Her apartment felt bare and confining, though.

If Varberg's hold on sanity was slipping, did he try to murder Chairman DalLierx? The entire micro floor knew DalLierx sentenced Varberg to serve an additional half G-year at the end his triannum—during which time his salary would be sent to Mahera's family as compensation.

But that was only a hand slap. G-years were brief, just over 190 circa-days.

Putting on a short jacket, she arranged Emmer on the collar and opened her door again. The corridor was empty. Graysha turned right, toward huge barrier doors between Housing and the cool hub. Passing through, she inhaled the damp, soil-rich odor of the central parkland. She hadn't taken samples from planters here, and she ought to check their microbial pops.

Beside a slender willow beginning to bend from its own weight, she sank onto a bench, hands in her jacket pockets. She thought about showing Emmer the truly warm water-purification sanctum, so different from the barren wilds outside Axis Crater, but she didn't feel like walking all the way to Wastewater. Emmer would only sniff, nibble, and sleep some more.

She crossed her ankles under the bench and reminded herself that solitude was better company than the wrong people. Eyeing the north arch, she wished a crèche couple might bring through a troop of young noisemakers. In a way, the hub represented Goddard's future, full of warm fertility and promise.

And above, now, it was all barren ground. Graysha rubbed her stiff neck. At times like this, with her spirits low, she felt like barren ground herself, all potential—and useful, in her way—but would her body bear fruit or go as cold as Goddard's uplands?

Paul Ilizarov had an easy answer for that question. For the moment, she didn't want it. Pushing off the bench, she cast a last look around the hub and then marched back toward her apartment.

She had reading to do for Duncan and Crys.

Dr. Yael GurEshel frowned down at the patient lying on her ICU cot. Unconscious, DalLierx looked pitiably young, even with a faint black shadow stubbling his cheeks and chin. A muslin sheet draped him from chest to toes. Drip packets of IV glucose and several drugs lay taped against his left arm. A blood-sugar sensor in his other arm fed data to a wall readout. A series of red dots on that wall screen gleamed like tiny drops of blood on a black background. Over the ten-minute period just past, blood sugar had crept upward almost to the normal range—but his condition seesawed wildly, letting him wake and then nearly killing him, over and over.

Come on, she urged the reading, *get up there*.

DalLierx shook his head and slit one eye open.

The last time, he'd been conscious eight seconds. She braced her arm against the bedstead. "Lindon," she said sharply, "do you have access to insulin?"

"Insulin," he murmured. His eyes closed.

He'd winked out again. Hope faded as red dots curved downward one more time.

She bit back unprofessional language, desperate not to lose Axis's Chairman for Colonial Affairs. His parents had caught a track-truck over from Center, and they waited in an HMF lounge. "Blood insulin," she said briskly.

A young nurse leaned over, drew blood for the test board, then shook her head. "It's rising again."

Yael slapped her palm with a diagnostic imager. Insulin readings were peaking in waves, suggesting an infection of some kind of insulin-producing organism that doubled its population every so often. Under Yael's direction, the room nurse and lower-floor medtech had run preliminary microbial DNA checks over every accessible centimeter of his body, turning up nothing but normal flora.

If he was fighting an infection, it was going to kill him, because broad-spectrum antibiotics, antivirals, and antifungals weren't touching it. If it wasn't an infection, she thought wearily, it would probably take him anyway, because they'd exhausted the med-op database, and though they had several treatments going simultaneously, none of them was breaking the cycle.

What else could she do?

"Medtech," she called into her intercom, "give me a complete genetic scan of every organism we've isolated from Lindon DalLierx in ICU."

"Complete?" The voice paused. "Yes, Dr. GurEshel. You know that will take six hours."

Yes, she knew. "Send up each individual scan," she ordered, "instantly." Red dots continued to drop.

"I have something," offered the unit nurse from her station near DalLierx's cot. "Not much, but something."

Glad for a distraction, Yael took two steps aside to the terminal.

"I cross-checked records for colonists licensed to maintain insulin-producing colony kits," said the nurse. "We have a short list—three females with diabetic graft-rejection syndrome. All are members of one family."

Yael read over her shoulder. "Hmm. Ling HoTung, Chenny HoNin, and Asabi HoLonge. Ling's the mother—"

"They all live at Hannes Prime," the nurse pointed out. "It's extremely unlikely they are involved."

"Let me . . . Excuse me." Sitting down on the nurse's high stool, Yael switched lines and ran a different check. This one alarmed her: Chenny HoNin recently visited Axis, and upon returning to Hannes Prime, she had reported her medical kit missing. A replacement was cultured from Ling HoTung's organisms.

"That's it!" Feeling triumphant, Yael dropped off the stool and pressed an intercom button. She'd worry later about repercussions. "Medtech, I want colony typing for genegineered staphylococcus 6-ICZ. Have Pharm send up any antibiotic specific for it, full dose, stat."

She looked down at DalLierx again. Surely he would last the five minutes it would take for that antibiotic to arrive, if they had one. The next supply ship would be too late.

Now, with the antibiotic ordered, she could think about forensics. If this antibiotic broke the infection cycle, that would confirm Chenny's kit as the assailant's *means*. But—trying now to work out a means-motive-opportunity triangle—how could she narrow down *opportunity* to a single occasion? Lindon DalLierx spent time in nearly every locale at Axis Plantation.

As for a *motive:* Ari MaiJidda, she thought instantly, his newly declared political rival. *But that makes no sense.* Why would Ari MaiJidda attack Lindon DalLierx when she hoped to beat him in a fair political fight?

Besides, Ari wouldn't have the foggiest idea how to use a bacterial kit to threaten a man's life. That called for medical knowledge . . . or microbial.

Two people on Gaea's microbiology floor had reason to resent him. One was Will Varberg, though truly, DalLierx had let him off easy.

The other was Yael's former patient, the microbiologist who shouldn't have been hired. If Novia Brady-Phillips's daughter was a Eugenics Board nettech, she might have come not as a spy but as an assassin.

Chenny HoNin agonized over the message on her terminal. Ari's news floored her. Her lost medical kit had been used for a murder attempt? It was inconceivable she'd been so stupid as to lose the kit. Evidently antibiotic therapy turned the tide for Lindon at the last possible moment, and for that she breathed a sigh of relief. He would, however, be confined to the HMF for days to regain some strength.

She flicked at a short braid. Where did she leave the thing? It had been over ten days since she left Axis. She shook her head, trying to remember.

Ari's last message gleamed. +Give me a list of every place you spent time, even routes you traveled.+ Ari promised to convey that information to D-group personnel assigned to investigate the incident. Chenny had started a list. She reread it, hoping each item might spark one more memory.

+Paul Ilizarov.+ Evidently she did Comrade Blue Eyes no favor by keeping him company that evening. He would be under suspicion.

+My temporary quarters were northeast corridor #25.+ The room would be searched, along with housekeeping records of whoever cleaned up after her.

+Business, CA complex.+ That had taken the greater part of her day. Then, +Dinner, Ari MaiJidda.+ At least Ari would be above suspicion. Then, the next morning, +Gaea building. Spoke with Dr. Brady-Phillips.+ *That was where I saw Dr. Brady-Phillips, wasn't it?* she wondered.

+Dr. Lee+—before finishing the sentence, she considered, then regretfully typed the name again—+and Paul Ilizarov.+

She called up a schematic map of Axis Plantation, drew in her routes as well as she could remember, then sent the message and went for a comforting molasses cookie. She'd sandblasted a pattern of triple spirals on her apartment's ceiling, walls, and floor. The Noetic faith used that symbol to honor humanity's triune nature—body, soul, mind.

A new message gleamed when she returned from her kitchen. +Did any of the Gaea people mention Chairman DalLierx to you?+

She set down the dark, chewy half cookie. There was an easy answer to that one. +Discussed him, yes. With Dr. Brady-Phillips. The vote to bring her here, specifically. Assured her most of us wanted her!+

When that message arrived at Ari's terminal, Ari shook her head. Yes, most of them wanted Brady-Phillips . . . before they knew her name. She touched her pocket memo to the screen, transferring her question and Chenny's answer. This narrowed her personal list, eliminating Varberg.

Paul, then, or Brady-Phillips. She had little doubt who she'd rather accuse.

She typed, +That should help. Sorry to drag you into this. We hope to put something together soon.+

+You don't think Dr. BP would have done it, do you?+

Ari ran the fingers of one hand through her hair, picturing Chenny's innocent-looking square face wrinkled in a frown. Chenny refused to realize that EB agents could travel anywhere cross-space shuttles went.

+If she's innocent, she'll be cleared,+ Ari typed. +Don't worry.+

Trev fidgeted in an HMF examining room. A nurse wearing a starched expression was about to set him loose. Maybe. "I'll want to see you in twenty-four hours," she declared.

Trev lifted a hand to touch his jaw. The ache had dulled once the nurse gave him a shot of whatever. Bandaged from lip to Adam's apple in white muslin, he felt more ridiculous than usual. "Yeah. Sure—okay."

By following exit signs, he escaped the Health Maintenance Facility. A desk clerk waved him past, evidently thinking he might mean to pay for medical services.

If anyone was going to pay, it was Will Varberg.

At the hub's far end, five small boys scattered out for a rowdy chasing game. Trev touched his bandage again, remembering that when he was a kid, this kind of battle wrap would've been the equivalent of military decoration. He'd been protected from tumbling with boys his own size, as if he were fragile or something.

He wasn't fragile. Just ugly.

He found a concrete bench. There he sat, staring at walls. Near walls, far walls. A high convex skylight.

About now, his father might be learning his whereabouts. Sending a crew to pick him up. Maybe even deciding to humiliate him and send police. Blase wouldn't think twice about inventing some offense and having Trev brought in. Of course the charges wouldn't stick. It was just the kind of game Blase liked.

And what would he do to the colonists?

Clearwater Plantation, back on Mars, wouldn't have clear water ever again. Blase had it reallocated to another hamlet, scattered Clearwater's population, and hauled Trev's host family back to Earth to stand trial for sheltering a fugitive.

Goddard was farther away. Blase was even more apt to play hardball, if Trev guessed correctly.

Should've thought of that before you left Earth, Trevarre.

Oh, shut up. I didn't plan to get caught, you know. By the time Blase showed up here, he had to vanish—for everyone's sake. Even Graysha wasn't bad, when she could escape her perennial teacher mode.

He wriggled, seeking comfort on the cold concrete. She'd commented, when done with her relief week, how much she enjoyed the Lwuites because they didn't coddle her. And DalLierx said Goddard observed a 20/16 voting/marriage legal-age split. An eighteener might be eligible to serve on that defense thing—at another locale. One without a spaceport.

Anything, *anything,* that might convince the colonists to keep him here.

Two boys spotted a black-and-white shorthaired cat under a bench and flushed it, chasing until it bounded up a corridor.

Trev stroked his aching chin. Defense group. He had to insinuate himself into some kind of position, convince someone to shelter him, if Blase was coming. Axis's D-group could transfer him elsewhere. Didn't military people always complain about being reassigned?

Taking long strides to look tall, he marched across the hub and up the northbound corry toward the defense barn. He'd found it one evening when he went for a walk. A greasy-wheeled grader was parked across from the building's entry.

The cavernous interior echoed back his footsteps. "Hello?" he shouted into the darkness. "Hello?" the building repeated. Pressing one hand against a concrete wall, he followed it until he met a door. He tried it. Locked.

Maybe there'd be someone after hours in the CA building.

At its entry he paused to check the directory. He felt conspicuous. The nurse could've at least bandaged him in browncloth instead of lily-white gauze.

Once he found the proper floor, a secretary had him wait while she asked if Ari MaiJidda was available. He sat and fidgeted, watching the communal office. These Lwuites worked weird hours. Five women and two men remained at concrete desks this evening. Heavy cables connected the desks like obscenely thick spider webs. The windows were dark, and his head throbbed. Aday felt like it'd lasted a week, but he wasn't going back to his room till he accomplished something.

The woman called, "Sir?"

He stood up.

"Vice-Chair MaiJidda is free to speak with you now." She nodded at a door on the waiting room's right side.

Trev went to it, knocked, then pushed it open.

The woman he'd seen only at town meetings sat watching, resting her chin on the back of one hand. Slim but stern. Not cuddly. "Yes?" She raised an eyebrow.

"Are there still openings in our defense group . . . ma'am?" It was time to play submissive again, but not incompetent.

"I don't think I know you. Are you Gaea personnel?"

"No, ma'am. Well, not exactly."

She flicked a finger toward a chair.

He sat. "I'm the stowaway, ma'am. But I'm determined to work. Can you use me in the D-group?" Start at the bottom, that's how they all said it was done. Get into an organization however you could, then make them need you.

MaiJidda's office had cloth hangings on the walls, dyed bundles of rough-spun rope that was woven here, braided there. The office seemed artsy for a Goddard dig.

Her eyes moved back and forth, plainly scanning his face. "What happened?"

Mentally he cursed the white gauze bandage. "I fell," he grumbled.

"Mm-hmm." She nodded twice. "Most people catch themselves with their hands when they fall forward."

Blast her. "I did fall. This happened on the way down."

"How old are you?" Her voice, achingly feminine, negated the hostile body-speak.

"Eighteen."

"And acting like it." She wagged her hand when he leaned forward to deny. "Oh, so did I when I was eighteen. It's no crime to act your age." She reached down for her keyboard. "I see we're to call you Trev, not George."

"Oh yes, ma'am." Too eager. He realized it as her lips went stern and wrinkled.

She crossed her arms. "Before I consider giving you a place in my group, Trev, I want to know your full name, identity number, and place of birth."

If she didn't like eager, closemouthed was also out. She'd get his ID soon enough, when ExPress's tissue typing went through. It was confession time. "Trevarre Chase-Frisson LZalle. My ID's TL38–72812. Born on Venus, Novaya Moskva. Raised there."

Tap, tap, tap on the keyboard, and then the woman's eyes widened. She looked back up. "LZalle."

Oh, chips.

"Your father's the performer."

"Are you familiar with his work?" He tried not to growl it. He was gambling a lot on this meeting.

"I had two of his early vidis, back on Einstein. I hated to sell them."

Worse yet, an admirer. One who might try to ingratiate herself into Blase's favor —and save her own skin—by returning Trev to him. What had he done? *Backpedal, and make it fast!* "Ma'am, he's an incredibly talented man, but he's not much of a father."

Ari MaiJidda sat loose in her chair, hands roving from keyboard to supply cubby, touching her face, then returning to her lap. "You're eighteen, you said."

"Yes, ma'am. I've got sixty hours in as a private pilot. Planetside." That kind of work had its compensations, including getaway-ready vehicles.

She clasped her hands on the desktop. "Trevarre, I'm not sure I would trust a stowaway with a plane . . . or a weapon, for that matter, and all our D-group squads are taking handgun training. But I do need some contract work on the side. Personal. For me—as a favor to us both."

He slumped. This was getting worse, not better. "What is it?"

"My private greenhouse is being neglected, and that's a crime. I grow ferns and other tropical plants I brought over as spores. My professional position is requiring more and more of my time. If I had an assistant, my hours there would be more efficiently spent. And I'd enjoy having someone to talk with."

About Blase LZalle, he understood. He could tell her touring stories that would curl her short hair, and he might gossip about the other entertainers who'd been in and out of his Venus home all the time he was growing up. Probably the closer he stuck to rigid, swear-to-the-earth-gods truth, the less she'd admire his father.

Then—hopefully soon—he'd have to make the second confession. "Certainly, ma'am," he said. "That would be helping the D-group, wouldn't it, freeing you from other concerns?"

She stroked her keyboard again. "Tell me your Gaea schedule so I can dovetail it with my own."

"One more thing," he said, screwing up courage. "Ma'am, it will be awkward for me—and for Goddard—if Blase finds out I'm here."

She eyed him sharply, as if trying to drill holes in his skull with her dark eyes. "What did you do?" she demanded.

Blast. He never should've tried this. "He's . . . hmm . . ."

"Are you saying," she asked, "that the only safe thing I can do is send you back?"

He thought fast. "No! He's just not . . . sane," he said carefully. "Lots of talented people don't look good up close. It'd be better for everyone if he just didn't find me."

"I will not be used." She stared back at him, letting both hands rest on her keyboard. "I will do nothing that endangers my people."

"But I'm here." He set his jaw. "You can't just hand me over to him. It wasn't good enough back at Mars, anyway."

"You pulled this once before?"

He nodded.

Glaring, she poised her fingers over the keys. "In that case, you're probably right. The best thing you could do is disappear."

Trev's throat tightened. He didn't like the sound of that.

Yael GurEshel rearranged her patient schedule so she could report to MaiJidda the next morning, and she felt small and dumpy as she stepped up to the Coordinator's desk. "He's recovering," she opened. "I assume you want my help with the investigation."

A message light blinked on MaiJidda's screen, but she ignored it. "We have circumstantial evidence against two persons at this point, both of them Gaea personnel," she said. "Can you furnish any possible connections between DalLierx and either Dr. Paul Ilizarov or Dr. Graysha Brady-Phillips?"

"We'd rather suspect Gaea than our own, wouldn't we?" Yael declined MaiJidda's extra chair, preferring to stand. Her back, never strong, had been bothering her lately. "As a matter of fact, the HMF receptionist says Dr. Brady-Phillips attempted to see Mr. DalLierx late yesterday afternoon."

"Really." MaiJidda arched her eyebrows and half pursed her lips. "The criminal, revisiting the scene of her crime?"

"If she's guilty," Yael said, "it would be more accurate to accuse her of returning to finish the job. Particularly if she's a Eugenics Board agent."

"Yes," said MaiJidda, "the notion occurred to me."

"It's probably occurred to a lot of people."

Ari shrugged. "Have you heard anything that might implicate Dr. Ilizarov?"

"I never met the man." Yael clasped her hands behind her back. "I dislike him on principle, though. He's been accused by two of our teeners of sexual harassment."

Ari MaiJidda's hands stiffened on the desk's surface, turning her knuckles white. "Which teeners?"

"I'm sorry, Ms. MaiJidda. That information is confidential, on a need-to-know basis." *Mind your own business, Coordinator. You're already too involved in our lives.*

"Why did you tell me about the harassment claims, then?" MaiJidda asked, scowling.

"They might have a bearing on the case. If Mr. DalLierx threatened to discipline Dr. Ilizarov, Ilizarov might bear him a grudge. We must not exclude any suspect from scrutiny."

"Gaea people," Ari muttered so softly Yael barely caught the words. "If one of them did this, she should be sent naked into the wild on Dropoff."

"She," Yael answered, "or he. Have you eliminated Dr. Varberg from your suspect list? After all, he—"

Ari's fingers jerked spiderlike on the desktop. "We must act first, I think, to ensure Dr. Brady-Phillips does not constitute a threat. Evidence against her is beginning to come in."

"What have you found?"

"I'm sorry, Dr. GurEshel." She smiled coolly. "That information is also confidential. On a need-to-know basis."

Yael stepped back, irritated. Lacking Jerusalem to fight over, her people coexisted well enough with MaiJidda's after they left Earth. Still, the woman's personality grated at her. She seemed determined to fight her own small holy war, and she'd baited Yael into asking that question. *Work with her,* Yael told herself. *We must work together or fall separately.* "She has a medical condition, of course. I can call her to the HMF at any time, where she could be questioned."

"I know about her syndrome." Ari MaiJidda tilted her head. "We may be able to use it. Be ready."

Yael started to turn away, then remembered a thread of conversation that had slipped past. "One other thing," she added. "The HMF greenhouse and distillery have only a limited amount of gamma-vertol available."

Ari MaiJidda leaned back on her desk chair. "How limited?"

"One dose available, a second under distillation for use within a month or two." Gamma-vertol was the "truth drug" used most often in police investigations, a precious commodity here.

"That's unfortunate. It must be a slow, inefficient process."

Yael inhaled, determined to ignore the insult. "We can only do so much to accelerate green-plant synthesis, Vice-Chair MaiJidda."

Ari sat and stared after GurEshel shut the door. If Paul tried to kill Lindon DalLierx, whatever his reason, she wouldn't mind. Let them have at it, man to man, and may the better man win.

But if Graysha Brady-Phillips had begun an assassination campaign, Ari could be the next target, as the Vice-Chair who posed an EB agent the greatest risk.

Clenching both hands, Ari worked them against each other. Innocent or guilty, the elimination of Brady-Phillips would be no great loss to Goddard . . . and accusing her would distract attention from Paul, giving him another chance at Lindon.

Then there was Blase LZalle's son. She could use him, too, she guessed. One move at a time, she must arrange puzzle pieces.

Graysha had plenty to keep her from reading that morning. Engineering delivered a modified incubator for checking transgenic bacteria—newly created organisms—for survival under different levels of wind stress. Trev dubbed it the "wincubator." Yesterday, she had Libby plate three subspecies of genegineered azotobacter, a free-living nitrogen fixer, and she'd set them inside to dry. Opening the door, she wrinkled her nose. Yesterday, this steel contraption smelled clean and metallic. Now, somewhere between earthy and foul, it was at home here in the micro lab.

No wonder she never bothered mixing perfume for work.

On her way back from the clean room, she poked her head in at Jirina's lab. "Good morning, Black Goddess."

"Ho, Blondie." Jirina pulled off a black fabric hood that connected her with a high-contrast low-light microscope. "Has tight-lipped Libby told you the latest about DalLierx?"

Graysha leaned against a wall, drawing a deep breath. "Please don't tell me he died."

"Haven't heard that. They're not telling Gaea *nuthin'*. But there's a great rumor. One of us is supposed to have done it—a Gaea person, probably micro. Use of insulin—it was an infection."

Graysha blew out the breath, wondering if she should tell Jirina her admittedly farfetched suspicions about Varberg. "Where'd you hear that, from a tech?"

"An HMF virologist. Techs aren't answering questions. Nice to know we're trusted, isn't it?"

"Go away," Graysha said.

"Go away yourself. You're in my lab."

"I'll bet there are other rumors, too."

"Six to ten of them. My money's on the woman who challenged him to a fresh election."

"It couldn't be one of us—do you think?"

"I doesn't think, honey. I listens, I waits, and I watches. And I keeps my mouth shut. 'Cept to friends." She winked.

Graysha winked back, then slipped out into the hall and back into her own lab next door. Near the bright window, Libby sat hunched over the scanning scope, balancing one hand on a colony counter. Trev's schedule had him feeding yabuts. Graysha waited until Libby stopped counting and pulled her head away from the eyepiece, then said, "Libby, what do you hear about Chairman DalLierx?"

"Nothing today." Libby gave her only a glance as she reached for the next prep, but Graysha saw suspicion in the tight set of her lips.

Saddened, she pulled an azotobacter-inoculated culture plate out of the wincubator. The growth gel medium's surface had crusted, as expected. Sparse growth, distinct colonies—probably once shiny on this medium—had gone dull and dry-looking.

Well, her work was before her. She would spend the next hour comparing and cataloging spore samples.

After tea break, though, she had trouble concentrating, preoccupied with Chairman DalLierx's condition and the rather exciting notion that her entire floor was momentarily under suspicion.

Another mysterious murder attempt. Wonderful.

And she couldn't feel too excited, not until she knew DalLierx would pull through.

It could've been a colonist, she mused, staring out the break-room window over the water purification facility's broad, flat roof to a dull-brown geometry of plowed ground. It would be interesting to find out if this attack fit a pattern, and she had recently met a sociologist.

Instead of returning to her lab from the break room, she walked straight to the elevator and waved at its call button.

In a second-floor office that smelled faintly of burnt vanilla, she found sociologist Benjamin Emerson standing beside a monochrome screen, idly scrolling it along while he smoked a straight-stemmed pipe. She'd known eleven-year-olds taller than this man. Maybe that was why he stood at the desk instead of sitting and why he chose to smoke. The scent evoked pleasant warmth in her mind.

"Graysha," he said, brushing long black hair from his eyes. Instead of glassware and lab equipment, his shelves were lined with potted plants, subtly framing a collection of ancient scholarly books. "Good morning," he exclaimed. "What brings you down here into the realm of irreproducible results?"

"A question." Graysha sank onto a low stool to look him eye to eye. "About the Lwuites."

He clasped the pipe's bowl and exhaled. "Ah. You and three others this morning."

"I suppose the poisoning brought them over, too."

"It appears that way. Would you like the standard analysis?"

"We'll start there."

Dr. Emerson rested his pipe on a tabletop. "Our department's main concern is with social dynamics—childbirth records, et cetera. The Axis Settlement appears well balanced, with a highly educated and artistic element and a conservative, righteousness-oriented element. Each is trying to prove it's more polite, more willing to sacrifice, and so forth. We have factions, yet in a frontier culture, people are fantastically interdependent for survival and progress. Already they find their Gaea employees too liberal."

"I would think any group that would come this far out and commit themselves this deeply would be strongly unified."

"They do display signs of a persecution complex. And," he added, "they're determined to grow their own society in their own way."

That made her laugh softly. "Not cooperative with Gaea sociologists, you're saying?"

Emerson turned sideways, pulled on his pipe, and smiled.

"Have you sent anyone over to their church services?" she asked.

"I went myself. Twice."

"Oh! And . . . ?"

He blanked the desktop screen and glanced out a window. From down here, the CFC plant's smokestack looked even taller, reaching up out of the window's frame. "The core of the services I visited seemed to be Noetic, as near as I could tell. The faith of human reason. Really, nothing one needs to join a church for."

How true. Abandoning Novia's Church of the Universal Father left gaping holes in Graysha's thought habits. Still, she hadn't joined Einstein's other major religious group because Noetics had no one to pray to.

She tucked her feet behind a stool rung. "Don't the Lwuites have reference works?"

"Not on any files we can access. And every time we send an official query, they clam quiet and claim the Religious Liberties Act. Graciously but firmly."

She eyed his bookends, a pair of medieval horse heads. "Why'd Gaea let them sign on?"

He shrugged. "Gaea, you may recall, was desperate for laborers. We did everything by the tutorial—notified them of official investigation. They gave every appearance of cooperating. Really, they don't seem the least bit interested in spreading their own variant of truth."

"Has anyone actually tried to join them?"

Dr. Emerson cocked his head sparrowlike, pulled on the pipe again, and made a fragrant tobacco-and-vanilla-scented cloud. "What are you considering?" he asked.

What *was* she thinking? Accomplish two goals at once, maybe. Find out if they're lunatics—and stay visible. "It occurs to me that they might give a sincere inquirer more information than they'd give an investigator."

"We're not interested in costumed espionage."

"I understand." Graysha stared out the window. North of the CFC plant, a domed rise—the underground hub's roof—bulged up out of a rock pile planted sparsely with dwarfalfa.

She had promised to tell Emerson's wife, Antonia Fong, if she learned anything definite about the cooling. So far, she'd found only what seemed to be a defensive virus on the Gaea net. "Then what about this poisoning business?" she asked.

Emerson's voice came from behind her. "DalLierx seemed the perfect charismatic leader figure. We thought most Lwuites were happy with him."

"Most." A gust of Bday—Sunday—wind flattened the dwarfalfa. "But they voted against him and hired me over his protest, and it takes only one malcontent to make trouble. Does this attack make him a martyr to the rest of them?"

"It might, or it could weaken his image. Difficult to tell. We're glad, for stability's sake, that it looks as if he's going to survive."

"Does it?" Graysha spun around. "I mean, the micro techs won't tell us anything. He's going to make it?"

The sociologist frowned, resting both arms on his desk. "Yes, he is. We've had a standing call to the HMF. They upgraded his condition this morning from serious to stable."

"I'm glad," she said, and she meant it. Of course she wouldn't wish death on anyone, but there was something else. As hard as this was to believe, here she was, attracted to another dominator-type male.

At least she could admit it to herself.

Emerson held his pocket memo against his mouth. "Enter, poll, DalLierx. Pro," he said. Then to her, he added, "Are you? That makes three for, one against."

Amusement distracted her. "Gaea's having its own election? Jirina Suleiman, on my floor, said she heard a rumor the Lwuites suspect us."

"Naturally. Just as we suspect them. Humanity is like that, you know." He waved her out.

The second floor's hallway, like the fifth's, made a loop around the elevator, stairs, and a pair of prep rooms. Its single long window looked north-northeast. Sunlight glistened off the vast crop shelter. She walked past Nonliving Soils, just to be able to say she'd been there, then boarded the elevator again. Riding, she ran a hand back and forth on the cold metal door.

Now, unfortunately, she was alone with her feelings. She almost regretted finding out Chairman DalLierx was widowed. He opposed her very presence on his planet. Even if he didn't already despise her, or at least suspect her, he wouldn't look twice at a woman who'd be dead in fifteen terrannums. For that matter, she didn't need the distraction from her work.

As for religion, if Lwuites would explain their beliefs to sincerely interested parties, she did have someone to approach.

She could give Crystal a call.

Ari MaiJidda ran stairs two at a time back up to her office. "Look what a cleaner found," she announced to the secretaries as she burst through the arch, dangling a small leather bag from one finger. "The missing insulin kit."

The nearest secretary gasped. "Where was it?"

Ari waited until the room fell silent. Once she had everyone's attention, she answered. "In a D-group locker."

The room sprang to life. "Someone in D-group?"

"Who?"

"That's terrible."

It was close enough to the truth. Over the chorus of denials, Ari heard the near secretary speak again. "Which locker?"

"We'll see." Ari had already researched locker assignments, but for appearance's sake, she slid around the desk, punched in a locker number on the woman's keyboard, then stepped back. The others could draw their own conclusion.

"Oh dear." The secretary raised a hand to her cheek. "Dr. Brady-Phillips seemed like a pleasant woman. But they're often the worst, aren't they?"

17. ACCUSED

Graysha crossed the southern arc of the hub on her way home from work that afternoon after spending a frustrating hour on the Gaea net. The cooling references she managed to find followed no discernible pattern. The best of them merely posted snippets of data without comments or accompanying graphs.

She had jotted several onto a sheet of paper, starting a graph of her own, but so far it was so full of blanks that she couldn't interpolate anything significant.

Someone called her name, and she stopped to look around. Crystal DalDidier waved from a bench near the hub's central circle. Deciding she still had plenty of time before she needed to eat, Graysha walked toward her D-group friend with a spring in her step. "How've you been?" she asked, buttoning her overshirt against the hub's pervasive coolness. She sat down.

"Better now, thanks." Crys wore an embroidered smock over her browncloth pants. Pink spots bloomed on her cheeks.

"Morning sickness?" Graysha asked, smiling.

Crystal raised a hand off her lap, then replaced it. It was a helpless-looking gesture. "Oh. That's right, I guess you wouldn't know. I was born Crystal DalLierx. Lindon is my brother."

Brother? Scooting back on the concrete bench, Graysha stammered to cover what felt like a terrible faux pas. Now that she looked for it, she saw the resemblance in Crys's straight chin and innocent-looking brown eyes. "No, I didn't know. . . . I'm sorry. You say he's doing better?"

"Thank heaven."

"I'm glad to hear it." She'd hoped to befriend Crystal. Was that still possible? She looked around. No one appeared to be in earshot. "Crys," she asked cautiously, "is there anything I can do to help with the poisoning investigation? I know I'm an outsider and not particularly trusted, but . . ." She trailed off, hoping Crystal would accept the wish, if not the ability, to support the Lwuites.

Crystal drummed her fingers on her legs. "Oh dear. Graysha, you'll . . . you'll probably be getting a call."

"Oh. From the . . . you have a police force, don't you?"

"More or less. It's been consolidated with D-group."

"Oh." That made sense. "Well, I'm due to practice, not tomorrow evening but the next. I'll—"

"Um, Graysha?" Crystal raised her hand again. "You probably aren't expected for practice."

That didn't sound good. "I think I am, unless I'm remembering the schedule all wrong. Isn't tomorrow Windsday?"

Crystal clasped her hands. "I can't believe no one told you," she said.

"Crys, don't play guessing games."

"I'm not. It's just that . . . this puts me in an awkward position."

"I'm sorry," Graysha said. "I don't mean to. I honestly didn't know."

"I believe you." Crystal laid a hand on Graysha's arm, then said, "All right. Don't go for D-group practice, because you're being conditionally discharged."

"What do you mean?" She pictured her hopes, blown away like dry leaves by a Windsday gust.

"You're specifically under suspicion." Crystal spread her hands on the bench. "As far as I'm concerned, it's ridiculous, but . . ."

The gist of Crystal's hints hit Graysha like a concrete block. It was bad enough they didn't want her in D-group, but— "Me?" she exclaimed, incredulous. "Your brother?"

Crystal nodded.

"I . . . What am I supposed to have done? No, wait." She raised both palms. "You probably shouldn't tell me."

"If I don't, somebody else will. It's common knowledge. They proved that his nasal passages were infected with insulin-producing bacteria."

"Infection," she repeated numbly. No wonder—

"Evidently, microbiologists are especially suspect, since they'd know how to create that kind of infection."

"Sure. But . . ." Graysha shut her mouth and swallowed. She might as well hope for immortality as try to convince these people to accept her. "Crystal, I'd never dream of—"

"I know you wouldn't." Crystal said it with conviction. "I think Ari MaiJidda did it. She's the one person on this planet who could poison Lin and get away with it."

Graysha fingered browncloth wrinkles alongside her knee. The hub seemed stuffy, cool though it was. "Why?"

Crystal's loose braid slid past her shoulder as she leaned forward. "There's bad blood between them from a long time back."

"But—"

"She used to be pretty hot for him, but he turned her down. And I think she has more against him than the old grudge."

So this was Crystal's private suspicion, not general opinion. "At first byte," Graysha said, "the idea makes sense. But don't you think it's pretty wild? There have to be others who—"

"MaiJidda's got a hard reputation. She'll never be suspected, because she's supposed to want to beat him in a fair fight. But she's also the one most likely to head up the investigation. It makes me furious."

Graysha tried to imagine Coordinator MaiJidda as a poisoner and found she didn't know the woman well enough, though she did tend to distrust anyone who reminded her of her sister, Asta.

But there'd been that missing protein-fiber meal on the first day, and the "accident" in the firing range. "I suppose any of us is capable of murder. Not that speculating would have brought your brother back if . . ." She let the thought go unspoken.

"He's going to be all right," Crystal said with a firm snap of the last word. "I just saw him. They're going to let him go home in two days if he promises to rest. Fat chance of that. Once he's loose he'll work harder than ever, trying to catch up."

"You're probably right." Everything she heard about him pointed to an amazing work ethic.

No! Do not admire that man!

As the thought flashed through her mind, a couple in their thirties strolled by. Graysha watched them pass, considering Ari against her own favorite suspect, Will Varberg. "Whoever did this is stupid to even think about killing a person. Coordinator MaiJidda isn't stupid." Neither, of course, was Varberg. She caught herself fiddling with browncloth again and folded her hands in her lap. "Well, maybe not stupid. But they must have no moral underpinnings at all."

"There you have it. Ari MaiJidda. And she resents Lin for his morality."

What did Ari do, try to seduce him? Graysha raised an eyebrow. She'd hate to be known for a lack of morality. Still, no one could base a murder accusation on such "evidence." She nearly said so but decided against it. Having suspicions probably gave Crys a shred of comfort. "If she's guilty, she'll be caught."

"Not likely." Crystal shook her head. "But even if she is, Lin'll want the charges dismissed. He'll want her forgiven, since no harm was done. That's the problem with our 'moral underpinnings.' According to the recompense law, crimes are committed against individuals, not the government, and victims can refuse to prosecute. Lindon introduced the law."

Graysha tried to wrap her mind around a fistful of questions. Should she ask about the Lwuite religion that those "moral underpinnings" suggested? HMF visiting hours? What was a recompense law?

She decided not to ask any of them. Crystal had brought out word of her brother's condition, and that word was encouraging. Now that Graysha was certain he'd survive, she could concentrate on her own work.

Would *her* family have visited her if she'd been poisoned?

Forget it.

"Do you have other family, Crystal?" she asked. Somehow, she needed to end this encounter gracefully.

"Besides Duncan and our three-and-a-half? Lin and I have a brother; and our parents live at Center, west of here. They've just gone back. Now, on Duncan's side I've got three nieces and two nephews," she said with unmistakable pleasure, "though I have to admit Lin's girls are the beauties."

"I'll bet," Graysha murmured. An instant later, she wished she hadn't spoken.

Either Crystal didn't notice or she simply considered her brother's looks a simple fact of life, like water and gravity. "Bee and Sarai lost their mother when Bee was only two," she said. "Freak accident—she was on an observation deck, right in a meteor puncture's kill zone. Six months pregnant. The doctors barely saved Sarai."

"Oh." Recalling the chill that fell on their conversation while watching the overflight vidi, Graysha grimaced. "The poor man. Why hasn't he remarried?"

Crystal's eyes narrowed. "Too busy. Always too busy for small things. Maybe this little incident will remind him he isn't immortal. If so, Ari MaiJidda's done him more good than harm."

"If she did it."

Crystal brushed dust off her pants. "It's all right. You have to talk that way. But I'd appreciate your not casting aspersions on me for being convinced."

"Heavens, no. I'm a newcomer. He's your brother, and you know them both."

Crystal toed the concrete under the bench. "I have to go."

"So do I." Graysha watched a young man push some kind of mowing contraption out onto a lawn. "Do you think I should go speak with Coordinator MaiJidda? I want to clear myself."

After scrunching her pursed lips toward one cheek, Crystal nodded. "I guess you'd better. Just be ready for an inquisition."

Ari MaiJidda had already tried twice to silence her, if her own suspicions were correct. This time, Graysha guessed MaiJidda meant to have her sent away regardless of guilt or innocence.

Maybe Ari *had* done it, in order to frame Graysha. That thought gave her a shiver.

She crossed her arms for warmth. No one would force her to leave this planet without a fight. Goddard was starting to feel like home. Its concerns were her own. If necessary, she'd go all the way to the top—and she didn't mean Melantha Lee. She would speak with Chairman DalLierx and make her own accusations against Vice-Chair MaiJidda.

On second thought—she stood up, feeling slightly silly—she couldn't see herself doing that. She needed to smooth things over, not ruffle them worse than ever. "Thank you, Crystal," she said as she held out her hand. "See you again?"

"Hope so. I'll miss you at D-group." Crys touched Graysha's fingertips before hurrying off.

Graysha turned toward the Gaea wing. Emmer probably wanted company, or at least body warmth. As Graysha picked her up off the pillow and settled her onto her shoulder, the gribien's little clicks made Graysha feel appreciated. She found a table alone in the cafeteria, where she could slip Emmer nibbles and think uninterrupted.

Torn between her suspicions of Varberg and MaiJidda, and angry at the notion of being suspected of a horrible crime, by the time she left the cafeteria she had warm shoulders but a cold, knotted stomach. She probably wouldn't be allowed anywhere near Chairman DalLierx, and she didn't feel like going to Ari MaiJidda, and she wanted even less to spend the evening in her room trying to correlate obscure research abstracts. Nor did Jirina's company, or Paul's, appeal to her. She wouldn't sleep that night unless she exhausted herself.

She took Emmer back to the apartment and then jogged down to the quiet lab. Maybe she could catch up on some of the productive time she'd missed over the last few days.

Once there, she found reasons to be glad she'd come in. Three test plates in the wincubator showed strong delayed growth, but the rounded lumps that were bacterial colonies hadn't run together. She could do a fast count that would be impossible later. Setting the first plate on a grid, she started at bottom left and set the digital counter to Auto.

That gave her more time to think than she really wanted.

They suspect me, specifically.

Well, of course they did. She was Novia Brady-Phillips's daughter. They probably suspected she'd been trained in all kinds of nasty skills. They probably thought she was heartlessly devoted to her mother's institution. They had no idea how many times—and how deeply—she'd been hurt by her mother, her mother's church, and the all-powerful EB.

She stared at the readout until it settled at a count of eighty-eight colonies, then recorded the data on her pocket memo. She ought to concentrate. She carried the memo into her office, interfaced it by a tail-like cord to the computer, and let it transfer, then keyed up another research abstract to read.

Groggy from a lack of sleep and still on edge, she arrived at work the next morning. Libby waited beside the sink, wearing a somber expression.

"Looks like you want to talk," Graysha said.

Libby nodded.

Sighing, Graysha opened her office door. "Come in. What is it?"

"I'm . . ." Libby looked everywhere but into Graysha's eyes. From her brief work with Novia, Graysha recognized that as a bad sign. "I think I should resign my position."

"Why?" Graysha asked bluntly, wanting to hear the accusation—if it was coming—in Libby's words.

"Vice-Chair MaiJidda called it a 'conflict of interest.' I'm cooperating with the investigation."

Graysha sank into her chair. "Of course, Libby. That's fine," she said, determined to conduct herself in a way that might win individual Lwuites' acceptance, even if their power structure rejected her. "Tell the whole truth. When the smoke clears, I suspect there'll still be a position here for you."

The girl's smile, a hasty pulling back of cheek muscles, looked neither real nor grateful. "Thank you," she said before she hurried out.

Tipping her head back, Graysha stared up at the ceiling. Last night, she had guessed at the colonists' suspicions: she might be an EB nettech. Not investigators but, more accurately, the henchmen who helped investigators, nettechs sometimes were sent to deal with troublemaking lab children and other offenders. Really, that suspicion was based only on guilt by association with Novia, but on Goddard, if they really had reason to worry, associative guilt might convince them to incriminate her.

A message light blinked on the monitor. Checking for a sender's initials, Graysha found a set she didn't recognize: DED. That felt ominous. Bracing herself, she touched a key.

+Graysha. Assume you've seen the weathersat report. What do we do now? Is it the CFCs? RSVP, Duncan.+

Duncan EnDidier—Crystal's husband was DalLierx's brother-in-law. Wondering what had come down yesterday, she touched three more keys and brought up meteorological data.

A daily high/low graph, superimposed over previous G-years' data, shocked her. The silhouettes paralleled each other, but they were almost three degrees apart. Not even Melantha Lee could scoff at this kind of temperature drop. According to a data string at the bottom of the display, the graphs were posted several hours ago.

Dr. Lee *must* know about it. New meteorological research must finally be under way, unless . . . unless Gaea Terraforming Consortium truly had a hidden agenda.

It would be easy to find out. Graysha opened a general floor connection to the meteorology department and scanned proceedings for the previous shift.

The report had come in yesterday midafternoon. After that, routine cloud studies resumed.

Appalled, Graysha yanked the cloth-elastic tie from her hair and shook her head. She looked up Duncan EnDidier on the net and tried his access code, but he didn't answer her call.

Maybe she should try to access the weathersat downlink. Uncertain how to proceed once she reached the main screen, she acted first on Duncan's suggestion, searching for current sampling and recent-past data on chlorofluorocarbons.

CFC concentration in the upper atmosphere, she found, had dropped 20 percent over the past G-year. The numbers were so low that they staggered her.

Her concrete work desk sat under two tiers of metal shelves. She blew at the lower one, raising a dust cloud. Melantha Lee unquestionably knew about this. And she was doing nothing? Either she was shielding someone or she was guilty herself.

Maybe Lee was responsible for the weird net virus.

Not only that, but since the Meteorology Department hadn't reacted to this new data, she had to assume *that* floor had knuckled down under "local consortium policy" just like Microbiology. At this moment, the entire colonial populace could be hostage to scientific foul play at the Gaea station.

Graysha clenched her fists on the countertop. Was there a link between this and the attempt on Lindon DalLierx's life? Graysha was shocked to be considering a new suspect, someone who ranked even higher than Will Varberg.

If Melantha Lee was guilty of criminal actions, to whom could Graysha report her?

Just then, Trev slouched in. Graysha checked her clock. He was right on time, bandaged more thoroughly than she thought necessary.

"Morning, Teach," he said in a jovial voice. "Like my new face mask? Which part of the planet shall we fertilize today?"

It felt good to see a friendly face—most of it, anyway. "You look charming," Graysha said. "Elegant. And this morning, we will analyze enzyme activities."

Trev groaned theatrically, laying the back of one hand against his forehead. "And I thought ground school was a pain. This is *dirt* school."

Lindon wished his HMF room had another chair, because sitting on the edge of his bed with Ari MaiJidda in the room made him profoundly uncomfortable. Her browncloth suit, set off with a deep green scarf, brought out a red-brown flush in her cheeks. Everything, including Ari MaiJidda, looked brighter and more alive since he'd flirted with death.

"Nettech," Ari proclaimed. "She has to be. If so, she's found something, and she's figured out we're stopping her offworld transmissions. Unable to get data off Goddard until the next supply ship comes, she's falling back on emergency orders. Key people will begin to die mysteriously. Before long, Lwuite longevity will become irrelevant. Unless, of course, we stop her."

"If that were the case, you're right. You would be in danger, too." Olfactory murder? It was a bizarre notion, but he had to consider it. Scarring of his nasal passages almost wiped out his senses of taste and smell. Dr. GurEshel's prognosis was for permanent damage.

Depressed, he pulled his browncloth robe more snugly over his hospital pajamas. Though blood weary, he was glad to sit upright. He'd looked in a mirror this morning. Other than purple half circles under his eyes, his color was coming back. "I can only believe parts of that scenario, though," he added. "It's impossible she could have found anything the rest of them haven't."

"Not if she's trained in investigation. Look at her behaviors, Lindon. She joined D-group. She eats at the co-op for no apparent reason." Ari leaned forward. "She's watching us. You can bet your life. Actually, you are already betting all our lives."

He couldn't do that. "You've questioned her?"

Ari draped one arm over the back of her chair. "Not yet, but we spoke with Liberty JenChee."

"The lab assistant? What does she say?"

"In her account of Brady-Phillips's activities, there are gaps that would be entirely adequate for the purpose of sneaking off to prepare cultures. There have been several evenings when she came back to the Gaea station and worked alone. Growing—" Ari raised her pocket memo—"growing staphylococcus 6-ICZ, maybe."

Lindon hated to accuse anyone of murder. "I've had no contact with her since her second day at Axis, except on the D-group firing line."

Ari looked side to side, glancing at the wall monitor, the window, and the door before looking at Lindon again. "Her hobby is perfuming," Ari said. "She probably sent you something using her kit. Or accessed your apartment while you were out with Bee and Sarai. Think. Think hard." She pushed up out of the room's only chair, and Lindon tugged his robe closer again. "Let me know if you remember anything," Ari ordered. "Odd odors, especially. Meanwhile, I'll question her."

Ari wouldn't do that kindly. *She saved my sister's life, Ari.* He almost said it, then decided against mentioning Crys's intimations. "Wait on that for the time being. We need her in the Gaea building. At least she's willing to work with us on the weather problem, and yesterday's data looks worse than ever."

She rested both hands on the back of her chair. "This may come down to priorities, Lindon. Or that could be part of her masquerade. What will it be? Do you think Gaea can kill us with the weather before Graysha or Novia Brady-Phillips wipes us out via something else?"

Lindon inhaled the oddly odorless air. Was Ari paranoid or had the universe truly turned against them?

Ari, at least, was doing something about it. "How goes the D-group?"

Ari lifted her chin. "It's looking more important than ever, isn't it?"

"It could be."

She shrugged and raised an eyebrow. "Oddly, we've had more homozygs join than heteros."

For an instant, he glimpsed the Ari he'd known nine terrannums ago: eager, curious, secretly playful. "Explanation?"

She walked toward the door as she said, "Either we're all still more aggressive than Henri Lwu intended—and if that's the case, we can close down half the Port Arbor Clinic—or else now that we have something to lose, we're even more determined to defend it."

So Ari, too, realized that the callosal treatments were worth less here than elsewhere. He started to slip off the bed's edge, but she stopped him with a pointing gesture. "Stay there. Get your rest. I can let myself out."

He nodded. Just sitting up straight reminded him how weak he was.

"Are you sure you want to wait," she asked, "and question her later?"

. . . Thereby endangering Ari, the next logical victim? Regardless of who tried to kill him—probably someone who lived at Axis Plantation, who might simply wait for another chance—the colony's fate rested on whether Commissioner Novia Brady-Phillips controlled her daughter. Novia could strike long before weather effects went out of control. Climatic disasters took months to develop. Novia could descend upon them in mere weeks.

An odd memory popped into his mind: Palila Lwu, revered by the colonists, had died suspiciously. Investigation suggested she was poisoned by a contaminated glass shard in her own lab. The Lwuites suspected a nettech assassination, but they had been powerless to demand justice.

"All right," he said reluctantly. "The First Circle can meet here, this afternoon."

"Good. I'll be ready with questions."

18. EXPOSED

Lindon nodded to Ari MaiJidda as she glided into the HMF lounge a few hours later. She took a chair between Taidje FreeLand and Kenn VandenNeill, who greeted him with a whispered "Praise God, Lindon." All four members of the local committee's First Circle constituted an emergency quorum.

After letting him dress, Dr. GurEshel had draped a heavy halter-wool robe over Lindon's shoulders. He shrugged it off and sat back against it. Over the last few days, he'd decided the physician used a perennially irritated attitude to keep patients in line. Sitting beside Ari, she firmed up her frown.

"I'm not going to stand on procedure," Lindon said. He touched one armrest of the HMF's motor chair. "Here's my proposal. Vice-Chair MaiJidda has raised the suspicion that Dr. Brady-Phillips may be working on the Eugenics Board's behalf. We have all worried this might be possible—"

"Ever since she arrived." Kenn VandenNeill rested his square chin on one hand.

"Yes," Lindon answered, and this was one of those times when he wished he were not Chairman. "I believe that learning whether she actually reports to her mother is so vital that we have to risk questioning her."

Kenn nodded. White-haired Taidje FreeLand folded his hands on his knees. Ari just kept watching him.

"The HMF," he continued, "still has one dose of gamma-vertol. By

USSC law, Dr. Brady-Phillips will have to consent to its use. Otherwise, any testimony we obtained would be illegal."

"If we had her word illegally," FreeLand said, "it might not stand up in court, but how important is that? We have to know the truth."

Kenn crossed his legs, nodding. "Yes. Illegal is one thing. Unethical is another. This is necessary. We're following the spirit of the law."

The law's spirit protected the weak. Who, this time, was the weaker party? Graysha . . . or the Lwuite population? "Do you all feel we should use it," he asked, "if we can find her and bring her here, whether or not she consents?"

"I do," Ari said instantly. "Too much is at stake."

Kenn nodded again. Taidje FreeLand frowned, drew a deep breath, and then nodded, too.

"Taidje," Lindon said softly, "would you go get her?" FreeLand would approach her respectfully. There was no need to let Ari confront her before it was strictly necessary. He didn't honestly believe the woman tried to kill him. She deserved a chance to prove her innocence.

To his surprise, Dr. GurEshel spoke up. "I'll go," she offered. "You people write up the questions you'll need. I'll call her in under the pretense of checking her tissue oxygen."

"Perfect," Ari said, crossing her arms.

"No." Lindon drew up straighter. "Tell her the truth."

"I'll use my own judgment." Dr. GurEshel made fists and strode out.

"Wait—"

Kenn raised a hand, cutting off Lindon's protest. "Dr. GurEshel is exactly the person we need. She really can check the woman's blood oxygen if you don't like bringing her in under a deception. But we need that information, Lindon."

Plainly, he was outvoted—and if she was a ruthless nettech, her seeming innocence would be one of her deadliest tools. "Very well."

Kenn pulled a memo out of his shirt pocket. "Let's have that list ready when she returns."

Graysha forced down a bowl of halfer noodle soup. Knowing she was suspected of murder—and worse—strangled her appetite. Really, she almost wished the colonists would hurry up and take the next logical step in investigating her.

Disappointed to make it through lunch uninterrupted, she plodded back to work. Trev still hadn't returned from his own lunch break. She pulled up a file on soil-layering, including the organisms needed to break down organic materials at various depths, and split her screen to display Gaea's bacterial inventory.

Someone knocked firmly on the hall door.

"Come," she called, squaring her shoulders. She might have known. Getting interested in something else was the surest way to nudge events.

Her door swung open, and she recognized the pigtailed physician. "Dr. GurEshel," Graysha said, trying to sound warm and friendly. "What can I do for you?"

"Would you come with me to the HMF?" GurEshel rested one hand on the doorframe. "We really ought to have gotten a baseline tissue-oxygen reading for your medical records. You're feeling well today, aren't you?"

"Pretty much." *If you don't count a bad case of nerves while waiting for you people to make your move while trying to look as innocent as I really am!* Graysha saved the split-screen document for further reading. She'd better not think much beyond the questioning she was about to get. The Lwuites weren't evil. They would give her a chance to clear herself . . . so long as they didn't leave her alone with Ari MaiJidda.

She snatched up a handful of sour candies from the bowl on her desk and patted her pocket to make sure the glucodermic was there. Then, hanging her lab coat on the door, she followed the doctor.

Lindon watched Graysha walk into the HMF lounge, hands hanging stiffly at her side. Her footfalls clicked on the hard, plain floor, and her silver-blue eyes looked dark and determined. Once she saw them waiting for her, she turned reproachfully to Dr. GurEshel. "I did wonder if you truly wanted a baseline reading, right after a meal."

He liked her straightforward admission, which didn't seem like something a nettech would say. He motioned for her to sit on a chair they'd pulled into the circle beside Ari. "Dr. Brady-Phillips, this is an emergency session of the Colonial Affairs Committee's First Circle. Certain charges have been leveled against you in secret, and this group has decided you should be given the opportunity to clear yourself from suspicion."

"I agree," she said quietly. "Next time, call me in honestly. I'll come."

"Certainly," Lindon said. She was right. They owed her that dignity.

Ari glanced up but kept her head down as she spoke, as if studying her pocket memo. "First," she said, "a few questions we're asking a number of people. I'd like a detailed account of your activities during the three circadays previous to the day Chairman DalLierx was taken ill."

"I'll try," she answered. As she listed the trips and activities she could remember, his discomfort came back. Long gaps did exist during each day, when no witness would be able to confirm her whereabouts. Kenn

VandenNeill checked his memo and showed it to Ari, who nodded and asked, "Are you familiar with genegineered staphylococcus strain 6-ICZ?"

"No." Graysha's forehead wrinkled. "I could look it up on my computer if you need information."

He'd suggested they skip that question. Even if she were guilty, she would not admit familiarity with the bacterium. He stroked his chin.

One corner of Ari's mouth twitched. "Your file lists your hobby as perfuming. What does that involve? Obviously, we're not asking everyone that one."

"You're investigating people's hobbies?" Graysha threaded her fingers together, then clenched the doubled fist between her knees. Again, he observed she looked much too nervous to be a professional detective. Again, he reminded himself that could be part of her role-playing.

At least he wouldn't have to decide alone whether she was guilty.

"Little details," Ari answered, "sometimes prove fruitful in any investigation."

"Well . . . yes." Graysha smoothed her browncloth pants. "I have an ester kit, and I mix fragrances."

"For personal consumption, or do you supply others?"

"I've put gifts together, but not here."

"Would you be willing to surrender that kit to the HMF for scrutiny?"

Graysha's eyes widened. In that instant, he guessed, she realized how he'd been attacked—if she wasn't guilty. She shot him a pained glance, then said softly, "Of course. Send someone to my apartment with me if you want to make sure I don't take anything out of it."

Ari's mouth twitched again. "I think not. Your turn, Chairman."

A distracting tic started at his right eye. "You have the legal right to decline to proceed any further, Dr. Brady-Phillips. We propose to administer gamma-vertol, a substance used in law-enforcement questioning, and ask you a list of questions. Coordinator MaiJidda, show them to her."

Graysha accepted Ari's pocket memo and started to read. Her right hand closed around her left thumb, and she rubbed the thumbnail. "If you'd like, I'll answer twice. Once now, once with the gamma-vertol. You won't like all my answers, but I . . ." Trailing off, she exhaled. "All right. First, I came here on my own behalf, no one else's."

He nodded. She would have denied EB involvement in any case.

She pulled off her browncloth overshirt. Beneath it, she wore a sleeveless black blouse that fit her body snugly. "Go ahead," she said to the physician. Graysha raised Ari's pocket memo to read off the next question.

Lindon leaned forward.

"I came to Goddard of my own volition," she said. "I came to accept a field researcher's position. Originally, I anticipated taking a teaching position at Halley Habitat.

"I last spoke with my mother approximately three months ago. She said nothing at that time about Goddard, the Lwuite group, or anything else connected with—" her voice caught as Dr. GurEshel injected the drug—"with my present assignment. But I do have general instructions to report to her any time I see anything of reasonably suspicious nature."

A chill tickled his shoulders.

"I have, in the past, accepted Eugenics Board money for reports of this type."

Ken VandenNeill squirmed.

"Hold on," she said firmly, "I'm not done. I have no intention of reporting to Commissioner Brady-Phillips, regardless of our personal relationship, because I came to Goddard for my own reasons.

"And, finally, I did not try to kill Chairman DalLierx."

She handed Ari's pocket memo to Kenn, looking as steady as anyone could under this inquisition. Kenn took the memo and turned to Lindon, raising an eyebrow. Lindon frowned. Graysha was right—he did not like all her answers.

Dr. GurEshel motioned Ari off her chair and sat down on it. "About one minute more," she said. Grasping Graysha's left forearm, she touched the green tissue-oxygen implant. "It does appear that your condition has stabilized."

"I feel fine," Graysha said softly.

After a few more seconds, Dr. GurEshel asked, "Have you had any symptoms since we released you?"

Graysha shot Ari a dark look, then said, "Nothing serious. Pale fingertips, occasional cold spells. I think that's . . . that's normal. Yes, nothing serious. Attacks of Flaherty's syndrome come on gradually, over a period of weeks. Generally precipitated by lack of exercise, fasting, or low gravity. But at the D-group firing range, there was an accident I'm not sure was—"

"That's enough, Dr. Brady-Phillips," Ari interrupted.

Remembering Crys's accusations, Lindon tried to relax against the chair. GurEshel nodded across at him. "Go ahead, Chairman."

Kenn passed back the pocket memo. Lindon cleared his throat and repeated the first question. "Did you come to Goddard of your own volition, Graysha, or were you assigned here by a party other than Gaea Consortium?"

Her answers, though rambling, matched the ones she'd given earlier, until he came to the final questions.

"Report to my moth-her," she repeated. Her eyes gleamed unnaturally.

"Report to my mother. Yes, of course. Listen, all of you. My mother already killed me. She wrote me off before I was even born. How hard could it have been for a woman in her posi-shion to find someone willing to tweak the chromosomes of a diagnosed genefective fetus? It wasn't too late. But it is now. When I came here, I didn't know what I'd find. I'd heard the rumors at Einstein—come on, you've all heard them—about how Henri Lwu figured out how to repair genefects. I didn't know what I'd find . . . but I hoped . . . I hoped. I didn't expect *good* people. And now you hate me. Can't you imagine it? My own chromosomes are . . . they're killing me." Her voice sank to a whisper. "Can't you guess what that feels like? I want a child, someday." Her eyes softened and her voice began to croon. "A baby of my own, a normal baby. Not a defective mutant, not one that carries one single defective gene. I am through with Novia. Through. No child of mine will—"

"Stop," Lindon said, relieved and alarmed at once. "Graysha, stop."

She halted in midsentence, looking stricken, then bent over and softly, achingly, started to weep.

"Dr. Brady-Phillips," Ari said in a passionless voice.

Graysha raised her head, wiping her eyes with both hands.

"Answer one more question, if you would. Did you learn anything at D-group that you would consider reporting to your . . . to Novia?"

Graysha glared at Ari. "So you have guns. So use them if the EB comes for you. But if it comes, it won't be because of me."

"I have another question," Lindon interjected, hoping to defuse the hostility rising between the two women. "Does your mother know, or do you think she might guess from past experience, that you wish to have your genes repaired? Is there a chance," he pressed, "that she could have sent you here without your knowledge of her plans?"

"No. No, Chairman, that is . . . I . . ." Graysha stared over his shoulder, slack-jawed, eyes wide. "I haven't the faintest idea," she said at last.

He slumped slightly. He had no doubt that was an honest answer, but it shook him to the core. Kenn and Taidje exchanged worried looks.

"Administer the antidote, Dr. GurEshel," Ari said.

"Wait." Lindon roused himself from his thoughts, but already it was too late. GurEshel moved away from Graysha's chair.

They'd left off a question.

He spoke quickly, knowing the antidote didn't take effect instantly. "Dr. Brady-Phillips, why did you try to kill me?"

She met his stare with a pleading expression. "I didn't. Absolutely not."

"Relax, Dr. Brady-Phillips," said Ari. "Try to relax now. Thank you for cooperating."

A minute later, Graysha sat with her head drooped, blinking and glancing side to side, obviously mortified by some of the things she'd said.

"We will adjourn." Lindon pressed his hands together. "There will be nothing said outside these doors about our discussion. Not yet."

Kenn stood and left, walking with a sway, as if his legs hurt. Taidje and Ari followed him, talking softly.

Graysha sat tight-lipped, as did Yael GurEshel beside her.

"Doctor," Lindon said, "I want to talk with Dr. Brady-Phillips."

"Not alone." GurEshel leaned as far from Graysha as she could sit on that chair.

This protectiveness was not necessary. "Use the observation window. Privacy, please."

"Chairman—"

He lowered his chin and spoke her name firmly. "Dr. GurEshel. Please." The physician slammed the massive metal door as she left.

Graysha watched the committee members go. The giddy half drunkenness was passing, but she was acutely aware of Lindon DalLierx's presence. He—the entire Lwuite colony—now knew exactly what a risk she was to their secrets.

She'd cleared herself, all right, but at what cost to her pride?

Unless . . . She stared up at the wall again, seeing her mother's smirk in midair. Was it possible Novia did somehow send her here?

It was possible. She knew that now. It was barely, grimly possible.

And her own hopeful suspicions were all but confirmed. Either the Lwuites were illicit gene fixers or they did something else just as illegal. Otherwise, they never would have risked questioning her in this way. Medico-religious, were they? *I'll bet*, she reflected, thinking about all the data she hadn't been able to access—data lock-coded behind the Religious Liberties Act. More than likely, the entire "religion" was a sham.

Weary of Novia's preaching, she wouldn't mind that at all. She'd had enough of religion to last her whole life.

Lindon leaned on one armrest. His face looked thinner, his cheekbones more prominent than before. "I apologize for invading your privacy, Dr. Brady-Phillips. The Eugenics Board's reputation is not sterling, either. I am pleased to know you are not employed there."

She crossed her arms in front of her, still slightly dizzy, guessing that now, if ever, Chairman DalLierx would believe her claims of concern. It was time to speak up. "I've come across something you ought to know," she said stiffly, "about Goddard's cooling. It's chlorofluorocarbon depletion. I got that directly off the weathersat this morning. I want to help your people if I can. But if I do, will you do what you can about healing my problem?"

"We can't," he said, frowning. "Those rumors are false. Isn't CFC depletion a matter for your supervisors?"

"Not if they're involved in it."

He sat silently. A clock on the wall hummed. He stroked his chin, then said, "You'll have to explain. Carefully, please. My head's still a little muddled."

She didn't want to sympathize with him at the moment, but she did. "How are you feeling?"

He rocked one hand. "It would have been an easy way to go home. One moment, I was lying down. The next thing I remember is waking up here."

He did look tired, sitting with his shoulders hunched forward. "I spoke with Crystal last night," she said. "I didn't know she was your sister. I like her. We got to be friends at D-group."

His mouth crinkled, and one slanted eyebrow rose. "I rather like her myself."

"You're lucky to have that kind of sister," she said, stabbed by jealousy. "Crystal's got a suspect, if you want to know. I have another."

"Oh?" He leaned several degrees toward her.

Graysha gave the depolarized observation window a sidelong glance, then faced away from it, not knowing whether Dr. GurEshel could read lips. "Crystal suspects Coordinator MaiJidda," she whispered, "and—"

"No," he interrupted. "I've never known Ari to run from a fair fight."

"Oh? Then why wasn't she going to let me clear myself of the murder accusation?"

His eyes narrowed slightly. "Anyone could make a mistake, and I think she did. I believe you were asked in time, and I accept your answer." He hesitated, then said, "I'm sorry. You were going to tell me something else."

Another point scored, she guessed. She dropped her attack rather than lose this bit of momentum toward getting him to accept her. "It's only a suspicion, Chairman DalLierx, but—"

"Please, *Lindon* is fine."

The man had nearly died. Maybe he tolerated her now because of that experience. "I've been thinking," she said slowly. "For terrannums, Gaea Consortium has offered a major reward to anyone who could develop some means of breaking down atmospheric CFCs. Those molecules linger far longer than they're needed, and they prevent the development of a UV-protective ozone layer on a terraformed planet. Any organism they developed here—a bacterium that could break down CFC—could be used back on Earth by Terra Two."

He sat up stiffly, arching his back as if stretching it. "Go on."

"I once had a prof who claimed that for every substrate, there was—or could be, genetically made—a microorganism that would break it down. I wonder if someone in the Gaea building has been going for that reward."

Lindon crossed his legs, pulling farther away from her. "Creating bacteria that would . . . eat our greenhouse gases out of the atmosphere . . . deliberately?"

She nodded.

The dark eyebrows lowered. "As an experiment? Whatever happened to professional ethics?"

"It's only a guess, but I can think of ways to check it out."

He struck the arm of his chair. "This is exactly the kind of development we've been looking for." His voice dropped lower. "Who else have you told?"

Graysha shook her head. "Only you. It isn't safe to tell anyone in the Gaea lab," she added flatly. "Here's something else. I tried to research the cooling, but my research files keep getting gibberished. I can't help wondering whether Jon Mahera was curious about the same thing. And that trail doubles back toward Dr. Varberg and Melantha Lee."

He shut his eyes and groaned softly, then looked around at Dr. Gur-Eshel, who stood staring down through the observation window. "That would explain why my going to Supervisor Lee accomplished nothing."

"I tried that, too."

He fingered his upper lip. "This is not a pretty problem."

Now, while she had his sympathy, she had to press the other issue. "Neither is the fact that I took Eugenics Board money in the past."

His head pulled back slightly, but he didn't respond. Evidently the man feared Novia Brady-Phillips like the wrath of god she thought she was.

It was clear that somewhere on this world, there were secrets that must be kept from the EB.

She was glad to know it.

"I'll work on the CFCs," she declared. "If our culprit is a microbe, it can be destroyed. They all have weaknesses."

His black eyes glistened. "You'll need help. Alert us through Liberty JenChee when you do. I'll ask her to cooperate with you. Tell her you've been cleared of the murder suspicion."

Graysha spread her hands. "Libby quit."

"I'll send her back. As I said, you've been cleared."

Something else was tickling the back of her mind, though, something far more vital than Libby JenChee. A materializing idea hovered barely out of reach. "Here's a thought. I can ... theorize a spontaneous mutation, something that simply happened up there in the ultraviolet. Yes, and if I say the bugs appear to result from normal pre-ozone UV, I don't see how Dr. Lee could think I suspect her. She couldn't stop my investigating, really. I'm supposed to be working in Soils, not Airborne, but they don't have an airborne specialist. And that," she added, feeling distinctly triumphant, "that in itself is suspicious, isn't it?"

He shrugged.

"I think it is. Listen, if someone is going for Gaea's reward for developing a CFC breakdown organism, he—or she—could still collect it, because they still could be first to come forward with a supposedly natural organism they 'isolated' out of the atmosphere." Already, she was wondering who really did it. Varberg, Paul, Melantha Lee?

And what about Ari MaiJidda? Who tried to murder this man?

Lindon pursed his lips, looking dubious. "Is that the way things normally work in a scientific laboratory?"

"Sometimes. Hard work is 95 percent of the job, but there's always inspiration."

"Will you feel safe going back to work?"

How about that—he'd gone from suspicious to concerned. This session, painful though it was, really had gotten her somewhere. "Um, mostly."

DalLierx grasped his chin, covering his upper lip with one finger. Even under glaring fluorescent lights, his pale face was beautifully boyish. "If there's Gaea money at stake, once you go public your co-workers will become competitors."

"But I'm not actually going for the reward. I only want the truth. If they find the organism quicker, that will be good for Goddard." On the other hand, if she could lay claim to even 1 percent of the reward money, it would help clear her debts. *Don't get greedy!* she ordered herself. *And stop admiring him, for heaven's sake.*

"Depending on what you find," he said, "we might be able to send word out to Gaea's Copernicus Office. We wouldn't dare go over Lee's head for anything less than solid proof." He sat motionless, staring at a spot on the concrete floor.

His thoughts, she realized, had taken a different track from hers. When it came to Goddard's weather balance, he was not going to forgive blindly, the way he might refuse to prosecute someone who tried to kill him.

Fascinating.

She glanced at the observation window again. "I think I should go."

His head came up. "Oh. Yes, we've kept you too long. I apologize once more."

"I'm glad to see you ... up." She pulled her overshirt back on. "I think I see now why the USSC outlawed human genegineering. Splicing a bacterial gene is relatively easy. Controlling its effect is impossible."

Lindon shook his head. "Don't apologize for what you said about your mother."

"I need to let you rest," she said again. Mentally she stood him next to Paul. Lindon's attractiveness had a gentler, more persuasive quality. He wasn't constantly pushing at her libido or her loneliness—not deliberately, anyway. She found that attitude much more appealing.

He pushed up to stand, then clasped her hands. "We do thank you." He paused there, looking as if he wanted to say more. . . . Looking, also, like a little boy who desperately needed a nap.

She stepped toward the door, tugging her hands free. "I'll let you know if I find anything."

Lindon raised one slanted eyebrow. "Please be careful. I will be praying for you."

Her stomach lurched. Novia generally used those words as a reprimand. "I'll be careful," she said, frowning.

19. COPERNICUS

Novia Brady-Phillips stood by the docking area's stippled gray wall, waiting for her assistant to process their baggage. That tended to be a lengthy procedure, and her left knee throbbed.

Fortunately, Copernicus Habitat furnished entertainment for those waiting on the docks. Projected onto a nearby wall, a real-time image of the hab's huge toroidal shape rotated slowly, filling the screen with shining metal struts, antennas, and hatches.

She'd seen similar donut-like images. Newer than Einstein or Newton, Copernicus's design was the latest in habitat technology, with the toroid's inner "ceiling" walled in transparent composites to let in more light energy than a cylinder's window strips could admit. Larger than Newton or Einstein, Copernicus's new design made it an ambitious project. Its location, orbiting Epsilon Eridani at one of Goddard's stable Lagrange points, made it isolated.

She checked her watch, guessed that Jambling might be halfway through with his task, and pushed along the docking area.

Copernicus customs would probably allow all her gear, no matter how arcane its circuitry (not to mention the military hardware), because a Eugenics Board seal covered each of its locks. Usually some bureaucrat flexed muscle at her nettechs, but Jambling knew how to deal with bureaucrats. That was part of his training.

Farther along the Immigrants' Wall, she found a semitransparent, three-dimensional habitat map. Clustered around the ring's fifty-kilometer "floor" were offices, laboratories, the green cubes that symbolized schools, and yellow stripes for transport facilities. Between those clusters, an inner reach was partially planted in crops and parklands, dotted by subground accessways to the shielded outer skin.

It looked emptier than she'd expected. Evidently Copernicus was having trouble attracting settlers.

She spotted Jambling by his height, walking toward her between clusters of passersby, and she gestured him toward the nearest elevator. Following a boxlike baggage cart, brandishing its remote control in front of him, he steered it into the elevator box.

When they emerged at Roosevelt Settlement, she was glad Nettech III J. L. Jambling sauntered beside her, showing troublemakers his alert eyes and all-business expression. This neighborhood was crusty with light industrial sprawl, two-story warehouses, and thriving saloons. She'd never smelled so much liquor in broad daylight.

Lovely, she observed, *the businesses that grow up around spaceport docks . . . even when those docks are built down a level, out in the habitat's skin.*

She eyed her escort. Jambling stood 190 centimeters tall, but he was so thin, with pale skin stretched over prominent bones, he looked unhealthy. His curly black hair looked greasy, though he'd just shampooed. His "muscle" consisted of deadly toys concealed on his person.

She did wish she'd told him to rent something they could ride, not just a baggage cart. Paced by his remote, the cart slid along tracks embedded in the walkway. A door opened on her right, exuding fumes of industrial composites.

Novia stepped up her pace.

Within five minutes, they reached the governmental plex. Novia checked into a two-bedroom suite with central office room, showered, and then waited for Service to bring up the lunch she'd ordered upon check-in. The sooner she washed the artificial cherry taste of protein-fiber meal out of her mouth, the happier she would be. Not liking to waste time waiting, she pointed her keyboard's short antenna at a wall socket. Jambling already sat in front of his. "Are you working on Goddard?" she asked.

"No." Cracking his knuckles, he squinted at her. "Checking out Copernicus. Major social groups—Daughters of the Crossing, Alphan Knights, and two lodges of Freemasons. Sixteen trade unions, three churches, his-and-hers correctional facilities, four prep schools, and a tech-ed. What else would you like to know?"

"Nothing." Sitting this close to Goddard and the expected fruits of her labors, she felt that exploring Copernicus was wasting time. She logged in her priority code and added the Gaea reception number for that nearby planet. "All right, Mr. Jambling. We have a Goddard listing for a Gaea net, open, and a Colonial net, closed. Which do you want to tackle?"

As she expected, that got his attention. He cracked his knuckles again, stretched his elbows, and reached for his keyboard. "Colonial for me."

She resisted the urge to smile. The door chimed. "That will be lunch, I think."

Jambling kept poking keys.

"Lunch," she repeated. "Jambling."

Frowning, he pushed away from his station and sauntered across the room's gray carpet. Daylight from a single square window puddled at center floor. It was the only bright spot in an office that was otherwise decorated in institutional fade.

Before pressing the Lock button on their doorframe, Jambling slipped one hand into a pocket. Novia knew he was armed. She hadn't come to like him during the shuttle trip, but she respected his attention to detail.

The door slid away. When Jambling reached forward with both hands, plainly satisfied that the caller posed no threat, she turned back to her work.

Gaea net opened immediately to her codes. Divisions: Botany, Engineering, Entomology . . . She skimmed downward. Medicine, Meteorology, Microbiology . . .

There.

Jambling set a covered plate beside her. Mumbling thanks, she pulled off the cover. She'd ordered chicken or "an acceptable local substitute," and the cubed meat steaming in thin brown sauce looked sufficiently like chicken. She forked down a bite, then reached back over and keyed in a division search for Graysha.

The automated net kept a running account of on-line activity. Graysha's personal file also opened to Novia's executive code, and it showed that at first she'd done settling-in research, then checked microbial balances at various sites. There was a search of abstracts, then more routine activity.

Novia flexed her fingers, warmed by a sense of watching a fast-forward scan over her daughter's shoulder, retracing the weeks since she arrived. It was good to see that the girl had been working and even better to see she'd started researching the Lwuites right away.

Novia ate several more bites of chicken, sopping up sauce with narrow noodles, then exited Microbiology and picked up Medicine. She keyed back to the day of Gray's arrival. To her dismay, an account logged by a Dr. Yael GurEshel recorded Graysha's immediate hospitalization. Novia read details, saddened by the realization that one day she would read of her daughter's death this way.

Scrolling down hastily, she observed log-in data on other patients, men and women whose names, injuries, and ailments meant little. One entry did catch her eye, a classification change from "illness" to "attempted murder." That piqued her professional curiosity, and she recorded the patient's name, DalLierx, to check later.

The name turned up promptly again, though—on an authorization code used to block Graysha's attempt to send a personal letter.

DalLierx. Novia noted the name and his title: *Chairman for Colonial Affairs.*

Bingo.

Working away at her chicken cubes, she eyed an overview of clinic activity at the Axis Plantation site and let her instincts absorb patterns. Later, as her subconscious digested that information, she would realize where something was amiss.

Next, she started checking to see if these Lwuites maintained another major clinic. The main one, there at Axis Plantation, wouldn't be the site of any illicit activity.

Aided by a hard-copy map from EB Einstein, she accessed the other settlements' medical data. Center's clinic was pitifully small and appeared to send its critical patients elsewhere. At Hannes Prime, slightly higher per capita activity offered promise. Most of the clinic admissions there were listed as "mining accidents." That, too, she would check later.

When Port Arbor's admissions data appeared, she stabbed her last noodle in triumph. Port Arbor admissions were double Hannes's, but major causes usually weren't listed. There, if anywhere, the colonists were conducting illegal activities.

Unfortunately, Graysha's name didn't appear on the patient roster.

Novia had arrived in-system too early.

She could wait. It would be amusing to extract as much data as possible from this distance.

"Anything interesting on the Colonial net?" she asked Jambling.

He raised one shoulder, twisting his neck sideways in a weird asymmetrical stretching motion. "I'm not in yet, but it feels like a standard access lock. I'll have it momentarily."

Graysha slept little that night. Rolling over and over, she tried to formulate arguments that would persuade Melantha Lee to let her start looking for a CFC-metabolizing organism. She guessed the colonists monitored her computer now, though she'd spotted no sign of it. When she dreamed, her mother chased Lindon DalLierx down an endless concrete corridor, brandishing a hypo full of gamma-vertol over her head. It glowed like a torch.

Awakening in a sweat, she lay staring at swirls on the concrete ceiling. If Novia had sent her here, she must look no closer at Lwuite secrets. Instead, she had to solve the atmospheric crisis—if that was possible—and leave immediately. That would protect the colonists, but it would end her fading hope for gene healing.

But if Novia wasn't involved, she would be needlessly throwing away the best opportunity of her lifetime by leaving Goddard.

"*I will be praying for you,*" he had said. Maybe he didn't mean that she needed to mend her ways or change her mind. She'd seen concern, not antagonism, in his eyes. She envied his apparent ability to forgive his assailant. How much more like the Christ she'd read about, long ago, than anything her mother ever said or did.

Mother! Graysha rolled over again. What, she wondered, should she do now? She was risking other lives, not just her own, by staying here.

Welling up from under her thoughts came an inexplicable sense of assurance. Justice would be served despite her fears, it whispered. Ultimately, she was responsible for her own actions and the task destiny gave her. She must not endanger others deliberately, but she must not live in terror of making a mistake, lest she prove unable to act when the time was vital and right.

Was that man praying for her right now, this minute? *Wouldn't it be nice if life were that simple,* she observed, clutching the feather pillow. Still, that moment's reflection snipped the threads of tension that kept her awake. Too tired to fight sleep any longer, she pressed her eyes closed and let the threads fall away.

The next morning, she fought Dday darkness and the temptation to doze with a double dose of coffee, lurching through catch-up work sent down from Varberg's office. Trev vanished from her awareness once she set him to washing glassware.

"Good morning, Graysha."

Rubbed *r*'s and the scent of lime made her suspect Paul, and swiveling in her chair, she saw him. He lounged against the doorway, indolently examining his fingernails, then raised his eyes to examine her. "You've been the busy one," he said.

She hoped she looked presentable, resisted straightening her hair tie, then wondered why she felt so uncomfortable when Paul looked at her in that intensely sexual way. Maybe she should just enjoy the attention. "Being a murder suspect is time-consuming," she said lightly.

"Yes, isn't that ironic? I probably want him dead worse than you do, and you were the one accused." His teeth gleamed when he smiled.

Prickly discomfort settled between her shoulder blades. She disliked such talk. Paul really might have tried to murder Lindon. . . .

Or it might've been Varberg. Even Jirina!

This was awful. All her co-workers were suspects, and she honestly cared who tried to do this awful thing.

Carefully, she said, "His sister thinks it was Ari MaiJidda."

Paul returned his attention to his shapely fingernails. "Have you checked Wastewater lately?"

"No, I guess I haven't. I probably should."

"Let me know if you'd like company. I can probably break free."

There it was again, the ache deep in her body from too many nights alone. "Thank you, Paul. You are a gentleman and a scholar."

But as soon as he'd gone, Trev poked his head in. "He's the one who tried to off DalLierx," he whispered loudly. He glanced into the hall. "I'd bet a week's pay."

"Nah," she whispered back.

Trev wrinkled his nose and pulled at one edge of his straggly new mustache. "Think Paul's too nice-looking to have done it?" He ducked back out, then reappeared. "Either him or Varberg. Remember the gribby that died?"

Graysha bit her lip. Suppose Varberg tested his organism on an animal first, one whose immune system was genegineered to resemble a human's.

Rattled, she plunged into the effort of composing her research proposal. Though drafting it took the rest of the morning, she simultaneously watched three automated spore counts in the outer lab. With that accomplished, she tabled it onto the *Ellard* file to let the wording rest awhile.

Varberg poked his head in just before quitting time. Trev scowled, seized a tube rack, and hurried out behind Varberg's back. "What's this I hear about your being questioned?" the big man asked. "Are the Lwuites trying to deprive me of another soils person, or is the position sheer bad luck?"

"They're a strange gang," she said, trying to look straight at his eyes. Libby's inability to meet her gaze had been her own confirmation they suspected her. "Really strange."

"Well, if you need a character witness, just call me."

"Thank you." Not at all pleased by his offer, she forced a smile. Varberg grinned.

After work, Graysha accepted Jirina's invitation to jog in the hub. The black woman's legs were so much longer that they couldn't run together, so Graysha brooded her way alone around two long laps.

"Don't slow down, Blondie," came a dark voice behind her. Jirina shortened her stride to match Graysha's, then accelerated again. "Come on. You're stronger than you think."

Graysha submitted to being run hard one more lap, then staggered off the unofficial track at the hub's edge, near the bench where they had left a pair of towels. As Graysha picked hers up, one corner flicked a bush with broad green needles. A whiff of rosemary startled and invigorated her.

"How goes it?" Jirina reached for her own towel.

Graysha wiped sweaty rivulets off her forehead. "Oh, Jirina," she gasped, "life has never been so complicated."

Even sweat-streaked, Jirina's long dark face had an uncanny beauty. "Tell!" she exclaimed.

Puffing out her cheeks, Graysha exhaled and draped her rosemary-scented towel over her shoulders. "Well. You know this man I'm supposed to have tried to murder?"

"Right. I know you, woman. You'd pull the wings off butterflies if you could find any."

"That's me. So tell me how stupid it would be to fall for Lindon Dal-Lierx."

"Oooh." Jirina turned around and walked backward, facing Graysha. "It wouldn't be hard, Blond Woman. It wouldn't be hard. With a face like that, mmm. Are you?"

Graysha shook her head. "I don't know. It must be the pressure of the situation. You know, the accusations, the worry about being framed for trying to kill him. But I've been intimidated by a man before. Never again. If I did, it would be back to the old downward spiral."

Jirina dangled her towel over one shoulder and shifted her pace to a hip-swinging strut. "You don't see this lady in any hurry to bed down permanently with any given male."

"No, I don't. And I'd appreciate your keeping what I just told you a secret."

Jirina made a sealing gesture over her mouth.

"Thanks."

"What happened to Paul? I thought he lit your fire."

Am I that obvious? Graysha wondered. "He's still around," she admitted.

"Don't forget," Jirina said, "that sweeting with a colonist would have some pretty serious ramifications—such as the privilege of living on Goddard, Eps Eri System, Nowhere, for the rest of your life. And your life isn't going to be so short that you shouldn't spend it in the nicest place possible."

Graysha laughed, glad Jirina had learned to speak casually about the illness that drove so many of her friends into a pained silence. "Thank you, Black Goddess."

The next morning, Graysha decided it *was* high time she rechecked the water purification plant. Paul's invitation leaped into her mind, and she seriously considered it for about one second. It took five minutes to pack Mahera's black box with materials she might need, and she was gone.

Walking up the corry, she found herself relaxing in anticipation of the green, fertile environment. The colonists had the hub for a parkland, which was pretty enough, but if a person wanted solitude, already she preferred the waste marsh.

She let the door clang shut after her and took a deep breath of warm, moist air. Overhead, bands of light gleamed to simulate daytime. There was a new odor today, bracing and sweet. Eyeing the raceways, she spotted a clump of tiny white flowers blooming on miniature spikes. A jungle would smell like this, she guessed. Kneeling near the door, she drew a water sample from that raceway with a sterile pipette, paused a moment with one finger over the top of the tube to marvel at the clarity of what had been sewage effluent mere days before, then dropped the sample into a labeled nutrient tube.

"Hello?" called a man's voice.

Startled, Graysha clutched the nutrient tube. Had Paul learned to lurk? No, that didn't sound like him. Maybe one of the colonists had discovered this place. "Good morning?" she answered cautiously, backing closer to the door, carefully tucking the broth tube into her pack.

From the first branch in the path, Lindon stepped onto the straight walkway. He wore a loose hand-knit red sweater that was fading with age.

"Good morning," she repeated, heartily this time. "You caught me at work. Do you come here often?"

He tugged down the sweater's hem. "Occasionally."

"When you want to be alone," she guessed. "I'm sorry for disturbing you. I'll get my samples and leave. Shouldn't take long."

"Oh no, don't hurry." He walked closer. "Would you mind my watching?"

Amused, she opened the pack again. "You won't find this particularly interesting, but you're welcome to watch." She strode straight up the long walk toward a fluorofoam raft of wire-braced tomato plants. He followed. She knelt, pulling out a fresh pipette. Several of the tomato plants had star-shaped yellow flowers with a faintly acrid odor.

To her astonishment, Lindon knelt, too. He touched a blossom with one finger, flicked it up and down, then reached for another.

Graysha drew her sample. "What are you doing?"

"Tickling," he said. "Pollinating, actually."

"Why doesn't the fruit mature? I've won—" She broke off the word, realizing there could be only one answer.

Lindon grinned. "Because greedy colonists pick them green, take them home, and let them ripen." He rocked back on his heels. "Wastewater fruit isn't budgeted into our food allowances. The few of us who know about it covet it for one another."

For one another? What a remarkable idea.

Graysha did a reverse knee bend back to her feet. "Now the marsh," she said, leading down the path. Paul Ilizarov's label, *too pretty,* floated back to the top of her consciousness. The man had beautiful eyes, framed with long dark eyelashes and exotic slanting brows. . . .

And she was rebounding from Ellard, hungry for male companion-ship—particularly sympathetic, intelligent, generous male companionship. Lindon DalLierx had a plantation to administer. She must create a lifetime's legacy in forty or fifty short years.

But there it was. She'd admitted it to Jirina, so now she had to admit it to herself. It would be easy to think too much, too often, about this man.

At any rate, he never would trust or accept her now. He knew about her EB involvement, and he had something to hide.

And he was praying for her, like Novia.

For the moment, she must enjoy their fragile truce. She knelt beside the grove of green cattails, keenly aware that this time he remained standing over her. Brown leather shoes and heavy browncloth trouser cuffs stood at the edge of her field of vision.

"When I despair of seeing Goddard bloom"—his voice came as she drew more water—"I come down here. If terrestrial plant life flourishes in the worst waste, that gives me hope for the wild."

"I haven't made much progress on the cooling issue," she said softly, looking up, "but that'll take time. Now I have to check the aeration tanks."

Pocketing both hands, he strolled up the walk and around the corner toward the massive cylinders along that wall. By the time she caught up, he'd already opened a sampling port. "Icch." He wrinkled his nose. "Hurry."

"You aren't supposed to open that," she said, attaching a clickdraw to the final pipette, "until I get here." She sucked up a few drops and nodded. Lindon screwed the sampling port shut as she dropped the sewage into her last tube. "There," she said firmly.

He leaned against the tank, which rose almost to the high ceiling.

"What do you do with those samples?"

Was he speaking as an administrator, she wondered, or was he just curious? "Certain bacteria ought to be present at each stage of the treatment, breaking organic molecules down, then down again. I'll send these samples through either a DNA scanner or a 'smart' filter programmable to recognize bacteria by the molecules in their cell walls. If any of the 'good bugs' are missing, I'll reinoculate the appropriate waterway." Aware she was addressing the gravel walk, she raised her chin and saw Lindon nodding. "I'd train Trevarre to do it, but I like coming here."

"I understand." He clasped his hands behind his back. "How is the boy?"

"Doing well." Graysha strolled back toward the cattails. "Trev's bright. Undereducated, though, and obviously unloved. I've seen kids like him, rebels for no reason. If you can make them care about what they're doing, they're just as strong-minded about their work as they were about rebellion."

"That sounds wise."

She shrugged. "Just good teaching technique."

"There are good teachers and those who don't care. I think you were one of the first group."

She turned her head away, hoping he wouldn't see her smile.

"Did you ever get out of him what he's doing here?"

She had promised to keep Trev's secret. How much could she say? Reflected skylight streamed through the cattails from behind, giving the illusion of natural greenery. Grandma Brady would have loved this place. "He's . . . running from a bad home situation."

Lindon paused to tap the side of the next glass tank. The water inside this one, green with algae, roiled with shrimp and tiny fish. "Too much wealth, I'd say from the little we talked."

Excellent guess, but she couldn't say so. "Were you . . . planning a campaign speech for the election?"

"I was thinking things through. Making sure I believed I was the person for the position. I couldn't campaign honestly if I wasn't sure I deserved my people's confidence."

"What were you really doing?" She hoped she didn't sound scornful. "Praying?"

"No." His voice fell, as if he were ashamed to deny it. He stared at the path pebbles as he walked on. "Sometimes it's hard to get an accurate perspective on my own desires. Sometimes I want a thing so badly that it would be hard to hear God's directive if He wanted otherwise. My comfort is that if I'm serving consciously, in all the ways He commands, my desire probably is right."

Maybe there was no Lwuite faith, but plainly this was a religious man. Just as plainly, he couldn't be CUF. He never hinted that he held the human organism sacred. "You probably think of me as an unbeliever," she said. "I'm not, not exactly."

"Maybe not, but you're not a member of any church."

"Oh?" This guess, as accurate as the other, made her strangely uncomfortable. Really, she shouldn't care. "What makes you say that?"

"What would you be doing here, so far from your communion?"

"Good point. I . . ." She fumbled for words. "I would like to know more about your beliefs. Not for Novia," she added hastily, "for myself. But I realize I'm trespassing by asking about them. Would you prefer not to answer?"

"I'm sorry," he said quietly.

She bit the inside of her lip, wishing she hadn't mentioned her mother. *Oh well. So much for that opportunity.*

"I don't think it would do any harm to warn you," he added, "that you're being watched for any attempt to contact her. Please don't."

She laughed harshly. "I don't want to. I swear it."

"Good." He glanced toward the door, then looked back into her eyes. "What happened at the firing range? You were going to tell the committee, but Vice-Chair MaiJidda stopped you."

Oh, mercy. Did she dare . . . did she want to accuse Ari MaiJidda, now that she'd cleared herself of conscious EB involvement? MaiJidda no longer had cause to fear her. "Some mild leg cramps," she said. That was part of the truth, at least. "I had to move suddenly. Ask Crystal. She was there." She skipped back to the previous subject. "And whether or not you're the deity's man for the job, good luck in your election." She adjusted her shoulder strap. "And thanks for your help."

"I didn't do anything, really."

Why are you people so afraid of the Eugenics Board? She wanted to shout it at him. Instead, she waved and walked out.

Even the primitive little dugout they'd given Trev for an apartment had a Gaea net terminal. He bent to examine a news burst that evening. +Search,+ he ordered, as he always did, and then, +LZalle.+

Usually, a burst took ten or twelve seconds to scan. He stroked his mustache hairs while waiting, wondering if his father—

+LZALLE.+ It appeared almost instantly. +Blase LZalle and Solar Blases. Tour Canceled. . . . +

Chilled, he read on. Within two weeks of Trev's departure, Blase had called off his tour, offering as explanation a "family emergency."

Chips. Oh chips, chips, chips. He raised a fist to pound his desk, realized once he started the downswing that he was about to hurt himself, and tried too late to pull the stroke. "Eesssh," he hissed through his teeth, shaking the painful hand.

You ought to be touched, he reflected grimly. *Look how many maxims the old man gave up for his ugly kid.*

Holding the aching hand against his chest, he stroked it.

But the old man's desire was to make Trev into a file copy of himself, to hide the born ugliness he passed to his son . . . and he wouldn't take no for an answer.

Trev had to dig in. His father might not be far behind him. He had four or five spare hours every day, after work and before sack time, hours he currently wasted reading articles for Graysha. He'd agreed to report two days from now to Ari MaiJidda's green room, but he ought to be investing more time on the colonists, "making himself valuable," as Graysha put it.

Hastily he keyed over onto a chores-wanted directory. Off-site work would be best. It was hoping too much to think Gaea might let him transfer to another Goddard locale, but if he wanted to hide, it couldn't be at Axis. Axis's spacefield made access too easy. Prospectors and explorers were out there in the wild, some Lwuites and some working for Gaea. Didn't any of them need part-time help?

Evidently not, he soon realized. But here was a listing, placed by a Yukio HoBrace—a Lwuite tech, working for the Consortium—and it looked like this Yukio needed someone with just about Trev's qualifications.

It also involved travel. Ignoring his hand's rhythmic throbbing, Trev punched up the advertised net code.

20. IN CONFERENCE

Lindon knocked on the door of an aboveground dwelling, then thrust his hand back into his warm pocket. While waiting, he gazed out into the Sunday cold. Heavy machinery was operating somewhere. Grinding and pummeling noises competed from two directions. Shimmering breath condensed near his face. Across the track, which would be a street one day, two more rows of yellow-tan brick houses stretched north and south. A blockhouse at the end of this row provided tunnel access.

The door behind him opened with a pressurized *whoosh*.

He spun around. "Mrs. TollHeyer?"

She reminded him of his mother, with a halo of salt-and-pepper braids and straight-shouldered poise that suggested she, too, had left behind a prosperous life. "Come in," she said, "please. I'll have tea for you and Vice-Chair MaiJidda in a moment."

"Thank you." He pulled off his coat. His hostess seized it and vanished into another room.

Her living room measured about three meters by four. Windows of Goddard-made, nonpolarized triple-pane glass provided a view of open sky. No pictures hung on the room's white walls, but the floor, swept clean of pervasive upside dust and sand, attested to Mrs. TollHeyer's industry—and reminded him he owed his own parents a visit now, though he had lain unconscious most of the time they were visiting.

"I didn't mean to rush you," he called.

The woman hurried back out of her kitchen. She'd fastened on a white-bow choker, and her work clothes had the stiff, unwrinkled look of new browncloth. How small the notions they considered nicety now.

Lindon sat down on her blocky couch of darkly dyed linen over synthetic foam, and he stretched up one knee. He and Ari could have thrashed out their differences over the net, but even with privacy circuits, neither liked that notion. He also could have met her in the hub or at the co-op or in a vacant office. Still, at a randomly chosen private house, there would be someone within call if either needed a witness for binding agreements. As it turned out, Mrs. TollHeyer was even a notary.

Crystal's accusation niggled at the back of his mind. He rubbed his chin, wishing he'd never heard it. His sister had been unable to prove her accusations, so he couldn't believe them 100 percent.

Still, Graysha Brady-Phillips had risen considerably in his sympathy. *"Ari tried to crush her, Lin,"* Crys had claimed. *"She nearly got me, too."*

Through a window, he watched Ari stride up the lane, holding her shoulders stiffly forward under her coat. "Shall I let Coordinator MaiJidda in?" he called toward the kitchen door.

"I'm coming." Mrs. TollHeyer carried a brown pot steaming between two fine china cups on a ceramic tray. She set it down, then unsealed the narrow metal door.

As Lindon rose, Ari stepped through, already tugging at her parka sleeves. She stretched out a slender arm to clasp his hand, then sat down in a chair close to his couch. Mrs. TollHeyer poured. "This is the last of my real tea. I'm honored to share it with you. Please consider our home your own, and call me if you get hungry."

Ari tilted her head. "Thank you." Her elegant figure and stance, and her politeness with the other woman, reminded Lindon she had a deeply feminine side. Why, he wondered, had she remained so contentedly unmarried? Many Lwuites wed at sixteen. Her heterozygous status wouldn't prevent her having pure-gened children now that the Port Arbor clinic was in full operation.

Maybe she, too, considered Goddard her highest priority. Realizing he'd fallen into that trap niggled his conscience. His first priority should be much higher.

Once they sat alone, he leaned forward. "I'm glad for a chance to hear your opinions concerning our differences, Ari, regardless of which way the election goes."

She matched his posture. "That's good. First, though, I think you might be glad to know we're about to make an arrest in the attempted-murder case."

Varberg, Lee, or someone else? he wondered. Their single dose of gamma-vertol was gone now. If Ari was guilty of the attempt on his life, she would feel safe arresting some other suspect. That poor person wouldn't be able to prove his or her innocence.

Crys, why did you open your mouth? He needed to stay objective.

"We think now," she went on, "that the case against Dr. Brady-Phillips is as strong as it can be."

But Graysha cleared herself! "What?"

"You'll be pleased to know," she said, lounging on her chair, "that we anticipate Gaea's defense countering our accusations. They'll try to send her offworld, as we originally wanted, but I think we'd be safer keeping her in custody until we're absolutely certain she won't run to her mother."

Evidently Ari had transferred her justifiable fear of the EB directly onto Graysha Brady-Phillips's shoulders. "She doesn't work for the Eugenics Board," Lindon reminded her. "You heard her testimony."

Her dark eyes narrowed. "Has it not occurred to you that a nettech might carry counteractive measures to questioning drugs?"

He sat up straight. "Then why in this world did you waste that one dose on her?"

"I'm not perfect, either. I thought of it too late."

Did she, really? "I think she's innocent," he insisted. Ari might not recognize guiltlessness if she saw it.

"Of course she *seems* innocent. She has a perfect face for espionage—the poor thing—and perfect connections. You won't deny either of those, will you?"

"She's innocent," he repeated.

Ari snorted. "We have evidence, Lindon. We found Chenny HoNin's insulin kit in her D-group locker."

"You did?" Stunned, he demanded, "Why didn't you ask about that when you questioned her?"

"No need," she said coolly. "It will come out in her trial. It's possible that she's bait, just as you suggested—whether or not she volunteered. Whether she knows it or not, the EB could be watching to see what we'll do for her. You wouldn't put that past the high and mighty Novia, would you?"

"No . . ."

"Well, then. If we suspended eligibility rules and instigated experimental procedures, her mother could present her own daughter's Strobel Probes as evidence against us."

Lindon lowered his head. "So the innocent must suffer along with the guilty."

"Spare me the theatrics." Ari reached for a teacup. "She is not innocent."

"There has been . . . another new development, Ari." Carefully choosing his words and hoping his growing attraction to the microbiologist hadn't clouded his judgment, he explained Graysha's offer to search the Gaea building for evidence of environmental sabotage. "I think," he concluded, "that for the moment I would like you to hold off making your arrest. Give her a week, at least, to try."

"That only makes things worse. Don't you see? She probably already knows what's wrong." Ari sipped from her cup. "Melantha Lee is demanding a minute-by-minute account of D-group training, thanks to her. If you hadn't gone to Lee again, accusing her of not doing enough about the cooling, we wouldn't have a new pile of busywork."

"Is Lee on your suspect list?"

"God, no. I'm not the only one displeased with the way Melantha Lee has gotten harder to work with. Can you imagine how nasty she'd turn if we tried to question her? Anyway," she continued before Lindon could tell her that had nothing to do with Lee's guilt or innocence, "we came here to talk about the election, not the affairs of *my* office."

Good idea. "We can at least agree to present issues to the colonists, not accusations or personality differences."

"Our people," she said icily, "are quite aware of the differences between us, both chromosomally and behaviorally."

"I apologize if you thought that was an insult. Tell me how you think Goddard could be better run."

Lindon sipped tea—wasted on him, for he might never taste nuances again—and listened. Ari wanted more aggressive exporting of the heavier raw materials. She wanted to accelerate his schedule for bringing in additional asteroidal resources. She meant to suggest tighter work schedules.

"All excellent points," he said. "If Mars had moved more aggressively into export markets, it might not still be an economic backwater."

"I'm fully aware history was your field of study. I know as much about space colonization as you do."

"I meant nothing of—"

"And if you are going to let sexual and genetic politics enter into this discussion, I am going to leave."

What had he said to draw that barb? "I meant nothing of the sort."

"What platform do you intend to run on, then?"

He'd thought this through carefully. "We have surplus food and energy stored against the chance of missing a supply ship or two. Somehow it has become vulgar to remind one another we all could starve waiting for assistance."

She raised one thin eyebrow. "You're not going to bring religion into your campaign?"

"People know our differences."

"I assume you've prayed about running for reelection?" She didn't quite sneer.

Lindon drained his tea and set down the cup. "You don't need to ask."

"Since you haven't withdrawn, I assume God told you you're the man for the position."

No answer would satisfy Ari MaiJidda.

"Good." She smiled frigidly. "I think we have accomplished the purpose of this meeting." She rocked forward to stand.

"Just a minute."

Ari reached for her parka but did not slip it on.

He had to ask. "There are fresh scars in the firing-range floor. Dr. Brady-Phillips says there was an accident . . . now. But she was going to say more as we started to question her. What happened?"

"For once she's telling the truth." Ari pushed one arm down a coat sleeve. "There was an accident."

Who should he believe . . . Ari or his sister?

"Don't you want her locked up?" Ari dangled her parka over a lace table runner.

Crys is only guessing. "We need her help at the Gaea station. Maybe Dr. Ilizarov might assist us? Do you trust him 100 percent—when it comes to planetary affairs?"

Ari laughed coarsely, then poked her head around the corner into the kitchen. "Good day, Mrs. TollHeyer," she called, then she lowered her voice and whispered, "Very well. Give her a week. But leave Paul Ilizarov out of this." He gave her a long head start, draining one more cup of warm flavorless tea in his hostess's company before slipping on his coat.

Slowly, he walked back to the blockhouse. Though some snow had melted, darkening the ground, most had blown away. Plowed drifts remained packed beside the road. Raising his head, he looked beyond the settlement, between the tall textiles plant and the low, flat-roofed heavy equipment garages. A dark track-truck crawled up the Port Arbor highway.

He had dreams for this colony, dreams of vast fertile tracts of land, dreams of free trade with Copernicus and other colonies, a university, cultural centers—everything he once enjoyed at Einstein.

Everything he gave up to come here. How many of these dreams might he live to see?

None of them, if the warming trend reversed. Goddard, for all its vastness, supported an unspeakably fragile net of open-air life. *We're playing God*, he reflected. *Are we overstepping?* When it came to terraforming, he didn't think so. All they hoped to build here seemed like a logical next step of human civilization.

Still, Goddard—even his people—must never take God's place of priority in his heart. He felt obligated to respect Graysha's spiritual curiosity. She had asked politely, making it easier to decline than to speak. Her life, too, was unspeakably fragile. If she died one step short of salvation after he refused to speak with her, he might be held accountable for all he didn't say.

Was she sincere? Was their single remaining dose of gamma-vertol squandered on a person who would not be affected?

He walked on, trying to convince himself Graysha was an EB plant. He couldn't. Her manner was too sincere, her sympathy too genuine. Ari's manner was another story entirely. The insulin kit could've been planted in Graysha's locker. If Crys was correct, Ari was blaming someone to cover her own guilt.

Ari was right about one thing, though. Trying to heal Commissioner Brady-Phillips's daughter could be a deadly act of charity.

Yet the issue of faith would not lie quiet in his mind. Graysha ought to know that for some Lwuites, faith was no quasi-legal camouflage.

That knowledge might make her less hostile toward the colony, less likely to change her mind and report to her mother after all. Already they'd tipped their hand by questioning her.

But he was not a private person. Here, too, he must use caution.

He checked his watch. Five-thirty. He was late for his Sunday appointment with Bee and Sarai. Plunging into the blockhouse, he hurried downside.

The brass desk plate read *Flora Hauwk, Ph D, System Supervisor, Gaea Terraforming Consortium.*

Novia eyed the woman. Flora Hauwk's dark gray hair, severely pulled back from her face, accentuated high cheekbones and a strong, narrow nose. Though Hauwk had to be eighty, her manner was feisty and young. Novia had come this morning to Dr. Hauwk's Copernicus office, formally requesting investigation privileges at Goddard.

Through an open window drifted a weird petrochemical smell. Copernicus Habitat's new-hab industry made it heavy on construction sounds and smells. Pounding noises on the sidewalks and composite in the air had given her a headache before she even arrived at this field office. She would be glad to leave this place.

"Besides being a money drain," Hauwk continued, "and a drag on Consortium resources, the terraforming itself is going poorly. I can't imagine what System Supervisor Bennett did with his time. He was supposed to be world-building." She pointed over her shoulder toward a set of bound hard copies. "These transcripts show laissez-faire on a grand scale."

Novia considered asking for copies of the transcripts, then changed her mind. Goddard's troubles weren't her concern. Its colonists were. Graysha hadn't reported since arriving on Goddard, not even a quick note. She'd hoped Gray would earn her gene fix with better grace.

Surely the girl suspected. She might be keeping a low profile, increasing her chances to connect with the colonists. "How long have you been at Copernicus, then?" she asked Supervisor Hauwk.

"Less than a week. Melantha Lee, site supe over on the rock, requested a change in management when Bennett was ready to quit anyway. I transferred over, almost without a chance to pack. I'm telling you this because I think it will be out of the bag soon anyway, Commissioner, but Gaea is about to reorganize. Our hab offices are sick of bearing the brunt, constantly digging for outside corporate support. The investment value of terraforming is on an outslide. Many of us think it's time to consolidate closer to home and wait out the slump, then move forward again when the maxims loosen up."

Novia didn't like the sound of that. "What does this mean for Goddard?"

Hauwk shrugged. "Evidently I get to decide."

Novia pursed her lips. She'd arrived just in time, then. "What about the rumors of planetary cooling? Graysha, my daughter, is doing on-site work for Gaea, if you haven't heard."

Hauwk nodded.

"She has been researching a depletion in atmospheric chlorofluorocarbons."

"Yes, we monitor Goddard's Gaea station. Has she turned up anything she hasn't reported?"

"I haven't communicated with her yet."

"It's all so complex." Hauwk reclined her chair, dangling one arm over its edge. "We've known from the beginning that it would take generations to craft a living planet. We can't be alarmist. But if we drain today's company of resources, we can't afford to be there in the next generation."

"I understand," Novia said.

Flora Hauwk slid a pocket memo from one corner of her desk toward its center. "You're the second visitor I've had this morning, you know."

How, pray tell, was she supposed to know that?

"That, you see, is why I rather have money on my mind." Hauwk eyed the memo. "A new major stockholder is in the Eps Eri system, looking for his runaway son. It would be nice to have that kind of money. He found out the boy is on Goddard, so first he bought a fast private ship, then he bought into the Consortium. He could afford a private pilot to get him here. He has other motives, too, as I understand it. He lives on Venera."

"Oh?"

Hauwk nodded. "He wants Gaea to 'finish up' over there. I tried explaining that we've done all we can to terraform Venera, but he doesn't listen."

"He could be useful. What's his name?"

Hauwk eyed the memo again. "LZalle. Blase LZalle."

Graysha stayed late in her laboratory, cleaning out the smelly wincubator. Charges and countercharges aside, she had to hold down a job. Tomorrow, she'd start wind-testing another genus of altered microbes, *Streptomyces* strains. First, she ought to see what Will Varberg already did to them. Once she'd sorted her discard tubes and plates onto Trev's processing racks, she settled at her computer.

Working down the Gaea net, she passed through upper levels to Varberg's culture inventory. His records were personally coded with abbreviations, but they were common ones. She read them easily. He'd been gene-splicing decomposer streps used in the middle stages of terraforming's microbial phase, bacteria that would break down plant and animal matter and help build fertile soils. DNA maps told her nothing, but she was used to working in half-light when it came to Varberg's genetics. She cross-referenced his soil streps with the media he'd used to grow them on.

Halfway down the second screen, she felt her heart do a little flip. Besides conventional sugars and amino acids, he'd requisitioned several kilograms of reagent-grade chlorofluorocarbons.

CFCs . . . as bacterial media?

Hardly daring to consider what that order might mean until she double-checked it, she saved the entry to a personal file and then keyed over to Stores. Their records confirmed the order.

She slumped over her keyboard.

Oh, Lindon. Duncan. Crystal. Varberg wanted the Gaea reward, all right. He'd been trying to grow—or create—an organism that broke down CFCs for nutrients, one that could survive in the poisonous presence of the free chlorine this breakdown would liberate. This data all but proved it.

Microbiologists didn't order media chemicals unless they meant to grow bacteria on them.

Still, it didn't prove he released these bacteria into the wild.

Her hands went limp in her lap.

Gene-spliced organisms were infamously delicate, she reflected. Few survived in natural ecosystems, even after several toughening generations in the laboratory.

Still, as she'd hypothesized to Lindon, *something* appeared to have robbed Goddard of 20 percent of its CFCs. She already knew bacteria could flourish in the atmosphere, suspended in cloud droplets and using atmospheric substances as nutrients.

But could Varberg have treated this planet as his private laboratory? What about Gaea's investment and the colonists' hopes to establish a new home?

He could. He'd made it clear that he didn't play by others' rules. Everything he lost at Messier might have made him vow that humanity never would see a planet overheat again. Melantha Lee could be covering for him, maybe for a cut of the Gaea reward.

She shook her head, half hoping she'd guessed wrong, half certain the seemingly disparate facts—cooling, depletion, and this otherwise irrational supply order—mandated only one answer. He must be monitoring the bacterium out there, waiting to claim it as a natural mutation he might "discover" and patent. But it had already destroyed 20 percent of the fluorocarbon shield. What was he waiting for?

For Lindon's death, maybe. Lindon insisted on asking tough questions. Varberg might be afraid Lindon would dog his trail out into the USSC's academic community. She wished Jon Mahera's files hadn't been purged, but she guessed she'd have found similar inquiries on them.

She must publish her proposal quickly, but not until she eliminated every hint of accusation. If the bug existed it probably was a streptomycete—since she found it in this subinventory—but the proposal mustn't say so.

She released her hair from the tie, slicked it back, and pulled the cloth band tight around it again. Varberg might have a perfectly logical explanation for all this.

Jon Mahera probably thought that, too. Cross-correlating this data might have been his last professional act.

"*I don't want to lose another soils person,*" Varberg's voice echoed down her memory. "*Dr. Mahera was sampling a duricrust Streptomyces seeding up on the wild when he—*"

Something creaked outside her door. She froze and listened—to nothing but her own heart thumping. Was she starting to imagine footsteps in the hall?

She stared at her screen again. If she couldn't eliminate this mysterious organism out there on the clouds—soon—so many greenhouse CFCs might be destroyed that the cooling would enter the critical phase. Yet she mustn't unbalance Goddard's frail young ecosystem with broad-spectrum antimicrobials. Those kill-it-all chemicals could eliminate beneficial soil bacteria as they rained down out of the sky.

Furthermore, before she could discover how to field-attenuate the mysterious strep, she must grow it in her own lab.

She must do all that without help or approval from her supervisors and without one metabolizing bacterium to work with, as yet.

So. She sat up straight, stretching her arms and staring at her monitor. The effort called for another sampling trip, this one into Goddard's open sky for airborne organisms. If her suspicions were correct, Varberg might sabotage that effort once he sniffed what she was up to. She must be extremely careful.

So how do I bring in an atmospheric sample?

She attacked the Gaea net with renewed energy. In a Transport file, she learned that Axis maintained three fixed-wing planes for spraying regolith with bacterial cultures, processed organic waste, and the seeds of higher plants. For her purpose, the small hovercopter would serve just as well and be more economical to run. The contact person was a man named Tate, Bryan Tate.

This, then, was the place to start. She gave her proposal a layer of polish, saved her evening's work in the *Ellard* file, and stumbled back home to Emmer and her bed.

21. DUTCHY

"So you have too many yabuts." Trev leaned close to a darkened monitor in Zoology's break room. "So why don't we just fly up there and hunt them off? I hear they're edible."

Yukio HoBrace, unlike the other male Lwuites Trev had met thus far, sported a tiny braid dangling along one sideburn. "The yabut population out in the wild isn't a food crop," he said, sounding disdainful. "What we need out there is a natural system of checks and balances so eventually the planet will take care of itself. The world itself lives. That's what terraforming is all about."

Stinging from the scorn in Yukio's voice—the tech was no older than he was—Trev swallowed his urge to retort. He had too much riding on this potential job. "Yeah, right," he said.

"Okay, then." Yukio touched on the screen, then typed so quickly Trev didn't catch his password. "This is what we're looking for." He painted a catlike figure in muted yellow.

Yukio, an animal handler, claimed he had slipped last Goddarday on ice and broke an ankle. He couldn't fly south alone, and his supervisor wanted a breeding nucleus of the vanishing predators—Van Dyk weasel-crossed lynxes on the books, "Dutchers" on Yukio's tongue—transported to a location up on the unsettled flatlands. Some place called Lower Infinity Crater.

"Size of a large house cat, just big enough to kill yabuts. Cream-colored with black-tipped bobtail, yellow eyes. Big ruff around the neck." Yukio sketched in fluff below tall tufted ears. "Big feet."

Trev smoothed his mustache, interested in spite of himself.

Yukio pulled back to eye his drawing, then stroked a series of panels to broaden the image. "That's more accurate," he pronounced. "Slim's nice for warm-weather creatures, but cold tolerance means fat layer."

"Uh-huh."

"To reestablish the Lower Infinity Crater zone we'll need a young male and two, preferably three, females. They pride, like lions."

"Pride. Yeah." Since when was *pride* a verb?

"You're sure you can handle a twin-engine Mathis?"

Trev flattened both palms on the desk. "You take me for a habber. I've always lived on a planet. I prefer planets. The first place I stopped on this trip, I couldn't breathe. I had to find a little room."

"Huh." Yukio checked his watch. "Okay. If we leave in half an hour, that'll give us eight hours to overfly the southern region, find some kitties, and hopefully release them before solar noon."

That wasn't going to leave much time for sleeping tonight. But he wouldn't have to lick Varberg's shoes for a whole day. The floor supervisor hounded him constantly when Graysha wasn't around. "Yeah, fine."

Yukio gave him full control of the Gaea plane. After an unimpressive takeoff, the Lwuite youth made no comment other than to guide him toward a notch in Axis crater's southern wall. A huge strip mine passed below. "Surface oxides," Yukio remarked as they overflew a dust cloud with a track-truck underneath it.

Vast stretches of bare rock lay to the left and right, and Trev gazed at them in satisfaction. Goddard had mountains, real craggy ones, on the port-side horizon. He would've liked to see the ocean, too, but evidently that was off in some other direction.

This place felt like home. He hadn't realized how cramped and confined he had felt in habs, in spacecraft, and even down in Axis crater.

He might be able to hide out here, but not alone. He didn't have God-dard survival skills yet. As they flew south, he watched the ground for signs of the prospectors he'd heard mentioned.

An hour later, Yukio stabbed one finger toward his window. "There. Bring us down about half a K from here if you can find a runway inside the fenced zone."

Runway. Right. Suddenly the ground looked less hospitable, pocketed with craterlets and pimpled with boulders. Yukio gasped when Trev started his first approach, so he pulled up, demanding, "You see any better place?"

"No," his partner admitted.

Trev saw one, though, closer to the cluster of boulders Yukio had pointed out. He headed for it, crossed his fingers, and nosed down again.

A few meters off the stony ground, he flared up to let the rear wheels drop. The first touchdown felt like he'd blown off the landing gear, but he held steady until the Mathis shook to a halt.

Yukio unbuckled. "Yeah. Next time, maybe I fly." Crouching, he shuffled toward the craft's back compartment and sorted out several heavy cloth bags, two pairs of gauntleted leather gloves, and a small rifle. He racked it once. "Tranks. Won't hurt them a bit."

"I know what a trank gun looks like. What do we need gloves for?"

Yukio tossed him a pair. "Don't put them on and you'll find out. Oh, and bring the first-aid kit."

Sounded serious enough.

They jumped down. Trev helped Yukio unload a pair of unwieldy metal crutches invented during some dark period of human medicine. The Lwuite planted them under his armpits, then swung forward on them, keeping his heavily casted left ankle off the ground. "Look." He pointed with a crutch.

An apricot-blond cat crouched atop the highest boulder, tufted ears forward, watching them. Trev shivered at the baleful expression in the creature's yellow eyes. They'd been modified with weasel genes, right? For compactness . . . or was it for fierceness?

Yukio braced his good leg and crutches to form a tripod, shouldered the rifle, and pulled off a shot. The cat bounded down behind a rock into the nesting area.

"Got it?"

Yukio grinned, his face comical behind UV goggles. "Easy. It's flushing the rest of them that'll take time." He dropped the rifle and let it dangle from its sling, leaned onto his crutches again, and hobbled forward.

Trev adjusted his own goggles, guessing he looked just as insectoid. "Want to let me try that rifle?"

"Not if you've never shot one before. We've only got so many cartridges. You go around to the other side of the nest and throw some rocks in at them. I'll put them down for their nap when they come out on my side."

Trev set down the first-aid kit and pulled on the long gloves. They came almost to his neck, where shoulder straps secured them front and back. Then he picked a way to the other side of the nesting ground. Human feet, he realized, had probably never walked this gravelled sand before. He liked the sensation. Eps Eri rode halfway up the sky, red through his goggles.

He could call this place home. Easily.

He picked up a fist-sized chunk of volcanic stone, hefted it, and tossed. It landed loudly at the center of the boulder pile. Immediately, Yukio fired the tranquilizer gun. *Crack . . . crack, crack*—

A black-tailed yellow creature bounded out of the shadows faster than Trev would have believed—straight for him. Another one chased it. This wasn't in the plan! As he bent for another rock, the first creature leaped at his face. He screamed, ducked his head to protect goggles and eyes, and flailed both arms. In the icy cold, something dug like knives into his scalp. Something unbelievably strong seized one glove. "Yukio!" he shrieked.

The trank gun crackled on.

One cat clamped jaws shut on his pants. Bracing his legs, he pulled both hands into fists inside the gloves and flapped empty leather fingers at the cat on his leg. "Shoo!" he shouted, "get away!"

"Don't move!"

Impossible—but he did it. Two more crackles echoed off the rocks, and flapping blue darts sprouted from both kits' rumps. Expecting the creatures to go limp, he waited for an instant, then beat at them again. Blood splattered from his chin onto one cat's fur.

They were bigger than he expected, the size of large *overweight* house cats.

Using both crutches, Yukio flung himself down the boulder pile. "Two minutes," he shouted, "and they'll be out." Dropping one crutch, he bent for a stone and tossed it toward Trev. A cat loosened its grip. Trev kicked it off his pant leg. Yukio hurled another stone. The second cat merely went for Trev's head again.

Icy little knives raked one cheek, then across his nose. He yelled. Startled, the cat drew back its paw to strike again. Trev slugged it with his other glove. It dropped, shook its head, then batted at his bleeding leg.

"Shoot it again," he cried to Yukio.

"Overdose'd kill it!" Yukio shouted back, half-kneeling, flailing both crutches to create a cat-free zone. "And I think it's a female."

Trev kicked at her, and finally she lay on her back panting. He would have liked to stomp her.

Instead, he drew off one glove and pressed a hand to his cheek. It felt warm and greasy, the deep gouges in his nose full of fire.

Maybe it'd scar. Wouldn't that just suit his father? If Blase found him before his face healed, he'd get one good look at something really ugly.

At Trev's feet, the Dutch cat curled into a wide-eyed ball.

Yukio climbed back onto his feet. "What'd you do, throw a rock into the middle of the nest? You're supposed to hit the entrances!"

"You never said so." Now he could look around. An icy breeze fluttered the fur on the limp little cat near his feet. Between him and the boulders were four more of them. "What do we do now? How long will they be out?"

"'Bout forty-five minutes. Get the sacks. I checked the nest and threw a trank bomb in—the mommies and the littlest kits we want are in there."

"What's wrong with these?" Besides the fact that they tried to kill him!

"Too old. There should be some barely weanables in the nest, and they'll suit us better." Yukio wrinkled his nose. "You look pathetic. Can you walk?"

"Oh yeah." Trev took an exploratory run at the boulder pile. Nothing felt broken, but he did visit the first-aid kit before doing anything about bagging cats. He smeared greasy salve onto his cheek, nose, leg, and the back of his head, where his hand came away streaked with blood.

Then he clambered into the rocks, taking the shortest route up and over the rough surface. Again, the eerie sense that no other human hands or feet ever touched this stone thrilled him.

Yukio knelt down in a hollow, near a furry pile that was apricot-blond with occasional black bobtails. "That one." He pointed toward a slender creature, smaller than the ones that had attacked Trev. "Put him in his own bag."

Trev made sure his gloves were pulled clear to the shoulders before bending toward the kitten. It hung limp when he lifted it onto the bag. He drew heavy browncloth over its body, pulled drawstrings, then slid the clamp tight. Hefting it, he guessed the kitten weighed four or five kilos.

"They're not very big." He joined Yukio. "You sure these are mature enough to take from their momma?"

"And feed them yabuts? Yeah, they'll make it. That one, and her, and her. They could go in together, but that'll make a heavy load. Give me the male."

"Huh? Oh." As he handed over the small sack, a weird thought struck him. These fierce babies were *cute*. Did their mommas think so?

Did *his* momma ever think he was cute? He'd seen pictures of her, but he didn't remember her. Not at all.

Clenching his teeth against a sudden urge to cry, he bundled the females, two in one bag and one in the third. Then he hesitated. "Can, uh, these kitties be tamed?"

Yukio looked up. "Only if you get them so young they still need milk, and they can draw a lot of blood looking for it. I wouldn't try it."

"I would. Find me one."

Yukio stared him up and down. "You're bleeding crazy."

"Yeah. Find me one."

With one foot Yukio flipped a large mother cat, exposing three kittens. "Take your pick. But get a male. They're surplus out here."

Trev reached for the smallest. "You, runt. C'mere." The kit didn't put up any fight as he placed it in a bag.

"Starve it for a day or two," Yukio advised him. "It'll be glad to see you then, if ever. I'll take this little guy. You take the females."

Trev balanced the bagged females over his shoulders. Yukio dangled the two smaller sacks, and they both hobbled toward the aircraft.

"Easy ride, girls," Trev told his own burden. "You're heading for the cold country."

Down here out of the wind, it felt warmer than at Axis. When he bent his arms, the parka folds didn't feel frozen. His right leg was getting stiff, though. He laid his bags in the Mathis's rear compartment and then re-opened the first-aid kit. From a bottle labeled Sulfas, he shook out a horse pill and gagged it down.

"What are you doing that for?" Yukio asked.

Trev choked once more, swallowed, and got the pill unstuck from his esophagus. "I've been handling animals, and I could have brought some-thing along on my skin. I work for Micro, you know." He opened another bottle and popped two pain-killer caps.

"Yeah. You've spent too much time on the Micro floor with the crazy people. Latch that grate. The big ones aren't supposed to wake up, but . . ."

"Yeah. But. Should we bag some more while these are asleep?"

"Mmm, no. Too territorial for more than one male at a release point, and three females to one male is the optimal breeding ratio."

"Sounds good to me," Trev said. Yukio snorted agreement. Trev man-aged the lock, then plunked down in the pilot's seat and took a deliberately slow breath. So this was frontier life. He couldn't remember feeling this excited, alert, and alive. "Leaving the rest of the nest asleep's okay?"

"I do know what I'm doing." Yukio stowed his crutches beside his seat. "How do you feel?"

Every claw mark burned. "Like I took a bath with three Veneran eels. Let's finish and get home."

He started the engines and took off.

Half an hour later, Yukio asked, "So what's Venera like?"

Gripping the Mathis's yoke, Trev stretched his shoulders. The pain pills had taken effect, and really, he probably shouldn't be piloting. "You don't have to call it Venera for my sake," he said. "Warmer. More plants, but we have to irrigate. Most of it, between domes, is desert or scummy ocean."

"Home sweet dome?"

Trev grunted. He'd heard that joke too many times.

"You descended from settlers, then?" Yukio raised one eyebrow, a smile beginning in the set of his mouth.

"No," Trev said shortly, and reality crashed back down on him. He eyed the Lwuite youth, wondering how much he should say. "My old man has too much money. I grew up in a guarded compound on a hilltop. Lots of water, plenty to eat, and nothing to do except watch the old man's vidis."

"Huh," Yukio said as they passed over a series of low buff-colored hills. "Sympathies, I guess. You obviously didn't want to stay."

"Right." Smoke rose from a hill off on Trev's left. "What's that, a baby volcano?"

Yukio stared. "Probably prospectors. We sent out a few less sociable souls, mapping and looking for valuable minerals."

Prospectors! He didn't expect them to look this obvious. Hastily he checked the location, noting it on the map panel. "And beyond? Is that Center's haze out there?"

"Probably just dust. Center's a small settlement."

"How come?"

Yukio shrugged. "We picked up a few Einsteinians before the crossing who wanted to settle Goddard but really didn't belong to our group. Adventurers, mostly. That's what the Colonial Affairs people call them, anyway. Nearly all the outsiders live at Center. Except Gaea staff, of course."

Another tempting possibility!

On second thought, that might be the first place Blase would look. "Your people let them come?"

"Gaea needed twenty thousand."

"Huh. DalLierx makes it sound like extra bodies aren't welcome."

"Oh, they have their place. There's room for other colonies on this world. Whole countries, really. Some day."

He tried to imagine Goddard broken up into petty little countries, like war-torn old Earth. "What gives DalLierx authority, anyway?"

"Election, of course. He's only in charge at Axis, not the whole colony." Yukio rubbed the back of his neck. "You don't like him, do you?"

Whoops. Did he say too much again? "I don't know him. Not really."

"Well, I don't like him. He's always asking for extra projects in our spare time. Okay, correct your course half a degree east."

By the time Yukio directed him to Lower Infinity, which was a double crater with rims that touched, four distinct voices yowled in the rear compartment, scarcely pausing for breath. Blase could use them for backup harmony.

Yukio glanced backward.

"What do we do?" Trev asked. "Drop the sacks, slit 'em, and run?"

Yukio grinned, showing lots of teeth. "You'll see."

Incongruous metal fences guarded the craters' rims, forming a compound of several hectares. The fenced area had been planted. Sticks protruded from the ground inside, leaves fluttering from some. Brown yabuts the size of his Dutch cats scattered like roaches as he swooped down to land.

"I assume someone fixed the problems with the fence?" Trev idled the engines.

"Yeah. Stay here." Yukio worked his way toward the plane's tail and opened a hatch. Then, from a shelf, he took down an aerosol can and sprayed all three of the large brown sacks. He slid the squirming cat bags toward the opening, then eased each to the ground. "Right," he said after resealing the hatch and limping back to his seat. "Taxi about a quarter klick away and turn the plane around so we can watch. You'll like this."

As Trev swung the Mathis's nose around, a dust cloud streaked down one edge of the crater. "Over there." He pointed. "What's that?"

"Happens all the time. Little quakes, little rockslides. Clears the crater walls."

He didn't mind that at all, so long as the rocks missed his plane. Once in position, he watched incredulously. Yabuts swarmed the bags, a brown mass writhing and wriggling.

Yukio leaned back and grinned. "They're going to nibble our kitties to freedom. I sprayed the sacks with their favorite flavor. Vegetable puree."

"You rat." Trev grinned, too.

"There's too many cats for us to safely cut them out and too many yabuts here for the plant cover. Once cats eat in a place, they decide it's home."

Trev filed that bit of information at the back of his mind.

"We're doing the yabuts a favor," Yukio added, "thinning down the population. Pretty soon the greens will come back. Everyone will be happy."

"Except the yabuts that get to be kitty food."

"That's life, Trev."

How true. Sometimes you got to eat. Sometimes you got eaten.

One cluster of yabuts scattered like an explosion of fur. A female Dutcher made a dash for freedom, then saw dinner running alongside her. She pounced, tearing joyfully at the creature.

"The trank doesn't hurt their appetite, does it?" Trev's stomach lurched.

Yukio laughed. The second and third female burst their sack. Their chase landed them on top of the male, still a captive in his bag.

"Poor guy." Trev rested his chin on the Mathis's control yoke. "If the females chase all the yabuts away from his sack, it might be a long time before he gets loose."

"Never underestimate a hungry herbivore."

Sure enough, more yabuts swarmed the remaining sack. They looked bigger, with brighter eyes, than the ones in Varberg's experimental-animal cages.

Naturally. They were free.

Both other bags lay almost consumed. "Is that cloth good for them?" Trev asked.

"Not particularly. But it'll go right through."

Out popped the male's little head. Trev snickered. One small he-cat, with three mates and plenty to eat, wouldn't have such a bad life. Its short black tail stood sassily straight up as it pounced on easy prey. "Get 'em, big guy!" Trev yelled, then he glanced back into the cargo compartment. His own cat bag wriggled.

"You're going silly," said Yukio. "Must be those pain-killers. We'd better get back and show you to the HMF."

If the quiet mail alarm in Graysha's bedroom had sounded five minutes later, she would have fallen asleep and missed it.

She rolled off the bed and stepped over to squint at the keyboard on her little desk, under the gathered wall hanging.

+If you're awake, may I talk to you? Lindon DL.+

Graysha blinked. What could he want at this hour? Standing, she typed, +I'm awake. Certainly.+

+Would you meet me at Wastewater?+

This was a surprise. And she had news for him. +I'll be there,+ she answered. +Ten minutes.+

She dressed hastily, ran a brush through her hair, reached for a hair tie, and hesitated. Most men liked loose hair.

And all the Lwuite women braided theirs. With one smooth motion, she rewrapped the tie.

He already had arrived when she reached Wastewater. The air smelled musty after the evening influx of baths taken and toilets flushed. Planetary daylight gleamed on, though by her body clock it was time for sleep. Lindon waited at one end of a raceway, a gleam of sunlight reflecting almost blue in his black hair. Standing with both hands thrust into his pockets, he looked tired.

"Hello," she said, stopping several meters away.

"Graysha. Thank you for coming. I wanted to speak with you privately."

"What can I do for you?" she asked. It was useless to wish they could simply talk frankly, one person to another, representing no one but themselves . . . but she wished it anyway.

Lindon pulled one hand out of a pocket. "You wanted to know about my faith, I think."

"Oh." She caught her mental balance. Was he *really* saying what she thought he was saying? "Oh, well, I don't want to trespass on the RL Act. Your group's privacy is your right."

He looked down, then from side to side. "Ah, there's nowhere to sit, except on the gravel."

"I've sat on gravel before." She matched action to her words and lowered herself onto the walkway.

He made a seat out of the gravel beside her, clasped his hands, and then rested them against his lips.

She held a breath.

"We are not a homogeneously religious people," he said, then paused again.

Her groping hand found a pebbly area smooth enough to lean on. "And you've done something to your genes," she stated. "Please don't tell me about it, because I can't pass on what I don't know, even accidentally. But I am curious as to why people—at this point in time, with all science has discovered and proven—why some people maintain belief systems. I think there's more to the universe than an accidental spray of atoms, but a lot of my colleagues don't."

"If that were all this world is about," he said, "I don't know how I could live." He reached for the breast pocket of his muslin shirt. "The deeper that science—real science, not assumptions—delves, the more mysteries it finds. Or so I'm told. You'd know better than I, I think."

She recalled her family's interminable discussions of unified field theory. "I think you're right."

"Here, take this." He drew out a black text capsule. "The gist of it is that a human born on Earth spoke with all the authority of the universe's creator. This is one of several records of his life, death, and teachings."

This sounded sickeningly familiar. "You're what, a Christian?"

His expression blanked. "Yes."

He couldn't have known she was raised CUF. Boldly, she asked, "All of you?"

"No."

At last a crack appeared in that wall of secrecy, but of all the horrible things, she never expected . . . She frowned, inhaling the room's heavy green scent. "Novia is, too."

He seemed just as shocked, staring back with huge black eyes. "What denomination?"

"Universal Father."

Slowly his head drooped, and he leaned back on both hands. "Oh." His voice sounded sad. "That makes sense. Are you?"

"Once."

"Not any longer?"

"I have to admit, Lindon, that I despise that church."

His eyes regained a bit of their gleam. "Does the word *apostate* mean anything to you?"

She shook her head.

"Never mind, then. Let's just say that I've never considered CUF a Christian denomination."

"They do."

"I know. Would you be willing to take a fresh look at old data for my sake, without bringing any of the CUF's commentaries into consideration? Could you just read the unadulterated text?"

"I work with raw data. I could do that."

"It's John's gospel." As he passed the capsule, their hands touched. "It must've taken courage to leave Novia's church."

"It didn't feel like courage. I simply stopped showing up."

"Breaking faith with your mother—professionally, too—would be a difficult step."

Plainly, he was fishing for information. "Do you really believe I've broken away from her?"

He stared into the cattail marsh. "I don't know," he admitted.

"You have too much at stake to trust someone like me, casually."

"You put that well, Graysha."

She sighed. "I reported to her four times," she said, deciding honesty might win him where subterfuge would fail. "There aren't many cases of genuine homogenegineering."

"Did you follow those reports?"

"The only one that looked serious was the Endedi case."

He sat up straight, crossed his legs, and eyed her. "You gave information on Rebecca Endedi?"

She didn't like the hard alert set to his eyes. "One of her former students enrolled in my lab. The girl drove off half the class with her crazy stories, but some of them were too wild to be fabricated. So I mentioned her to Novia."

He shut his eyes for several seconds. "Endedi was convicted," he said. "It was merely enhancement, trying to breed superior athletes. Six boys had been altered genetically, eight little girls. They were all between the ages of two months and three years. The EB subjected all fourteen of them to full-body irradiation so no clones could ever be made, then isolated them for the rest of their lives from contact with any humans other than their guards. When we left Einstein, one had already died of leukemia. Three others were dying."

Horrified, Graysha tried to moisten her dry mouth. Toddlers . . . mere babies.

"Endedi can't practice medicine again, of course," he added. "She's now a programming assistant at the women's prison in Graham's Reach."

It was hard to care about that, compared with the horrible fate imposed on fourteen innocent children. The only crimes were committed by their parents and a lawbreaking doctor.

"Novia's your mother," he said, staring straight at her with narrowed eyes. "She can pressure you in all kinds of ways. And you must still have some loyalty. I'm sure you love her."

Graysha shook her head, feeling filthy inside. "I didn't have to do it because of her. I was . . . I still am trying to pay off a lawsuit my ex-husband slapped me with. And no, I don't love Novia. Not with any kind of affection, anyway. If only there were some way I could make amends to those children." She fought down a choking sensation and pocketed his text capsule.

He kept staring at the raceway. "You need to know," he said dispassionately, "that Ari MaiJidda wasn't convinced by your gamma-vertol testimony. I can't go into reasons, but there's still a chance you'll be arrested. If you are, though . . ." He reached toward her shoulder but didn't come close to touching it. "It will not be because of what you just told me. I asked her to wait until you can finish your atmospheric research, if she decides to pursue the case. I won't mention Rebecca Endedi—if you don't try to contact your mother."

Graysha felt shattered inside. So much for trying to level with him! "You can't tell me why she thinks I was lying? You gave me gamma-vertol."

He shook his head. "I'm sorry."

If they thought she was an EB nettech . . .

She didn't want to even use the word, in the faint hope they didn't already suspect it. She looked hard at his face. To her surprise, she saw genuine regret in the softly raised set of his eyebrows, something she'd never seen in Ellard. Maybe she was seeing Lindon's keen sense of responsibility, to his people and his faith.

Or was it sympathy? "On that account," she said, "if I'm going to be arrested as soon as I finish, I would take my time with the CFC study. But

I think there's something serious going on in the atmosphere, and I want to see it resolved, and I need to hurry. Whoever's doing this doesn't want to be caught."

Lindon's head turned, and once again, his dark eyes focused on her face. "I appreciate your dedication."

"Good." Graysha drew a deep breath, steadying herself to plunge into even deeper water. "Because I have a solid theory about what's going on."

"You said you would tell me as soon as you—"

"It's only the barest bit of evidence," Graysha explained, "but it's something concrete at last. Dr. Varberg ordered a quantity of chlorofluorocarbons for laboratory use. On the Micro floor, what we use chemicals for is growing organisms that will use them for food."

"Exactly what you suggested before." He crossed his arms. "What do we do?"

"If there's an—" The term that crossed her mind sounded ridiculous, but she decided to use it. It was something a layman would understand. "If there's an atmospheric infection, we have to bring in some of the organisms."

"How?"

"As soon as I can get a proposal through, I hope I'll be able to use a Gaea plane for atmospheric sampling."

He reached over, and this time he rested a hand on her shoulder. "I won't report this to Ari until you tell me to go ahead. The fewer people who know what you're doing, particularly people who plainly don't like you, the less risk you run of this getting back to Varberg and Lee."

To her embarrassment, she wasn't thinking about Ari MaiJidda at all but rather the warmth of that hand on her shoulder. What if the Lwuites weren't gene healers but gene modifiers after all? In that case, Lindon was more—or less—than human in every cell of that hand. For an instant, she had the eerie sensation of touching an alien.

Then more immediate concerns crowded her mind. Whether or not Ari MaiJidda arrested her, her own D-group comrades might lynch her if Lindon spread the word that she reported Rebecca Endedi.

Information flow could be deadly. Both she and Lindon now held the power of life and death over each other. She shivered.

"It's late." He rocked onto his feet and stood. "I don't need the book capsule back anytime soon. Give it a chance. Even as literature, it's a masterpiece. Your mother," he added, "did she encourage you to participate in church activities?"

Please, not Sunday school. Not from him. "Always."

"You resent her."

"Bitterly."

"She stands in need of forgiveness, the same as you or I."

"Not to hear her talk about it."

"I'm sure," he said, glancing skyward, "but she does, whether or not the CUF would agree. Good night, Graysha."

Back at her apartment, Graysha didn't feel like sleeping and didn't want to try. Behind all the mystery surrounding the Lwuites, this. How could Lindon DalLierx share a faith with his mortal enemy, Novia Brady-Phillips? His people denied the perfection of God's creation.

Unless . . . *were* they healers?

Confused, she shut her eyes, remembering a soft touch on her palm and a hand lying on her shoulder. It had been so long, so long.

And it was so late, and she was being so stupid. In Lindon's eyes, Graysha was the worst kind of traitor. Did this chain of accusation and suspicion have no end?

Rubbing down with her warm rough washcloth relaxed her muscles, and then she brushed Emmer. The gribien squirmed, trying to escape. "Stop that," Graysha chided her. "You need this." Her pet's long, nearly flat body contorted once more, and then, to Graysha's surprise, the gribien rolled over and offered her belly.

"Oh, old girl," Graysha murmured, "I'm glad you're here."

She had learned one vital thing in her conversation with Lindon. There was no Lwuite religion. It was a sham after all, a show for the sake of the RL Act. Lindon had volunteered information that might doom them all, showing her that his faith mattered more than any possible charge of wrongdoing.

And in almost the next breath, she told him how deep her treachery ran . . . by his standards. Lindon would never trust her with anything now, no matter what the Lwuites really could offer. What a stupid mistake she'd made, thinking honesty might dispose him to accept her.

She decided she would inquire no further. What she didn't know, the Eugenics Board couldn't learn from her.

She twisted tension out of her back, then clutched her prickly feather pillow. She'd like to read that text capsule, but if God existed, she had a bone to pick with Him.

He didn't play fairly.

She went through the motions of work the next morning but without producing much new data and finally retreated to her computer station. The research proposal was basically finished. She'd started deleting and reinserting the same words and phrases. All she lacked was the nerve to send it down to Melantha Lee. "What do you think?" she asked Trev, who slipped in for his morning instructions. Then she got a good look at him and exclaimed, "What did you do to your face?"

He touched a new mask of bandages that covered his nose and both cheeks. "Cat scratches. I'm okay. Let's see what you wrote." He read a few lines, then shrugged. "You're asking the wrong guy. I—"

Someone rapped on the door behind her. Before she could fully turn around, Will Varberg stood at her other shoulder. "What are you working on?" The big man wore a new fragrance today, something musky with an off-acid contrast.

She might as well get this over with. She let him finish reading.

Atmospheric task force proposal.
Submitter: Graysha Brady-Phillips, Ph.D.
Abstract: It is proposed that current atmospheric cooling experienced on the planet Goddard is due, at least in part, to a thin-air ultraviolet mutation of some organism used in terraforming, a mutation critically dangerous to the future of the Goddard project in that it utilizes chlorofluorocarbons, either C–11 or C–12, as a carbon source. Such an organism might survive suspended in polar stratospheric clouds (PSCs).
Proposal: A high-atmospheric survey shall be undertaken, and all organisms obtained will be inoculated in a chlorine-rich medium. Any organism demonstrating survivability in that environment will then be inoculated into a medium consisting chiefly of chlorofluoro-carbons, to see if the suspect organism exists in fact. . . .

The screen ran on with suggested procedures. Graysha watched them scroll past with mixed feelings of professional satisfaction and personal dread. She'd drafted a solid proposal, but her relationship with Will Varberg was about to change radically. Starting today, she would either work progressively closer to Varberg or establish a professional rivalry.

Or follow Jon Mahera into the soil.

Varberg pushed away and leaned one shoulder against the doorjamb. "Going for the reward, are you?"

Now was the moment. She had to try and enlist his help. "Well, certainly. But the whole floor could work on this. We could share the reward. There would be plenty to go around."

"I don't think I'd publish that." He stared down his nose, shaking his head.

Dread danced at the pit of her stomach. "Why not?"

"I tried something like that once," he said. "My computer picked up a virus that took the techs a week to cure. I'm almost surprised you got that far with this. Don't forget how long that Gaea reward has stood. It's not going to be easy."

She almost mentioned the gibberish that had been made of her files. Her next thought was of Jon Mahera. It silenced her.

"There's nothing wrong with Goddard's atmosphere, Graysha."

What could she say to answer that?

Trev spared her. "Hey. Leave her alone." Trev stood, feet wide apart, ready this time for Varberg's temper. "She knows a lot about this planet."

"I'm only playing with ideas," Graysha put in hastily. She saved the proposal back onto the *Ellard* file, then realized too late she'd just shown Varberg where to find it. "As I understand it, Chairman DalLierx is deeply concerned about the notion of cooling. It's almost an obsession on his part," she added, guessing Varberg's preoccupation with overwarming on Messier might make Lindon's concern seem ridiculous. Humorous, even, if she gave it the right tone of voice.

Varberg didn't laugh, but he backed off a step. "Mmm. And since he's been on our butts all G-year about the cooling, he has suddenly adopted you as his Gaea favorite. Lovely. Keep your nose clean. If you're that short on work, come up to my office. I have all sorts of projects that need attention."

His back disappeared around the hallway corner. "Thanks," she called with a sinking sensation.

It would take him a minute, more or less, to reach his lab, and if he was the culprit, she could kiss the *Ellard* file good-bye.

"What a roach," Trev said, stamping one foot. "What a—"

"Hey," she said briskly, "thanks, Trev, but we've both got to work with him." She eyed the boy's bandaged, lopsided face. "Okay?"

Abruptly she realized she still had not changed her password. Varberg had never shown her how to lock a file on this net, either.

It was publish, then ... now! Or else the idea and the hope would perish.

"Right," Trev said. "I try and help you, and since I don't have a degree—"

The text alarm sounded on her monitor. "Excuse me for a minute, Trev." Graysha lurched toward the screen as Trev slouched out.

A message from the Zoology supervisor appeared. Zoo, it seemed, was pleased with the quality of Trev's work at Lower Infinity Crater. She had no idea what the message meant, but obviously it had to do with his new bandages. She relayed it to Trev. Within seconds, before she could reach for the keyboard again, Will Varberg reappeared.

"What's he doing, taking days off from his assigned work to fiddle around on the other floors?"

He'd keyed his computer to her branch of the Gaea net, all right.

Infuriated by the intrusion, she clenched her hands. "I had no idea Trev was doing anything," she said evenly, "other than his work for me. I wouldn't be surprised if he did it for the scenery. He grew up on a planet. Staying inside probably gets a little old for him."

Varberg *hmmph*ed and left her lab. Anxious for Trev, she listened as Varberg's heavy footsteps clomped back up the hallway.

Angrily, she pulled up the *Ellard* file, copied the proposal, and bracketed it. Three key strokes later, it was on the net and public.

Graysha sat back and exhaled heavily, realizing she was committed now, for better or worse. Melantha Lee would see this as soon as she checked on the station's declared research. That could be anytime during the next week. If Lee wasn't trying to cover something, the notion—logically and hypothetically supported—wouldn't arouse a moment's suspicion.

Proposals like this surfaced all the time, in every hab large enough to support a university with doctoral candidates.

She must have Jirina show her how to change a net password, though. Today.

She was walking back from the break room when Paul poked his head out into the hallway, looking tousled, as if he'd had his head in a lightproof hood. "What is this?" he called in a stage whisper. She stopped near his door. "A new proposal? More work? You need a break. Let's pack lunch from the cafeteria and sunbathe at Wastewater."

Why had Paul spotted the proposal so quickly? The weight of his hand on her shoulder, fingers curled toward her throat, made her as uncomfortable as the proposition itself.

"I shouldn't," she said. "I have so much work to do."

"You'll work better if you relax when you eat. Trust me."

"Well . . ."

"Good. I'll put in a lunch order. You pick it up at the cafeteria and meet me at Wastewater. All right? Good," he finished without waiting for her answer.

He ducked back into his workroom, she into hers. It seemed like too much trouble to refuse.

And now, alone, she dared speculate about what specific chain of events might have set Varberg's submerged fears against Jon Mahera. If Mahera caught Varberg deliberately environment-testing his bacterium, the notion of reward money might have dulled Varberg's conscience.

But the colonists had cleared Varberg.

Was Paul involved in illicit research, too?

She felt almost dizzy. *Dear God, are they all out to silence me?*

And DalLierx, deeply concerned about the cooling trend, had been poisoned. Varberg had access to genetically altered bacteria, including insulin producers, easily and legitimately.

That would explain the dead gribien.

Proof, though: she had no proof of anything but the CFC order. She paused to crack her knuckles, then settled in to read more abstracts.

Communication time between Goddard and Copernicus Habitat, close by in the Eps Eri system, was approximately six minutes. Melantha Lee rarely saw responses to anything published on Goddard until at least a day passed, so she assumed the message on her terminal originated on Goddard until she saw its originator's name. Then she skimmed back upscreen to reread its header.

Gaea Terraforming Consortium
Flora Hauwk, Ph.D., System Supervisor
Roosevelt Settlement, Copernicus
Melantha:
    Am curious regarding Brady-Phillips's research proposal. Do new data suggest a more severe cooling trend?
                                                    Flora Hauwk

Lee frowned at the monitor. What had Graysha Brady-Phillips published that caught the new system supe's eye? She punched up current research, read the new abstract carefully, then read it again.

This, she decided, must be answered immediately. She reached for her keyboard.

Dr. Hauwk:

No new evidence of cooling, simply a new theory. Brady-Phillips hopes to explain the minimal cooling we do experience. She is inexperienced at on-site terraforming. We're letting her try this as a learning experience.

Melantha

P.S. Welcome to Eps Eri system.

That, she hoped, would keep Dr. Flora's long nose out of the issue long enough for Lee to ensure that Graysha's research failed. Melantha had worked with the woman, years ago. She liked to snoop and throw her weight around.

So she'd have to deal with Graysha quietly.

Trev lifted the frond of a delicate fern and ran a finger up its underside. Covered with tiny bumps, it looked infested with some kind of insect. His hand stung. Searching for food, Dutchy had pounced hard. According to Yukio, it would be okay to offer a bottle tomorrow. Trev hoped so. Maybe the kitten wasn't desperate yet, but he was.

"Ari," he called, "is this one all right?"

Laying down a compact handheld sprayer, the tall Vice-Chair crossed her damp dugout and eyed the frond. "Yes, it's all right." She laughed. "That's where it grows its spores. I was only able to bring my collection because of the minimal weight of propagation cells."

"Ferns don't have flowers, then."

"That's correct." Her sensual mouth looked solemn, but her eyes seemed to laugh every time she looked at the mess of new bandages half covering his face.

When he frowned at her, one long cut stung sharply. He was starting to hate his father for an entirely new reason. Evidently his education had holes a man could drive a track-truck through.

Ari examined the pot. "You haven't fed this one."

He couldn't believe the way she spotted tiny grains of fertilizer. "Not yet."

She set the plant back in its spot and returned to her frond misting.

Was this a good time to ask her how a person might put in for a transfer to live at Center, with other non-Lwuite immigrants?

No, she wanted him under her eyes. She might report him to DalLierx for asking about Center, and he didn't want to get Yukio in trouble.

Still, he couldn't wait too long. He needed to make a move.

A few minutes later, she spoke while she continued to work her way down the row. "Rumor has it you've no love for our CCA."

Where did she hear that? Did Yukio report him? "DalLierx," he answered, "treated me like a retarded criminal. At least I thought so at the time. He's—"

"He's a self-righteous prig. Any suggestions you can give me on how to beat him in the election?"

Oh, the election. He'd forgotten these people had their own pressing concerns. He dug his spoon into the beaker of plant food. "Graysha Brady-Phillips would be the one to talk to about that. She's spoken with him more recently than I have."

The rhythm of Ari's spraying faltered, then resumed. "Oh?"

"Yeah." He sprinkled crystals onto the potting medium. "She's sweeting a little bit on him, I think. And she's commented about religion a couple of times. Something she's nosy about, I guess. I know how to respect the RL Act."

"Keep it that way," she said softly. "What else can you tell me about Dr. Brady-Phillips and Chairman DalLierx?"

He couldn't see around the freestanding shelf, but he heard her stop working while he answered. "Well, when he's on screen during town meetings, she *watches*."

"Oh?"

"She's been married. You know how divorcées get sometimes. Desperate. DalLierx is pretty, but so's Paul Ilizarov."

"Now, that's an interesting observation."

"And she told me she met his sister, trained with her, at your D-group."

"Yes, I saw that. I'm surprised she made the connection, but perhaps I shouldn't be."

Ari set down her sprayer with a thump and walked to the end of the row, close to where he stood. Browncloth lost some of its wrinkles in this humidity, he noted. Her lightweight off-duty clothes suited that long, well-curved body. She smiled, but it looked predatory, not kindly. "I like you, Trev. You're the most honest person I've met on Goddard. We need to water that fertilizer in. Then, if you have time before lunch, I'd like to show you my other hobby."

"Other hobby?" How was he going to escape this woman and get out to Center or into the wild?

She ran the back of her hand down his arm and finished the caress at his fingertips. "I dance. I hope you didn't know that. It's my darkest professional secret."

On the other hand, he had a weakness for deep-voiced women. "Oh?" He cleared a catch out of his throat. "Well, I sing. Sometimes. People say I sound a little like Blase."

"I'd love to hear you."

An hour later, Ari ladled a measure of water into her steam shower's intake port, then pressed a button and leaned against her wall to let the water heat.

It had seemed only sensible to consolidate her hold on Trev LZalle in the quickest, most effective way. She'd guessed he would fall to a blatant come-on. He was old enough to appreciate beauty but too callow for caution.

Besides, she'd found out he really could sing, with sublime expressiveness and an incredible range.

A high-pitched whistle told her the steam bath was ready. Quickly she slipped through the door and shut it firmly behind her.

LZalle, Brady-Phillips, DalLierx: she couldn't afford to let any one of them go unwatched. DalLierx was a fool to hope Graysha Brady-Phillips didn't report to her mother. Thwarted in her attempt to send information offworld through personal mail, she plainly published that proposal, now on its way outsystem, as a message to Novia's spies. Couched in scientific doublespeak, there could be any number of prearranged keywords.

One round to you, Brady-Phillips.

It would take time, though, for other nettechs to arrive. Ari would up D-group readiness. She must ensure Graysha learned nothing more and that she did not report again. Now Ari had Trev on watch.

The little he'd said was cause for alarm. If Graysha was inquiring about religion, she was probably on the track of deeper secrets. Dul Lierx, Ari knew, would sacrifice group security for one clear chance to influence an immortal soul. That was a poor bargain for the rest of Goddard.

Ari frowned as she reached for shampoo. Lwuites did need a unifying faith. Her own fledgling progressive ideology fit Henri and Palila Lwu's original writings well enough. Separated from other people groups, they might be able to gradually drop away religious pretense. Eventually, once D-group had enough muscle to guard this world, they might declare themselves openly. One day, when Lwuite life-spans stretched to millennia, she hoped to be remembered as a spiritual guide of the immortal race during its infancy. It was her hope—her dream—to release Goddard's next generation from all the old combative faiths.

She would make up the new religion as she went along. Converts would flock to Goddard as to the fountain of youth.

With the exception of a few truly religious men and women, most colonists would be glad to have an on-file faith to be "discovered" by inquirers. That would be a relief after all this head turning and mouth shutting.

Gathering threads from all religions would help ease the transition for all but a few diehards, whose children would be raised in crèches anyway.

One generation of crèche indoctrination would finish the job.

After her bath, she called up her ideology file and spent an hour refining a loyalty precept. She would introduce it as part of her election platform. When group security was compromised, consequences must be serious.

Brady-Phillips had to be stopped.

It had to be done soon, and it must look like an accident.

Ari's mother had called it "the prophet's prerogative."

Graysha almost decided not to meet Paul at lunchtime, but she just wasn't comfortable doing a no-show. She unwrapped the cafeteria's lunch parcel beside the settling marsh. Paul sat close by, lounging as comfortably on pebbled concrete as he would lie on a bed. That, at any rate, was the image his languid posture projected. "Soy spread?" she asked, handing him a sandwich. "And greens. Good idea."

"Too bad we don't have any ripe tomatoes."

"You checked?"

"Of course," he said.

In fading Windsday sunlight through shielded roof panels, cattails swayed in the ventilator's breeze. "You could almost imagine yourself in a park," she said. "Will you be returning to Einstein someday?"

"Difficult to say. It's been pleasant working with real oceans. I might be so bold as to make the pilgrimage back to Earth for my next stint."

Graysha swallowed, then said, "I don't know where I'll go. I meant to teach at Halley, and if I last the triannum here, I'll probably reapply for a university position. I'll have to wait and see where there's an opening. But that's three terrannums away. Do you think you might settle on Earth?"

"I'm not a settler."

No, he wasn't. He was a free spirit if ever she met one.

"So tell me." He dug into the box for one greens tray, popped its lid, and squeezed on reddish vinegary-smelling liquid. "What will the logistics of your proposal entail?"

How much could she tell him? She considered, thought twice, then three times. "Well," she said, "I'll need a sampling aircraft and someone to man it. Trev, probably—"

Paul raised one eyebrow. "The way I hear it from colonial sources, you think there's been environmental sabotage—by one of us."

But she told no one! No one but Trev—and Lindon, who certainly didn't socialize with Paul. "Colonial sources?" she asked, feeling stupid.

"Mmm."

She ate silently, not wanting to pressure him. Water trickled over pebbles close by. A water bug bobbed past, then dove under the surface.

"Finished?" Paul nested his cafeteria boxes.

"Almost," she said, tipping her own box to show him that half her greens remained.

"If you hurry, we have time for dessert." He eased closer and rested a hand on her thigh. Catching a whiff of citrus, she felt the old longing press down inside her heart and body.

"I don't think dessert is on my diet," she said, staring at the greens.

"But you need it. Here." He took the salad away from her and laid it on the walkway. "Only a nibble. Main course when you're ready, but you ought not to say no when you haven't tasted."

"Stop it." She scrambled to her feet. "Stop condescending to me. Please."

"You've changed." He arched one eyebrow and clasped his hands around one knee. "From that, I assume you have an eye elsewhere. Dal-Lierx, as I hear?"

Did Jirina tell him? It didn't matter. If she gave him a millimeter, she'd end up stuck on the old familiar path of scorn and conciliation. She held her tongue.

"Go find your dessert in the refrigerator with the rest of the dead and dying, then." He waved one hand toward the door. "Go on. Go."

"Hey," she said, "when you set up this lunch, you didn't even give me the chance to say no politely."

His eyes flared. "I'm so sorry. What did you bother coming down for, then?"

"Because I thought it would be rude to simply not show up." She spun on one foot and stalked toward the door.

"Graysha."

She turned. He was crumpling lunch cartons between strong hands. "About that proposal of yours?"

"Yes?"

He dropped a carton onto the path. "Watch your back."

23. TRIDENT

Lindon sat up on his bed, disoriented and unsure what had wakened him. Fading westerly sunshine streamed through the skylight, and his eyes ached. He hadn't slept nearly enough.

"Mr. DalLierx," repeated an urgent voice.

He rolled toward his bedside intercom. "Yes?"

"We need you on duty as quickly as possible. It's an emergency."

Lindon checked the time. It was almost midnight. "Keep talking," he said, "I'm getting dressed. What kind of emergency?" He'd laid out a clean shirt next to yesterday's pants. He yanked them both on.

"Volcanic." The gruff voice wobbled. "I'm in the Gaea building. It's Thad Urbansky, Geology."

Lindon fastened his pants. Poking his head through the neck of a pull-over, he asked, "Where's it going off?"

"Sixty K northeast, along the Storm Sea pipeline. I'm getting either one huge or several small hot spots on satellite and seismic triangulation."

Seizing shoes and socks, Lindon dashed out.

In the bright, eerily quiet CA building, he swung into his office, dropped his shoes, and went on audi line. "Urbansky, DalLierx here. What do you have?" He pushed one toe into a shoe.

"Nothing I didn't have before," said Urbansky. "This is insane. We had no seismic warning at all, not even a wobble in the magnetic field. Can you see out to the northeast?"

Lindon jabbed the polarization control for the nearest window. A plume of ugly gray cloud billowed past Axis in the northerly wind. He started activating alarms to bring in the rest of the CA committee and its office staff.

Two terrannums ago, they had lived under concern that the removal of overburden might liquefy rock under Axis Crater. They had expected it to happen sooner than this if it was going to take place, and people had slowly relaxed.

Office staff arrived before the other CA Committee members. For white-faced personnel, he reviewed procedure. "We're not evacuating yet, but this is a full evacuation watch. Track-trucks ready to go within ten minutes. Port Arbor is out of the question—the activity's in that direction. Send some northwest to Hannes Prime, some west to Center. Anyone unable to get on a truck should head southwest on the wild with emergency supplies and await pickup. The children will go first, supervised by crèche parents. But before that happens, we have to know if a single volcanic vent has opened, or more. Also precisely where they lie and the severity of the activity." He shifted on one bare foot. "Evacuation orders, if they come, will come from this office."

Once the staff filed out, he opened a line to the airfield to request a pilot. To his surprise, one copter was already off the plantation. Checked out to—could this be right?—Trev LZalle. "Controller?" he asked. "Is anyone on duty?"

On the line he heard footsteps, then: "Tate here. What's that smoke?"

Trev tossed another pirated halfer leg bone, then watched with delight as all four of Dutchy's fat little cousins pounced at once. Three tugged it one way as the other chased, jumping and growling. He guessed he shouldn't try to tame the creatures—and they looked plump enough!—but Dutchy had refused the bottle when Trev finally offered it, and he had to feed *some* animal *some*thing.

This early on Dropoff it still was light—barely. The sun hung low, almost at the horizon. He'd have to head back soon.

Lower Infinity Crater's norther tore at his parka. He adjusted his goggles, which was tricky in long gauntleted gloves. He'd love to stroke all that coarse blond fur. Would they attack if he tried? Surely they weren't hungry anymore.

Maybe next time. Meanwhile, Dutchy needed Pops. He pivoted on one foot and started to walk south, back to the Mathis hovercopter. The odd gray cloud he'd noticed fifteen minutes ago on the horizon looked bigger. Had to be his imagination.

Ever since it snowed, he'd seen nothing fatter in the sky than a Veneran mare's tail, but that looked like the granddaddy of all storms. He'd intended to return to the spot where he and Yukio saw the prospector's smoke before he went to bed tonight, but maybe he'd better get the copter back to Axis before bad weather grounded him. He broke into a run.

The cockpit radio chattered as he yanked open the hatch. ". . . please respond, Trevarre LZalle." Three seconds of silence. "This is an emergency, please respond, Trevarre LZalle."

Without pausing to shut himself in, he jumped onto the seat and shouted, "I'm here."

"This is Axis ground control. LZalle, we have a volcanic event under way near Axis Plantation. Two recon pilots are getting ready to take off, but we have you triangulated close by. Would you do a flyby before it gets dark? Repeat, would you do a flyby?"

Then that was no storm. He stared out the hovercopter's windshield. He wasn't as familiar with this model as with the Mathis twin-engine, but this was a chance to insinuate himself into the colonists' good graces in the biggest possible way. "Yeah," he snapped. "Hang on while I shut the hatch."

Eps Eri shone red near the right-hand horizon, sinking lower into a close purple haze. For him to see those clouds at all, they must be incredibly high or incredibly close.

Three minutes later, he crested the sandhills between Lower Infinity Crater and the billowing cloud. "Yyah," he shouted into the microphone pickup, "I can see two, three vents in a line. Hardly any lava, just smoke blowing away from me—no, wait, the left-hand one's spraying red at the base."

"Confirm, left-hand vent shows lava activity, others throwing ash. Is that the east vent, LZalle?"

"Yeah. The farthest vent from Axis."

"Can you estimate their distance, one from the others?"

"Uh . . . " There ought to be instruments for that on his panel. "Gahh, I don't remember how."

"Touch the control that says Triangulation." That was a new voice. "Then sweep both points with your cabin mouse."

Trev found Triangulation, then the onboard computer's small remote. "Yeah. Uh . . . sixty klicks from me, and it's nine klicks between the eastern vents and twelve on the right."

"Confirm." The distant voices conferred, then the first spoke again. "Don't get too close. Be sure and stay out of those ash clouds. We can see them from the CA building."

Lightning snapped from one gray cumulus swirl, striking a small crater's rim. Trev leaned hard on the stick. "No problem with that order."

"Do you have a camera control below your throttle?" That was voice two again.

Trev checked at his instrument board. "Confirm that."

"Switch it on. You've got an anxious audience in the CA and Gaea buildings."

He activated it, then swung the copter back toward the three vents, fighting the norther to hover steadily. "You're not going to believe this, people. The hills closest to the vents are melting!"

"Yes, we do," said a gruff new voice. "Water's bound up in surface regolith all over this planet. Mudflow is the first thing we expect. Good pictures. How's your fuel?"

His hands were starting to shake. "Half up."

A woman's voice, warm and deep, asked, "Can you see the Storm Sea pipeline from there? It's not coming through on your pictures."

Trev pushed the controls to gain some altitude. "Is that you, Ari?"

Brief silence, then, "I'm Defense Coordinator, Trev. Civil defense, too."

"Oh." He pushed down a vivid distracting memory. "No, can't see the pipeline."

Evidently Ari turned aside, because her next words were unintelligible at first but got louder as she returned to the mike. ". . . panic about our seawater inflow just yet. Trev, can you remain in the area and let us observe, so long as there's light? We'd like to recall our own pilots to prepare for the possible necessity of evacuation."

Yes! They needed him now. "Sure," he answered, "I'll do it. Just recall *me* if things look dangerous, all right?"

"Certainly," answered the gruff voice.

In the large room outside his office, Lindon stood shoulder to shoulder with other committee officers and stared at pictures relayed from Trev's cameras. Taidje FreeLand had arrived first, his steadiness reassuring. Kenn VandenNeill's square jaw worked as he pursed his lips. Ari MaiJidda scratched her neck.

The sight of those mudflows wrenched his stomach. The triple vent would destroy hectares of painstakingly seeded regolith. For oxygenating organisms to establish an effective worldwide hold, 20 percent of the planet's surface must be inoculated and maintained.

Supply flights might stop for a time, too. Axis Plantation had goods on hand for two G-years, which they hoped might be stretched for five, but that assumption barred sudden catastrophes.

If Axis was evacuated, Gaea's terraforming would grind to a halt. So would Graysha's investigation of the cooling.

Ari MaiJidda touched his shoulder. "Give the word and we'll send the children to Hannes," she muttered. "It will take one call and about ten thousand maxims' worth of fuel."

Bee and Sarai . . . and Crys, with her crèche. Lindon looked at Taidje FreeLand, who nodded.

Lindon swallowed, wishing he had time to squeeze the girls. Sarai would especially need reassurance. "Do it," he said.

She stepped toward a desk.

It couldn't be real. Volcanoes erupted on vidis recorded light-years away and decades ago, and in his history texts: Pompeii, Krakatau, Rainier. Humans had lived in volcanism's shadow for centuries—but not here. Seeing that shadow fall on Axis Plantation made Lindon wonder how they braved it.

A speaker beside the screen crackled, then came the gruff voice he recognized as Thad Urbansky's. "Still nothing in our deep well but rumbles from the active site. If magma were forming under us, we'd have indication."

Kenn VandenNeill sighed loudly.

"Put a twenty-four-hour watch on that," said Lindon.

"Already have."

"Why is this happening?" Lindon asked.

"Several theories. Redistribution of weight on magma reservoirs—by the new oceans—is one possibility. Our attempt to reactivate crustal subduction is another. Neither was predicted to cause volcanism so early on, though. It's highly likely that early volcanism is due to our cratering. Crustal stresses from the splash phase."

Lindon pursed his lips, then said, "Tell me these eruptions will be beneficial in some way. Please."

"It's outgassing volatiles we would've had to bring in from asteroids. Ashfall will also provide soil nutrients."

Graysha's alto voice answered next. "It will also be excellent enrichment for bacteria, what organisms it doesn't heat-kill."

It felt good to hear some optimism in those voices. "Thanks. Dr. Lee, are you on?" Lindon asked.

"I am" came the Gaea head's smokier alto.

"Would you recommend upgrading the evacuation?"

"You might consider sending away nonessential adult personnel, those whom you don't need for life support."

Lindon picked up his pocket memo. Plant and animal production could largely be put on autofeed and self-water, but complications—

calving, lambing, robotic failure—might cruelly decimate the colony's food supply.

He could send away concrete production workers, artisans, light-manufacturing personnel. "Taidje," he said softly, "put a second evac group on alert." He handed over the pocket memo, then nibbled a corner of his lip. Volcanic activity was figured in atmospheric simulations as a cooling factor. Dust clouds increased albedo and prevented sunlight from penetrating to warm the ground.

Why now, he groaned silently, *with CFCs already depleting?* Tons of imported water only increased the possibility of cloud overproduction, and now additional water vapor belched skyward. Taken together, they foretold an icy apocalypse.

Something changed on his screen. LZalle's voice whooped. "Hope you're seeing this, people. What is it?"

A dark flat cloud surged downhill from the central vent and fanned out like water. The hovercopter rose sharply, then tilted to observe again. Urbansky's voice rumbled from the other speaker. "Pyroclastic flow—superheated ash, mixed with steam and other gases. We can be glad we've got crater walls between us and the active zone."

Lindon backed away from the screen. Others elbowed into the place he vacated. He sat down on a desktop and folded forward, hands pressed over his eyes. *Protect us,* he prayed. *Don't let this be the end, already.* He remained hunched over a minute longer, then realized he still had one bare foot.

Melantha Lee sniffed at the message glowing on her screen. How like Flora Hauwk—though she sat sixty degrees across the Eps Eri system—to panic. Hauwk had ordered her to poll Gaea employees immediately and see if they wished to wait out the volcanic event at another orbital locale, such as Copernicus. Had USSC evacuated Earth when Rainier surged down during abnormal wind conditions and took out Seattle?

On the other hand, she was tiring of Goddard's little problems: alarmist colonials, an atmospheric imbalance she was no longer certain could be controlled, and now volcanism.

She drafted a calm, brief reply in her mind, then revised it twice on screen before sending it off.

> Neither immediate nor long-term danger indicated at this point, and we are monitoring no seismic activity beneath us. I shall query other staff regarding possible temporary relocation outside Axis Crater. It might be wise.
>
> Melantha

Hearing the order given to evacuate Lwuite children, Graysha ached for the sundered families, then reconsidered. These children, already living communally, would not be so terrified by separation as nuclear habitant families.

She hopped down off her stool and refilled her coffee cup, half wishing she'd snatched up Emmer when she dashed back to work. Never before had the break room held everyone who worked on the floor yet been so silent. The rancid odor of nervous sweat smelled almost as strong as the coffee. There would be no sleep tonight. Paul's techs had scooted off for their crèche at word to evacuate. Varberg sat brooding in his deep chair, fingers steepled in front of his face, thumb ring catching rays of the overhead light. Paul leaned against a wall, staring into the darkening northeast. Apparently calm, Jirina sat at an auxiliary monitor.

For two days, Graysha had thought of little else but CFCs and the fear Ari's colonists might arrest her. Now this—the realization that Goddard itself was imminently dangerous. "Anyone else for a refill?" she called softly.

Negative grunts. Holding her steaming cup, she ambled over to peer at Jirina. "Don't you ever panic?"

The black woman shrugged. "Heat doesn't bother viruses, and they positively love poison gas. Only puts their host pop down. They just go dormant. My job grinds on."

Behind Graysha, the screen bleeped. Dr. Lee's voice came on. "Attention, floor heads. Please survey your employees. If the adult colonists evacuate Axis Crater, do your employees wish to leave or stay on duty?"

Varberg erupted out of his chair. "Who objects to leaving with the Lwuites?"

Messier . . . He had to be remembering those catastrophic floods. Hastily she prayed this emergency would not trigger his old desperation. She could think of nothing binding her to an empty Axis Crater, and she said so. No one else spoke.

"Fine," Varberg said. He leaned forward. "Lee?"

"Listening."

"Microbiology floor will leave. And can't we get that LZalle kid off the vidi net?"

Staring at Varberg's back, she found she could pity him. How many friends had he left on Messier?

Mentally, she started packing. Three changes of clothes and her few personal belongings wouldn't take much time to throw together.

Ten minutes later, the elevator doors swished open. Dr. Lee stepped off. All the curl was gone from her gray hair.

Varberg wheeled around. "Don't tell me. The other floors voted to stay, so we're staying, too." Graysha saw his right hand tremble.

"No," Lee answered. "Seismology and Meteorology remain on alert. If they see any danger signs, we'll all start to evacuate. Vice-Chair FreeLand is allocating transportation."

The big man's cheeks lost their color. "Wait for danger signs? We can't risk that!"

Melantha Lee dipped her chin, then looked sharply back up at Varberg. "Prevailing northerlies are blowing gas and ashes past us on the east. Don't worry, Will. We're fine. If the winds shift, we'll start loading trucks."

Varberg rocked from one foot to the other, then said, "I'm going back down with you. I want to talk with my wife."

Lee and Varberg strode toward the elevator. Graysha uneasily poured another cup of coffee. She'd learned plenty about volcanism in the past half hour, and now she tried to project her imagination half a kilometer down into bedrock. Long weighted, it had been partially cleared when ejecta blew out of the crater. If unweighted and adequately heated from below, solid rock could melt. Liquefied, it might stay in place, but it also might start to ooze upward.

At any sign of upward channeling, Thad Urbansky—suddenly elevated to supreme importance in the Gaea building—would give the order to evacuate all personnel, livestock, and gene stores. Varberg's concern made sense. How much warning would they have if the ground shifted?

The hand that dropped on her shoulder smelled like lime. "Exciting." Paul's blue eyes sparkled.

Her skin crawled. "For this, we left a safe, warm habitat."

"And won't you have stories to tell your grandchildren?"

Her mind performed a wild four-way skip. Children. Gene-fix. Lindon's dark eyes, apprehensive. Atmospheric cooling. "You tell your grandchildren. At the moment I think I'll do some work. Call me if anything develops or Trev comes in. I want to congratulate him. He really came through."

Paul's hand slid off. "Did he have a choice?"

24. PROBABLE CAUSE

Will Varberg spent that long dark morning in his laboratory, sealing down instruments and setting refrigerators for cold storage. Lee had granted him permission to take his wife, Edie, out of Axis with a track-truck of Lwuite children. A good thing. He was leaving this *world* with or without permission, and Lindon DalLierx—who had sentenced him to spend extra months facing Goddard's intolerable dangers—had been lucky to survive.

He checked his pocket memo. From its place under the packing list, Graysha Brady-Phillips's research proposal peeped at the bottom of his monitor.

He couldn't gibberish this one. He'd moved too slowly, and she'd managed to publish. Yet he had a hunch Graysha would be too busy with three volcanoes to worry about hypothetical organisms. His single freeze-dried atmospheric culture, carefully bonded into one seam of his favorite lab coat, was safe for the present.

Strange how his ethics changed after Mahera's death. He'd barely been able to live with himself for weeks after that accidental miscue. He felt better about it now. He never meant to hurt the man, but in the time it took MaiJidda's ferrets to trace that memo, he'd come to realize everyone died sometime. Mahera's turn would have come sooner or later.

So would DalLierx's.

Despite Graysha's interference, he would be absolved of the CFC matter, too. He'd been subtle, releasing those organisms on a cloud spray. With Melantha Lee's approval—and her 5-percent cut of his salary—he'd inserted a suicide gene onto their DNA. Their growth would peak after two cold seasons, just about now, and then they'd all die off.

He closed his fist, shutting off the pocket memo. Either Brady-Phillips had a brilliant intuitive streak or he missed incriminating data when he purged Mahera's files. "Who's going to watch Graysha?" he'd asked Lee down in her office.

She'd answered with a narrow smile. "Paul owes me 5 percent for keeping secrets, too. Besides, he's been more than willing to watch her. I can't imagine that will change."

The knowledge she was also blackmailing Ilizarov didn't surprise or bother him. He just wished he could figure out a way to be clear of this mess.

If only Graysha had waited just two more months to start investigating, there would have been nothing to find. His suicide gene would've destroyed all the wild-released bacteria, Goddard's warming would have resumed, and he could've left Goddard with a guaranteed early retirement.

For Edie's sake, he would try to stay invisible until they got offworld. After all, he had created the means by which the Messier disaster could be prevented from ever recurring. It was a breakthrough of heroic magnitude, and Lee promised the whole floor would benefit—all but Graysha, whose official connections were too delicate to bring her inside. Maybe now he could sleep without being tormented by survivor guilt.

He shut his eyes. Rivers of dark mud flowed across his vision, then catastrophic walls of water. Haggard forms huddled together on Messier's high ground, some unmoving. Children cried for food. Adults longed to sleep.

It could erode a man's sanity.

Dday, Dropoff, settled in. The first wave of track-trucks rumbled off into dark distance, then the colony went on alternating watches. To Ari MaiJidda's amusement, Melantha Lee changed her mind and authorized expenditure of Gaea funds for additional auxiliary fuel so individual Gaea employees could depart on a second evacuation convoy if they chose. Barring catastrophe, that group would leave early Aday morning for Center.

Ari double-checked Brady-Phillips's schedule on her apartment console. The woman had checked out for the first sleep shift as evacuating Gaea employees prepared to travel. This could be Ari's last chance.

She shook two sleep-replacer capsules from her nearly empty vial. Clutching one capsule, she swallowed the other and lay down on her bed.

Two capsules and two hour-long naps roughly equaled a full night's sleep, and she was willing to live with depressive side effects in order to deal with Brady-Phillips.

When the first trance faded an hour later, she swallowed the second capsule and closed her eyes again.

She woke to deep, gloomy darkness. Refusing to dwell on the futility of her efforts—this profound depression was simply a side effect of the sleep-replacer trance—she dressed, pocketed a pair of gloves, and slipped out into the quiet hallway. Everyone was either working or sleeping. With volcanoes erupting to doom Axis Plantation, it was no hour for casually strolling the corries.

She waved her D-group master key across the apartment's lock. Silently the door slid open.

Doomed, she repeated to herself, eyeing the woman sleeping on the bed. *She has doomed us all.* Brady-Phillips deserved to die.

A dim desktop monitor lit a knotted-rope wall hanging. Ari glanced from that to the sleeping scientist's throat.

It would be easy to outmuscle and strangle the smaller woman, but she couldn't get away with that. On the countertop near that monitor, in a pile of pocket paraphernalia, lay a glucodermic whose existence Ari had suspected ever since that day on the firing range.

She slipped on her gloves, snatched it up, and backed out. Up the corridor in a dark supply closet, she waved on a ceiling light. She laid Graysha's labeled syringe atop a pile of clean linen and pulled a confiscated glass ampule from her breast pocket. A topside rancher had intended to illegally euthanize several sick sows. Brooding, Ari held the glass bubble up to the lamp. That pale, cloudy liquid was death—consummate sleep, the ultimate futility of existence stated fully and finally.

She snapped the glucose ampule from its housing and carefully inserted the other. If the HMF performed an autopsy, its own glucodermic would be implicated as the source of poison.

Even that didn't cheer Ari.

Silently she returned to Graysha's apartment, and she laid the glucodermic back where she found it. She was certain Brady-Phillips would need glucose once she struck out over the wild with evacuating employees. But was that certain enough?

She eyed the body's attitude of sleep. Brady-Phillips lay limp on her stomach, one arm clutching an extra pillow. Her furry creature looked like a stretched-out black hole next to her head.

Should she—could she—try to hit one of Graysha's self-injection points with that glucodermic? That still would make it look like Graysha accidentally poisoned herself.

No, she decided. *I'll be here at Axis and she'll be gone when it happens.*

Maybe it was only a side effect of the sleep-replacer trance, but Ari fled with her heart thumping.

Graysha actually enjoyed reporting to work with Varberg gone. Now she could work on her project in peace. She watched the second convoy roll off, standing at her laboratory window. It irritated her that the Varbergs left when no adult Lwuites, except crèche parents, had gone. Surely Lindon would understand that when Graysha refused a spot in the second convoy she meant it as an atoning gesture. Even Novia might be proud.

Whether or not her efforts won Lindon DalLierx's trust, the cooling issue had become her own. She would not rest until she proved what caused it.

But all Gaea's planes were grounded today. She could do nothing but her reading.

She skimmed abstracts with a vengeance.

In Trev's sleeping room, there barely was room for a bed shoved up against the side where the slanted ceiling hung low. Underneath the bed frame, Trev knelt beside a cage he and Yukio liberated from Zoology. He pulled on one leather glove. That wasn't exactly *his*, either, but Zoology wouldn't miss it for a while. His bandaged face still stung. This time, it was no shallow scratch on his chin. Slices of flesh were gone. He'd considered asking if the IIMF doctors could remove those long gouges.

Then he reconsidered. Those linear scabs were badges of honor. "All right, Dutch," he crooned. "It's Pops. Cage that weasel temper for a while, will you?" Gingerly he lifted the latch. "I've got milk for you. Milk?" When the little weasel cat hissed, he shifted his hand to hold the borrowed bottle by its bottom end, as far from the nipple—and Dutchy—as he could without dropping it. A few drips spilled on the kitten's nose.

The long pink tongue snaked out.

"Nice milk, kitty. Kitty, kitty." He felt like an idiot pitching his voice this high. "Come on, guy." He shoved the nipple inward again.

Dutchy's hissing fit made him drop the bottle.

"You want to starve?" he growled, then plucked up courage again and reached back into the cage. The poor creature really was nearly starved. It had refused food for three days. Trev couldn't remember feeling so terrible. If he hadn't gotten that stupid urge to adopt a pet, little Dutchy would be out there in the wild, gorging contentedly on cat milk.

He shook the bottle so a tiny drop clung to the nipple, then held it close to the kitten's nose. "Kitty, kitty," he sang. The kitten crouched, flattening his ears against that tiny, tawny head.

When the bottle didn't move—when Trev's arm ached and trembled so badly that he had to prop it up with his other hand—the rough pink tongue reappeared. It cleaned the nipple tip. Resisting a powerful longing to shake another drop loose, Trev held still.

After two more licks, the kitten bit down on the nipple. A stream of drops appeared. Trev was beyond caring if Dutchy's cage got milk puddles, but it would've been a groundless worry. A frosted muzzle closed on the nipple. A chain of bubbles started to rise toward his hand, and to Trev's disbelieving joy, little Dutchy started to purr.

"Kitty," he crooned, "good kitty. Good milk. Pops will feed you." He eased his ungloved hand alongside an apricot-blond flank while pulling away slightly with the bottle. Dutchy followed the source of manna. Trev's bare fingers touched wiry fur. Finally!

Instantly, the kitten let go of the nipple and closed sharp teeth on Trev's unprotected hand—but he didn't bite hard enough to draw blood.

"No milk here," Trev said through clenched teeth, holding his hand rock still. "Up here. Look, Dutchy. Up here." He wiggled the bottle temptingly.

Dutchy lunged for the nipple.

Graysha settled in with Jirina to watch the weekly town meeting begin right on schedule in the dark middle of Freezeout afternoon. Ordinary concerns were discussed, and though officers postponed several until the crisis ended, the committee members presented an admirable illusion of normalcy.

Ari MaiJidda glided into the live zone when the scheduled time had nearly passed. "I have a question for the Chair," she said.

Lindon gestured that she should speak.

MaiJidda wore her snug D-group uniform. "In light of the upcoming election," she said, "I would like Chairman DalLierx to explain a comment of his that was reported by Marta CerRetti, a crèche parent. I will quote." She lifted her pocket memo and began to read. "'I've wondered if it might be feasible to discontinue neonatal treatments. I don't see much effect, considering the risks we subject them to.' End of quote."

"Ooh," Jirina said. In Varberg's absence, she'd appropriated the big chair. "He oughtn'ta said that."

"Shh." Graysha perched on a stool, watching Lindon's face. He didn't answer immediately.

MaiJidda looked down at Lindon's table, then aside at one of the operator stations. "Does the Chair recall making that statement last Windsday?" she pressed.

"Vice-Chair MaiJidda makes it sound like an accusation." He slowly folded his hands. "Yes, I said that. I assume we all have considered the possibility. All of us are normal humans, with propensities toward greed, selfishness, and yes, violence. The aggressiveness we're skimming off might be vital for survival now. Our very existence has become a struggle."

"Your faith becomes you." From Ari's fierce grin, Graysha guessed she felt she'd damaged Lindon's chances in the postponed election.

"He's right," Jirina muttered. "For a supposedly gentle group, they sling enough mud."

Lindon was speaking. "Don't I remember your making a similar conjecture at the HMF?"

Ari made fists on the tabletop. "Never."

"Even if we were biologically identical to other humans, we would remain a people," he said. "I have no desire for reintegration, and I have made no statement in favor of the cessation of those neonatal treatments. I raised a question. That is all."

"We don't need questions, Lindon. We need certainties."

Even if those notorious fetal treatments were discontinued, whatever they did to their genes would still set them apart: that, Graysha guessed, was the thrust of Lindon's argument, though both scrupulously avoided the subject of genetics.

"Hoo," Jirina breathed when the set dimmed, "I thought he had re-election sewed up. Now I'm not so sure."

Graysha shook her head. She wasn't sure, either. Why—if he wanted to stay in office—did he admit his doubts?

When daylight broke again, small lava cones showed around the volcanic vents. Still Urbansky sent no warning of impending magma rise. Gaea and the CA building held an audi council, and Graysha listened from the privacy of her lab. As when he was publicly accused, Lindon's voice remained calm when others shouted, accepting correction without showing temper. Admiring him came easily, particularly from this safe distance.

All aircraft were allocated to Geology while daylight lasted. Between conferences, she mapped the three-dimensional circumpolar regions and memorized streptomycete data as groundwork for atmospheric study. The floor was quiet and calm without Varberg around. She urgently wanted to sample his streps bank, but Melantha Lee rode the elevator constantly, even sleeping in her office, and Paul became a friendly nuisance. At least he stopped making suggestive comments and gestures.

When Graysha retreated nightly to the housing wing, sleep eluded her. She read Lindon's book twice straight through. For that man to share the same fundamental faith with her mother seemed unthinkable. Novia's church claimed God vested all humanity with holiness by sending Christ in human flesh. But everywhere Graysha looked in the book, Christ seemed only to say that He—alone—had holy power and authority. And each time she came to the eleventh chapter, one line struck her: " . . . *it is better for you that one man die for the people than that the whole nation perish.*" The words, mightily profound, came from the lips of a villain. If early Christians invented the whole story, wouldn't they have attributed that bit of wisdom to Christ—or at least a disciple?

At least the book kept her mind off her current danger. Even, sometimes, off Lindon. Long prayers for protection became her substitutes for sleep-replacer capsules.

Other Gaea people, and the Lwuites, had had time to realize they faced uncontrollable planetary phenomena. For Graysha, the realization that this was no normal human-friendly environment came a little harder.

Yet plantation life went on. On the third circaday after eruptions began, the ground hadn't melted beneath her. It was time to sample compost, a job previously performed by young Lwuite techs.

Like the halfers, the compost-aging beds smelled less foul than she expected, and the layers of bacterially active material kept her hands warm.

She rested against a concrete post, Lindon's book fresh on her mind. The Jews of occupied Palestine had lived every day under threat of death— by starvation, plague, or the whim of foreign conquerors. Most of human history had passed without assurance of survival . . . for anyone. Recent generations owned a new hope: the reasonable expectation of long, untroubled life. Perhaps that accounted for the general decline of religions.

Long life. Ha. She closed up the black satchel and brushed dirt flakes from her muslin shirt. She really ought to give Lindon's book back, thank him, and avoid seeing him again.

When she spotted him crossing the hub toward her, her cheeks flamed. "How are you?" she asked when they met halfway.

"Good enough." His short-sleeved shirt made his arms look bony, as if he'd lost more weight. Two call bands on his left wrist accentuated the thinness.

"Are you in touch with your daughters?"

"Indirectly. They enjoy camping out. Do you have a minute to talk?" He tilted his head toward a bench.

"Do you?"

"About that long." But when he sat down, stretching out his legs in front of him, he didn't speak right away.

He definitely did not look good. She wondered if he might be skipping meals. According to Novia's pastor, primitive believers sometimes fasted. Was he—?

"Graysha, I need to ask you something that I haven't been able to get Lee to answer. What is Gaea going to do if we evacuate Axis Crater?"

She'd been ordered not to discuss this with any of the colonists. "Dr. Lee," she said carefully, "wants to relieve you of the responsibility for Gaea staff."

"That's no answer."

"I know," she said. "I'm sorry."

He leaned back, exhaling and closing his eyes. Someone hurried out of the HMF, down the shortest hub path, and vanished in the northward corridor.

Once again, her compulsive honesty defeated common sense . . . and Dr. Lee's orders. "Most of the Gaea staff have elected to evacuate when you people do. But some have left already, and we're free to go at any time, as individuals or by full truckloads. The . . . um . . . rest of us will keep things running as best we can, as long as humanly possible."

His eyes opened, showing dark lights. "You aren't staying."

"Actually, I am."

He straightened, facing her, and the concern she saw in his eyes made her want to jump up and cheer. "If the crater starts to infill with magma, you won't have enough warning to get out."

"I don't want to waste time running away when I could be useful." She rocked onto her feet.

"Wait." He reached toward her hand.

This was the time to give back that text capsule, to thrust home the shame in her past and say good-bye, but she'd left his book at home . . . and she couldn't say it.

She slid her sampling satchel's strap down her arm, set the cloth bag on the bench beside her, and remained standing.

"Living like this," he said, looking down at his feet, "each one day as I get to live it, changes my perspective. It's time I apologized for the way I treated you when you arrived."

She never expected that! "I think I forgave you several weeks ago."

"And the Rebecca Endedi children are not your responsibility."

Her throat tightened. "Yes they are. Partially, at least."

"Their parents accepted the risk." He stared across the hub again, and she stared down at him. "What do you think of Goddard now?"

Relaxing, she sat down again. "Frightening," she admitted. "Impressive.

Uncontrolled. But I can visualize it, one day, as a home for humans. You'll never live to see it the way it will be, nor will any of your generation. I'm sorry for you."

"Moses never crossed the Jordan."

She folded her hands and eyed him, daring to smile. "Is that who you'd like to be? Moses?"

He uncrossed and then recrossed his ankles. "In a way," he said at last.

So deep a confession called for her to answer in kind. "I never wanted anything quite so lofty. To teach, to encourage people who need me, who are willing to learn. The satisfaction of bridging the gap between ignorance and learning. But life threw me a curve before I was born. And truly, I hope, I wish, I could have children of my own, but gene-pure, before I'm too old to see them grown. There has to be some way I can make amends for damages I've done."

"Have you read—" he began, but one of his wrist alarms buzzed, cutting him off. Graysha slid away on the bench. He touched the thin band. "Yes?"

A tinny voice said, "Ag Subcommittee wants to harvest all nearly ripe vegetables. Requests staff to get it done."

"I'll be right there." He stood up, brushing wrinkles from the back of his pants, then looked down over his shoulder. "Your goals are every bit as lofty as mine. Please be in touch."

"Yes," she said, "I've read your text capsule. I'd like to keep it awhile if I may. I'm finding things I'd forgotten."

"Of course. Keep it as long as you'd like."

Why had she said that? As he jogged off, she sat staring at the nearest bit of lawn, trying to reconcile this depth of attraction with her first impressions of Lindon. Even when he showed her that reconnaissance vidi, his silences could have meant only attentive observation and the certainty she'd soon be gone.

He hadn't asked about her new research. Either he'd forgotten, with so much on his mind, or he assumed she'd tell him if anything came up.

There was nothing to tell. She pulled her satchel back onto her arm and plodded back to the Gaea building.

Novia passed a hard-copy sheet to the third person in Flora Hauwk's spartan field office. Hauwk sat in the only reclining chair, next to a window she insisted on keeping open. Blase LZalle, ebony-skinned and resplendent in absolute-black fabric, lounged sideways across an office chair. In the course of her career, Novia had dealt with many different kinds of people. She'd never disliked anyone as much as Blase LZalle. If power corrupted, this man was positively rotten with decay.

From the too-black shade of his skin and his flaming red hair to the length of his legs, the shape of his cheek, jaw, and fingernails, everything about him had been altered. He reeked of jasmine perfume. And his demand, that his only child be remanded into his custody for similar cosmetic surgery, capped it all. She'd taken a devil's advocacy stand against him with Flora, insisting the boy was old enough to decline elective surgery and therefore ought not to be bound over. Thus far it successfully delayed the necessity of declaring her Goddard investigation complete. Yesterday, Jambling found all the evidence she needed in Port Arbor's files. All that remained was to obtain physical confirmation. If all went well, Graysha would suffice as a living specimen.

LZalle stroked the vocal enhancer implanted alongside his Adam's apple. As she understood it, he could use the enhancer as an octave doubler or for producing instantaneous harmonics. "That settles it, Hauwk," he said. "I won't rest easy about my investment on that planet with volcanoes popping up *and* atmospheric imbalances. It's time to regroup, rethink, and relieve ourselves of the Goddard project."

"Supervisor Hauwk has limited jurisdiction." Novia clenched her hands in her lap. J. L. Jambling stood beside the office window, a black-haired wraith conveying the impression of not listening. "If Dr. Hauwk feels it necessary to evacuate—"

"The true difficulty," Flora Hauwk interrupted, "is that volcanic activity was not predicted so close to the settled region at this time. Really, Dr. Urbansky's job was supposed to involve mineral exploration. His most exciting work involved sediment samples—to see if Goddard is regularly bombarded from space, or often swaps poles."

Novia rolled her eyes.

"Perhaps Goddard's crust is less stable than we thought," Hauwk said, "more easily fractured by magma upwelling. It could be time to cut our losses. Even Melantha Lee seems to think so, between the lines."

Novia nodded. She'd drawn the same conclusion from Lee's reports.

"I shall contact the home office, requesting permission to cancel the project," Hauwk continued. "That will take some days, you understand. Commissioner, wouldn't evacuation simplify your investigation?"

"Yes," Novia admitted, "though with this crisis underway, illicit medical activity has halted. I would like to wait for more data."

"I thought you had enough data already."

Blase LZalle rested two fingers against the double cleft in his chin. Novia hated that chin, which didn't look even slightly natural. "Good," he said.

Novia directed her answer toward Flora Hauwk. *Stall, stall!* "Yes, I do. Their privacy right can be suspended long enough to obtain chromosomal samples with or without their permission. But I still would like to wait."

"Chromosomal sampling should be easy if they're contained shipboard for an evacuation." Hauwk pointed at LZalle. "Trevarre will have to leave Goddard, too, if the closure order is given. Because he is only eighteen, you may take custody."

LZalle tucked his chin to one side, mocking her. "Why, thank you."

Novia stared at him through narrowed eyes. The poor child wouldn't get a chance to resist. "Supervisor Hauwk, please reconsider. I'll take him if he's unwilling to go with Mr. LZalle. I am all for the rights of parents, but not when those rights infringe on their children's identities. If that boy wants to keep the face he was born with, Mr. LZalle, it is your responsibility as a parent to praise his maturity."

"To despise his cowardice."

"Mr. LZalle—"

The singer sat up squarely in his chair, laying elegant hands on his thighs. "Ha. Commissioner Novia Brady-Phillips, Mrs. Virtue in a blue dress, sitting in your chair"—his voice lowered, becoming wicked and sharp—"and drooling for the chance to sterilize and irradiate fifteen thousand people. You would criticize me for trying to give one son, my own flesh, a decent chance at—"

"I will not sit here and take—"

"Mr. LZalle. Commissioner." Flora Hauwk leaned forward on her desk chair.

"You're the kind of woman who lays down the law and loves it," LZalle continued. "You—"

Furious, Novia barked, "Jambling. Quiet him."

"Just you hold on," LZalle shouted, "you, Mr. Bodyguard. I have no intention of hurting the lady, so relax. Go ahead, Commissioner Brady-Phillips. You think humans are so perfect. So explain to me what gives you the right to go in there and—"

"Humanity, as it evolved under the Creator's hand, is flawed." Novia took a low tone of voice to keep from shrieking. "I'll admit that. We are flawed in the sense that while we have the ability to save ourselves by doing good for others, most of us don't bother to try. We are flawed in the sense that we have the ability to change our physical nature but not yet the wisdom to forestall the dozens of lethal disasters that step could create. We—"

"Are you opposed to artificial eyes, too?" LZalle imitated a pair of eyeglasses by looping both hands in front of his face and peering through them. "How about limb transplants? Wart removal?"

She kept her voice low. "I do not expect you to understand the fundamental difference between constitutional repair and chromosomal alteration. I expect you to dance around it. It is enough that—"

Flora Hauwk raised a hand and calmly said, "The boy should go with his father. Now, both of you—until I hear from Einstein, in order to prevent any difficulty with this defense group Dr. Lee reports and Mr. Jambling confirms—please avoid mentioning my decision to anyone outside this room. Mr. Jambling, that goes for you, as well. Novia, can you continue your investigation from here for the time being?"

LZalle leaned back and sneered, as if he'd enjoyed baiting her.

"Yes, Dr. Hauwk." Novia regained her most dignified tone of voice. "Mr. LZalle, I'll forgive your ill-informed accusations if—"

"You know what the old faiths call you people, don't you?" LZalle grinned and spoke the hideous word. "Apostate. Even evil incarnate, claiming to speak for God—"

Novia flew up out of her chair, abandoning all hope of dignity. "Call me tomorrow, Flora," she cried. She wanted to strike the man. Shoulders aching with the effort of resisting the urge, she strode out.

"Hey, Teach, Zoology wants me to do another predator redistribution. Can I have Windsday morning off?"

Trev's bandage mask was missing today, and the long slash marks across his stubby nose and blotched cheeks had scabbed over. Beyond Graysha's northeast window, the billowing gray ash cloud had become part of the landscape after eight days of steady eruption. The sun stood high in the sky, surrounded by a ruby corona. "Bishop's ring," someone in Meteorology had called it. The high tension that followed the original evacuation order no longer affected work in the Gaea building. Among those who remained, life went on. The microbes multiplied, and still all the planes were allocated.

Graysha had just learned that she needed medical clearance for high-altitude flight, anyway. "Go ahead." She washed her hands thoroughly at the counter sink. "But I may want you to help me do some atmospheric sampling near one of the poles, and I'm your priority employer. Are you going with Yukio again?"

One hand pocketed, Trev leaned against the door arch and scratched his scalp through unruly black hair. "Yeah."

"I think you're starting to care about the Lwuites and their planet," she said.

"Nah, I don't think so. Maybe I'm beginning to understand all that self-respect stuff. Maybe I like the way I feel when things get dangerous and I cope."

Good for you, Trev. But instead of commending him, she nodded and said, "Drive carefully."

"It didn't take long before."

Early the next morning, Trev found Yukio in the fourth-floor break room. "Ready to go check those smokers from the air?" Yukio called.

"Yeah. First. Then we can go kitty hunting again. Going to let me use the trank gun this time?"

Yukio rinsed out his coffee mug and replaced it on a shelf. "Maybe."

Trev boarded the elevator. Really, it wasn't predators he had on his mind, nor simply self-respect. It was survival—his own, and the colony's.

"Got the coordinates?" Yukio murmured once the door slid shut.

Silently Trev touched his pocket memo.

He would visit Lower Infinity Crater if there was time, but finding one of those prospectors mattered more today. Yukio was being real decent about taking a look. They planned to drop out of Axis's audi net and sweep the area with infrared to find the cabin—if one existed—and make contact. If Blase did arrive, it would be a good place to run. As for volcanoes, he and Yukio had seen them closer than any of these people. The smokers no longer frightened him.

Airborne, Yukio steered for the cloud. Green streaks crossed the landscape below, promising springtime. "Doesn't look all that much colder down there," Trev observed. "What's all the fuss about?"

"Short year. We're almost to equinox. Summer will come, ash or no ash. It's next winter that worries me."

Flying over a shallow rocky lake, he spotted a section of the upland wild seeded with something—clover, maybe?—that was actually blooming through thin gray dust. Channels dug from the mudflow area settled out water, though ice ringed the lake.

Trev leaned the top of his head against the glass bubble. There, below, was another seeded patch gone green. From its medium-dark shade, he thought he recognized cold-kudzu.

Yes, he could live here. No scummy poisonous lakes. No claustrophoboid domes or habitats.

Once they performed their official geology overflight, Yukio set course south, overtly toward the Dutch cats' breeding area. Trev fingered his mustache carefully, avoiding scabs. Twenty klicks north of where they first spotted the prospectors' smoke, he unclipped audi and tracer controls from the panel. They were supposed to be fail-safe.

But this kid had been raised with electronics by people who liked to kludge. Brandishing a scalpel blade he'd liberated from Graysha's lab, he studied the circuit board, then carefully inserted the blade. "Long as I leave that there," he explained as Yukio peered at his work, "we're out of contact. Soon as I pull it out, contact again. That simple. It's not actually breaking any circuit. It's creating a field and diverting current."

Yukio pursed his lips and raised both eyebrows. "Not bad. Whoops." He lunged for the control yoke.

"Can't you get more speed out of this thing?" Trev asked several minutes later.

"In case you hadn't noticed, we have a head wind." Yukio clenched the control yoke.

Trev waved one hand from side to side. "I'd notice from all the trees blowing around, maybe?"

Yukio didn't answer.

Their locator dot eased along the plane's small onboard map. Flying almost due south under audi silence, they nearly reached the map coordinates before he saw that thread of smoke from a prospector's cabin: 2.15 degrees south of the equator, 4.7 degrees west of Axis meridian. With Yukio along, he figured he'd stand less chance of being run off just because of sheer ugliness.

He was switching on infrared when the plane's ground speed shot up so abruptly that Trev felt as if he'd seen a vidi go into hypermotion. "Wind die?"

"Uh-huh." Yukio banked to the right. "See anything down there?" he asked as the craft veered sharply.

Trev visually raked the boulders for evidence of human activity. "No, but—Yuke, what's that?"

A cloud wall, white above and gray beneath, stretched across the northern horizon. Yukio's ruddy cheeks went pale. "Get your knife out of that circuit."

Trev yanked it free. From the long-silent speaker, grumbles of static filled the cabin.

"This is Foxtrot Alpha two-six-three," Yukio said sharply. "Axis airfield. Come in, Axis."

More static.

"Atmospheric interference," Trev said, realizing it was not useful information.

Yukio performed the triangulation maneuver. "It's coming on too fast. We can't get home around it."

Trev didn't like the panicky note in Yukio's voice. "Okay. Calm down. We'll put her down. We've got time. Yukio, we've got plenty of time. Don't lose that much . . . Pull up!" Trev lunged for the control yoke.

Yukio slapped him away. "There's a good spot right under us. I'm going to circle back for it if you'll get your greasy hands off my yoke."

He was coming down too quickly, losing too much altitude without shedding airspeed, clutching the yoke and banking hard left. The cloud was closer than it had been a minute ago.

And so was the ground. "Yyah," Trev muttered, grabbing for his ankles. Who was going to feed Dutchy if he didn't make it back?

As Trev wedged his head between his knees, Yukio shouted, "Hang on!"

Graysha spent that afternoon at her computer, filling out forms to requisition a sampling hovercopter. Just before four o'clock, her screen came alive.

+Heavy snow mixed with nonlethal ashfall predicted within the hour. Recommend suspension of aboveground activities.+

Hmm, she thought. It was Windsday, after all. Sounded like a mud storm coming in.

The message faded, then a second one appeared, this one personal. Dr. Lee had diverted her request to the HMF for high-altitude clearance.

Either Lee was worried she might have an attack at that altitude or this was more interference. Delay after delay, and still Goddard cooled.

She checked her wincubator cultures, made notes, and recorded requests to Will Varberg, asking him to try creating drought-resistant specimens of two strains as soon as he returned.

Trev ought to be back soon.

Trev blinked. What was he doing lying on his side clutching his ankles?

They'd been dropping too fast. Had they crashed? He couldn't remember.

He took sensory inventory. Engine silent, no sense of motion—they were down. Gray mud dribbled in streaks down the windscreen, obscuring his view. Smoky light filtered into the cabin. The storm must have just hit. If this stuff had been coming down for long, he wouldn't be able to see out at all.

Uphill from him, Yukio sat slumped over the control yoke, his tiny braid dangling oddly alongside his sideburn. Blood welled from a cut on his forehead and dripped onto his browncloth pants. He'd misjudged the landing. Badly.

"Yukio." His companion didn't answer. Trev undid his seat harness and thrust himself up toward the Lwuite youth.

He was breathing.

Relieved and shivering, Trev let gravity pull him back down onto his own seat. They'd both stripped off coats in the heated cabin, but already he could see his breath. He climbed behind his seat, found the coats, pulled on his own, then stared at Yukio's.

He shouldn't move Yukio until he knew the extent of his injuries.

Crouching, he shuffled to the rear of the cabin. There lay the Dutcher bags. A minute later, Yukio sat blanketed in browncloth with his hooded parka topmost. Trev dabbed salve from the first-aid kit onto Yukio's forehead. That stopped the bleeding.

Now what?

He eyed the control panel. From the locator map, it looked as if they were almost on top of his prospector.

He couldn't go yelling for help in this storm.

Not for a while, at least.

Trev pulled his hood down farther and frowned up across the tilted cabin. "Yukio!" he shouted. "Hey, Yuke?"

An hour. Maybe in an hour the storm would ease off.

Maybe he should have gone for Blase's surgery. This was going to be one cold, lousy place to watch a friend die.

Graysha and Jirina weren't the only joggers in the hub Windsday afternoon. Jirina was not fastest—a lanky settler lapped her twice—nor was Graysha the slowest anymore. She felt strong enough to leave her candies and glucodermic back on her dresser.

After eight laps, which almost equaled 5K, Graysha pulled down to a walk, her chafed underarms stinging. She steadied her hands on her hips to let perspiration dry and kept her stride long. Overhead, the hub's single skylight was clogged with ashen mud. "Stone snow," Jirina had dubbed it.

Her circuit led past the grove of small fruit trees, where green apples made young branches droop. Nine fruits dangled on one tree, twelve on another. A woman sat on a bench nearby, guarding the national treasure.

Plums blushed purple on the next tree north. How had time passed so quickly? The trees were doubtless fed an optimal N-P-K mixture and transgened for a rapid bloom-to-fruit time.

Genegineering. She arrived on Goddard thirty-eight days ago, with little else on her mind. Was that still her ultimate priority?

In one way, it was. She was desperate to locate and destroy one particular transgened organism. In just over a month she had become a crusader in her own right, the Novia Brady-Phillips of Axis Plantation.

Amused by the comparison, she smiled wryly and strode on. How cost-inefficient, and time-consuming, too, to try isolating the organism from the wild, when it had to exist—if at all—in Will Varberg's culture collection.

Before trying the long route, she might attempt a little judicious piracy. All she had to lose was her job, a triannum at triple pay, the chance to get out of debt, professional honor, and possibly her life.

She reloaded Lindon's book after bathing, this time curled up on her bed with a cup of alfalfa tea on the nightstand, the viewer on her pillow, and Emmer under one hand. It would take about an hour to read the text once more.

Universal Father swore by this book but rarely quoted it. In context, Jesua's fruit and livestock metaphors fit an agricultural mentality, like ancient Palestine . . . or Goddard.

She skipped sickening medical notes on the process of crucifixion.

Emmer wriggled up onto her shoulder, and Graysha tilted her head, pushing her ear down into warm fur. If Lindon didn't have to evacuate, she'd familiarized herself enough with the book to ask questions, such as how much of it he literally believed and how many of these I am God statements he thought the man actually made.

Because if the story was literally true, that changed her perspective on the entire universe.

Her thoughts returned to Lindon. She believed she had put aside her desire for the colonists' genetic healing, so why was he still so much on her mind? She only wanted the best for Goddard, but at some hopeful depth of her subconscious, did she still hope he might influence the colonists to help her? She hated to think she might be pursuing this friendship out of ulterior motives.

Discouraged, she shut off the room's main light and changed into a nightdress by the dim glow of her monitor. Gently she lifted Emmer to one side, then lay down in the middle of the bed. Ellard had always lain on her left. She pulled her blanket to her chin, creating the cave effect Emmer liked best.

Amazing how they all could pretend nothing was wrong when privately everyone admitted jumping for the ceiling with every microseism. With the storm still blowing, satellites couldn't even record activity in the volcanic zone. Seismology continued to insist that all epicenters were northeast near the Trident and all these little "Goddard shakes" were to be expected.

The "microseism" that night nearly rolled her off the bed, and she dashed for her desktop monitor. Three seconds later, the standard message appeared. *Epicenter 59 kilometers northeast. Crater floor stable.* Graysha stumbled to the bathroom, sure she wouldn't sleep until morning. One more time, she checked in on the net.

For the first time in days, Melantha Lee's terminal was down. The woman finally must have decided she needed to sleep.

The thought woke Graysha up like caffeine. Keying hastily, she brought up Varberg's streptomycete inventory. Notations beneath some cultures gave her hope. She transferred their filing numbers onto her pocket memo. If only Lee had gone home—and slept through the quake—she might carry this off. Lab doors didn't lock. She dressed quickly and slipped out into the hallway.

In her own lab, she seized a few sampling items. Diffuse daylight filtering through swirling ash-laden snow made her feel as if someone could see her, though of course everyone was home. Quietly she opened Varberg's door far enough to slip through, then took a moment to get her bearings.

His lab suite was laid out differently from hers, with the inner room directly behind the door. It was open and as dark as Freezeout. She walked farther in.

A heavy metal door interrupted the wall beyond his office. She tried its huge latch. It, too, opened easily, chilling her with rancid-smelling air. She waved on a light. Clusters of capped tubes sat in metal bins on wire shelves, each bin numbered. Hesitantly she lifted one tube. Opaque green broth half filled it, with a tiny glass tube inverted inside. A bubble of gas showed through the inner tube when she held it up to the light.

Hurrying now, she selected tubes from the appropriate bins, thumbed the flash switch on her loop dropper, and dipped it into the first tube, then into a tube of enriched broth from her own incubator. She labeled that tube #1. It wouldn't do to have Varberg's inventory numbers found on her pocket memo. Yesterday she'd saved a scrap of paper from a floor meeting. On the back, she recorded culture designations in minuscule numbers.

An hour later, she'd pirated the entire public streps inventory, 192 species. After all, the best place to hide a treasure was in plain sight. Stealthily, she returned Varberg's tubes and let herself out. The cooler's light winked off as she shut the metal door.

It wasn't what Trev wanted to do, but darkness was falling and he had to try something. After one last check to make sure Yukio's wrapping hadn't slipped and one last pause to be sure his friend was breathing, he sliced the plane's auxiliary nonelectronic compass off the control board. That prospector ought to be three degrees west of south, just about half a klick away.

He pocketed the compass and started knotting sack-tying ropes together to tie to the rotor for a guide back. He wondered who he was trying to fool. They wouldn't stretch half a kilometer. And it was still snowing. Once he let go of the rope, he'd lose it.

But he had to try to get Yukio help. If he didn't come back, the rope would at least give searchers a direction to look for his body . . . come the next thaw.

It did not comfort Graysha to learn that a rescue party was being sent out for Yukio and Trev. On her work terminal in early Dropoff darkness, the message gleamed coldly: their last known location, before cabin electronics apparently failed, was being searched first.

Her stomach ached with dread as she depolarized the window and peered out. There were no stars—it must still be cloudy—but the wet spring snowstorm had passed, and she couldn't hear any wind. Lights gleamed off white humps down at the AnProd range.

Well, then, her tubes from Varberg's inventory ought to be clouding up with cell growth. She pulled one from the water bath. The broth looked suspiciously clear, but she might be checking too early. Carefully she sniffed one . . . then sniffed again.

Phenol!

Someone had disinfected the tubes. How was that possible? No one knew she'd been here last night, unless her lab was monitored twenty-four hours a day. Who could be doing this?

Someone, she concluded, who needed to protect Varberg's lab. She bit her tongue in frustration. It was back to atmospheric sampling. That, at least, would be part of a registered research program. Before she secured a copter, she would need to rig up some kind of collecting device.

She stared out her window. *Who?* she demanded of the darkness, wishing it might answer.

Hannes Chair Chenny HoNin slowed to a walk and nodded greeting to several people she recognized as Hannes residents, then started to trot again, short pigtails slapping her shoulders. It would help if somehow she could be in three places at once. Assuring evacuees, maintaining calm among her own residents, keeping the e-net warm with requisitions for foodstuffs and waste pickups—her life had become one single mad run. If Ari could see her today, she might withdraw from the challenge election.

Hannes's strained corridors housed nearly two thousand Axis children, not to mention crèche parents and frightened Gaea personnel. She slowed down again, approaching one such corridor. Her presence reassured refugees far better than visits from staff or personal messages.

Intended for storage, this corry had no skylights, but it was warm and dry, and far from seismic danger. A young woman crouched near the main doorway, taping a little girl's bloodied knee. "You can't stop here as quickly as you can at home," the woman was saying. "This floor is slicker than Axis concrete."

"When can we go back?" The small girl caught sight of Chenny, then widened her eyes in chagrin.

Laying one hand on the child's shoulder, the young woman straightened. "Chair HoNin, good morning."

"No offense taken. Home is always better," Chenny assured the little girl. She thought she recognized the slant of the woman's eyebrows. "Crystal DalDidier, isn't it?"

Crystal looked pleased to be recognized. "Yes. Go play, Kristin." The girl scooted off. "Good afternoon. Other than minor accidents putting on brakes while playing tag, everyone is doing well."

"You're coping wonderfully." Chenny extended a hand and shook Crystal's. "If anything comes up, please send word to my office."

"Somehow I suspect you're too much like my brother, Chair HoNin. You probably never sleep."

"I see your brother in you, Ms. DalDidier. You govern compassionately." Chenny offered a tired smile, then walked on.

Crystal DalDidier's resemblance to her brother reminded Chenny of that painful incident with her insulin kit. There still was no word of Graysha Brady-Phillips's arrest, which seemed odd. Ari usually kept her informed. It was good to know that a suspect in the DalLierx murder attempt had been found, though Chenny hated to see Dr. Brady-Phillips accused. She liked the woman.

Up the next corridor, eight to an apartment, evacuated Gaea staff waited out the crisis. Their fears gave Hannes a tone she didn't like, a sensation that something was bound to go wrong. She wished she could separate them farther from the unruffled children. Her oldest son had recently asked when they'd have Hannes to themselves.

Chenny had invited several couples to dine at her apartment over the previous few circadays. Will and Edie Varberg attended last night. That man was so jumpy, he frightened her. She hoped Axis's geologists took the problem in hand soon. She sensed trouble in Varberg. Might as well check on him while she was in the area.

She knocked on his door.

"No," answered a Gaea man she recognized as Rik McNab, an AnProd specialist, "the Varbergs aren't here. They left about an hour ago, flexcase and all."

Chenny stood stock-still, confused. Where was there to go?

Graysha shut off her computer with an open-palmed *whap*. The HMF had finally returned word on her request for medical clearance. Because of the altitude she'd have to reach in a sampling plane to sample polar stratospheric clouds, and because of the danger of oxygen failure to someone in her condition, the HMF said no.

She couldn't go over their heads, either. Melantha Lee had routed the request.

And there was no word from the rescue team, six hours gone. They must not have found any wreckage at or near the location where Trev lost contact.

That lack of news heartened her. At least there was still hope.

His cat! Graysha realized she'd better go feed Dutchy. No one else knew about him.

26. MARIGOLDS

The taller prospector's name was Kevan. Not much older than Trev, he held an impressive handheld metal detector, and though he scowled at the scabs striping Trev's face, he proved willing to march back through wind-driven drifts to search for the plane and Yukio. Kevan's partner stayed in the dugout.

Gripping a high-beam light and squinting against a driving gray blizzard, Trev stamped through filthy shin-deep snow behind Kevan. Ice stung his face and hung from his mustache. His earlier footprints had already filled. Kevan waved the metal detector from side to side. At a large gray hump, he slid the detector into a belt holster. "Dig," he yelled against the wet wind. ·

Trev yanked the young prospector's folding shovel from his own belt and thrust it into snow. It clanged. Several minutes later, they squeezed through into the plane's cabin.

Trev bent over Yukio. "Still breathing," he muttered thankfully. "Look at his forehead, though." Blood had crusted over a swollen lump. "You know anything about first aid?"

"Only enough to be a danger to injured people. Let me take a look."

Trev fell down into his own seat. Kevan pulled off thick gloves, did something to Yukio's head, and ran a hand up his neck. "Concussion, I bet, but there doesn't seem to be anything wrong with his spine. Hypothermia's the immediate danger. We'll have to get him to the dugout."

"I'll carry him," Trev offered, "if you'll take the equipment."

"We'll both carry him. I'm going to unbolt the chair. Hold this."

After slipping Yukio into a coat, they lifted him, chair and all, without letting his neck twist. After freeing him from the plane, carrying him the half kilometer to Kevan's dugout was easy. Eventually, Trev hunched close to a catalytic furnace, drinking hot water while Kevan adjusted blankets over Yukio on his own bed, a foam pad on bare rock floor. "That's about all I can do for now," Kevan grunted. He stepped over to the fire and poured hot water into his only other cup. "I don't have any of the right drugs. We'll have to wait for him to wake up."

"How long will that be?"

The other man, a dark figure who sat cross-legged on the stone floor, finally spoke. "Minutes, hours, days. Or maybe never." He bent back down over a capsule viewer on his rock-slab table.

"Nick, my cheerful partner," Kevan said.

Trev shivered. "Can you call Axis?" The HMF probably could help Yukio.

"When the storm's over, sure. But this isn't what you'd call a licensed establishment, and we're not pleased to announce our location. What are you doing out here?"

He'd hoped to have Yukio along, conscious, to talk to the prospectors when he finally contacted them. "Uh, looking for you people, actually. We work for Gaea, and our business took us this way one day. I saw your smoke. I'm looking for a place to get away from Axis if I need to. You see . . ."

He explained his predicament without emphasizing the code-red threat his father posed. When he finished, Nick had swiveled around on the stone floor to sit staring. Kevan scratched his stubbled cheek. Black whiskers and eyebrows gave the husky young man's fair skin an even whiter cast, but other than that, he had the features of another pretty Lwuite.

"We don't want Gaea company," Kevan said at last. "This is our claim, even if we haven't registered it yet. I could run you off, but you're probably going to report the locale anyway."

"Mmm, no. I won't report you." Trev set down his borrowed cup and rubbed his hands close to the heater. "I know what it's like to want to hide."

Nick fingered his auburn beard. "Oh? How are you going to get your friend back to Axis without reporting where you are?"

"Get the plane flying again. Maybe." Kludging a break in communications was one thing. Heavy repair was another.

Kevan snorted. "Sure you will. But maybe Axis will be busy enough worrying about those volcanoes not to bother with prospectors until we're ready to register this strike."

"Strike?" Trev thought he knew what that word meant.

Kevan leaned away from the heater. "If your father's who you say he is, what's the chance he could offer a little financial backing for a start-up mining operation? The colony would pay for extraction, but finding the best offworld markets can be tricky from out here."

"Hey-ey," said Nick. Finally, he smiled.

Terrified by the thought, Trev reconsidered. Blase liked power. Wealth bought it. Maybe he could *buy* the old man's forgiveness—for himself and Goddard colony. "But . . . but then he'd have to know where I am," he protested anyway.

"Sounds fair to me," Kevan said. "Axis is going to know where we are because of you."

Nick nodded.

On the other hand . . . "Nobody changes your face if you get found," Trev snarled, flooded by the old fear.

Kevan looked significantly at his bed. "Look, I'm not going to let your friend die from lack of attention. But someone's going to have to pay for that attention. I'd just as soon it wasn't me."

Trev sucked the last cooled drops out of his cup. Nick and Kevan's hideout, shelved with broken rock slabs and lit by one small lamp over the heater, didn't look like much to give up.

But fair was fair.

Startled, he picked at a scab on his chin. Where did that thought come from . . . Graysha?

Buying off Blase might be his only chance—better than trying to hide from him, anyway. "I'll make you a deal," he said. "Call help. Show me your operation. Then, uh—" he bit his lip—"give me time, a month or so, to contact Blase." Actually, he'd probably show up sooner than that.

Kevan raised one black eyebrow.

"But if Blase backs you, help me work on him. Grovel if you have to. It'll be worth it. You've got to trust me on this."

Nick picked up a shard of stone from the floor, tossed it spinning toward the ceiling, and caught it. "That's doable."

Was that daylight at the end of his long, long tunnel? "Deal?"

Kevan scrunched up his mouth, then said, "I'd buy it, if you're really who you say you are. Nick?"

Nick shrugged. "We'll write it up later. Call Axis for a medic, then take Trev LZalle on his tour. I'll watch whatshisname."

"Yukio," Trev mumbled, glancing down at his Lwuite friend. If that guy died he'd never forgive himself.

Kevan lifted a dusty cover from a compact transmitter, made sure its leads were secure, then turned it on. No one answered his hails, neither at Axis nor at Center. Trev heard only steady chattering static.

Looking relieved, Kevan shut it off. "Okay, I tried. For now, let's go below."

Ari MaiJidda let her dunked sandwich drip back into soy broth before taking another bite. The D-group building was eerily quiet, a private place for the First Circle to gather before tomorrow's town meeting.

"It's good news," Lindon said quietly. For the first time in days, she saw him eating. The man must have called off his fast, deciding God heard him. "Urbansky was able to ascertain solid rock beneath us for at least 2K. That means our only lingering danger is heavy ashfall. It's probably as safe as ever to bring the evacuees back."

He probably missed those homozygous little daughters. "As safe as ever" was a good term, too.

"I'm not certain," said Kenn VandenNeill, "no matter what the Gaea people say."

Ari swallowed her bite, then said, "Gaea people don't have to remind us about overcrowding, the risk of disease spreading under those conditions, or the strain we're putting on Hunnec's stores. I agree. Bring them back." She wiped her mouth with a browncloth square, then added, "Don't you think it's odd Brady-Phillips didn't evacuate with the children? Any sensible person in her condition would have gone, given the choice." If Yael GurEshel hadn't confirmed the official diagnosis, Ari would have suspected the "syndrome" of being only part of Graysha's cover. Ari was doing her best to forget having switched glucodermics. It just put her on edge. "Is she sensible, Lindon? I understand you've spoken with her quite a few times."

That little bomb had an immediate impact. "Why?" Kenn asked, setting down his sandwich.

Lindon narrowed his eyes enough to communicate displeasure. Let him. The election was tomorrow, and this was her chance to consolidate Kenn and Taidje's votes. "She is staking her professional reputation on investigating Goddard's cooling," Lindon replied, "and trying to accomplish as much as possible before Dr. Varberg returns. Evidently he attempted to block her research in the past."

"Oh, is that it?" Ari asked in knowing tones. "I think her decision to remain at Axis Plantation fits the pattern we've discussed. Be careful around her. Kenn, haven't you heard that nettechs can beat gamma-vertol if they know it's coming?"

Kenn shook his head. "Yes. We shouldn't have wasted it on her."

"She requested a high-altitude sampling plane." Lindon frowned over the tabletop. "The HMF denied permission."

"You let Yael GurEshel get away with that?" Ari injected scorn into her voice.

"I'm no physician. I don't claim authority over medical personnel."

"There are times when you should." Ari raised one eyebrow at Kenn.

He nodded slightly.

Ari exulted. VandenNeill was hers.

If Ari got to serve as Axis's CCA, Yael GurEshel would knuckle down, too—or find herself working at another settlement.

"Any word of LZalle?" Ari asked. She'd had precious little information out of her spy thus far.

Lindon shook his head.

So the children were coming back. That was good news, Graysha decided. But Varberg would be returning, too.

Her computer came back on with an electronic burp and a wobble of letters: +Speak with you privately? Lee+

Startled, she pushed back from her desk. Maybe Dr. Lee had gotten the message about her clearance being denied and meant to ensure that she wouldn't go off on her own. With Trev missing, everyone's panic threshold had dropped about eight points.

Frowning, she headed down to the first floor.

As she entered the crane-watched sanctum, Dr. Lee swept one hand toward the extra desk chair. "Sit down."

Graysha pulled a good deep breath and sat.

Melantha Lee wore a tailored blue offworld suit this morning. "Tell me," she said. "How is progress on the alleged CFC-metabolizing organism?"

Graysha crossed her hands in her lap to hide a triple row of fresh scratches. Dutchy had been glad to see her, all right. "Not so good, Dr. Lee. I haven't been able to do my sampling, and the HMF is being sticky."

"Perhaps then it's time you turned your full attention back to soil studies. With a full day's work lost when the Trident first erupted, and so many of our technical staff gone to Hannes, we've fallen behind on spot-checking agricultural areas."

"I'm sure," Graysha said. "I'm glad they'll be back soon."

"Please get a start on the project today. They'll—"

Lee's message alert screeched at full emergency volume. Graysha leaned closer to Dr. Lee's desk and read, +Chenny HoNin, calling for Gaea Consortium, Dr. Lee. For Colonial Affairs, Chairman DalLierx.+

Dr. Lee touched her Acknowledge key. "I wonder if something's gone wrong with bringing our evacuees back." On the screen a second +ACK+ appeared, followed by +LDL+.

+Dr. Lee, Lindon: Need your help. Hostage situation in progress. Varbergs are barricaded in a storeroom with two children, demanding you call ExPress Corporation and shuttle them offworld.+

"That lunatic," muttered Melantha Lee, seizing her keyboard.

+Which children?+ Lindon came back. Graysha held her breath. The monitor stayed blank for five agonizing seconds, and then a third message appeared.

+Merria HoBrace and Sarai DalLierx.+

Lindon felt as if he'd been knifed in the stomach. +Of course they cnaa go,+ he typed, tangling his fingers in an effort for speed. Under his reply, Melantha Lee's message appeared: +Promise him anything, Chair HoNin Gaea will cover shuttle fare to Copernicus.+

He rubbed his forehead, then wiped his palm on his thigh. Bee was capable and generally calm, but Sarai, so sure she was delicate, might fall to pieces. The man must be berserk.

Someone knocked at Lindon's office door. He ignored it.

Graysha could feel her heart pounding inside her rib cage. Poor Lindon! And why—now—did Lee seem so willing to give Varberg whatever he wanted?

Lee typed rapidly again, using the *Gaea Terraforming Consortium, Goddard Office* heading. "If Dr. Varberg sees me send off the message he wants," she said over her shoulder, "maybe he'll release those girls right away."

The same hope made Chenny HoNin bite her lip. Once the request for immediate shuttle service was formulated, committed, and sent, she keyed over to the terminal Will Varberg had appropriated. +Done, Dr. Varberg. I'll send a woman over for the girls.+

+Send her with food for four,+ he came back, his typing speed surprisingly slow. +Notify us when the shuttle reaches parking orbit.+

Graysha gulped when she saw Varberg's message. *No*, she pleaded, *not that long.*

Melantha Lee shook her head and typed, +That's not fair to the children or their parents, Varberg. Release them now.+

Letters reappeared instantaneously as Varberg retransmitted his previous message. +Notify us when the shuttle reaches parking orbit.+

"That's it, then." Lee sighed. "For now, we wait."

Graysha's heart kept pounding. "Dr. Lee, he's not crazy enough to hurt those children, is he?"

The Gaea supervisor folded both hands on her desk. "Will Varberg is not crazy."

Oh, but he was. Half of him had wanted to kill Mahera; he might do anything now, "by accident." The words echoed in Graysha's mind as she reentered her own office. He was capable of ruining Goddard's thermal balance. What else might he do? *You just called him a lunatic, Dr. Lee. You were right.*

Spurred by anger, she punched up the Micro floor's inventories program, then coded in for Dr. Varberg's cultures. Again she searched his streptomycete files—backward this time, hoping something might be coded to come up only that way. She almost knew the list by heart.

Nothing new appeared. Her stomach hurt. She dropped both hands from the terminal to rub it. Varberg's inventory continued to scroll past, backward, in alphabetical order.

Staphylococcus 6-ICZ . . .

What? She grabbed the keyboard. This was the bacterium that nearly killed Lindon. This entry, on Varberg's private inventory, was the evidence everyone had been looking for. Varberg did resent Lindon enough to try murder, particularly if his conscience had been seared back at Messier.

Now she wished they hadn't recycled that dead gribien.

She paced to her door, then back to her seat. Would it be safe to take another snooping trip up the hall into Varberg's lab? No. She shook her head. After this much time, even a half-sane person would have destroyed all possible vectors of deliberate infection. She wouldn't find any clue as to how he infected Lindon.

Even blank walls had flaws, though. She saved that page of Varberg's list onto her pocket memo.

Then she sat down, flexed her fingers, and reached for the keyboard. All right, then, what about . . . She'd been assured the net wasn't monitored, but it looked as if everyone between here and Copernicus Hab could peer over her shoulder at net activities. Might there be some kind of visual record of events in the Colonial Affairs building, too? Suppose . . .

Keying over to the medical branch, Graysha pulled up a staph–6-ICZ entry. The organism could only establish nasal infection if it was administered as an aerosol, she learned. Onset of symptoms occurred four to six days after administration.

Good, good! That gave her an exposure vector and time frame.

She dashed from her chair and out the door.

Lindon's secretary did not want to let her through.

"I'm well aware his daughter's a hostage," Graysha said, panting. "I think . . . hoo . . . I think there's a chance . . . that other charges could be brought against Dr. Varberg."

The pigtailed woman raised one eyebrow.

"There's a strong chance Dr. Varberg *is* the one who tried to murder the Chairman." Exaggeration maybe, but it made the secretary reach for her keyboard. Moments later, Lindon's door opened and he leaned around the corner to beckon Graysha in.

He didn't wait until they were seated. "How could he have done it?"

It felt good to see him again. "I don't know," she admitted, "but I have a definite incubation period. I don't mean to snoop into your security, but if you have a record of things that happen in this office, check around five days before you were taken sick."

"I can do that." He tapped at his keyboard. "We have a visual. . . . Here. I brought it up fast-forward, without sound."

Graysha watched, clenching one hand down at her side. On the monitor, a tiny version of Lindon sat at his desk, talking to the pocket memo. A secretary flashed in and out. More sitting. He left. Soon he was back. Three Gaea people entered, including Will Varberg—

"Freeze that," Graysha cried. Beside her, the full-size Lindon was already reaching for the keyboard.

Varberg held a tumbler stuffed with marigolds.

"Flowers," Graysha whispered.

Lindon shook his head. "Varberg brought flowers for that monthly floor meeting, for 'color.' I thought nothing of it." He touched a button set into his chair's neck rest.

"MaiJidda." Ari's voice came from near his ear.

"Can you come over, Ari? Quickly?"

"Is it about your daughter?"

"Yes and no. There's more."

Graysha walked to his window and peered out. Varberg! How dare he? "I suppose those flowers were destroyed. Recycled."

"No," he declared, "I was supposed to save the seed heads for Dr. Varberg. And I was busy—"

Ari MaiJidda burst in, her short hair rumpled on one side. She spotted Graysha and frowned.

"Look." Lindon thrust one hand toward his screen. "This record was made exactly five days before I took sick. Will Varberg set a bouquet on my desk. Graysha, tell Ari the incubation period for that staph bacterium."

"Four to six days." Graysha stared back at Ari.

Lindon's black-haired rival rested one arm on his desk. "That's very interesting."

"I wanted you here as a witness, Ari." Lindon stood up. "Somewhere in this office, I saved those flower heads. I don't believe I ever took them over. I . . . Yes." He slowly crossed to a set of shelves. Graysha held her breath.

He opened a cubbyhole. Instantly his back straightened. "Here," he exclaimed.

"Well, Dr. Brady-Phillips." Ari crossed her arms, wrapping long fingers around her shirt sleeve. "You're the expert investigator. What do we do with them?"

"We take them to Jirina's office. No," she said quickly, "to the HMF. Let your people do this. Dr. GurEshel should wash them, then filter and examine the residue. She should be able to tell, within the twenty minutes it takes to run a differential filtration, if these were used in a . . ." She looked at Lindon. He raised one slanted eyebrow. "In a murder attempt."

Yael GurEshel shook her head ruefully. "Eighteen thousand cells per gram of staphylococcus 6-ICZ. That simple a solution. Dr. Brady-Phillips, we all owe you an apology."

"And our thanks," Lindon said soberly. "I think I can guess why he did it."

Ari stood several meters from Graysha, crossing her arms over her chest. Graysha knew that as Ari's favorite suspect, she'd better not feel too relieved, not yet.

"Revenge for that restitution sentence," Lindon suggested. "He's desperate to leave Goddard. He'll even try . . . kidnapping," he finished in a weak voice. Graysha wanted to take his hand and try to comfort him.

"Shrewdly planned on his part, though," observed Dr. GurEshel. "Some owner of a staph kit was bound to be brought forward as a suspect."

Or else, Graysha thought, *someone who didn't own a staph kit and who could easily be framed.*

Ari wrinkled her nose. "Did you sniff them, Lindon? Marigolds don't even smell pleasant."

"I must have." Lindon's head drooped. "We have a new charge to transmit over to Chenny HoNin."

"Tell her to be careful," Graysha put in. "I don't think he's emotionally stable." She inhaled a deep breath of HMF ethanol-and-phenol air. *Poor*

Lindon. Now he has fresh cause to worry for his little girl.

Ari MaiJidda planted one hand on her hip. "Wait. Don't transmit anything yet. If Varberg learns we suspect him of a second crime, he could easily panic."

Lindon laid both hands on a centrifuge and shut his eyes.

Novia raised her ringing pocket com. Stalled in her research and wanting to warm up that aching knee, she'd walked Copernicus's reach for an hour. Far ahead, a green parkland sloped up and vanished in a typical morning haze. Despite stringent air-quality regs, habitat air always looked slightly misty. The horizon sloped up on both sides here, as well, thanks to Copernicus's toroidal design. It made her vaguely uncomfortable. Habs should slope along only one axis.

"Novia," said a filtered voice on the com unit, "this is Hauwk. Are you willing to travel without a pre-takeoff fast?"

Novia looked up and down the broad residential avenue. Only Jambling stood close enough to hear, and these skinny trees couldn't hide spies. "I'd prefer not to," she answered. "Why?"

"We have a situation developing over on Goddard. Evidently, Will Varberg of Microbiology demands shuttle evacuation to a hab. Lee sent an urgent request, and I'm going over myself. Mr. I Zalle is coming along. Can you?"

"Yes." Novia's stomach bottomed out. Too soon! Graysha probably had the information Novia needed but was not yet genetically healed. Novia wanted posterity as badly as anyone, and Asta had no intention of marrying. Obviously Graysha wouldn't reproduce either, until she was sure her children would not carry mutant genes.

Acid guilt burned Novia's stomach. If Graysha felt so strongly about not wanting genefective children, she must resent Novia for having brought her to birth. Again, Novia decided she should've taken her pastor's advice and terminated that genefective pregnancy. Graysha was approaching the long, slow end.

More than once, Novia wondered if Gray might consider shortening those difficult years. Euthanasia might be a welcome act of mercy, even if Gray couldn't bring herself to ask for it. That might be a loving mother's last kindness—better than letting her die by millimeters, clutching life like a sick animal.

She keyed off the com. "Back to the plex, Jambling," she said with forced cheerfulness. "We're finally headed over."

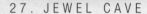

Trev picked a way along jewel-crusted stones, dazzled by the sight. They'd passed less than five meters into the cavern, and visions of wealth already kick-stepped in his brain. "What is this stuff?"

"Just calcite." Kevan rapped a boulder covered with grape-size white crystals. "Calcium, carbon, oxygen. Valuable, maybe, in quantity. But I'm hoping to find better. What we're after is Buyout, the point where Gaea is paid back for all services. Up to that point, a miner's take is under 50 percent. After Buyout, it could be more like 90."

Trev's whistle echoed in the narrow passage.

"Watch your step." Kevan started to wend down an incline. "And don't get lost."

Five steps later, Trev reached the point where Kevan started to disappear. Awed, he gulped and swung his head lamp around. Kevan's helmet light shone against more crystals, five meters down in a room that gaped like one of the cargo holds where he'd crouched, hiding, just a few weeks ago.

A flash from below momentarily blinded him. Kevan must've turned his head back. "You coming?" the prospector called.

"Okay. Yeah." Trev scrambled on. In one place, his foot slipped as he stepped on a crust of crystals that sheared off its rocky base. "Yyah!" he yelled, but before Kevan's head lamp swung his direction, he got his balance back.

"We can go back if you want to."

"No." He picked up a fistful of crystals, fascinated. This world was full of surprises.

"Listen," Kevan commanded.

Trev strained his ears. "To what?"

"Nothing." Kevan's voice sounded triumphant. "Absolutely nothing. It can be blowing a gale up top, and down here it will be warm enough to thaw meat—slowly. Cave temp is a constant three above. I've done wind measurements of the part of the cavern I've explored so far. Unless I slipped a decimal, given current atmospheric pressure, this is a half-million-cubic-meter cavern."

Trev blinked. "That's a lot of calcite."

"Not enough to sell offworld."

So why was the young prospector so excited about this place? Half an hour's scramble from that spot took them to a wall so flat it looked unnatural. "This is a fault line." Kevan slapped it. "End of the limestone, end of the passageway, so far as I can tell. Faults are prime mining sites."

Oh. "Fault lines? With all these quakes and volcanoes going off, aren't you afraid the thing will slip?"

"It's possible. But this one looks like it's been inactive since Goddard lost its first water."

Only slightly mollified, Trev peered closer. "What's all over the floor?"

"More calcite. I knocked it off the fault wall."

It seemed a shame to destroy such jaw-dropping beauty, but Trev understood the prospectors' urge to hurry Buyout. It would make the colony free—and maybe make them rich.

"We're exploring along this wall," Kevan went on. "There are several narrows close by where we've blasted but haven't gotten through. Maybe you could."

Squaring his shoulders, Trev frowned. So what if he wasn't as big as the Lwuite prospector. "Sure," he said. "I'll try."

The first passage back toward the fault defeated Trev's efforts at wriggling in, despite Kevan's instructions to rotate, twist, and turn. A scab on his forehead scraped loose, and a fresh warm trickle of blood started down beside his nose.

Deep down the second side passage, Trev found the fault again, a solid straight wall at the end of the line. "It goes to the fault," he shouted back at Kevan, "but there isn't much surface showing."

"I'll check it out later." Kevan brushed him off once he reached the main passage again. "Think your old man might be interested in our chances?"

"Yeah, maybe. Probably." Trev wiped his forehead and hoped it was true. "He goes for the exotic. This qualifies."

When they reached the dugout, Yukio's condition hadn't changed, though Kevan's sheets needed to be washed. "Saved them for you," Nick said. "I tried calling both Axis and Center. Still too much storm interference."

"Thanks." Trev ran a hand across his forehead and cheek. His palm came away marked with a red smear. "Can I have some salve?" he asked.

After gooping his scrapes, he ran Kevan's sheets through a small sanitizing unit. He felt thoroughly wretched about their predicament. Yukio crashed the plane on his own, but it was Trev's idea to disconnect communications. Otherwise, they might have had warning of the storm.

After sharing a pot of plain noodles, first Nick and then Kevan stretched out and fell asleep, side by side on Nick's narrow bed. Trev could no more sleep beside Yukio than stand on his head. From the rock-slab shelf where Kevan hung his tools, he pulled one of the lamp helmets and a rock hammer, then eased down through Kevan's access hole at one end of the dugout, back into the cavern.

The endless crystals reminded him of one of his father's costumes. Blase might be interested in the claim—might be intrigued. But how to get him out here before he took his revenge on Axis?

Dazzled, Trev followed Kevan's well-scuffed path to the fault line. Backtracking along piles of blast rubble, he found another crevice too narrow for Kevan to have entered.

The silence was eerie. He almost felt as if ghosts were watching over his shoulder, yet this world was too new to have ghosts.

Except Jon Mahera's, he decided. And please, not Yukio's.

That passage ended within a few meters, and he tried another one. Fired by the drive to go where no human had ever entered—Blase might relate to that!—he twisted sideways and edged in, first one arm and then his shoulder. His head wouldn't go. He turned it back into the passage as far as his neck would stretch, then tried worming up and down on his toes. It hurt, but he kept pushing—was through!

Kneeling, he tapped crystals from a boulder and piled them beside the crack where he'd entered the new passage. That way, he might find his way back.

Cautiously, he went on. His head lamp threw short eerie shadows that kept startling him as they moved close by.

For a few meters, he could walk upright. Then the ceiling dropped again, but he could crawl. At every junction point, he stopped to pile crystals. Stone everywhere, above and below him, hung like oppression visualized. The main passage seemed obvious, a rounded floor that looked as if water flowed through it for centuries. Before long, he could walk upright again. Not far beyond, the ceiling leaped out of lamp range.

This passage, this room—this view—was all his own. An exclusive. Of course the whole claim belonged to Nick and Kevan, but they had never seen this. The ceiling here was even higher than that of the first room Kevan had showed him. One flat wall obviously was the fault. With his borrowed hammer, he slammed hard at the crystal face. Hundreds of tiny jewels sheared off and fell to the floor. He was picking up a handful when he realized that the rock wall was a different color here—black, like glittering jet.

Impressed, he hammered off a chunk of the new stone and stuffed it into a pocket. Then he sat down with his back to the faulted wall and stared up at a crystal-coated ceiling.

The sense of oppression melted away. If a person really wanted to hide, this was the place. This was exactly the place.

He followed his trail of crystal piles back to the main path, struggled through his narrows, then retraced Kevan's path to the dugout. Yukio lay still, so Trev tried firing up Kevan's audi rig.

There still was no signal.

When he showed Nick and Kevan the black rock the next morning, Nick took it casually. "We'll know in a minute. Where was it?" He lifted a piece of electronic gear lashed to a pack frame from one shelf along the wall.

"On your fault line. What's that?"

"X-ray crystallography. It's for"—Nick touched something, and as the unit started to hum, he scratched his cheek, parting his thick auburn beard—"atomic identification." He touched something else and then reached for a rock hammer. With practiced ease, he flaked one crystal along an axis. "In you go." He dropped the flake into a chamber, then leaned close to a binocular eyepiece.

"All right," Nick announced, pressing his forehead to the instrument, "we have carbon . . . no surprise . . . traces of calcite . . . dust, probably . . . and bor—" His narrative ended midword. "How much of this was there?"

"I only knocked crystals off one section of the big flat wall. I don't know how much more there might be."

"Kevan, get a look at this." Nick backed away and let his taller partner lean over the eyepiece.

Kevan bent down, gazed briefly into the eyepiece, then straightened up, staring at Nick. Nick raised an eyebrow. Kevan barely shrugged.

"What is it?" Trev doubted that instrument would tell him anything, but he did know one thing. Boron was something people wanted. It had something to do with stabilizing cross-space drives—and not the little ones that drove ExPress shuttles. They kept habs stabilized, too.

"It's a boron compound," Kevan confirmed. "One I never saw before."

"LZalle," Nick added, "this could be a high-temp rock vein. There's so little boron in the free state you can't even mine it on asteroids."

"Hey, I know that." Trev tossed his head. They didn't need to talk down to him.

"It's . . . where?" Kevan asked.

"Show us," Nick demanded, thrusting one arm through a pack strap.

"You big guys will have to blast a wider way in." Trev glanced at the bed. "And who's going to stay with Yukio? I need to show you how to get there."

Kevan made a strangled noise. "I will," he said, "but get back quick."

Two hours later, they sat at the table again, drinking coffee Kevan had stirred together. To the top as far as Nick's hammer would throw, and clear to the bottom, and to both sides of the wall, the black vein went on. "Gaea would get 30 percent—that's the contract, no matter what we find." Kevan's wide eyes and little-boy face made him look ten years old.

Nick nodded.

"Of the rest," Kevan explained, "40 percent goes to the colonial treasury, the rest to the claimant."

"So you get 60 of 70," Trev murmured. "Too bad it isn't more."

"It's fair," Kevan continued, "because the colony pays for developing. Depending on how deep that vein goes, we might not be worrying about the price of shoes for a good half century."

Trev glanced down at Yukio. "All I want is enough to buy Blase LZalle off my back. After that, it's all yours, for all I care."

"Freedom. Yeah. Small enough item." Kevan picked dust from under his thumbnail. "Yeah. Really, forty of the seventy, after Gaea takes its cut, could be enough—if the vein goes—to put a substantial payment against the colonial loan's principal."

"Why does that matter?"

"Because." Nick rolled his eyes as if he were addressing a small and stupid child. "After Buyout, the next strike is almost all ours."

Kevan eyed Nick, pointedly excluding Trev. "You know who really wants freedom?" Kevan asked. "My brother. And the rest of them, back there in the crater bottom."

Nick nodded somberly.

Trev decided he might as well play along. "They'll put up statues of you, maybe."

"If it weren't the law," Nick said, "we'd love to keep it all for ourselves."

"Rocks won't do any good in our pockets." Kevan reached deep into his coveralls and pulled out the frayed inner pouch of a hip pocket. "We haven't got the connections, or the technology, to independently transfer this stuff offplanet to industrial markets. And I don't guess even your father could manage that."

"Don't bet against my father's pile." Trev rested one elbow on the table-top. Could this be happening? Could he actually be glad to be related to Blase LZalle?

"Nick, where's your pocket memo?" Kevan asked.

Holding the memo on Record, Kevan roughed out an agreement between himself, his partner, and the LZalles. Trev would be loaned two thousand maxims as soon as extraction began. After that, 2 percent of all profits went to Blase if he helped market the colonists' share offworld. "If there are any profits," Kevan added.

Snorting, Trev agreed. He typed in his USSC identity number, then his name. Nick did the same, then Kevan. To Trev's shock, the big man's surname was DalLierx.

"Your brother." He gaped.

"Yeah," Kevan said, "you probably know my brother. You're not the first one who wanted to leave home."

Lindon fidgeted with the handle of his coffee mug. Sarai's face seemed to hover in the air in front of him, frightened eyes accentuating her thinness. He saw her everywhere he looked.

Taidje FreeLand sat in the CA office's extra chair. His white hair, freshly cut, lay almost invisibly on his head. "Chenny HoNin's office assures us Hannes is doing all it can." He turned toward Lindon, who saw compassion in the sad set of his gray eyes. "I'm sorry," he added softly, "but I have to agree with Coordinator MaiJidda that we should not involve the D-group."

Lindon nodded. "I understand." He'd called another emergency meeting of First Circle members. "Kenn?"

Kenn VandenNeill stood near the door, tapping his square chin with his pocket memo. "As much as I'd like to see the girls rescued immediately, I agree. It's a police matter, not a D-group issue. Hannes has its own police."

Lindon thumbed a button and erased one section of notes on his pocket memo. "But we shall demand immediate extradition if Will Varberg can be taken into custody before his shuttle arrives. He must serve out his manslaughter term at the very least." It wasn't recompense he wanted this time but revenge. Varberg had dared to scar his young daughter's mind, and that scar would never go away. He knew he should forgive. He knew vengeance belonged only to God—but he also knew letting go of this debt would take all the charity in his soul . . . and more.

There had to be consequences.

"Definitely." Ari seemed to agree with him.

"Of course—" Taidje said, then he hesitated—"I do wish we could press attempted-murder charges immediately." .

Kenn dropped his pocket memo on the table. "You already have the vote for this one, Lindon, but I'll make it unanimous."

"Thank you." Lindon touched the Erase button again. "One other thing seems urgent enough to consider today, and I'll let you go. This regards Graysha Brady-Phillips. We've been concerned for some time about the lingering possibility of her reporting back to the Eugenics Board." He paused, glancing at each of the officers. Late last night, his heart had made peace with his mind . . . though his spirit still whispered doubts.

For this matter—unfortunately—he also needed to consult the committee. "Yet we've known for some time that she wants her own genes fixed if possible. I think I've thought of a way we might ensure she does not report to her mother."

"Go on" stares from all, even Ari, encouraged him.

"If this committee would approve Port Arbor research into treatment for Flaherty-syndrome chromosomes, and then a gene-fix for her, she would be so deeply indebted to us that we might lay the worry to rest."

Kenn took a step back. Taidje folded his arms over his chest. Ari frowned, leaned one forearm on the table, and said, "She is not one of us, nor is she eligible by . . . by . . . Good God, Lindon, you're not suggesting . . ."

Kenn cocked his head. Taidje's expression, closed like a door, defied interpretation.

"Perhaps I'm being dense," Kenn said. "Lindon, what does she mean? What do you mean?"

He was committed now. "If the procedure would be okayed by this committee, I would be willing to . . . qualify Dr. Brady-Phillips for the procedure."

Ari pushed back from the table. "He means, VandenNeill, that he would propose marriage."

"*If* she's willing to make a spiritual commitment first," Lindon murmured. She'd already rejected the apostate church. He saw the deep hunger left in her heart. He could not feed that hunger, but he knew Someone who could.

Still, it was a terrible risk.

Taidje laced his fingers and said nothing. Lindon couldn't read his expression. Kenn gaped.

"Ari is correct," Lindon added quietly. "Attaching her to the group by marriage would make her eligible, by our laws, for gene work. It would ensure she stayed on Goddard."

"Not here at Axis," Ari insisted, jabbing the table with one finger. "Not with the spaceport right here."

"I think," Taidje said, "that it is a proper, worthwhile idea, provided both you and Dr. Brady-Phillips are willing and that she accepts the idea of marriage *before* you mention genetic alteration."

Ari whirled aside. "Taidje, you're crazy. The woman is probably an EB agent. Look at the way she solved the . . . the attack on Lindon. She knows far too much about investigative methods."

Kenn pursed his lips.

"She's a microbiologist," Lindon said.

Stepping closer to Kenn, Ari drew up tall. "Kenn, Lindon can't vote a measure he proposed. Break the tie."

Kenn tilted his head left, then right, then shook it. "I can't," he said. "You both have valid arguments. I propose we table the matter until after the election."

Lindon drained his black coffee. Kenn probably hoped Lindon would change his mind. He also followed trends, in the congregation and at work. If Ari won the election, Kenn would side with her.

Well, that was that. At least they didn't force him to justify his feelings for Graysha. How did a man explain the moment when he realized that he cared too deeply to turn aside? Didn't the great apostle Paul say that "the greatest of these" was love?

He pushed Graysha out of his thoughts. "Other new business?" he asked softly.

None was suggested. Taidje scooted back his chair. Kenn hurried out.

"May the best candidate win tomorrow," Taidje said on his way to the door. "Good luck to you both."

Ari lingered behind the spare chair, barely smiling. Lindon raised an eyebrow at her.

"When the count comes in," she muttered, "remember you did it to yourself, last meeting."

"Some aggression is important," he answered. "There are things worth dying for."

"Ooh." She raised both eyebrows. "Too bad you didn't say that on the vidi net, too."

"I said that for you. Males do not need to be repaired. You and I are supposed to complement each other."

She balled a fist on one hip. "That is a part of your religion I don't need."

"You want this colony to 'stand behind the D-group and declare itself,'" he reminded her. "That would take a good deal of aggressiveness."

Ari rolled her eyes. "That's a rumor, Lindon."

"It started with you."

"No one can prove that," she said darkly as she strode out the door.

He stared after her. Ari never would win the sympathy vote. It might swing his way, with Sarai in Varberg's hands. Still . . .

He squeezed his eyes shut, wishing he could trade away every sympathy vote, along with every vote of confidence in his abilities, for a chance to hold his child.

Carrying additional explosives and their crystallography unit, Nick and Kevan squeezed down through the dugout's floor hole. Trev washed Yukio again, then returned to the audi rig.

Half an hour later, voices started to gibber through static in Axis's direction. Repeatedly Trev tuned them down to speaking pitch and tried to break through. All channels were locked tight.

Something to do with the volcanoes, he guessed. Twisting the dial on the prospectors' antenna rotor, he tried listening for Center. In that direction, he heard silence. Encouraged—at least it wasn't static—he called, "Hello, Center?" He leaned closer to Kevan's button mike and tried again. "This is Trev LZalle. Emergency. Center, do you copy?"

Into his fifth pause came a faint voice. "LZalle, we read you. This is Center, Echo Five 632. Where are you? Do you have an operating number?"

Elated, Trev whooped. "Echo Five 632, yeah, um, I'm at . . . 2.15 degrees south, 4.7 degrees west."

"We read you, LZalle. Operating number?"

"Jeez," he exclaimed. Were the idiots going to stand on procedure? "I have an injured man here. Concussion. Repeat, my friend has a concussion. Possible brain injury. He's been unconscious almost twenty-four hours. Can you send a medical team?"

Edie Varberg stared at the two children who lay sleeping alongside the wall in the "room" she and Will had found—a half empty medical storage area. Their own daughters, long grown, long gone, had been this small once. It would've nearly killed her to have had them kidnapped, no matter how happy the outcome.

These children wouldn't be harmed, of course. But she understood why Lindon DalLierx needed to suspect they might. Will had explained carefully. Since the Trident's first eruption, her night terrors had returned, wakening her screaming and sweating. If Chairman DalLierx didn't perceive a threat, the shuttle coming to fly her back to hab life might not have been launched.

One child rolled over, whimpering.

"Will," she called softly, "they're beginning to move."

Her husband sat cross-legged in the corner nearest the door, mumbling to his pocket memo. He put it down. "Take care of them. Best if they don't wake up all the way."

Edie pulled the whimpering one—Sarai, the smaller—to her feet. With her arms around the girl's shoulders, she sleepwalked her to the chamber pot they'd set up behind cargo containers. Helping the little girl with her needs reminded Edie of the sweet days when she had toddlers of her own.

She covered the pot with a plate-shaped lid. Then from a distilled-water flask, she filled a small beaker and reached into her pocket.

Her groping hand didn't find what she needed. "Oh. Sit down, Sarai. I'll be right back."

The groggy child obeyed, sliding down the wall to sit against it. Edie handed her the beaker. She held it two-handed, staring.

Edie approached her husband.

"Now what?"

She looked down at the concrete floor. On second thought, maybe she could find them herself. "Oh, nothing," she said. "I'm sorry I bothered you."

Will scowled, and she realized she'd better explain. He was so jumpy these days! "I forgot and repacked the pills. She's still not quite awake."

To her relief, he grunted and went back to work.

Now, where did she put that prescription? She rummaged into the large flexcase she and Will had packed. The vial wasn't in the side pocket where she expected to find it. Perhaps, by mistake, she'd tucked it into Will's kit bag. She opened the small leather pouch. Several prescriptions were in there, normal for a man his age. . . .

What was this? She lifted an aerosol inhaler wrapped in offworld plastic. A typed label read *Staph 6-ICZ.*

She almost dropped it. Why, that was the organism that had nearly killed Chairman DalLierx. What was it doing here? She turned the inhaler in her hand. It would be easy to hold this to the mouth and nose of a drugged, sleeping child. . . .

Her hand fluttered. For weeks, she'd wondered if Will needed psychiatric help. She'd been afraid to admit it to herself, terrified to suggest it to him. She needed to get him away, safely off Goddard, before he hurt someone.

It looked as if he'd already tried.

Horrified, she repacked Will's kit, then searched her own. The sleeping tablets were tucked into her hairbrush's hollow handle.

Prying off the cap as she crossed the little room, she returned to Sarai. The thin child blinked. "Here," Edie murmured. She shook out half the pill she'd broken earlier, presenting it between thumb and middle finger. "Swallow this. Good girl."

Sarai gulped the white half-tab with water and let Edie guide her back to her sleeping spot. It hadn't been this easy to drug them the first time. Merria HoBrace slept on; since she was larger, they'd forced a full adult tablet down her throat. Edie shuddered at the memory. Poor things.

Edie freshened her lip gloss, then lingered, screened behind the cargo containers.

It was one thing when Will hit *her*, because she'd married him knowing his wild, romantic nature. But others . . . It might be easier to use that aerosol a second time. She wanted to leave Goddard—desperately—but not so desperately she'd let her husband harm a child.

She peered around the barrier at him. This was the man who'd fathered her daughters, who'd bought them pretty things, who'd wept openly at their graduation and weddings. He'd felt so bad about what happened to Jon Mahera. What happened to him on Messier and now here in this terrible place? He needed rest and a chance to escape the hideous planetary environment. If this was the same organism that was given Chairman DalLierx, it would take time to act. Antibiotics, promptly administered, would prevent tragedy.

Unless he'd already made them breathe it, while she slept? That thought made her gasp. No, no, he wouldn't!

Even if he hadn't, they could be arrested as kidnappers.

It was a little late to think of that, but she ought to try to free the girls. It would be difficult, since they couldn't run.

Then she pulled back behind the screen, reconsidering. Will was so frightened. He hated Goddard, hated it when she questioned his plans, and he was determined to stay with Gaea. The tension had become so bad she'd had to hide one bruise for weeks. She couldn't have lied if Melantha Lee had seen it.

She ached to do something, but her brain just didn't seem to function independently anymore.

28. GOD'S ELECT

Trev swung through the hall door into Graysha's lab. Ignoring the sudden dig of Emmer's short claws, Graysha wrapped her arms around him. "You made it!" she cried. "You're all right!"

"If you're going to hug people, do it right." He kissed her enthusiastically, his breath heavy with smoked meat.

Emmer growled. Graysha pulled free, stroking Emmer to calm her down. Today, feeling as if she'd ignored her pet too much, she wore the beast. Emmer would help her stay awake, too. She was sleeping less every night, then dragging around her lab all day—even on this sunny Bday. "What happened? Where did you go down?"

Jirina hurried in, clutching a marking stylus. "Did I hear Trevish?"

"You did." He seized Jirina, kissed her, too, then backed up to a countertop planted his hands on it, and sprang up to sit. "We set down out in the wild when we saw the storm coming. Ran into a couple of loners, prospectors. Waited out the storm there. Yukio got a concussion," he added, tucking his chin sheepishly. "It wasn't a good landing, and it wasn't until Center flew him out that he came to."

"Is he hurt?"

"Yeah, but he'll be all right. Got dishes to wash?"

Startled, Graysha eyed him, looking for some outward change to match this sudden shift in his attitude. He seemed downright eager, as if he'd made peace with some demon of inward terror.

Jirina crossed her chest with one arm and curled her fingers around her biceps. "You heard Varberg snatched those two little—"

Trev nodded vigorously. "I told you he was schizic. Are they sending D-group over?"

If only you knew how crazy, Graysha thought, *and for how long.* But the new theory of attempted murder was still secret. "Not that I heard," she said. "But they're finally holding elections today."

Trev snickered. "I'll bet DalLierx is so hot over Varberg he's toasting the ceiling."

Graysha shut her eyes, disappointed. "Oh, Trev. Have a heart. That's his child." Then she remembered how Trev felt about his own father. "He really loves his little girl," she added.

"Okay." Still looking mightily pleased with himself, he jumped down. Jirina bumped him with one hip, spun around, and headed out.

"Trev, wait," Graysha called. "Come here." When Jirina's footsteps had faded and Trev stood close enough to hear her whisper, she added, "I tried to inventory Varberg's organisms. Someone sterilized the entire tube rack, right here in my lab. I'm almost ready to give up."

"That's too bad." He glanced over his shoulder toward the glassware racks. "Hey, when you make CFCs, what's the hardest ingredient to get hold of? Did you tell me it was carbon?"

She no longer cared if he really listened or learned. She had life-and-death matters to worry about. "That's right, elemental carbon. Why?"

"Because I think we might've found some." Whistling, he opened the ion-field sterilizer and started unloading glassware.

Graysha signed on the net and sent a message to Lindon's office. +Prospectors, where Trev came down—carbon source? GBP+ Really, it was just an excuse to contact him. She needed to communicate with someone who cared. Yesterday, she'd sent one last message to the HMF, appealing the denial of her clearance refusal. Yael GurEshel was not answering her queries.

Lindon didn't answer right away, either. He had to be busy with election affairs. Yawning, she checked her t-o button, popped a sour candy into her mouth, and returned to her workload. It had been so long since she'd felt rested. Recent tests on the drip greenhouses showed the beginnings of a mycotic infection. Keying up the appropriate sample, she set a DNA analysis to run.

Evidently, she would contribute nothing more here than what Gaea Consortium hired her for.

She made it to lunch, then dragged through the afternoon. At four-thirty, she switched her terminal on to the colony net and lugged a scope from her lab into the office to count spores on stained bacterial slides. At 4:45, letters started appearing on the screen. She made herself watch the counter finish before looking up.

General Election
Colonial Affairs Chair, Axis Plantation
Lindon DalLierx, 1425 votes, 48%
Ari MaiJidda, 1459 votes, 49.5%
Write-in candidates, 59 votes, 2.5%

Graysha leaned back in her chair, stunned. She'd never expected this. Lindon worked himself ragged for these people, and—by thirty-four votes, which the write-ins might have affected—they tossed him out. He should demand a recount.

She knew Lindon too well, though. He wouldn't do that.

Just like that, this suddenly, the rules in this little planetary drama had changed.

He might leave Axis for one of the other settlements. She might never see him again.

That shouldn't bother her. She shouldn't waste emotional energy on someone who had other priorities, and she'd wasted too much time this afternoon. Springing to her feet, she pushed back her desk chair. On her way up the corridor, mentally planning to tidy up details of her granary check, she stumbled to a halt. She'd shut off automatic watering in that drip greenhouse two days ago and never switched it back on.

She wheeled around so quickly Emmer dug in with all twenty again, and she jogged the other way.

Just inside the greenhouse's door, she paused. "Look, Emmer," she whispered, "it's all right." The gribien answered with soft throat clicks, the kind she often gave if intrigued by some scent or sound.

"Wheat," Graysha explained. "Here, smell." Carefully she plucked one stalk and held it to Emmer's nose. Tiny white teeth showed momentarily, latching on to the stalk. Graysha sank down on the walkway, relaxing. Crisis upon crisis might drive humans to distraction, but the gribien's perspective never changed. If food existed, life was good.

Slowly, Emmer munched her way up the stalk toward the seed head. Slowly, Graysha's eyes closed.

When Ari MaiJidda arrived after dinner at the Colonial Affairs office, one secretary sprang up to shake her hand and said, "Congratulations, Chair MaiJidda." Others stayed at their desks, some smiling approval, some turning away from their work to nod at her. Lindon's door hung open.

Hitching her briefcase higher under one arm, she strode toward the office door and knocked on its frame.

"Come in," he called. As she stepped in, she saw him sweep something from a wall cupboard into a well-used cargo box. "I'll try and be out before the swearing-in." He glanced at his wristwatch. "Oh, there's been a carbon find where Trevarre LZalle was stranded. You'll want to check it out."

"That and ten thousand other things. Take your time." She leaned against the windowsill, reviewing mental lists of people whose jobs she wanted shifted and programs she meant to change. She had new incentives in mind for metals prospecting. Without better ores, D-group would never achieve respectable military status. More research assistants for Port Arbor. And new religious education would start immediately at the crèche level. That excited her most of all.

When he started rolling the cargo box toward the door, she pushed away from the window. "What plans do you have?" she asked. Not that she cared, but she was curious.

"For now, to take a few Goddardays off and finish recovering. Yael GurEshel has been chasing me with sleeping pills."

And then what would he do? She studied his back as he packed another compartment. He didn't look as slump-shouldered as she had hoped.

So what? The point wasn't to beat him. The point was to win.

What to do with him now? He'd often said he considered the Chair a two-person job, but if she needed an assistant, she would not hire him. She'd designated an aide to maintain the accelerated D-group training schedule, for now. "Quick trip to Hannes?" she guessed. "You must feel rather awkward about the situation over there. Maybe you could help free Sarai."

"Awkward," he said brusquely, "isn't the word. When you have children, you'll understand."

"Don't hold your breath."

"Anyway," he said without turning around, "I wouldn't accomplish anything. I'd get in Chenny's way. Do let me know," he added, shifting his feet to reach for his precious antique books, "if you think of positions where I could be useful."

She despised his accommodating nature. "I will." The first position that came to mind involved dry-waste recycling.

Another knock at the door preceded Kenn and Taidje. Half a dozen other colonial officials—Second Circle committee members and advisers—followed them in. She straightened up, smiling. If the Noetics were right and she had an aura, it probably glowed.

The swearing-in lasted five minutes. Taking possession, she sat down in the tall chair and clasped her hands on the desktop.

Strain lines showed at Lindon's eyes. Events had swept along quickly, and she guessed he needed to be alone for a while.

Taidje FreeLand touched his arm and turned to his successor. "Ari," he said, "no matter what's still on record for your use, this man has two ter-rannums of invaluable experience. I suggest the Colonial Affairs Committee retain him as senior advisor, to ease the transition."

Kenn VandenNeill lifted his square chin. "I would second that if you made it a motion."

She hesitated. They'd think her arrogant if she refused in front of so many people. "Yes, Lindon," she said smoothly, "stick around. I want to talk to you before I turn in tonight."

In his glance down at his cargo box and the hand that twitched, she saw that he wanted to escape. "That would be fine," he said.

One by one, the others congratulated her and moved toward the door. She heard "Good work, DalLierx," from a secretarial worker whose name she'd forgotten.

Ari caressed the chair's armrests, letting Lindon wait a few moments longer. If he stayed at Axis Plantation and had time on his hands, he might spend time with Novia Brady Phillips's daughter, courting her toward that commitment to Goddard, telling her dangerous secrets.

It was high time Graysha rejoined the D-group.

"Would you close the door?" she asked when the last of her congratu-lators slipped out.

Lindon shut it and took the side chair. She smiled, liking the look of him sitting down there.

"I want a full report on Dr. Brady-Phillips's atmospheric research to date," she said bluntly. "Also, have you supported it from this office in any material way? It's imperative to have that work completed rapidly."

He frowned before he started talking. She didn't care. Let him suspect her motives. He had to support her in this. It was very nearly his favorite cause, and she wanted that research wrapped up quickly.

At Graysha's next D-group session, Ari's aide would make sure the woman was pushed hard enough to need that glucodermic.

Half an hour later, Trev LZalle stood on the other side of Ari's new desk. The light of purpose shone in his eyes. His news about the prospec-tors encouraged her. Maybe he would also help her tap the LZalle resources.

First, she had to find out if Graysha already knew—or guessed—what Lindon planned for her. Those gene-pure children he wanted to give her would be *his* if she had probes done, and Ari bristled at the thought. "I have a job for you this evening," she told Trev, "one I think you'll enjoy. But you'll need Dr. Brady-Phillips's assistance. By the way, has she ever implied she might consider a permanent change of residence to Goddard?"

He wrinkled his pug nose. "Implied? Huh. That's a pretty loose word. Maybe. I don't know. Don't think so. I think she still feels Goddard is dangerous to her health."

If he only knew. Under her desk, she drummed the fingers of her left hand on her knee. Carefully, casually, she winked. "Is she still sweet on DalLierx?"

He didn't hesitate. "Visibly."

A chill tickled her between the shoulder blades. If Trev was that sure, she had every reason to go ahead with her plan. "How quickly could you assemble gear for this atmospheric sampling she wants to do?"

Wrinkling his nose again, he pursed his loose lips, then tilted back his head. "I know the systems pretty well. I'd say thirty minutes."

"If you and Graysha work together and make it twenty, I can get you a plane. Tonight." Daylight was strengthening outside the window.

He thrust his scabby chin forward. "What?"

Yes, she realized, a high-altitude flight might suit her better than a D-group tragedy. She would be absolutely elsewhere when it happened.

Ari stroked the desktop's leather cover. "One of Urbansky's planes is coming back to refuel. It should land in seventeen minutes." She lifted a square of precious paper and waved it in his direction. "I have an order—forged, but who will know if Lee's signature is genuine?—granting you priority requisition. Just don't crash this one."

He whooped.

"That's the spirit." She dropped the paper, then flattened her palms together and touched fingertips to her forehead. "Go sampling. Go now. You'll have daylight for thirty hours. But be sure to take Dr. Brady-Phillips along. You know how badly she's been wanting this."

He seized the sheet of paper. "The HMF doesn't want her to go—they're afraid high altitude might worsen her disease—but she's not going to let that stop her. Thanks!"

Worsen her? Absolutely. She would need extra oxygen and glucose to make it home this time. Lowering her hands, Ari smiled. "Hurry, then. My people will meet you two at the airfield in nineteen minutes."

Graysha dashed into the Gaea cafeteria just as the dinner lines closed. Jirina stood at the dump window. "Where've you been?" Jirina demanded. "Your little Trev bounced off both sides of the hall looking for you."

"What did he want?"

"Didn't say."

"Where is he now?" Waking disoriented in the greenhouse after an unexpected two-hour nap, she'd clutched Emmer to her shoulder and run straight home.

"He went out. Said he'd leave you a message."

Graysha cajoled soup and bread from a server wiping down her station, then hurried back to work. She couldn't believe she'd done such a stupid thing. Sure enough, her monitor blinked. When she punched in her personal code, Trev's message appeared.

+North polar area, stratospheric clouds—isn't that what you said? I went out, since you aren't around. Ari got us the plane by forging Lee's sig. Know you wanted those organisms ASAP so didn't wait. I've got your gear, and I know more about how to use it than you think I do.+

Trev relaxed his hands on the steering yoke of the little plane, letting calm settle. He was tired in this eerily bright night-shift hour— exhausted was a better word— but two sleep replacers would get him through tomorrow.

He had no idea if the sampling he'd done over the last six hours yielded a viable specimen, but at least he had done it right. Gray's proposal, published in well-outlined teacher talk, was easy to follow.

As for the stratospheric clouds . . .

Sparkling like fresh, pink, iridescent ice, they conducted some kind of acid chemistry—if he understood references she'd made in the lab. It had been the most exhausting six hours he'd ever spent, and the loneliest, but also the most beautiful.

"Okay," he said aloud. "A direct course home will take me more or less directly past the Trident. That ought to be wild."

He still suspected Chair MaiJidda was only his ally because she wanted to meet his father, but she was eagerly cooperating with Gray's research. It was a welcome change from DalLierx's hesitancy.

Working to stay awake, he reran the memory of returning to Gray's lab, fairly bursting with news about the glittering caves backing up to that boron deposit, however big it was. She'd been busy, though, like everyone else at Axis. He actually had an easy time keeping Nick and Kevan's secret. He'd done nothing, in fact, but mention the carbon in passing . . . and drop a rock sample on Yukio's lap in the Axis HMF for luck.

Nick and Kevan would prefer to put off official invasion of their claim, anyway.

About an hour later, he spotted the vents by their steam and ash clouds.

Already Etna, Fuji, and Lee were dark cones dribbling red-orange lava. Trev shook sleep from his head. What a wonderful world—a young world, where mountains and people could grow free.

If the people could learn to survive. And if other people let them stay, instead of yanking them offworld—

A wild pitch of the plane jerked him out of his reverie. Too close! Prevailing winds had pushed him almost to the vents. Like in the bad old vidis, Trev's life flashed through his mind. This would *not* be a happy ending. Regaining control, he banked away from the hot updraft and steered back upwind on to course for Axis. The fate of a planet might be sloshing in his sample flasks.

Though she'd been sleeping soundly when Trev buzzed her room, Graysha jumped into her work clothes at two-fifteen and beat him to the lab, leaving Emmer on the pillow. Undoubtedly Melantha Lee knew Chair MaiJidda had commandeered Urbansky's plane by now. She would be hopping mad. Graysha wanted as much work done as possible before Lee interfered again.

The elevator door whined open. "Ho, Graysha," Trev sang out, his baritone voice turned tenor with excitement and exhaustion, to the accompaniment of a cart's rolling wheels.

She lunged off her stool and into the hall. They might be the only ones in the building, but she couldn't count on it. She raised a finger to shush him.

Comically biting both lips, he wheeled the cart into her lab. She helped guide it.

"Okay, lift the metal door." Carefully they unpacked the sampling rack. Graysha gasped softly. In three of Trev's culture flasks filled with chlorine-enriched medium, murkiness betrayed bacterial growth.

"You did it, Trev," she breathed. "You did it."

She opened one flask and carefully sniffed. Both the chlorine stench and the streptomycete soil scent were unmistakable. This was a strep organism, all right, and it thrived in an environment that would kill most bacteria.

Working rapidly, she drew a sample from one cloudy flask, dropped it onto a slide, and inserted the slide into her stain fixer. She breathed a prayer before switching the slide to her scanning scope's stage.

Filamentous rods, with chains of spores showing clearly at the end of long, thin mycelia: *Streptomyces*, confirmed.

Her back popped as she leaned away from the scope. Reaching for a marker, she paused. She'd been about to name the organism Sample One, but that described nothing. In her neatest print for posterity, she labeled the slide *Streptomyces varbergii.*

Trev hung close to her elbow, reeking of sweat. A day-glow grin lit his mustache from beneath. "Take a look," she said, and she stepped back from the scope. "All right, we know this bug survives at cool room temp and in our chlorine medium. So our next job is to confirm that it uses CFCs as its carbon source."

"Of course it does," Trev insisted. "Look where it was growing."

She smiled at her student. He'd learned so much! "Yes, but we have to confirm that. We have to try growing it in a medium that has no other carbon source—only CFC—and see if it survives. Would you inoculate— no," she said, shaking her head, "you've been up all night. I'll do it. Thanks so much, Trev. You're a trooper."

He raised both arms. "Hey, no problem."

"Go get some sleep."

"No problem with that, either." He wove and wobbled out the door.

Graysha ducked into her private office, intending to fire a message to Lindon's office, then remembered he didn't work there anymore. It had happened so suddenly. On the public register, she found his home code. +We found the organism,+ she sent.

To her surprise, he came back instantly. +I'll be down in the morning. Good luck.+

Now her mind leaped ahead. As soon as she could confirm *S. varbergii's* viability in CFC medium and find out what else it grew on, her next job would be to decide what would kill it. She would need something that would eradicate it on the clouds but wouldn't destroy streps in the soil if rains fell. This had to be a mighty tough bacterium, since chlorine didn't faze it—

Actually, she realized, her first job was to prepare multiple samples and hide them, in her lab and Jirina's—and in Varberg's, since he was gone. She would even hide some down in her apartment. She and Trev sweat blood and risked their lives to get these samples. Three 500-millileter flasks were too vulnerable.

From the glassware rack, she pulled several small sterile capped tubes, and she rapidly pipetted 10 mils of the cloudiest solution into each, quickly replacing caps one-handed. Two tubes went into her lab-coat pocket, propped upright with her pocket memo, as surreptitiously as she could get them there. She felt silly about that, but somehow, someone had learned about her piracy of Will Varberg's streps. Maybe each lab was watched electronically.

Then she pulled a handful of culture dishes from her refrigerated stock and inoculated those, too. She initialed each sample GBP, then tucked three into her lab refrigerator and carried two up the hall to Jirina's. She needed to stash these in cool spots because organisms that survived in polar clouds might not thrive at the temp of normal incubators.

It was 4:28 A.M., and still she'd seen no sign of Melantha Lee.

Home, then, quickly, with the other tube and one culture dish she palmed, and then one more trip back to work. She left Trev's flasks chilling in a ten-degree water bath and waved off her office lights.

When she stumbled into her apartment, everything looked the way she had left it, except that the mail light on her monitor blinked rapidly. She cued up the message.

+Please contact me ASAP. LDL.+

Didn't he ever sleep? She punched his code and an alert. A few seconds later, she read, +I've gotten HMF permission for you to set up a safe lab over there. Medtech PalTion is an old friend. She'll meet you downstairs at 7:30. I'll wait at Wastewater to talk at 7:45.+

Giddy with exhaustion, she wanted to laugh out loud. +Bless you, Lindon.+ It was perfect! Surely no one would sabotage cultures she filed at the colonists' HMF.

She punched up Gaea net and published the fact that she'd found her organisms, but before she typed in the name she'd given them, her courage faltered. She didn't dare accuse Varberg this publicly, now that he'd turned violent. *S. gaeaii,* she pecked out. Too many vowels, almost unpronounceable, but it would do.

Lee would be furious.

She moved Emmer to the pillow's edge and fell onto her bed fully clothed.

After four precious hours of sleep, Graysha met the medtech and took possession of a closetlike back lab burrowed under the HMF building. Then she hurried to Wastewater, where Lindon waited, stroking a young green willow leaf. She hurried up to him. "What have you heard about your daughter?"

He exhaled heavily, fingering the leaf. "No change," he said. "They promised to contact me if anything happens. Have you been by the medical lab?"

She ached for him. "Yes," she said. "It should work well. Thank you. I'll keep careful track of materials and see the HMF is repaid."

"If you give me a list, I'll cover that."

"Cover. . .? You don't mean pay for them personally? That wouldn't be right."

"I'll see that it's covered," he said firmly. "I should have thought of this earlier."

She hoped Axis had funds set aside for such purposes and he wasn't absorbing the expenses for her benefit. "We didn't have an organism isolated earlier, so giving me room to work on this would've been premature."

He gave the leaf one last tug, then turned away. "You're sure this is the one?"

"It looks right."

"How soon will you know?" he asked. "Ari MaiJidda has been ten times the help to you that I ever was, just by commandeering that plane."

She exulted. He actually wanted to help! Then, as before, she wondered, *Are my feelings toward Lindon true or am I subconsciously using him?* "You were trying to get along with Dr. Lee," she suggested. "I'm starting to suspect that she simply can't be humored."

Finally a wry smile appeared. "I'll say nothing."

It felt good to distract him from such horrible fears. "Anyway, my anti-microbial sensitivity tests should only take a day or so to run. I'll go in over my lunch break and finish setting them up."

"Have you had breakfast? You shouldn't skip meals." Two long creases furrowed his forehead, and dark circles ringed his eyes. With the surprising election defeat coming while his daughter still was a hostage, he must be resting terribly.

"No, and you're not supposed to go without sleep. But this is important."

"I'll nap this afternoon. Please go eat, Graysha."

Was that tenderness she heard in his voice? "Believe me," she said, "I've tried to figure out how I could get through to Varberg and talk him into releasing the girls. But he doesn't like me. He won't listen." She took a few steps away, studying the cattails. One head was starting to soften, releasing tiny feathered seeds to drift down into the raceways.

"Graysha."

She looked over her shoulder. This time, there was no mistaking his gentle tone.

"There's a church service tonight. Would you like to register an inquiry under the RL Act?"

Graysha gaped. He couldn't do this, could he? "Would I be welcome? I don't want your people to think . . . Well, Ari believes I'm spying for my mother."

"That's right. She does." Stepping backward, he tangled himself in a massive fern whose fronds overhung the path. She watched as he extricated himself without tearing a single leaflet.

"Well?" she asked after a long silence. "Would I be welcome?"

"To those whose intentions are sincere, you would be."

Even in her home church, where people loved to pass judgment on unexpected behavior, there were a dear few who didn't. "I don't want to make things complicated for you, Lindon."

"You've complicated things since the day you arrived," he said, and he reached for her hand. Hesitantly, she grasped his fingers. He pulled his arm in, drew her closer, and then dropped her hand so he could sweep both arms around her shoulders. "You're cold," he murmured. "Are you all right?"

His body gave off a warmth that made her want to stand closer yet. "I don't mean to be difficult," she whispered, disbelieving.

She felt his palms spread out on her back. Not daring to move or speak again, she locked her hands together, arms surrounding him. She could feel his heart beat a slow, steady rhythm.

"Graysha," he began—

Something clicked not too far away. Graysha let go of Lindon and turned to stare at the door, keenly aware that she still heard a heartbeat in her ears . . . her own racing pulse.

Paul Ilizarov backed into the treatment plant, dangling a towel over one arm. A short-haired young woman followed. As he turned, his shoulders squared with a sudden intake of breath and his demeanor became silk and oil. The woman's eyes grew huge. She backed out and vanished.

"Graysha," Paul greeted her. "DalLierx."

"Good morning, Paul." Embarrassed for no good reason, she brushed past him on her way out into the corridor. There she stood, waiting for angry voices.

Instead, the door clicked open again. Lindon slipped through. "I'll meet you in the hub at seven twenty tonight." He ran his fingers through his dark hair. "Is that all right?"

Her only thought was how much she wanted to hold him again. It probably was a good thing Paul had burst in when he did. She must maintain her professional objectivity—but was that possible anymore? "Where do I go to register this inquiry?" she whispered. "I'll do it before work."

"Can you find Kenn VandenNeill's office in the CA building?"

"I'm sure I can. I'll do it."

Varberg's continued absence meant she, Jirina, and Paul had to cover his duties, and she scrambled all morning simply to keep up with her third of the floor's maintenance routine. She decided to save time by seeding *S. gaeaii* from the flasks right there in her Gaea water baths onto CFC-enriched plates so she could run antimicrobial sensitivity trials. It meant a frantic morning, but soon, two dozen plates lay upside down in her cooled wincubator, evenly inoculated with broth from the flasks and then dotted with tiny paper circles. Each color-coded dot was impregnated with a known antimicrobial or antibiotic. By tomorrow, she might know if her job was going to be impossible . . . or just difficult. She hated to think of trying to convince Gaea Consortium to pay for a huge pharmaceutical shipment that might require refrigeration.

But if it meant saving the Goddard project, plus discovering an organism that would help with all future terraforming experiments, they probably would pay. It would be in their best interests, certainly.

She looked out a northeast window on her way out for lunch. This morning, in still air, the ash cloud resembled a giant cauliflower.

I must be hungry, she decided.

After lunch, she hiked up to CA and registered her inquiry. Mr. VandenNeill's secretary took down the information with a reassuringly nonchalant expression.

At one o'clock, her message alarm rang with a summons to Melantha Lee's office.

She latched the wincubator, swabbed her counters, and squared her shoulders. This would be her moment of truth. As soon as Trev came back from lunch—five minutes late as usual—she told him, "I have to go downstairs. Make sure nobody bothers the wincubator or the water baths, and see if you can finish that entisol inventory while you stand guard."

"Right, boss." He slung his lab coat over his shoulders. Graysha thought they looked broader than before.

Downstairs, standing outside Melantha Lee's closed door, she felt like a prisoner awaiting trial. The mottled floor tiles looked and felt chilly, even through her shoes. A dark-haired man typed rapidly at the reception area's keyboard. He had to be Edie Varberg's replacement.

What was life like for *her,* married to that man? Or was she just as loopy?

The door swung open. "Come in," Graysha heard. Bracing herself, she walked inside.

Dr. Lee sat at her desk. Once Graysha stood beside the extra chair, Lee touched a panel on her keyboard, and the door shut again. With its serene decorations and top-notch office hardware, this place was a far cry from Lindon's Colonial Affairs office. Graysha felt as if she'd come back home to the twenty-second century.

"Sit down." Lee rocked her chair in a slow arc forward and back.

Wishing herself anywhere else, she complied. "Good afternoon, Dr. Lee."

Melantha Lee's face remained placid as she pressed her palms together. "I believe I deserve an explanation for this . . . colonial hijacking of a plane we were using for geological survey work."

That stare would unnerve a statue, and a statue's stomach wouldn't churn. "As I understand it," Graysha said, "Axis's new Chair for Colonial Affairs commandeered that plane. I have no clearance for high-altitude flight from the HMF, and I would not have taken the plane without checking first with you. Trevarre is . . . impetuous." She leaned farther forward. "But I'd've been crazy not to take advantage of what he and Chair MaiJidda did. And you'll be pleased to hear I have antimicrobial sensitivity tests running. If all goes well, we should be able to start getting a handle on this cooling difficulty within a day or two." She had to tell Lee about the study she was running. Maybe it would draw attention close to home, and Lee—or whoever was the saboteur—would miss the fact that she'd started duplicate organisms off campus.

"I am glad." Lee granted her a dispassionate nod. "However, fuel consumed on that unauthorized trip was extremely expensive, not to mention dangerous to the plane. Mr. LZalle crashed one Gaea aircraft already. Fuel and repair costs will be taken from your salaries."

"The . . . both costs? Fuel and repair?"

"It would not be just for Gaea Consortium to absorb such waste from its limited resources."

Graysha's legs twitched. She wanted to get up and run far away. It was unfair, absolutely unfair to bill her. But if she argued, would Lee's sabotage program reach out even further?

Half a terrannum's wages wouldn't cover the cost of aircraft repair. Even at triple salary. "Doesn't Gaea have insurance?" she asked, recovering some semblance of intelligence.

"For authorized pilots." Lee crossed her arms.

"Yukio HoBrace crashed that plane."

"Then the colonists will pay damages, too. You have no idea," she said, then she paused to sigh, "how weary I have become of petty financial difficulties, of high-handed appropriation of Gaea equipment and materiel."

"As a Gaea employee, wasn't Yukio covered by *us*?"

Lee uncrossed her arms. She lowered her eyebrows and gave Graysha a dark look. "Go back to work, Dr. Brady-Phillips."

"Yes," Graysha said, feeling nauseated. "I will."

After calling the elevator, she stood staring at metal door panels. Gaea had spent the time and money to give them a satin finish.

Yukio HoBrace had to be insured. Melantha Lee was simply telling her, showing her, that the price for any further meddling would be exorbitant. In retrospect, she wished she hadn't been so quick to blame Ari MaiJidda and Yukio, giving Melantha Lee an additional reason to resent the colonists.

Too late. As she rode the elevator back to her floor, she knew the heaviness deep in her stomach wasn't due just to accelerating upward.

She wished she had something to fall back on, emotionally—the way Lindon leaned on his church. If only Novia hadn't spoiled religion for her . . .

Well, this evening would be interesting. She focused on her duties for the rest of the afternoon. Just before quitting time, Jirina slipped into her lab. The long sleeves and high collar of a black turtleneck shirt showed under her brilliant pink lab coat. "That must have been quite a conference with the Dragon Lady."

Graysha pressed her eyes to the scanning scope, where she was counting spores. "I don't want to talk about it."

Jirina laid a hand on her shoulder. "You okay, Blondie? How's that beautiful colonist of yours surviving his new unemployment?"

At the mention of Lindon, Graysha's cheeks warmed. She pushed away from the scope and eyed Jirina, who drew back to lean languidly against the countertop. "I'd guess he's too worried about the girls over at Hannes to waste time crying in his beer."

"Ooh. I do wish you hadn't mentioned beer." Jirina shook her head. "The Lwuites never bothered planting hops. If we pooled our petty cash, we could send for a keg from Copernicus and have a floor party."

"It was just an expression." Graysha lowered her voice. "But don't invite Varberg. And I think I'd leave Paul home, too."

"Wisely said, Blond Woman. That leaves you and me and Trevish."

It felt good to talk about something light, something irrelevant. She raised an eyebrow. "Maybe we'd better invite Botany."

"Maybe we'd better wait till we can go to Copernicus ourselves." Shaking her head in mock sorrow, Jirina strode out.

Graysha's eyes ached for a rest. She stood up and cracked her back, then pulled open the wincubator door to check preliminary growth.

The plates looked ominously clear. After five hours, some slight turbidity might confirm that the bugs were growing.

If these flasks, too, had been sterilized . . .

One still sat in the chilly water bath. Maybe *S. gaeaii* wouldn't flourish in any of these media, or maybe she was trying to grow cloud-borne organisms at too high a temperature or in too moist an environment.

Or maybe . . .

She could run an enzyme activity check on a 100-mil sample from one flask to confirm viability, or she could wait until morning. Running the titration would mean skipping dinner if she hoped to join Lindon at his church.

If the organisms were dead, knowing tonight would make no difference. At least she had cultures hidden where no one should suspect.

She pulled off her lab coat and waved off the lights. Since the HMF lay just beyond Gaea housing on the hub, she dashed downstairs and checked her culture dishes there. Glistening, lumpy growth streaks made her exhale hard in relief. Here, at least, the bugs seemed content.

That made the no-growth flasks up in her lab all the more suspicious.

She gobbled a bowl of stew and took a fast sink bath, then paused in front of her open drawer. Her offworld clothes were far dressier than anything she'd purchased here. Did she want to appear so obviously foreign—or try to fit in?

She lifted a soft fawn-colored pullover. If only she'd worn it this morning, when Lindon held her. She still wondered why he'd done it. Voted out of office, he might be vulnerable, needing sympathetic company. Or maybe the undeniable chemistry that drew her to him from the beginning pulled both ways and only now was he free to show it.

No. She still was Novia Brady-Phillips's daughter, a former Eugenics Board employee, the informant responsible for Rebecca Endedi's conviction and the misery imposed on all those children.

Emmer lay content on her pillow, stuffed full of dinner scraps. Graysha almost envied the creature's easy, risk-free life.

But not really. Not tonight. She wondered what Lindon's late wife had looked like. *Beautiful, probably.* Surely no one ever expected her to die so young.

Graysha's pullover looked dressy enough when she wore it with brown cloth pants that hung like long culottes. She took a few extra minutes with her hair, making sure every strand lay smooth along her head and snug in the tie. A touch of blue eyeliner to bring out the silver in her eyes made her realize she hadn't worn makeup since arriving on Goddard.

Then she pulled open her perfuming kit. Lilac again, she decided. Lindon seemed the kind to enjoy old-fashioned touches. She mixed the proper amounts from memory, then touched droplets to her wrist and throat and stroked what remained across her hair.

It was seven-fifteen. She slid on shoes and was ready. Rather than wait, she walked up to the hub.

He had arrived early, too. Standing between a bench and a young apple tree, he faced Gaea housing and watched her arrival. It gave her a chance to take a good look back. He wasn't tall, was more slender than muscular, but remembering the calluses on his hands, she guessed he was strong enough. Paul called him "too pretty," but there was nothing effeminate about Lindon's strong chin, his arching black eyebrows, or the possessive smile with which he met her. "I'd offer my arm," he said, "but you're going to create a stir as it is."

That was an understatement! "Did you sleep?"

"A little." He wore nubbly trousers and a pale blue shirt—local clothing, but finer than usual. "One thing you'd better know is that there will be a short communion service."

"Universal Father stopped doing that fifty years ago. We're not into blood."

"I know," he said. "That's . . ." He seemed to catch himself. "What I need to tell you is that it's open to all who consider themselves believers. There won't be any pressure to participate, though."

"That's good," she said. "I was, once. I think."

"That's all right." He guided her north. "There will be others who don't take the elements. But I need communion tonight." The desire in his voice became keen, almost hurting her with its intensity. "With Sarai still gone," he explained.

Not to mention the ego blow of an election defeat. "Here." She drew the text capsule from her hip pocket. "Thank you."

He took it back without comment and walked on. At a plain concrete arch on the corry's right, he touched her arm. It led a hundred meters farther on, past several rooms she'd never seen. Finally he pushed open a round-arched door.

She blinked into darkness that was barely lit by unscented candles. As she hesitated at the entry, Lindon let the door close. From speakers she couldn't see, soft, slow electronic music played a reverie.

Lindon slid into the back row of foam-covered chairs. She followed until he chose one, then took the seat beside him. About fifty people already sat inside, some whispering, some quiet.

To her right, light from the doorway flashed and faded as other worshipers entered. She'd never felt more like a spy. Yet if Lindon's own version of God existed, she, too, was being observed. *I want to learn*, she addressed Him. No one here would mind if she tried a silent prayer. *But please, nothing mindless.*

The first parts of the service—singing, group prayer—could have been Universal Father. Beside her Lindon stood up, then sat, then stood again, obviously at home with the routine and trying to cue her when necessary.

Graysha felt the room's atmosphere darken as the ritual began. "The visible reminder," intoned the leader, "that blood has been shed and we have been cleansed." Graysha cringed. This was a disturbingly effective method of reminding worshipers what they believed. Physical involvement was required, and everything shared was consumed . . . digested . . . became part of the participant's body.

Lindon winced as his teeth crushed half a cracker, just as if he were biting into someone's flesh. Acutely aware of being trapped in her own defective body, Graysha shivered. He really did believe this. She could be back at Einstein for all the attention he paid her now.

He accepted a tiny cup of red juice and sat staring at it. ". . . blood of the new covenant," the man up front finished. "Help us to live as those who have been forgiven."

Lindon drank, then wiped his face. Tears? she wondered. Lindon was no blood-sipping barbarian, but this smacked of ancient Rome and the lions.

Like a CUF service, there was more music and a speaker. Unlike CUF, the sermon focused on someone ancient and invisible. A queer sense of finally escaping her fears stole into her heart. She resisted its seduction, reminding herself there was no escaping the destiny fate—and genetics—had dealt her.

But was all this *real?* What if a way out really existed? A new purpose for this life, and something more—something perfect, without defects—afterward?

You don't need to be flawless, whispered a voice at the back of her mind, *if He really was.*

When the meeting ended, no lights came up. A few people left, while others remained seated. Some bent forward to rest their arms on the chair in front of them.

Graysha searched the room, this time noticing its stark plainness. Its yellow-tan walls were smoothed but not painted. At least there was rough brown carpet. "Don't you have emblems of some sort?" she whispered. "We had the three stars."

Lindon sighed, as if he were focusing his mind back on his chosen planet. "The cross is our sign. But this sanctuary is used by other faiths on alternating days." He stood to embrace a man who stepped in front of him—the gesture didn't seem to embarrass either one of them—then bent back down to address Graysha. "In the two terrannums since arriving here, we've admitted a number of new members. Perhaps they need to understand their human identity. Perhaps they've found that human nature hasn't changed so much, despite the . . . changes we've made."

She smiled inwardly at his near slip, feeling composed again. "Maybe living on a half-finished planet makes people more desperate to believe someone out there is on their side." *Particularly that Man,* she reflected, remembering the text capsule.

Instead of answering, Lindon touched her shoulder and nodded toward the aisle. In the corridor, several other people greeted him, shook her hand, and invited her to come back. They gave the impression of sincere welcome. At first it surprised her. Then she guessed that those who feared her had already left.

The gathering dissipated. Lindon glanced up and down the corry. She wished his wrist alarm would bleat with news that Varberg had released Sarai and the other little girl. Then he really might relax. *What about it?* she asked the supernatural one. *He just paid you a visit. This would be a good time to act on his behalf.*

Back at the main corridor, Lindon hesitated. "Would you come home with me for a while?"

Feeling as if a shuttle's thrust had just ended, leaving her weightless, she said, "All right." If all her old fears were about to come back, she could at least delay the reentry. Oddly, she didn't distrust his intentions. Was she so convinced of Lwuite nonaggression?

Not far from the textile plant, he led west at a narrower corridor, pausing at its end to unlock a door. A breath of spices and hot dough puffed out before he waved on a light. She stepped into a small carpeted living area. Other than a cluster of framed portraits straight ahead, his walls were bare.

Then she sniffed. "It smells wonderful in here."

"I have fresh rolls from the co-op. Would you like tea?"

"Yes, thank you."

Lindon crossed the room to a tiny kitchen. She let her eyes swing left, through an open door into a small bedroom, then quickly followed Lindon. His counters were bare—he probably ate at the co-op—but he did have a dusty glass of dried faded flower heads on a shelf over his sink. *Memento of his wife,* she guessed.

She took a seat by his table on one of two benches cemented to the wall. He switched on a small waterpot, then pulled a hooded ceramic tray out of his oven and a stoneware crock from the refrigerator.

Amused, she wriggled, finding a comfortable spot on the bench's thin cushion. "Are you still worried about my blood sugar?"

Lindon set the tray on the table in front of her. "It's called hospitality." He slathered butter over one roll and pushed it toward her on a plate, then returned for two steaming stoneware mugs. "Now, what can I explain about the service?"

Intentions, she reflected wryly. This man had designs on her soul. Her body could wait.

"You're an intelligent man, Lindon. Obviously, to you this is real.

Does it make you happy? Does it make your life . . . smooth?"

"Obviously not," he said softly, "or Sarai would be at Axis."

As would Sarai's mother. She glanced at the dusty dried flowers. "I'm sorry," she said. "Is your older daughter back from Hannes yet?"

A drip of butter pooled on the underside of his fingers. "Yes. Of my girls, Bee is the quicker. She tells me she turned and ran when Varberg broke into the crèche's hallway and started grabbing hands. Sarai frightens easily." He shook his head. "It will take her months to recover. If ever."

"The poor child." Graysha wiped her hands on a soft cloth napkin. "This must be one of the hardest things you've ever lived through."

He stared through his roll at the table, and she respected his silence. The table, she noticed, had a repeating wood-grain imprint on its brown-stained concrete surface. She admired the ingenuity that reused one precious board to give many colonists' tables the comforting look of home.

"It's not a matter of finding divine security," he said after a long minute, "or smoothness. It's an assurance that . . ." He leaned back, closed his eyes, then opened them and went on. "That when I have fallen short, or put my surroundings out of balance, the covenant He struck provides me with reconciliation. You read a gospel," he added. "Laying aside historical criticism and the CUF's deification of humanity for a moment, would you call Christ's life heroic?"

"Obviously." Here, she was on familiar turf. CUF study classes had discussed reasons to believe or disbelieve historical documents, instead of studying the documents' contents. She'd been taught since childhood that literalists lacked education, imagination, and intelligence. "But if you're going to take the man literally, he said he was returning to Earth. Doesn't it worry you that we're colonizing other worlds and it still hasn't happened? If you really expect it to happen, don't you want to be there?"

Lindon pulled off another section of roll and buttered it. "It took longer than anyone expected from the Abrahamic covenant to the First Coming. Thousands of terrannums longer. But from God's extradimensional perspective, He could manifest himself anywhere—or everywhere."

CUF teachings had no answer for that. Impressed, she decided not to ask what he meant by an Abrahamic covenant. Plainly, his was no mindless belief. "Do you think the man was God, then?" Really, that was the crux of the matter. If a person bought that idea, everything else had to follow. Every word he said had to be taken . . . well, taken as gospel.

"I do." He spoke as solemnly as a bridegroom taking his vows.

"Why?"

Lindon fingered his mug's glazed handle. "For one thing, He made the claim on record. CUF doesn't often quote that. Your former church stresses all the wrong things. Your mother thinks she'll win eternal life by hard work and legalism. It isn't done that way."

The strength of her defensive reaction surprised her. Evidently she did still believe—somewhere deep inside. "You aren't going to conquer Goddard without hard work," she pointed out.

"All I've seen here only proves that humankind doesn't change. That's my chief difficulty with the Noetics and your mother's church. Both make *Homo sapiens* something to worship."

Do it, urged the inner voice. *You have nothing to lose and everything to gain.* Instead, she leaned against the wall and took another large mouthful of the steaming nut-brown roll.

"Are those bacteria from the polar clouds working out?" He seemed not to sense her silent struggle—or was this just his impeccable manners?

"Too early to tell much." Glad to change the subject, she explained the beginning she'd made. Melantha Lee's financial threat seemed too absurd to mention.

Nodding, he wiped his hands with a cloth. "I hope . . . If there's anything else I can do to facilitate your research, don't hesitate to ask."

There might not be much he could do anymore. The election defeat had to weigh heavily on his mind.

He pivoted on his bench to face her. "About your mother, Graysha."

On to the next uncomfortable subject. "Go ahead," she said, bracing herself.

"What—" he began, then he pressed his lips together and flicked a loose thread on his pale blue shirt. "What promise, what assurance can you give me that anything you learned about my people will not find its way back to her?"

Not so difficult a question as she expected, but much more direct. He looked straight into her eyes, as if daring her to turn away. "You have my word already."

"That was forced from you."

A shiver started at her fingertips, passed up her arms, and dissipated through her shoulders. "Then I'll repeat it. I am finished with my mother and her schemes. Through. I would love to be reconciled to her someday," she admitted, "but only on my own terms. I swear it, Lindon." She longed to tell him exactly how she felt and be done with it. If he laughed her off, she wouldn't have to fight her feelings anymore. "I . . . need to tell you something personal."

He cocked one eyebrow. On him, it was not a mocking expression.

"I assume you know you're easy to look at," she said, rushing ahead, surprised to realize that a part of her heart wanted to test him, to see if she could push him away. "I admire you, and I enjoy your company. So tell me. Is that love?"

His soft exhalation sounded like the surprised ghost of a laugh. "A lot of people think so." He cleared his throat. "It's certainly part of love."

She pressed her shoulders against the bench's hard backrest. "I realize that wasn't graceful. I'm sorry. But in my lifetime, there won't be time to waste playing social games."

"Thank you," he murmured. "It's an awkward situation, isn't it? The closer you and I become, the more of a danger we pose to each other." He stared. His lips twitched, first frowning, then relaxing. He looked as if he were struggling with some decision. After several seconds, those firmed lips softened. "Have you ever considered remarriage?"

Good heavens! The rules to this game were changing too quickly to follow. Her cheeks flamed. "I have," she managed.

Dark eyes flicked up to meet hers for an instant, and then he dropped his stare again. "Assume for a moment—hypothetical situation   that your health would let you remain on Goddard, with or without Gaea. If you could choose a job, what would it be?"

At least that one was easy to answer. "I'm only masquerading as a researcher. I'm a teacher."

He looked up, arching one eyebrow again. "We need teachers, particularly those trained in sciences at the university level. Our children are the future of Goddard."

"You're not CCA anymore," she said bluntly, wondering whether she spoke out of defensiveness or sheer perversity. "You don't have to talk like a chairman. Any children I have will carry a genefect."

Shutting his eyes, he tapped one finger on the tabletop. "You want children, though, don't you?"

Graysha clenched her hands. "I was only deluding myself, trying to think I accepted EB standards for my life. I hate the notion of becoming an outlaw, but . . ." She trailed off, shaking her head.

Lindon looked straight into her eyes. "I think you've guessed what I'm about to tell you."

She almost stopped breathing. She imagined she could feel magma moving deep under Goddard's surface, the world slowly rotating, the swift sweep of Eps Eri orbiting the home galaxy's center.

His dark, bright eyes didn't waver. "We have a clinic on Goddard. It is as illegal as your wishes. It's possible, but not guaranteed, that we could help you . . . your children, anyway."

She bowed her head and covered her eyes with one hand, turning somersaults inside. It was true!

He reached across the table for her free hand and held it, caressing her palm with his rough thumb. That made her want touches she'd lived without for far too long. Warning sirens roared at the back of her mind. She lowered her voice. "What are you?" she whispered.

"It started innocently enough," he said softly, "with a study of certain families that seemed immune to most cancers."

Graysha's body went stiff, and her breaths came shallow. He really was going to confess!

"Dr. Lwu—Palila Lwu, not her husband—was able to isolate several fragile loci, strengthen supporting chromosomes, and to some extent, suppress the body's predisposition to die at around 120 years. She also worked with programmed cell death—apoptosis, they call it. She really did believe in nonaggression, but truly, she felt that increased longevity was the key. She hoped it would decrease the species' tendency toward self-destruction. And my parents—my grandparents, too—believed her."

Palila Lwu was the one they named themselves after? "Longevity?" she asked.

He dipped his chin.

"Just how long do you expect to live?"

"The second-generation average is 152 terrannums," he answered softly. Graysha groaned. So long . . .

Yet not that long, objectively speaking. "For an extra thirty terrannums—what, 20 percent?—you're risking so much."

Lindon's clenching hand relaxed, and she adjusted her fingers more comfortably. "Our people are working to extend it."

"You still have genetic diseases, like diabetes."

"Exactly. It's controllable, so that work is prioritized to the next generation, after we finish cleaning up deadlier hab-based mutations."

She nodded. *Like mine.* Did any Lwuites carry Flaherty's genes?

"It's genetically possible," he continued, "that humans could live for centuries. It's just not good for us, and I believe that with all my heart. If we were genetic immortals, we'd be so frightened of taking risks we'd spend eternity hiding, accomplishing nothing. The concept of life after death is healthier for the psyche."

So he'd been given a gift he could not give back. Plainly, it troubled his conscience.

"But if the Eugenics Board finds us . . ." Trailing off, he spread his empty hand.

"I know." His reaction to the Endedi case made bitter sense. Graysha felt a second chill. "Are any of the modifications dominant?"

"All recessive, like most altered genes. Six chromosome pairs are involved."

She nodded. "Are you homozygous?"

"*You* singular, or *you* plural?"

"Both."

"I am fully homozygous, with all twelve altered chromosomes. About half of us are. About a quarter heterozygous carriers, about a quarter non-carriers. But at the clinic, we're working on a better percentage for the next generation."

"That won't create conflicts with your own generation?"

His hand shifted again, and he let her go. Delicately, he fingered the kitten-soft edge of her pullover's cuff. "What do you think?"

One face sprang into her mind, a sudden epiphany. "Ari MaiJidda," she guessed, suddenly understanding the D-group coordinator at several new levels. "Heterozygous, jealous, and as aggressive as a killer bee. Since you've admitted this much, tell me how Palila Lwu eluded the Eugenics Board for long enough to create . . . what, fifteen thousand of you?"

"Eight thousand in the first generation. Her husband had a large staff. He was working on something else, you'll remember. Fetal work late in pregnancy, thwarting sexual dimorphism as expressed in the corpus callosum. That much is public knowledge."

"As Ari MaiJidda would be pleased to remind us all. I'm deeply impressed so many people kept such an incredible secret."

"They were incredibly motivated. Look at their choices—"

"Oh yes," she interrupted. "Full-body irradiation for themselves and all their children if they spoke up. Otherwise, long life and a hope for peace."

"Only a hope, though."

She kept thinking. "Did that town-meeting discussion swing the election to Ari?"

"Maybe. That, and my public insistence that your site supervisor knows more than she's admitting about the cooling. I'm supposedly responsible for a number of retaliatory restrictions."

"Ouch. So says Chair MaiJidda, I assume."

"Yes."

"I see." Graysha clasped her hands, remembering how gently his rough hands stroked them, then she forcibly focused her thoughts on this conversation. Whether or not he should speak, Lindon was answering questions. "Do you admire Palila Lwu and her husband?"

"Yes," he said.

"But doesn't their work conflict with your beliefs?"

"Did you ever read how vigorously some people opposed organ transplants? We've all but forgotten their objections."

Interesting. "Do you honestly feel that the callosal work has outlasted its usefulness?"

"Absolutely. Taidje FreeLand, of the CA committee, is one of Henri Lwu's last surviving co-workers, and he is almost convinced, as well."

So one reason they came here was to drop a deception and concentrate on another one. "You—a Christian—have to live inside a circle of lies." Did he dare deny that?

Nodding, he covered her hands with his own. "Sometimes we have to choose not to follow human law. Now that I've lost reelection, I'm free to express doubts I had all along. With all our so-called medical advances, we are still muddled, selfish people." He pulled his hands away. "Does it disturb you to know what I am, Graysha?"

She leaned her head back against the wall, glanced up at the ceiling, and confessed, "Only out of jealousy. I can't imagine what it would be like."

Lindon shook his head. "You have about twenty terrannums?"

"More or less."

"If you were isolated from medical care, how much would that shorten your life expectancy?"

"It shouldn't," she admitted. "I'll have adequate warning before I reach terminal hospitalization phase."

"Will you think about settling here?"

She mulled over his question carefully before deciding it wasn't a marriage proposal after all. "It's terribly far out," she said in a low voice. "You were right about that all along. I'm fine for now, but eventually I'll need full-time care."

"When that time comes, steps can be taken. Please consider it," he said, pressing down on her hands, "so we can consider helping you."

She still was free to leave, even free to report this man to her mother. Stricken by the thought, she shuddered. "It's possible you would have to protect *me* from the Eugenics Board."

"I would," he said.

"Oh," she murmured, then she realized Lindon had given someone else real grounds to eliminate her. "What will happen if Chair MaiJidda finds out what you just told me?"

"That will depend," he said soberly, "on how good you really are at keeping secrets."

She shifted her hands so she could grip his. "So, Lindon—how much does a person really need to understand before they can buy into this faith of yours?"

He drew away from her, wide-eyed, plainly startled.

Go on, she urged herself again. *Try it on. This could be your last chance.* "If the way you treat people is any sign of what old-line Christianity is about, I could just about sign on."

He exhaled hard, shaking his head. "Don't look to me for an example. Don't ever—" Abruptly, he pulled his hands away. A sudden clear smile spread across his face. "Oh, Graysha, forgive me for arguing. All you need is to admit your flawed nature—"

"No problem with that," she said lightly.

"And accept salvation as Christ's gift, not anything you could earn."

"Aha," she murmured. "Here, you and my mother's church part company."

He nodded.

"Anything else?"

"That's where we all start."

She shut her eyes. *All right, then. Here I am. As imperfect as anyone ever born. And there he sits, and I am not doing this just to please him! At least,* she added, slitting one eye open, *not exclusively. But if you want to give eternity as a gift, I would love to come home to you. Show me what to do next.*

Sighing heavily, she opened her eyes. "Now what?"

"Did you?" He leaned forward over the table, as earnest as she'd ever seen him.

She nodded.

He seized her hand. "Now we rejoice." To her astonishment, he drew her to her feet. "Let me walk you back to the hub."

30. SUICIDE GENE

Two minutes after Lindon's congregation dispersed, someone knocked at the door of Ari MaiJidda's apartment. Startled, she shoved the vest she was embroidering back behind her soft chair. "Come," she called, deactivating the lock from where she sat.

A woman slipped in. Ari recognized her from D-group. "I just saw something you'll want to know about," the stranger began.

Five minutes later, she had gone and Ari sat rigid on her chair. She already knew Brady-Phillips didn't fly off with LZalle—and that disappointment was cruel enough—but now the worst had happened. DalLierx had taken her to his church. And even worse was about to happen. Information concerning the Lwuites' actual religious practices, or lack of them, was about to pass from Lindon DalLierx to Commissioner Novia Brady-Phillips by way of the smoothest intermediary the Eugenics Board could have sent. News of that sort fairly flew—witness the visit she'd just had.

She pushed up out of her chair, clenching and unclenching her hands. If only she could shoot the woman and be done with it!

No, it must be absolutely, unimpeachably accidental—or suicidal—and immediate. That shuttle coming for Varberg must carry Brady-Phillips away, too, dead or alive.

Alive? If Yael GurEshel could be convinced to frame an evacuation-to-hospitalize order...

No. Surely Brady-Phillips already knew too much.

How close *were* they?

Close enough for the pretty boy to agree to marry her. The relationship was accelerating toward consummation.

And Paul Ilizarov hadn't been her would-be assassin, after all; it had been crazy-man Varberg. That disappointed her, but she would sleep it off. Varberg could be managed into bringing that atmospheric organism under control, particularly if his choices were to cooperate or be prosecuted for kidnapping. She would save the attempted murder charge as a final threat and use it only if necessary.

Ari shuffled back to her chair and carefully sat down in the dark. Tissue oxygen. She remembered reading about something that bound up tissue oxygen.

Carbon monoxide! The gas was greedy to bind hemoglobin, and though no longer plentiful in this post-petrofuel age, it was available.

And—most important, if her victim was to be Graysha Brady-Phillips—odorless.

Lindon hadn't fallen asleep, though midnight had passed. He lay staring at the skylight, his mind tugging in three directions. Perhaps Sarai slept, frightened but safe. Axis's future lay in Ari's hands now, not his, though he'd left so much undone.

And then there was Graysha!

Guide her, Lord. Don't let her lean on me. He had said far too much, from a human standpoint—but then look what happened!

Yes, but what if she chose not to settle? His confession would put fifteen thousand people at risk.

Did he do the right thing? Was one soul worth more than the future of a world?

If rescuing one soul from torment was worth his Lord's infinite sacrifice, and if infinity times fifteen thousand still equaled infinity, then each individual soul had the same value as the entire group. But heavenly math muddled his brain. He needed to speak to her again. Soon—

His message alarm sang out.

Distracted, he crossed the room and read, +Chenny HoNin. Security transmission. Please enter net password.+

This might be terrible news. His heart thudded as he keyed in his code.

Now letters appeared successively, indicating spontaneous transmission. +Re your news about Will Varberg and the charge of attempted murder, I agree. He makes a likely suspect. Would like to try an arrest. It will mean breaking into Varberg's room. Some danger to Sarai inevitable. Want your permission before we try it. HoBraces', too.+

His mind's eye created a horrible image: Sarai, caged with a man who didn't shy from trying murder. What would Varberg do if Chenny's forces tried to break in?

He scratched his scalp, remembering that Varberg's wife was also in that room. She was a mother, a steadying influence who might protect Sarai and Merria.

On the other hand, Varberg dominated her to an unwholesome degree. He reached for the keyboard. +How soon do you need permission?+

+We want to try before dawn, when we hope they'll be sleeping.+

+I'll be back within an hour.+

+Thank you, Lindon.+

The screen darkened. Lindon felt haggard and helpless. Should he ask them to wait, hoping Varberg would release the girls when his shuttle came? Varberg might decide to keep a hostage for travel, but it would be easier for police to snatch them en route to a shuttle than from a closed room.

At last, he lifted his leaden hands to the keyboard. +Chair HoNin: Permission granted. LDL+ He hesitated another minute, covering the message with prayer.

Then he sent it.

Edie Varberg woke panicked. Voices, lights, people rushing one way and another. Someone waved on the brilliant overhead lamp.

Will stood rigid in the corner, dangling Merria HoBrace by her shoulders. A beefy man in black aimed some kind of weapon at them.

"Let her go, let her go!" Edie shrieked at Will. She spun around. Someone carried tiny Sarai DalLierx from the room. "Wait," she called, "let me—stop, let me give you my medicine vial! She isn't hurt, she's only asleep."

The rescuer paused. "Mighty sound sleep."

Edie seized the kit bag.

"Edie," Will shouted angrily.

The staph-doctored inhaler—they would charge him with trying to kill DalLierx if they saw it! He was guilty and sick, desperately sick. She whirled back to face her husband. "Let the girl go!"

Will hesitated, fury flaring his nostrils.

"Please, Will." Her voice caught.

He threw Merria to the floor. Instantly, the burly man sprang. Someone else caught Edie's hands from behind and cuffed them. She relaxed, sobbing.

A voice behind her clipped, "All clear, Chair HoNin."

The door flew open. Chenny HoNin strode in, short pigtails wagging as she surveyed the room. She knelt beside Merria HoBrace, who lay slumped on the floor, and extended a hand.

"Wait," said the burly man. "Don't move her. She might be injured."

"We didn't mean to hurt them." Edie forced words through her tears. "Please, we . . . we . . . it's only . . . oh . . ."

"Spit it out, woman!" Will shouted.

She couldn't look at him but mumbled toward the floor. "We only want to go away. Back to a hab. Back where it's safe."

Chenny HoNin was a short woman, but authority heightened her. "That has been arranged," she said. "First, however, Dr. Varberg . . ." She stared up at Will with hate-filled eyes. "We have concrete evidence of a CFC-eating organism over Goddard's north pole, and rumor has it you created that organism. If you did release it, you'll be thankful you're in custody. Otherwise, I would not guarantee your safety when word reaches the rest of my people."

Instantly, Will seemed to come back to life. He pulled his shoulders back and his head came up.

"On the other hand," Chenny went on, "there's a possibility of the kidnapping charges being dropped if you will cooperate with an attempt to contain that organism."

"I see." Will smiled widely. To Edie, he still looked so handsome. So wise. "That, too, can be arranged."

"You'll cooperate?"

"They can put the trank guns away."

Edie slumped in relief.

Melantha Lee hunched over the keyboard in her apartment. She lived at the inmost end of the Gaea wing, separated by as much concrete as possible from hub and cafeteria noises. +Cooperate with them, Will,+ she typed, certain the exchange would be monitored by colonists—as well as Flora Hauwk at the Gaea System office.

+You'll need to get help for Brady-Phillips's research.+

Yes, help: help making sure it failed. Lee understood the hint. +Paul still owes me for past services,+ she returned. +I'll put him on it.+

Graysha slept like a corpse, without dreaming or moving. Emmer lay across her neck, clicking softly, when the alarm rang at seven.

She sponged off hurriedly while her memory replayed last night's conversation with Lindon, down to every touch. So much had changed, so suddenly, that she didn't know what to do. All she knew was that she must never ever see her mother again. *Please,* she prayed, trying out the new-old habit. If she felt different at all, it was only the confidence of having done the right thing.

Before eating, she spent twenty minutes in her tiny HMF lab. Two meters by three and windowless, it had a concrete countertop and a small incubator, and that was about all. She carried her loop dropper in her pocket. If she needed a sink, she had to go out into the medtech's domain; still, she inoculated two dozen more plates for antibiotic trials, then peered out into the larger lab. "Fresia?" she called, but the medtech had let her in and then vanished. Feeling guilty for snooping, she started searching cupboards for the small glass vials that normally contained antibiotic test disks.

She'd worked her way down one countertop when the medtech returned. "Antibiotics?" Graysha asked.

"Here's what I have." Fresia had broad shoulders that made her tiny waist seem even more pronounced. She pulled down an overhead rack, and Graysha felt her empty stomach lurch. At the Gaea building, she'd lain samples of 150 antibiotics on culture plates. Here were maybe 30.

She still might find something that was environmentally safe. "Thanks," she said, "I'll bring them right back out."

Inside her lab, she used a pair of sterile tweezers to drop five tiny drug-saturated dots onto each of six plates. Gingerly she flipped them, making sure the disks adhered.

Back in her Gaea lab, after downing cereal and cream, she hurried to the wincubator. Any antibiotic inhibiting *gaeaii* would create a clear no-growth zone around it. The rest of the plate would have clouded up by now.

She held the first plate up to the brilliance of her own laboratory light quickly, before condensation could cloud its cold surface.

Totally clear, with no bacterial growth anywhere.

Sabotage. Again. Shutting her eyes, she slumped forward long enough to swallow bile, then straightened. If anyone did monitor this lab, they would see defeat.

Maybe she'd have better news tomorrow, at the HMF.

She pulled her lab coat off a stool and slipped it on. As soon as Trev arrived, there were soil samples to run from Axis's protoforest.

"Graysha?"

She turned around. Paul stood gently knocking against the door frame. Was he the saboteur? "Come in."

"I apologize for interrupting yesterday, at Wastewater." He tucked his chin and gave her a knowing look.

"We were talking," she said firmly.

"Talking. Yes." Clasping her shoulder, he lowered his voice. "After this

I'll mind my own business, but I think you should know DalLierx's family made its fortune running illegal drugs."

Drugs? Lindon's family? Her vision went muddy. "I never heard anything so preposterous."

"They were never caught. Ask him sometime where the money came from."

"Is he wealthy?" she asked, curious in spite of herself. Was that why he offered to reimburse the HMF for whatever materials she used?

"Probably not anymore. Ask him," he repeated. "But don't trust his answer."

"Thank you, Paul." She tried to sound sincere.

He winked, squeezed her shoulder, and left.

Poison, she thought at him, *that's poison you're spreading.* If he wasn't sabotaging her experiments, he certainly was trying to ruin her relationship with Lindon.

She couldn't ask Lindon such a thing. Even if it were true, he might not know. How, then, would Paul?

+Dr. Varberg has returned. We need to set up parameters for completion of your research. M. Lee+

Graysha pushed back her desk chair and braced for a long elevator ride into battle. It was later that same morning—Dropoff, and Orion hung overhead. She walked cautiously into Melantha Lee's office.

At the near corner of Lee's desk sat the ever-present glass of marigolds. She wondered if Lee guessed what use Varberg had made of them.

Several extra chairs had been pulled into the room. Varberg sat between two Lwuite men wearing D-group name tapes, whose attention swung her direction before returning to their charge. They looked out of place in a room flagged with stone tiles and watched by an elegant mural.

"Dr. Varberg," Lee began, "Dr. Brady-Phillips has isolated a cloud-dwelling organism of the *Streptomyces* family. It metabolizes chlorofluorocarbons. She believes the organism is gene tailored. Reluctantly, she has stated that she further believes the organism originated in the Gaea microbial genetics laboratory. I would like to know if that is true and, if so, if you will assist us in eradicating the organism." With her fingers steepled in front of her chest and iron-gray curls pressed flat against her desk chair, Dr. Lee looked official enough. The speech sounded rehearsed.

"Dr. Lee," Graysha interrupted, picking up the cue she assumed Lee had dropped, "my cultures have died."

"What? Died?" Lee asked. Her eyes went round in her round face. "All of them? How?"

"I don't know." Graysha stood stiffly beside Lee's desk. "I still have Trev's samples. There could be viable cells in the flasks."

Varberg laid a palm on each of his knees. When he leaned back on his own stool, a tic in one knee made his leg shake. "This is all unnecessary," he said, "unnecessary. I'll tell you why.

"Yes, the organism originated in my office. I have called it *S. goddardii*, by the way, and I shall apply for patent under that title."

Melantha Lee crossed her legs. "I hope you are eligible for patent, William."

"Gah. Heavens, woman! You don't think I would release an organism into the environment—even a *planetary* environment," he added, sneering the word, "without making sure it wouldn't get out of hand. *S. goddardii* has a suicide gene. One locus cluster is altered to end the organism's ability to reproduce after two seasons below minus-twenty Celsius. It's all going to die anyway."

"You said nothing." Furious, Graysha barely kept her voice down. "You knew why Goddard was cooling, and you said nothing."

"You shouldn't have found anything," he said flatly. "It's pure chance LZalle filtered any organisms. As I said, they're dying off now. Next season, warming will resume."

"You thought you were going to conceal the organisms' effect as a—what did you call it?—a wobble in the equations," Graysha said.

"Or a natural ultraviolet mutation." Varberg smiled, showing teeth.

Let him gloat. He'd be called in on another charge soon enough.

"I will accept that," said Lee. "Dr. Varberg, you strayed dangerously close to criminal actions in releasing that organism. But if you can prove the suicide gene exists on those cells in Dr. Brady-Phillips's laboratory, you will have been a tremendous help to the Gaea project, and I shall formally request dismissal of kidnapping charges."

"The cultures *died*, Dr. Lee," Graysha repeated.

Varberg tipped back his head. "Viable or recently dead shouldn't make any difference. This should only take me a few hours. I'll fire up my scope and map chromosomes on the bugs in your sampling flasks. Would you like to watch?"

"No. Thank you." Feeling nauseated, Graysha stalked out, leaving Lee with Varberg and his guards.

Once back in her own lab, she formulated a report to Lindon, erased it, tried again, made fists in frustration, then stalked down the hall for tea.

All her work, all their worry over antimicrobial sensitivity, and Lindon's efforts to get her the HMF lab—not to mention Trev's dangerous trip into polar clouds—for nothing. She ought to be glad Goddard would recover, but at the moment, she didn't feel particularly enthused.

Trev was bent over an animal cage in the break room when she stalked in. Seeing her, he straightened. "I told you that man was evil. I told you. I've seen enough like him in my lifetime to know one when I see him."

"You were right, Trev." *Come on,* she chided herself, *be thankful for the suicide gene. Goddard will recover.* Her stomach churned with fury anyway.

In Jirina's office, a mirror image of her own, she spilled it. "Trevarre could have been killed. Any of us sampling those clouds could have been killed. And now he claims it's been under control all along." She dropped the *gaeaii* cultures she'd stashed in here into Jirina's sterilizer. If someone was watching, they would think she just burned all her bridges.

Jirina rocked her office chair. "He thought he wouldn't get caught," the black woman said, "or would get away with a professional reprimand at worst. But what does he care? He'll have the money, and terraforming's future just got bright. Hey, buck up. Want to get something to eat?"

Her stomach still ached. "I'm not hungry."

"You eat." Jirina wagged a finger. "It's almost eleven, nearly lunchtime, and you're under stress."

"I'd rather have co-op food than Gaea cafeteria."

"Good." Jirina stood up and flung off her lab coat, which she left draped over her chair back. "We'll get some exercise on the way."

Ari MaiJidda floundered in new business that morning. The matter of prospectors locating carbon in quantity had finally surfaced on her list, and she sent a pilot to check the location LZalle reluctantly named. Next evening, when she had an hour to spare, she must dance for him again.

She shut down her monitor, then hurried from the CA building. While crossing the hub, she patted her shirt pocket to ascertain everything was there.

It was time to act.

Brady-Phillips and Dr. Jirina Suleiman jogged north toward the corridor. Neither appeared to see her. Now that everyone on Goddard knew what Varberg had done, Gaea people walked the corries a little quicker.

All this was Lindon's fault, she reflected as she turned left into the HMF and hurried downstairs.

A woman was working at the medtech station. "I'd like to see these planet killers firsthand," Ari explained.

"I can understand that." The skinny medtech reached for a tube rack on her countertop with a gloved hand and carried it out.

Ari slipped through the narrow inner door.

After shutting off the room heater, she carefully slid a finger-shaped canister between heater vanes near the inflow. Intense heat would melt a thin coat of wax closing this special canister's port, and then it would start to leak. So small a canister held less than a lethal dose for most individuals. If it killed Brady-Phillips, fine, but she was banking on the poisoned gluco-dermic.

She tightened the inner door's spring mechanism to make sure it closed automatically. That was the kind of thing people never noticed. Holding it open between her feet, she shifted a tiny switch on her D-group key strip. Working patiently, she experimented with disengagement combinations.

There. From the outside, the door still opened. From the inside, it would not.

Lindon would be the only one who grieved Brady-Phillips. *Remember, Lindon, you're the one who made this necessary. You and your missionary urges.*

You told her too much of the wrong . . . truth.

"Graysha?" Jirina poked her head into the lab. "Dr. Lee wants you downstairs."

Riding the elevator, she rehearsed ways of telling Lindon his worries were over, that he'd confronted Lee and lost election votes for nothing. They all worried for nothing. The organism was already dying off out there.

At least Goddard was safe.

Once again, she found Dr. Varberg and his D-group heavies sitting in Lee's office, but this time Varberg wouldn't look up.

Drumming two fingers on her desk, Melantha Lee gestured Graysha toward a chair. "Evidently," the Gaea head said calmly, "an ultraviolet muta-tion actually has occurred. Dr. Varberg's suicide sequence evidently was destroyed in a single organism. That one bacterium appears to have mul-tiplied out of control."

All Graysha's self-righteous fury melted away. She gasped. She'd been a fool to think all her problems were solved.

Varberg kept his angry eyes lowered and drew a huge breath, then said, "Dr. Brady-Phillips, I authorize you to use all my code-locked data." His legs trembled.

Graysha sat staring. "All I want to know is what kills the organism."

"Antibacterials." She heard a note of hysteria in his laugh. "Spray a chemical disinfectant on those clouds, and the next time it rains you'll destroy every soil organism on the planet!"

"You've killed Goddard!" she exclaimed. She glanced aside. Lee sat motionless.

Varberg pushed up out of his chair. "I'll be in my office, transferring files to your access code. Then, evidently, I'm reporting to the CA building for another one of these pleasant little interviews with Chair MaiJidda."

His back filled the door and then shrank in the lobby.

Melantha Lee leaned on one elbow, glaring. "You've ruined him, you know. His research is seized. He's disallowed from reaping any profit from his experimental results, and the techs have brought in rumors of vigilante talk from our so-called nonaggressive colonists. I hope you're happy."

"I've ruined *him*? Dr. Lee, he's paranoid, he's . . . psychotic." Graysha touched the marigold glass. Thinking of Lindon, lying gasps away from death, kept her from summoning up one shred of sympathy for Will Varberg. "And what about the colonists? He ruined their world, Dr. Lee!"

"If that organism is multiplying out of control," Lee said, "I'm sure Gaea's System Supervisor will suggest evacuating the planet. It might be for the best. Copernicus Hab has plenty of open space, and I'm sure the colonists will be given a land grant."

"For the best?" Graysha feared she sounded slightly hysterical. She pictured Lindon's stricken face when she gave him this news. "I have one or two things left to try," she said. "I still might be able to pull it off."

Lee raised an eyebrow. "Oh?"

Graysha hesitated. If Lee knew about this organism all along, she would be scrambling to hide all proof. "Let me think, Dr. Lee. Let me think something through."

"I'm anticipating mail from Flora Hauwk within half an hour. If you can't give me anything specific before then, I'm afraid I will have to recommend evacuating. We can recoup some of our financial losses using asteroid-mining platforms, but at this point I do not think this world will ever be open-air habitable."

"Don't give up!" Graysha insisted. "I could start with another sampling trip."

Dr. Lee's black eyes gleamed. "Yes, you could." Graysha heard a threat of sabotage in that smooth voice.

As she rode back to her lab, she flicked a finger up and down the elevator's control panel. What could she do now—cast herself upon Lindon's mercy? As appealing as that sounded, it would solve nothing. Admit her extra cache of organisms existed and make them vulnerable to Melantha Lee—or whoever sterilized her other cultures?

No, she couldn't do that, either. If she came up with nothing new within half an hour, though, Hauwk and Lee might order Goddard evacuated.

That would mean certain death for Lindon and his people—if their secret got out.

And she'd found no HMF antibiotic that would safely kill Varberg's cloud-borne bacteria.

There was no time to lose.

When the elevator door slid open, she turned on one heel and jogged up the hall to retrieve Varberg's cache of Gaea antibiotics.

She didn't quite make it to the HMF with her clutch of antibiotics. Halfway across the hub, she decided to try contacting Lindon from her apartment. Once alone inside, she snatched Emmer from her pillow and draped the gribien over her shoulders as she turned to her keyboard. "Poor old lady, ignored again." Emmer clicked contentedly, oblivious to Graysha's tension.

Lindon answered her message alarm immediately. Her spirit sank. She'd hoped to send text and give him time to think about it. +Bad news,+ she typed rapidly with her keyboard set for simultaneous transmission. +Varberg admits creating the CFC-killer germ and releasing it into the environment, and Lee was definitely in on the project. He tailored it to die off after two cold seasons, but gene sequences he stuck on got mutated off in the UV. We've got runaway multiplication, with too many CFCs gone to easily replace. That's why Trev got his samples first trip out. And someone destroyed my Gaea lab organisms.+ She went on to explain her quandary with Melantha Lee and the threat of evacuation.

He didn't come back immediately. As she'd guessed, he needed time to think this through.

It wasn't his responsibility anymore, though. +Should I consult Chair MaiJidda?+ she typed.

Lindon clenched his fingers. Bee had sent a message this morning, asking him to release her from the new mandatory crèche religious ed. program. Already, a dangerous doctrine of physical immortality as a reward for persistently applied intelligence had crept in. It scandalized Bee, to Lindon's relief. At least Sarai was back, having returned yesterday to a celebrity's welcome. She was settling in with Crystal and Duncan.

As for Ari . . .

He blamed her for the new crèche program, but he felt he was starting to understand her. An avowed atheist, she had no external accountability, nothing to restrain her from setting herself up as the Lwuites' new spiritual leader.

But he couldn't let her reprogram his children's souls. How could he fight her?

First things first. Unless Goddard remained habitable, his people might cease to exist.

Graysha was waiting. He'd hoped to propose today, but now he didn't dare distract her.

Should she consult Ari? +That's up to you,+ he keyed, +but I wouldn't, not yet.+

+I'll check and make sure the HMF bugs are still growing.+ She went on to briefly explain the difficulty of killing cloud-borne organisms without sterilizing the environment below. +I combed every reference on the net, on abstract, and on tape. I think I know everything about strep's sensitivity to antimicrobials that there is to learn. But the really ironic thing is that the best defense against any bacterial growth is chlorine. An organism breaking down CFCs literally bathes itself in chlorine. It must be fantastically tough.+

+Surely it has a weakness. Keep me posted, and be careful in the corries. Some people are very angry about Varberg's actions.+

After signing out, he bent low over his tightly folded hands, praying. *Protect her, since I can't!*

Graysha exhaled a long, shaky breath. Was she thinking clearly? Was Lindon? The ache in her chest dissipated to become a dull sadness throughout her body. Steadying Emmer on her shoulder, she trotted on to the HMF with her stash. No one there looked particularly hostile, but she doubted she'd know if they were.

She didn't remember turning off the heater. She flicked it on, then pulled open her little incubator and held one plate up to the light. Though it was too soon to check these, she thought she could detect growth, if not clear zones. The next plate looked similar. She still had cause to hope, then. She set the Gaea antibiotic vials on the countertop.

She was examining the tenth plate when Emmer's soft clicking stopped. Her grip went limp.

"Sleeping hard, old thing?" Graysha asked, stroking soft black fur. "What is it?" She pulled the creature from her shoulders, alarmed by Emmer's lack of resistance. Emmer hung limp over her left hand.

"Emmer?" She tapped her pet's soft head, then caught a flash of yellow. On her forearm, her t-o button gleamed its pale warning.

Was that why she felt so relaxed, so drowsy?

She hadn't eaten much lunch. A breath of fresh air should help them both. She shuffled to the door, grasped the handle, and tugged. When nothing happened, she pulled harder.

She worked the handle up and down. "Fresia?" she called. "Hello! Is anybody there?" She pounded on the heavy panel. Metal and concrete, it accepted her blows silently.

Confused, she scurried back to her incubator and replaced her plates. She laid Emmer across her thigh, took a deep breath to calm herself, then another. This little room didn't have so much as a keyboard to call for help.

She was definitely sleepy. Deep in a lab-coat pocket, she always carried the glucodermic. Hurriedly she fished it out, uncapping it with trembling hands. She would never hit a vein with these shakes. It would have to go straight into a muscle. She pressed the point to her thigh.

A noise startled her. Was that someone out in the medtech station rattling glassware, or was she hallucinating?

"Hello!" she gulped, springing up. Emmer and the glucodermic fell together to the floor. Her legs crumpled in familiar agony. Pushing toward the door, she drew a deep breath and screamed, "Fresia!"

Cramps blazed up her body. Her arms collapsed when she tried to rise up on them.

Close beside her, the syringe lay leaking a small clear puddle. Desperate, she slid over a hand, dabbed it in syrup that was oddly thin, and thrust the coated finger to her mouth.

Hideous! She retched at the taste, tried to spit, then retched again.

And the world shrank away.

Ari MaiJidda keyed over to the D-group lidar simulation she'd had designed, then fed it downline to two techs in training. If it seemed abnormally realistic this time, that was deliberate. A threat could be approaching.

She'd locked Varberg up after his "interview," impounding the staph-doctored inhaler in case she needed murder evidence. On lidar, Copernicus's shuttle looked larger than required to remove him.

At least it looked too small to accommodate the whole colonial population.

Still, she was ready to activate D-group if a forced evacuation seemed imminent. After deploying personnel to defend Port Arbor, she must distribute extra supplies to crèche parents and assign track-truck drivers for possible scattering onto the wild. It was warm enough out there for survival. Since they weren't well enough armed to field a conventional force, they would have to use guerilla tactics.

At least Graysha Brady-Phillips would leak no more information to the Eugenics Board. An HMF monitor had shown her rushing through the medtech's station, letting the door swing shut behind her.

Finally, after three botched attempts, Ari had one victory.

She looked out her window. The long sunset was beginning.

Lindon was sitting on his sister's living-room floor when a knock sounded, but he couldn't stand up without thrusting Sarai from his lap. Lavished with too much public attention, she'd already started to withdraw. This was why he'd petitioned for Crys and Dunc to take custody. Under this circumstance, education directors would surely let him keep her out of the crèche.

As the door swung open, she jumped off him, shouting, "Uncle Kevan!"

The name soaked into his tired brain. Lindon rose, too. "Kevan?"

His brother, unshaved and smelling like the AnProd range, bent to hug Sarai. "Hello, Princess," he said, then shook his head at Lindon. "Tough news about the election."

Lindon thought he remembered his brother as being smaller—certainly not this much taller than himself. "You look well fed." He extended a hand.

"Going to be better fed, too." Kevan's flushed cheeks matched the gleam in his eyes. "I've got a vein of the best boron ore you ever saw."

"Boron?" Lindon asked. "Sarai, let Uncle Kevan go for a few minutes. We need to sit down and talk."

"I'll talk, too." Sarai tossed unbraided black hair while she clung to her uncle's hand. "What's boron?"

To Lindon's surprise, Kevan knelt down beside a pile of brightly colored plastic blocks. "Boron is a rare incompatible lithophile element. Can you say that?"

She jerked her head away. "I'm not a baby."

Kevan stood. "Your replacement in the Chair doesn't stall," he said. "I've been extracting since that Gaea kid dropped out of the sky on us, and MaiJidda just sent six track-trucks out for it."

"Do you think—" Small hands clutched Lindon's belt loops. "What is it, Princess?"

"I don't . . . don't know." Covering her eyes, she bent forward and started to cry.

"You're tired," he murmured, "and everybody's been fussing at you. Let me tuck you in for a nap. Kevan, please don't leave."

"Have to. More hoops to dive through. Imagine if we found enough of this stuff. Buyout."

"Dreamer," Lindon called over his shoulder as Kevan strode out the door, but the thought fired his imagination. To pay Gaea and be independent this early was worth dreaming. Quietly, they might vanish from USSC surveillance.

First, though, Varberg's work had to be undone.

He pulled Sarai's blanket up over her chest and sat for a minute, stroking her forehead the way she'd liked as a toddler. *Lord of wonders, heal her. Protect my people. And Graysha—*

Abruptly an urge came over him to get up and run, as if some inner sense heard a cry in the darkness. He'd heard it when Cassandra died, and it terrified him now. He drew away. When Sarai didn't protest, he hurried out her door into Crys's entryway. Fear nipped his heels like a nightmare that refused to fade.

Sarai was safe. Bee was protected. What about Graysha and the hostile Gaea supervisors? He called her office from his sister's terminal. She didn't answer.

The hub, then, or the safe lab. She said she was headed down there.

He jogged down the HMF stairs. "Hello, Fresia. Is Dr. Brady-Phillips here?" he asked the medtech.

"She arrived an hour ago. I've been in and out, though. She might have left."

Lindon pushed open the door and lurched forward. Graysha lay face down and still on the concrete floor, her arms bluish pale except for a t-o button so yellow it almost glimmered.

"Fresia!" he cried before the door could swing shut again.

Novia hunched close to the door of the shuttle's control room. Only two could fit inside with the pilot.

"We have all appearances of a runaway situation." That was Melantha Lee's voice. Closer after four interminable days' travel—much of which Novia spent feeling wretched, having traveled without a takeoff fast—now they experienced only a three-minute total time lag in transmissions. "Dr. Varberg's research was sound," Lee said. "I don't want charges brought

330 — KATHY TYERS

against him. It was only the worst kind of coincidence that led to this particular mutation."

Flora Hauwk glanced over her shoulder toward Novia. "I think I see your point," Hauwk said. During the last three-minute break, they'd discussed on-site personnel's attitude. Obviously, Varberg and Lee were pushing for Gaea reward money and hoped to see Goddard abandoned for other reasons. The notion of blaming finances pleased Lee just a little too much. If Goddard weren't abandoned, she and Varberg might face charges they thought to avoid by inserting that suicide gene.

And maybe Gaea ought to reward them anyway. That money would be nothing compared with the cost of continuing to run terraforming on Goddard—particularly with a new, potentially disastrous, geological problem. Gaea ought to accelerate the forestation of Mars, conduct more aggressive research into Venus's problems, or even—with the help of this new organism—assist Terra Two with atmospheric cleanup on Earth. Blase LZalle, his flame-red hair showing over the top of the first officer's chair, had loudly voted for Venus.

All that remained was to contain these colonists aboard evacuation ships and begin chromosomal testing. Professionally, she had to be pleased.

Personally, she wished things had turned out differently.

Hauwk was still talking to Lee. "I have a go-ahead from HQ to use discretion regarding whether to evacuate, and I think, from all you're telling me, that you can count on it. But don't start packing. Don't give the colonists any sign of what's going on. If they're not willing to leave peaceably, as you implied, herding them could be tricky. We may have to threaten. You have isolated bunkers for Gaea personnel, don't you?"

Supervisor Hauwk ended her transmission, then stood up, nearly bumping her head on a row of lights and switches. "I can't see using those missiles on the Axis site."

My daughter is there! Novia wanted to shout, but she had operated too long in this capacity to abandon her professional demeanor. "No, no," she said, "Port Arbor. That's where the clinic activity is taking place. It's too bad we won't have time or personnel to do a complete job investigating that locale. I'd like to have had their research for my files." *I tried, Graysha.*

"This still might be managed without a confrontation," Hauwk insisted.

Novia clenched her armrest. If the Lwuites hadn't dampened aggression, they might have taken Graysha in and healed her by now. Neither hot nor cold, they deserved double retribution. "As we all hope," she answered steadily. "It's a widespread loss of their lives that we're trying to prevent."

White light shone on white concrete walls, and Graysha's belly ached as if she'd been vomiting. What was she doing here? Where was Ellard? The dreams she'd been having ... alternately sweet and troubling ... about someone else ...

Feeling her cheeks warm, she rolled away from the wall. "Ellard?" she called.

Then she realized this wasn't her bedroom. It was a hospital or clinic, because it smelled ethanol-phenol medical. But the bed lacked autoinjection apparatus, and no drop-down mask hovered over her pillow. If this was a clinic, it was antiquated.

Disoriented, she pushed up to sit. Out the window near her bed's foot, floodlights bathed unfamiliar pale green fields that stretched away toward blackness. Blinking beacons marked the top of a huge distant crater wall.

In that case, her complex dream—and Lindon DalLierx—were real. Hurriedly she slid up the left sleeve of a flimsy hospital gown. At the center of its tiny floral tattoo, her tissue-oxygen button looked pale.

But not yellow. Relieved, she pushed up toward the head of her bed and flopped back onto her pillow. She'd had another Flaherty's attack—a terrible one—in her so-called safe lab, and whatever was in that HMF glucodermic, it wasn't glucose.

She reached for the call button in her bedside table, then hesitated. Did Dr. GurEshel try to poison her?

No. If GurEshel meant her harm, she'd have—Graysha gulped down a foul aftertaste—she'd have murdered her here without letting her wake up. She touched the call button.

Half a minute later, Yael GurEshel whisked into the room, pigtail flying behind her stocky back. "You're awake," she observed. "Any lingering muscle cramps? You slept a number of hours."

It was too late, then, to get any word to Melantha Lee before she and Hauwk conferred.

"I feel rested," Graysha said cautiously.

"When did you last eat?" GurEshel pulled a pocket memo from her lab coat and touched something up. "What meal?"

Dissociating dreamlike reality from her uncannily vivid two-terrannum-old memory took a few seconds. "Lunch, I ... I think."

"Lunch on what day?"

Graysha tried to remember. "Dday," she said after a struggle. "Dropoff."

"Yesterday." GurEshel worked at the memo again, then pocketed it. "Here's what we're going to do. The shuttle coming to remove Will and Edie Varberg will reach parking orbit midday tomorrow. I'm ordering a drip-pak for you immediately. We'll get your blood sugar and oxygen to an acceptable level while still maintaining your takeoff fast. Copernicus has an excellent hospital facility." Pausing for breath, GurEshel crossed her arms in front of a browncloth smock. "It's obvious now that your health is simply too poor for you to remain on Goddard. We'll stabilize your condition today and release you early tomorrow morning to finalize your affairs, turn over your research to your associates, and pack your belongings. By then we will be able to give you specific pickup instructions."

GurEshel seemed sincerely determined to protect her. After all, she'd had two severe attacks since arriving.

But Ari MaiJidda had deliberately provoked the first and probably the second. She wasn't as sick as Yael GurEshel had to assume. Still, Graysha hesitated to tell her so.

"I'll send a nurse to start the drip-pak and immune enhancement." GurEshel left as hurriedly as she'd arrived, without giving Graysha a chance to protest. Didn't anyone notice the broken glucodermic?

If they did, they took it at face value. Graysha pressed up from the pillow, tempted to cut her losses and let them send her back to Copernicus. It wasn't her fault if Goddard's environment failed.

That temptation passed quickly. She had to finish here. Where was Emmer?

She flung her pillows aside and examined the bed, under the bed, and inside the small bedside table.

Cold fear settled in her chest.

The door opened a crack. She steeled herself to resist the nurse. No one was going to stick drip-paks, which might be full of tranquilizers or sedatives, into her arm.

Lindon's solemn face peered around the door, then he eased the rest of the way into her room and shut the door. "Graysha, thank God, I was worried."

"Come in," she urged softly. "Lindon, I have to get out of here."

He shook his head, crossing the room rapidly to seize her left hand. "You need to rest. Whatever brought on that attack—"

"Listen to me," she exclaimed, letting him examine the pale t-o button. "Dr. GurEshel is determined to send me to Copernicus. If I stay in this bed, they'll have me on the shuttle for sure. I've got to get back to work." Heartsick, she pulled back her arm to grasp his hand. "They took Emmer somewhere. Do you know if she survived?"

"Emmer." His Peter Pan eyebrows arched. He reached into a jacket pocket and drew out a tight black furry ball. "It was a miracle I found you. There wasn't anything else I could do except take care of your pet. I don't know if it's . . . going to make it."

Graysha had never seen the gribien ball up so tightly. She held Emmer close to her face and exhaled, offering her scent as comfort. "Emmer?" she whispered, stroking.

Lindon reached down. Delicately, with the back of one finger, he stroked, too, but Emmer did not move.

"Is it . . . dead?" Lindon asked.

"Emmer." Graysha shook her head. "Her name is Emmer. No, they go limp if they die. I'll take her with me." She clutched Emmer against her chest. "I need some clothes. Please? I have to get loose."

He frowned, biting his lower lip. "All right. Cooperate with the nurse. It's painful to take out a drip-pak, but I watched them do it when they had me in here. I can manage for you."

"Come back with clothes."

"As quickly as I can." He brushed her forehead with his lips.

Graysha didn't have to wait long. Sulking, she bared her left arm for the nurse who arrived less than a minute later and gritted her teeth while a long, thin needle wormed into her vein. The nurse couldn't be older than nineteen. "I'm sorry," she said. "At Copernicus, they'll have better equipment."

"That's fine," she mumbled as the nurse left. One thought gnawed at the back of her mind: someone tried to poison her. The bulging liquid-filled bag against her arm looked more ominous by the moment. Finally unable to restrain herself, she started picking at the sticky tape that looped it in place.

Lindon returned, carrying a towel-size bundle under one arm. "Nothing fancy," he said, "and I had to guess your size." He sat on the bedside and pulled the last strip of tape off her hand. Graysha stared. "Are you sure you want to watch?" he asked. "It'll make you woozy."

Though curious, she couldn't afford to faint. She turned her head and studied a line of grooves in the near wall.

"Did you know," he said calmly, "that your oddbod tech turned up boron ore where he had previously only reported carbon? The plantation's buzzing with the find . . . and the hope of Buyout." His hand pressed down firmly on hers. "Ari sent out six track-trucks, and they're back. Urbansky is checking it—"

A long, painful slithering snaked out of her vein. "Ouch!"

"That's it." He tossed the bulbous sack into a waste can. "You're free."

She slipped off the bed and yanked off her gown before he had a chance to turn his back. Startled, he looked away.

"Sorry," she said, shaking out the clothing bundle. She pulled on the shirt and pants, and soft fabric shoes that were much too loose. "Boron ore?" she asked. "How much?"

"We'll know soon."

"All right," she said softly. He turned around as she gently lifted Emmer. "Downstairs," she directed. "It's the only place I have any bugs left."

"We'll take it slowly." Lindon offered his arm.

She grasped it. "No we won't. Hurry."

32. ON APPROACH

By the time they reached the bottom of the stairs, Graysha didn't have to lean so hard on Lindon. Her inner lab door hung open, held in place by a metal wedge.

"Lindon," she murmured, letting one loose shoe flop against the wedge, "I don't remember having to prop this before. It stayed open or closed as I left it." She turned all around, realization penetrating the fog in her brain. "Emmer went limp just before I had my attack. Something happened in here. Something is wrong."

Lindon crouched to examine the room at floor level. "I don't like it. Your research destroyed, and now this." He knelt, staring at a blank spot on the wall. "You're Novia Brady-Phillips's daughter, Graysha. More than one of us has worried about that."

"Well, I only know about one who's been openly hostile. And another thing. Where's . . ." She knelt to look for traces of the glucodermic. Not a shard or a dribble remained. "Have colonial police been in here?" she asked, sickened by her suspicion.

"I would assume so. Let me check." He hurried back out to the medtech station, where he spoke softly with Fresia. The young woman nodded and murmured something.

Graysha stayed where she was. When Lindon rejoined her, she told him about dropping the syringe. "I've never put anything in my mouth that tasted less like glucose, and I woke up with stomach cramps."

"The nurses said you were very sick to your stomach." As he stared into her eyes, his slanted eyebrows almost met at center.

"And I would guess that Ari ordered colonial police to clean up," she suggested. "I had another mysterious episode, too, besides the one at D-group."

"When the crates nearly fell on you? What else?"

For half a splintered second, she wondered if Lindon had thought he'd told her too much, then tried to mend his mistake.

No. Never. Not him. "When I first arrived at Goddard and fell sick, it was because Chair MaiJidda 'forgot' to bring me a can of fast-breaking food, then encouraged me to run across the landing area. Neither episode was a use of deadly force, but they both were plain warnings, Lindon."

His chin worked. "We found out who you were just before you arrived. I agree, that original incident wasn't so sinister, taken alone. But she—*someone,* let's say—has escalated the attacks. Wants to use the minimum violence necessary, but refuses to give up. If that's the case, her . . . the next attack will be more direct. Promise me you'll stay with someone tonight. Dr. Suleiman, maybe." He gripped her hands. "You mustn't be caught alone."

She felt vaguely disappointed, even though she knew she shouldn't. He had all but proposed marriage yesterday. Today, it wasn't "stay in my spare room tonight, you'll be safer," but "stay with someone." Was he so ethical, was she so unlovely, or had he changed his mind about that, too, even after she committed herself to his God?

"I'll try."

His lips firmed, making him look irked.

"I probably won't be leaving this room for a long time. I've got to finish this." She swept a hand up the lab counter, closing it on the antibiotics she found in Dr. Varberg's lab, all 150 of them.

"All right," he said. "Then as soon as I leave here, I'm speaking with your tech, LZalle."

"Speak with Ari," she said soberly. "She's persecuting an innocent person. She can't go on—" Graysha stopped speaking. "I'm sorry," she added. "I'm asking you to act aggressively. That's not your way."

Lindon's mouth firmed. "Do you think I'm afraid of her?"

"But," she began, then she shook her head, remembering Lindon's doubts about the callosal treatments. She'd barged into his life, sowing even more confusion.

Abruptly, she realized they both were staring. Heaven knew what he saw—maybe a woman who'd been very sick, wearing someone else's ill-fitting clothes—but this lonely man had lost a wife eight terrannums ago, and he was not looking away. He eyed her, in fact, with a kind of hunger she'd seen twice, maybe three times on Ellard's face. On Lindon, the expression was transformed: not a "Come here, woman," but a controlled ache he plainly hoped she might fill.

Very well, then, he got full credit for ethics, and she didn't need to feel unlovely! Smiling in spite of all danger, she pushed the antibiotics vial into her back pocket.

He stepped closer, and to her astonishment, he fingered the underside of her chin. "I'll save my anger for Ari," he said. He leaned down, closer, and kissed her.

It was the slightest touch, but he might as well have hit her with an earthmover or revectored the orbit of her heart. Maybe he didn't mean to clinch her loyalty for all time, but as she pulled her hands free, clasped them at the nape of his neck, and drew him closer, she knew she could never look him in the eye without remembering this moment.

Whether or not this choice was wise, she was committed. Her peripheral vision went dark. The laboratory vanished.

When she opened her eyes again, the quirk of little-boy eyes, dark and concerned, tore at her. "I'm sorry," he whispered. "I didn't mean to do that. We're both too vulnerable. But, Graysha . . ."

He shut his eyes, took a deep breath, and pulled her head to his shoulder. She stared at the lab's wall, incredulous. That one kiss obviously affected him just as deeply as it did her.

She stammered, "It's just that . . ."

"No, I understand." He backed away. "I love you, Graysha. Whether I should or not, I do. I'll talk with you later, when we're both steadier. I mustn't keep you from . . ."

"Lindon, I . . ."

He rushed out. Graysha followed as far as the outer door, then turned back. Her insides flamed. The afterimage of his face had scorched onto her vision.

Blinking, she drew her inoculated plates back out of the incubator one by one and stacked them on the countertop, then managed to focus her mind on her work and examine them.

Cloudy. Every one of them, without a single clear patch. *S. gaeaii* grew profusely in the presence of every antimicrobial the colonists kept on hand.

That brought her crashing back down. At least she still had organisms. *If the cultures had been destroyed,* she reflected grimly, *one trip into the cloud cover would yield more than enough bacteria to start a fresh lab colony.* She had more antibiotics to try, too, from the Gaea building—but too little time and too few organisms to inoculate more plates just now.

She hurried out into the medtech station, wondering if Fresia PalTion saw the afterimage of Lindon in her eyes. "Could you spare a large flask of TSY broth?" she asked.

"Heavens, yes." The medtech flicked a long brown braid behind her shoulder and gestured toward a cooler with her own loop dropper. "Help yourself."

"Thanks."

Moving like an automaton, she inoculated the flask with *gaeaii* microbes. They preferred a CFC medium, but she had to hurry. This general-purpose broth ought to give her enough organisms to start a new set of antimicrobial tests later today, or tomorrow. "May I leave this in your refrigerator?" she asked.

"Of course." Fresia might be preoccupied, but her smile looked sincere.

Graysha opened the metal door Fresia indicated and tucked her flask safely inside. "I didn't label it," she said dubiously. "Do you have a pen?"

"Don't bother. I label all mine. I'll know which one is yours. Say, I'm sorry about what happened yesterday. I didn't hear you call—"

"Not your fault," Graysha insisted. *Not even slightly.*

Back at her apartment, Graysha traded too-large clothes for a brown-cloth outfit in her own size, scooped up Emmer, and headed back to her own lab, where she pillowed Emmer on the floor, wrapped in an extra lab coat. The little gribien stretched languidly, then curled up to sleep.

Almost immediately, Trev skidded in. "Morning, Teach," he puffed. "DalLierx seems to think it was foul play that brought on your attack yesterday. Hope you can stand my company, because I'm supposed to stick with you like limpet glue."

She sagged against the countertop. "That's fine, Trev. Thank you. Where've you been?"

"Down at Geology." His lips curled up at both edges, then turned down again. "Introducing myself to Dr. Thaddeus Urbansky. He's been assaying samples from a few truckloads of the rock I found down south. Says it's good stuff. From the voice, I pictured him about seven-foot-three. Would you believe he's shorter than I am?"

It cheered her to talk to someone in such good spirits. "And how's Dutchy?"

Trev displayed his right hand. From knuckles to wrist, two parallel streaks flamed blood red. "He likes me better now that he's learned I'm the food source. These are just impatience marks."

Graysha whistled. Hearing cart wheels in the hallway, she peeked out.

To her surprise, a man in co-op whites pushed the cart along. "Dr. Brady-Phillips?" he asked.

She beckoned him in, and he parked the cart between her lab counter and the nearest wall. "Mr. DalLierx sent this over." He unloaded a set of covered dishes, then hurried away.

Graysha removed the covers. Beneath one, steaming grilled ham made her mouth water. Waffles dripping with honey filled the other plate. "Where are they growing enough flowers to keep a beehive?" she asked. Trev shrugged. Two bowls held yogurt and fresh fruit, and the carafe gave off a scent of fresh coffee. "Looks like enough for both of us," she said, "with leftovers for Jirina. Pull up."

Trev speared a slice of ham. "This will do me."

After eating just enough that Yael GurEshel could no longer declare her on a prelaunch fast, she tore off a strip of waffle and dropped it onto her napkin. "Emmer's sense of smell is very keen," she explained as Trev stared. "Maybe this will rouse her."

She knelt beside the gribien. "Emmer," she whispered, glad to see her pet stretched out again. "Here, I brought you breakfast."

Black ears sprang up, a black nose sniffed, then white teeth closed on the waffle. Deeply relieved, Graysha returned to the outer lab. Jirina stood over the cart of food. "Thought I heard my name," she said around a mouthful. "So I helped myself. Didn't want you overeating when you've been sick."

"Jirina," Graysha said suddenly, "has Dr. Lee put out anything about a change in the status of the Gaea station?"

"No, why? What have you heard?"

Graysha nibbled the torn waffle. "She's scared. Doesn't think we'll be able to restore the planetary greenhouse in time."

"It does look bad, but you'll do it. Invoke the Black Goddess if there's anything she can do to help."

Then maybe the decision to evacuate wasn't made. Chewing a multigrain mouthful, Graysha leaned against a countertop to consider her next move while Jirina chaffed Trev about his scratch marks. As soon as she left this lab for dinner, she would stop by the HMF with Gaea's test vials—now tucked deep into her pocket—and initiate that second series of sensitivity tests.

And there was, she realized dumbly, one other thing she hadn't tried. Streptomycetes, almost all of them, were notorious antibiotic synthesizers. If some other strain gave off a natural chemical that inhibited *gaeaii's* growth—but not the soil streps they were using to create arable cropland—

that might solve the problem without adding toxic chemicals to every rain-drop. It was possible.

But to find out if they had such an organism, she might have to carry Varberg's entire streps inventory down to the HMF—or else bring a viable *S. gaeaii* sample back across the hub to this lab.

The second option sounded easier. "Discovering" those TSY flasks might look suspicious, but she could worry later about Melantha Lee's sus-picions.

First things first. She had to ensure herself against sabotage. As soon as she and Jirina cleared the breakfast cart, she sent Trev to Varberg's refrig-erator for the streps inventory. Lee, she realized, hadn't come up to check on her this morning. The Gaea supervisor probably was tidying up Var-berg's records.

Would Lee order Graysha off Goddard on that shuttle? If so, she'd have to find some place to hide. Period. End of story. She was not leaving—

What, she wondered, was Ari MaiJidda doing at this moment? Laying another trap, deadlier than the last?

Trev returned. "We need broth cultures of every one," she told him, pointing at Varberg's array. "All 192 strains."

He groaned. "You have an idea."

"I have an idea." She switched on her flame sterilizer and went to work. One row of fresh inoculations was nearly filled when she sensed a frigid stare. She turned her head. Melantha Lee stood in the center of the door-way. Her round face seemed to float between her iron-gray hair and dark business suit.

"Dr. Lee," she said. "Good morning."

"Hello, Trev. How do you feel, Graysha?"

"Much better, thank you." *Reach for the next tube. Dip the micropipette. You will finish this job.*

"Dr. GurEshel has been looking for you."

Graysha watched her tubes. "I suppose she would be. I feel fine." Trev's head swiveled at the edge of her peripheral vision. She ignored his curious stare.

"I told her I hadn't seen you," Lee said. "It was true . . . then."

Sample into the tube, swirl. She glanced at Dr. Lee.

The Gaea supervisor held both hands at her sides, tilting her head to look down at Graysha like Varberg had done. "I have a priority soils titra-tion that needs to be done today."

"I'll get to it as soon as I do this. I need to finish my research, Dr. Lee."

"You will do the soils titration first," Lee ordered, "now. Or I will dis-miss you from employment and send you away with the Varbergs."

Plainly, Lee meant to delay this experiment until it was too late to influence Dr. Hauwk's verdict.

Not this time, she wouldn't. Even Jirina had offered to help.

Now, if ever, it was time to do a little judicious fudging. "Very well," Graysha said submissively.

Lee folded her hands, appearing to relax. "I had another transmission from Dr. Hauwk."

Sobered, Graysha sterilized her pipette and dropped it into its sheath. She swiveled on her stool. "Oh?"

"Trev," Lee said, "this concerns you, as well."

"Oh." He kept working, bless him. Tomorrow morning, all these broth tubes would be grown and usable for cross-inoculation.

"That shuttle launched to take away the Varbergs will reach parking orbit tomorrow. Gaea's Council of Supervisors sent two representatives with full authority to decide to continue or discontinue the Goddard experiment." Lee stepped farther in through the door. "Flora Hauwk is coming, of course. I'm surprised she stayed away this long. She will evaluate the situation from a scientific point of view.

"The other supervisor is apparently a member of Gaea Consortium's Board of Shareholders. A new *major* shareholder, I'm told."

Trev halted with one hand in the air. "Oh, please. Tell me it isn't my father."

"I won't," Lee said stiffly. "I can't. And I think it's time we concluded this planetary project."

Graysha let one hand go limp, releasing a soy-broth flask to shatter on the floor. It was safer than expressing her panic verbally. Glass shards settled in a puddle of fragrant broth that ran toward the floor drain. Seizing a browncloth towel, she slid off her stool.

Melantha Lee pursed her lips. "Graysha, Dr. Hauwk will wish to hear about the current situation from you publicly. Please prepare a statement."

Lee strode around Graysha to the counter's inner end. "And Mr. LZalle Senior will discuss with me—and with Colonial Affairs subcommittee members the financial feasibility of trying to maintain Goddard." She bore down on Trev like a predator. "Finish what you're doing, if it's genuine Gaea business, and then come to my office for the soils titration tubes."

Trev stayed late at work, helping Gray and Jirina finish Lee's titration and the CFC tubes. That gave him plenty of chances to keep trying to contact Kevan DalLierx. At midnight, after Jirina promised to stay close to Graysha, he made one last desperate call to the dugout. Maybe by now they'd arrived back home. He stared out the polarized lab window at Eps

Eri's face rising in slow majesty over the crater's rim. It took a long, long time. Bday was dawning. His forty-fifth day on Goddard.

Blase was coming.

He needed front 'money now, not after extraction was complete—for the colony's sake, as well as his own. He had to know how deep that ore vein ran, even if it meant tying Thaddeus Urbansky to a track-truck and driving him there. At least Nick and Kevan had finally recorded the claim. He'd checked the record yesterday. True to their word, they'd registered his name, too . . . and Blase's.

So there really was hope. But he needed a back door, some way to escape if Blase wouldn't dance to this tune. . . . Did he really dare stay and face the old man, to try talking him into taking a new kind of business risk?

Balling a fist, he pushed it against the window panel. If he made an offer and Blase wouldn't dance, Trev wouldn't have a chance to get away. He'd have to run—*now*—and let Kevan and Graysha and DalLierx fight their own battle.

His visit yesterday to Urbansky's office made it all the more urgent to contact Kevan or Nick. The bearlike little man confirmed Kevan's analysis. "What we're seeing come in on the trucks is as rich as anything I've ever seen. Better than any of Earth's important ores," he added, handing back a chunk of black rock. "Gaea's cut will bring the company a nice profit."

"I'll be getting a little myself," he'd explained to the geologist. He didn't tell Urbansky everything but explained there might be an offworld backer.

"Oh," Urbansky said. "Ah. Well," he added, drawing briefly at a straight-stemmed pipe, "if it's a good strike and it goes deeper still, remember me in your will."

"What about the calcite?" Trev asked casually. Graysha had infected him, too, with the urge to see Goddard's CFCs restored. "I thought I saw one truck dump crystals."

"You did." Another pull on the pipe. "But our estimates of the cavern size don't jibe with Kevan's. There isn't enough there to manufacture suffi-cient CFCs to replace what's been lost."

Maybe. And maybe Lee and her cronies fudged the new calculations. Surely nobody had mapped the whole cavern, not yet.

"What was your Varberg thinking of?" Urbansky had asked as a parting shot, "playing with CFCs up there?"

That had sent Trev sulking toward the door. "Don't talk to me about Varberg, and he's not *my* anything. If the colonists lynch him, it's what he deserves."

"This had better be important." Ari MaiJidda folded her hands beside her keyboard. "D-group has to be ready when that shuttle lands."

Lindon glanced aside at Taidje FreeLand. The white-haired elder stood in front of a dark tapestry Ari had hung in the CA office. Taidje said nothing. He'd agreed to escort Lindon here and stay with him just long enough to witness a brief statement. "It's important," Lindon said softly. "If Graysha Brady-Phillips were to die here, not only would you bring a USSC investigation down on our heads, but you would have committed an act of murder."

Ari pulled up straight in the tall chair, eyes wide, mouth open as if in shock. "I beg your pardon. Precisely what are you accusing me of?"

He kept his voice soft. "Of abusing your position with the colonial police. Of deliberately creating three situations calculated to aggravate Brady-Phillips's illness. Of—"

"If we don't get her sent away, there will be—"

"Listen to me." He all but shouted it. Ari closed her mouth and glared. Taidje looked at the brightening window, then back down to Ari.

"Did your officers enter the HMF lab after Dr. Brady-Phillips was taken upstairs?"

"They did," she clipped firmly.

He watched her eyes. "Did they remove all traces of a broken syringe, including fluid that leaked from it?"

Ari tossed her head. "I would hope they cleaned up."

"Did they run tests on that fluid?"

She looked up, eyes narrowing. "They did not."

"Why not?" Lindon leaned both hands on her desk. "Did you order them not to?"

Ari folded her arms, pulling away from him. "It was an ordinary generic plainly labeled glucodermic. Should we have analyzed her culture dishes, as well? The air in the room, the dust on her countertop? The woman is sick. Of course she carries a glucodermic."

"Perhaps other things were removed from that laboratory, too." Lindon looked at Taidje. The older man's head turned slightly, and he eyed Ari with a trace of skepticism.

"I would like to speak with the officer who cleaned up the scene," Lindon said quietly.

Finally she appeared to hesitate. Her eyes went to Taidje and then refocused on Lindon. "He left this morning for Port Arbor as part of our defensive posture."

Taidje raised one eyebrow, a good sign. Maybe he, too, doubted her innocence.

"Ari," Lindon said, "I will consider one more assault on Graysha Brady-

Phillips, one more 'accident,' one more 'attack' of Flaherty's symptoms, as confirmation of your guilt—and I will ask for a recall election. Taidje, I call you as witness."

Ari sprang to her feet, looking as if she wanted to jump over the desk at him. "Get out, DalLierx."

Graysha woke early from dreams that were dogged with urgency. The faint scent of sandalwood pervaded Jirina's bedroom. She dressed quietly, trying not to wake her friend.

Jirina's window looked out on the covered crop fields. Strengthening light reflected off the shimmering shelter cloth. So much had been accomplished out there, under the shelter and elsewhere. Despite the volcanoes, nearly 10 percent of the wild had been seeded for mineral liberation. That was only half what would eventually be needed, but it'd taken only eighty terrannums. Closer to the settled craters, thousands of hectares sprouted clover, dwarfalfa, and cold-kudzu; more grew experimental grains and other new crosses—fifty terrannums, overlapping the mineral-lib phase, all in preparation for colonization. Even in the short time since she arrived, the crop fields inside Axis Crater had been plowed farther out, inching toward the crater walls.

If her research failed, all this might vanish under an ice sheet that would last until Eps Eri began to burn out.

She slipped into shoes, then brushed her hair. She'd been told, but never really understood, the incredible amount of time and work involved in terraforming. One person, a thousand people, might spend their lives laboring and scarcely make a difference. It took unbelievable sums of money, all the knowledge and know-how humankind possessed, and time. Decades, if not centuries.

And people willing to spend their whole lives laboring, guiding, shaping—

For what? To have someone take it all away?

She should pray. Feeling a new intimacy, a sense of actually connecting, she formed words in her mind. *God, if you care about Lindon—and you do know he cares about you—don't let that happen. They say you raised dead people. That you own everything that exists. Would this be so hard for you?*

Like a voice in her ear or an echo from some philosophy professor, she heard what sounded like an answer—to some other question. *Your greatest fear is rarely your greatest real danger.*

Was that a quote? She couldn't place it. Feeling strangely haunted, she looked back at the bed, where Jirina's long blanket-covered body lay still.

Did Jirina want to leave Goddard? Was she afraid?

Graysha shook her head. No, Jirina wasn't frightened—but she would follow orders. So Graysha had to convince Flora Hauwk and Blase LZalle not to evacuate.

Novia Brady-Phillips lounged in her deceleration hammock, which hung from a bulkhead alongside Flora Hauwk's. Blase LZalle hadn't shown his face since turnaround signaled deceleration and the landing fast began. Jambling flitted in occasionally with position reports. Novia found these sleeping hammocks slightly more comfortable than the deceleration seats, and she wasn't heading down there until she had no choice.

"Copernicus simply doesn't have enough large ships to evacuate them instantly," Hauwk said. "We'll need assistance from Halley, or perhaps Einstein, where more shipping is conducted."

"That's all right," Novia answered, this time squelching her flicker of hope. She'd accomplished nothing for Graysha, and Goddard was rapidly becoming dangerous. The atmospheric imbalance made evacuation imperative. From this point, Gaea—and the EB—would do everything by the tutorial. "This shuttle will hold thirty, restrained, if we convert the cargo holds to steerage. We'll take their leadership this time."

"If they prove guilty." Hauwk sniffed. "You seem convinced, and you haven't done a single chrome scan."

"I have enough evidence," Novia answered. "Those people must leave sooner or later. It gives my board a better show of force to take the top percent into custody from the first, though of course, the suggestion can be made that we merely need their presence to renegotiate their labor contract."

"Let's stick with the truth, if we can," Hauwk said wryly.

Everyone seemed determined to protect these criminals! "For the present, the most vital operation from my standpoint is to confirm that Port Arbor is the site of illegal activity."

Flora Hauwk's hammock swung gently. "I'm almost sorry to have to evacuate," she said. "Goddard had so much potential. I suppose we must announce the failure publicly, in person. Perhaps we'll be glad to have your armed escort along." She grinned, indicating a joke had been made.

To Novia, it was no joke. The Lwuites had formed a defense group, after all. She'd seen no reports as to its strength or readiness. "They certainly seem to have gone after Dr. Varberg. Strangely, it seems he has done Gaea more good than harm."

"You people don't object to the alteration of a planet from its created state?" Dr. Hauwk's bright eyes narrowed. "Or genengineered animals? It's just humans, isn't it?"

Novia was ready for a change of topic. "Terraforming is borderline permissible if no native life is displaced. But the human organism is sacred."

Hauwk stared up at the dull gray bulkhead. "Is it our chromosomes that make us human, after all? I thought you church people thought it was something a little more nebulous. Our so-called souls."

"If genengineered creatures have souls," Novia said stiffly, "God will be able to tell."

"After you send them into his . . . dimension."

"They are dangerous here. Incredibly dangerous."

"Oh, I don't doubt that." Flora Hauwk adjusted her hammock cover. "In other words, we have recreated God, and he is us."

"That's reasonably close." Novia didn't feel like arguing theology any further. Hauwk plainly had no interest in converting to the CUF. Novia wanted to think.

"What's that?" Trev tapped a large new object, square metal with primitively welded seams, that lay beside Graysha's laboratory sink where the water baths used to be. He seemed nervous today, pacing and fidgeting.

Graysha raised one finger to her lips, then pulled a pair of small cloudy flasks from her lab-coat pocket. "Your friend Kevan DalLierx was here when I got to work," she whispered. "Lindon brought him by. It's a lockdown mechanism he put together to protect two water baths."

Trev's back straightened. "He was here at the plantation and you didn't call me? I've got to get ahold of him!"

Graysha wondered why it mattered so much. "He was driving a tracktruck, and he stayed only a few minutes. I tried to get him to call you, but they're making hay—so to speak—while the sun shines, so they can get speed out of solar engines. You've got to help me cross-inoculate these samples with Dr. Varberg's streptomycete inventory."

"No, I've got to call Kevan. Now."

"Trev," she said patiently, "I need about 500 tubes inoculated. I want duplicate tubes for backups, plus controls. This is too important to do carelessly. This is it, Trev. Our last chance to save a world."

He groaned, then ducked into her office. "Let me just try calling his dugout again. I'll leave him a message to contact me here at work."

"Go ahead," she said, sighing. "But please hurry."

She jogged up the hall and ordered the media she'd need. Bateson's broth would yield the fastest results, if *S. gaeaii* could utilize its carbon source. A normally blue medium, Bateson's faded to pale green in the presence of even a minuscule amount of free chlorine. If her samples grew out in Bateson's, she'd be able to monitor an infinitesimal color change within the few hours she had left. If any other strep species inhibited *S. gaeaii,* that tube would still be pure blue tomorrow morning. Surely Gaea would let her wait that long. Spectrophotometric examination would confirm whether *gaeaii* organisms still were present—and later, she could make sure any organisms that passed this test also let soil streps grow. Running 192 samples through Jirina's spectrophotometer would take . . . at two minutes apiece . . . over six hours, but she could at least start growing the cultures now.

Much to her relief, the media tech agreed that mixing Bateson's with small amounts of CFC wouldn't interfere with testing.

She needed a day and a half. So little time.

Surely, Dr. Flora Hauwk would give her that long—and delay her verdict.

To Graysha's relief, Dr. GurEshel didn't send for her that morning. She let Trev leave at ten, as soon as he finished the cross-inoculations. Shortly thereafter, Melantha Lee called all Gaea employees down to the stone-floored lobby. Graysha arrived last, feeling shaky and hoping the others' presence would divert Lee's attention.

It didn't. The site supervisor stood on a stool near the glass walls that separated her office from the lobby, and only seconds after Graysha walked off the elevator, she called out, "Graysha, if you need to try your sampling again, there is a hovercopter available."

Thirty heads swung in her direction. "Thank you, Dr. Lee," she called back, feeling conspicuous. Maybe they hadn't discovered the lock-down incubator. Whether or not they had, she couldn't leave the plantation now. She needed to hear what Flora Hauwk and Blase LZalle intended. Lee's offering the plane also might be a final act of sabotage.

Dr. Lee cleared her throat and spoke to the gathering. "There will be a public meeting in the Gaea cafeteria at twelve-thirty. It's our largest contained room, better equipped for mass communication than the hub. We'll bring in as many colonists as will fit. I suggest you all head home, shower, and have an early lunch."

Had Hauwk secretly ordered evacuation? Graysha shuddered, hoping her guess was wrong, but this could be a final good meal before confining them for a takeoff fast.

"I have one more suggestion," Lee add, "for what it's worth."

From Graysha's position at the back of the crowd, she saw heads turn toward one another. A few people jostled closer to Lee's stool.

"There are a number of rumors going colonial rounds," Lee called. "Unkind ones. It might be safest to sit together at the meeting. Please avoid antagonizing them."

Yes, Graysha thought, *Varberg already stirred them up against us.*

With the inoculations complete and locked down, she had no reason not to go back to her rooms and bathe thoroughly. It felt good to get the broth-and-spoilage work scent off her body. In an effort to look as professional as possible, she took an offworld dress suit out of her drawer and shook out the wrinkles. Emmer uncurled and stretched on the bed as she pulled on the off-white ensemble, and Graysha was reaching down to stroke her when someone knocked.

"Just a minute," she called. She adjusted her hair tie in front of the mirror, slipped a few essential items into one jacket pocket, then opened the door. Trev waited there, wearing local browncloth, but these were darker, more formal pants than she'd seen him wear before, and his shirt was embroidered with crimson floss in a parallel-zigzag design.

"An attempt to please the old man." He ran a hand along the pattern. "I went shopping."

She eyed him closely. He stood evenly braced on both feet, and his jaw twitched. "Couldn't hurt," she said. There was no need to tell him she saw his fear. She hoped he was overestimating his father's wrath.

"Thought you might appreciate company for lunch."

"Sure. I'm ready. Let's go."

She picked a pasty with gravy from the Gaea cafeteria's selection. Despite Dr. Lee's warning, Trev chose a table far from where Jirina and Paul were already eating. The big room was still almost empty. Apparently Lee hadn't called in the colonists yet.

Where, she wondered, was Lindon? "Trev?" She tipped her head in Jirina's direction. "Over there, with them?"

Trev frowned. "Today I think I'll take my chances with the colonists." He quirked an eyebrow, regaining a hint of the cocky Trev she knew. "But if you'd feel safer with Paul Ilizarov—"

"No," she said firmly. "This is fine."

Trev's first sandwich vanished almost instantly. The second went down slower. Watching the cafeteria's fanfold door, Graysha spotted Melantha Lee by her broad silhouette and curly gray hair. She spoke to someone, who immediately rapped a fork against a drinking glass. General conversation dribbled away to silence.

"The Gaea representatives' shuttle reached parking orbit roughly thirty minutes ago," Lee said. Hands behind her back, standing with her dark dress coat hanging open, she tapped a foot on concrete. "We anticipate lander arrival in about forty minutes. Please sit close together and leave tables for colonists who choose to attend. Thank you." She joined the shortest lunch line.

"Guess we can stay here," Graysha observed. "Or you can. Now that I think of it, I should pick up some hard copies over at the lab." *And check my organisms.* "Save me a place, all right?"

Trev grunted. His hands had started twitching again.

"You don't seem quite yourself."

He pulled back his hands and sat on them. "I wish you wouldn't put it like that. If he's got any kind of legal papers with him, I probably won't *look* like myself in about one month."

Despite scars and blotches, she'd come to like that face. "Why are you sticking around, then? Take that copter Lee offered me. Go find Kevan—"

He pursed his lips and said, "I don't know why I don't. Maybe I just hate to run again. Maybe I hope I can buck him this time. Graysha, he means to make things ugly for Gaea. For Goddard. And for me most of all, but . . . well, we'll see."

She eyed her young assistant. Maybe he wanted to face his father as a man instead of hiding. He really was growing up. "Good for you, Trev," she muttered. She folded her napkin. "I'll be back as quickly as I can."

Back in her lab, she waved Kevan's key across the lock of his water bath safe, and it popped open. Her cross-inoculated tubes sat in the water bath in neatly numbered rows, all 576 of them. Four hours after inoculation, it was too early for turbidity or color change, but she couldn't resist holding a few to the light. Every one remained as clear and blue as she'd left it.

She sniffed one, then smiled. Thanks to Kevan—and Lindon—this time she had no fear of disinfectant.

On her desktop, where she'd left it, lay a black folder. Fearing she'd find it empty, she opened it. Inside were several sheets of precious paper, hard copy authorized by Lee for the occasion and printed down at Lee's office. Graysha lifted them one by one. Here was her original proposal. Here was new scanning-scope and DNA-filter data on *S. gaeaii*'s rugged cell walls, which protected the organism so well from free chlorine, and a second proposal suggesting possible procedures for combating the *gaeaii* strain with by-products of whatever new bacterium inhibited its growth . . . if she could find one that did.

At least Lee was letting her hypothesize.

Ruefully she read the second proposal. *S. gaeaii*'s exponential multiplication could be intercepted before passing out of control, she was suggesting, if Gaea Consortium instigated emergency measures immediately: biochemical protection for soil streps already in place, if possible, followed by a massive cloud spraying effort. Even, maybe, comet harvesting to try replacing cloud water that the sprays could bring down.

Can we do it? she wondered. She almost wished she could stay here, on the job, instead of attending the meeting.

Before heading for the elevator, she locked everything down one more time and pushed her key deep into a pocket of her suit pants.

When she reached the hub again on her way back to the Gaea cafeteria, a crowd of colonists flowed toward Gaea housing. She let the press carry her. Shoves from either side, rougher than they needed to be, confirmed Lee's guess—the colonists weren't feeling friendly today.

At the big doors, she saw that someone had moved the tables close to the cafeteria's open end, creating standing room near the servers. Other people sat between tables on the concrete floor. Trev perched sideways on their bench, fending off interlopers.

"Thanks." Graysha slid into the spot he'd saved. Immediately, a woman wearing smudged coveralls wedged in alongside her.

Graysha peered around, searching for Lindon. Near the food lines, Melantha Lee waited with Thad Urbansky, Antonia Fong, Will Varberg, and Varberg's D-group bodyguard. In that group, no one but the guards looked at Varberg. Graysha didn't see his wife, Edie, anywhere.

After several minutes, a track-cart's rumble approached out in the corridor. The general roar of conversations died out. The track cart appeared at the broad doors, and several people stepped off. One woman wore the blue-and-green Gaea uniform Graysha hadn't seen since leaving Halley Hab. One man wore ExPress Shuttle gray. Behind them strutted a dark-skinned man with wildly incongruous red hair. He wore absolute black. Judging from Trev's slouch toward the table, he knew him.

So did someone in the back. A chant started over on one side: "Blase, Blase, Blase." Someone else shushed it.

The man's face, Graysha decided as he walked up an aisle toward the serving area, was neither strikingly handsome nor gruesome. She wasn't sure what she expected, but Blase LZalle, in person, wasn't the monster who chased Trev through her dreams. Slightly taller than Trev, he walked with a confident, swaying gait. *Trev comes by his cockiness naturally,* she observed. Two other arrivals, following the lead group, were dressed like techs. Graysha barely glanced at them before settling her stare on the uniformed Flora Hauwk. Gray hair pulled severely back from her face did nothing to soften a long thrust of nose, and from ten meters away the woman's flawless skin gleamed like ivory. Only her quick, shallow breathing hinted that she had to be in her seventies—or was that her reaction to Goddard's strange smell?

Graysha took a cautious sniff. She no longer noticed the odor.

The cafeteria quieted. Melantha Lee needed no amplification to make formal welcome. Hauwk shook hands with all the department heads but Varberg. When he was introduced, colonists sitting on the floor near Graysha whispered, heads nodding.

Lindon appeared out of the crowd, wearing a finely tailored gray wool suit, its short coat double-breasted with a pronounced waist. He, too, had to be saving offworld clothes for special occasions—expensive offworld clothes, she realized. Seeing him dressed like that, after what transpired yesterday in the HMF lab, made her wish she stood beside him, offering whatever support she could. Taidje FreeLand followed Lindon, then Kenn VandenNeill, both dressed tastefully, though Lindon would have stood out even if she weren't drawn to him like a needle to magnetic north.

Where was Ari MaiJidda, the colony's new CCA? Working feverishly at the D-group building, Graysha guessed. She was probably watching space for other arrivals and posting guards at sensitive locations.

Handshakes were repeated with the man in black. Colonists in the back and on the floors remained silent this time. Watching, listening.

"Gentlemen and women," VandenNeill said loudly, "I understand there are several topics on your agenda. One which we wish to add, and to discuss as early as possible, is the matter of possible refinancing."

A woman sitting close to Graysha on the floor leaned toward her neighbor, lips moving rapidly. Her sweaty neighbor glared at the Gaea group.

VandenNeill continued without pausing, "Extremely rich boron ore has been found south of here, and Goddard Colony would like to petition for the application of a substantial payment to the principal of our colonizing loan."

A few colonists standing in back clapped approval. Clearly surprised, Supervisor Hauwk accepted several sheets of paper from VandenNeill and scanned them rapidly.

Now, Graysha guessed, Hauwk would want to know where Ari was.

To her astonishment, Trev sprang up off his seat and climbed onto the tabletop. "Blase," he shouted. "Dad, whatever you're planning, I need to talk to you first."

"His son?" Graysha heard the loud whisper from a group of pigtailed young women near the end of a table. Heads turned, zeroing in on the famous performer's offspring.

"Hah," said Blase LZalle. "And you thought—"

"Wait," Trev called out. "Whatever you've got to say, hold it for five minutes. Let me talk to you."

A sea of sitting colonists parted for Trev to push his way forward. Flora Hauwk stood scanning VandenNeill's papers. Graysha held her breath.

By the time Trev reached his father, he was already talking earnestly, gesturing with both hands. To Graysha's relief, the older man cocked his head and gave every appearance of listening.

Hauwk raised her head. "These are indeed interesting, Vice-Chair VandenNeill. I will read them carefully, later. However, it is the state of the ecosphere we have come to discuss. That matter must be settled before we speak of finances—or of mineral mining, which can be done even on un-inhabited asteroids, using proper equipment. Dr. Lee, I believe you wished to speak?"

Melantha Lee produced her own handful of hard copy. "Thank you, Supervisor Hauwk. I will try to be brief." As Trev and his father backed away from the serving area—Trev was gesticulating now, waving one arm out toward the wild—Lee reviewed the state of terraforming on Goddard, listing growth and successes along with regressions and failures. Graysha noticed she said nothing about atmospheric tampering or Graysha's efforts to counteract it. Graysha's neighbor picked at a loose thread on her sleeve.

Lee called the department heads forward one by one. Urbansky insisted the volcanic eruptions posed no insurmountable threat and urged contin-uation of the Goddard project. Antonia Fong's testimony was more disap-pointing. The difficulty of fencing small ecosystem areas suggested a need to work with larger overlapping ranges. Ben Emerson claimed the only sig-nificant sociological problems had been friction between Lwuite colonists and Gaea employees, and he returned the floor to Dr. Lee on a positive note.

Graysha guessed she was being saved for last, like a banquet's dessert course. She wondered how it would feel to be publicly picked to pieces.

Seated in a chair produced by cafeteria staff, Flora Hauwk listened blank faced, letting her pocket memo transcribe. The gray uniformed ExPress pilot stared at his feet. And still, Trev and his father talked in hushed tones.

Rather than call Varberg as head of his department, Melantha Lee ended with the official version of all his actions. At this point, Flora Hauwk rocked forward on her chair and asked, "What disciplinary action have you recommended?"

Lee covered one hand with the other on top of her folio. "A transfer seems appropriate at this point. Kidnapping charges were dropped, pending his cooperation on attempts to undo the atmospheric alteration. I feel that this, in addition to loss of potential copyright of the CFC-breakdown organism, is action enough."

But he *hadn't* cooperated with her investigation, beyond discovering the loss of the suicide gene. Afterward, he'd vanished to some secret lockup.

And Lee said nothing about that sentence the colonists imposed on him for accidental manslaughter. He stood clasping both hammy hands in front of his legs, leaning backward with that maddening me-dominant gleam in his eyes. He was going to go free, the monster!

Taidje FreeLand rose and asked for the floor. "Dr. Hauwk, with due respect, the Lwuite colony of Goddard requests custody of Dr. Varberg."

Ah. The colonists had not forgotten. Graysha folded her hands tightly on the tabletop.

Melantha Lee nodded toward Varberg. "The kidnapping charge has been dropped, Vice-Chair FreeLand."

"I realize that." FreeLand dipped his white head. "But recent evidence suggests that a new charge of attempted murder must be brought against him."

Varberg's confident posture deflated. His mouth gaped, and he looked left, then right.

Lee waved her papers at FreeLand. "Dr. Varberg was cleared of voluntary intent in Dr. Mahera's death, as you'll recall. His punitive debt to Dr. Mahera's family can be worked off elsewhere."

"Your pardon, Dr. Lee," said FreeLand, spreading his hands, "but we must regretfully charge him with attempting to kill former Chair DalLierx."

"What?" Varberg barked. "That's ridiculous. Lee—"

Melantha Lee made a shushing gesture. Varberg closed his mouth. So did a woman near Graysha's feet, whose reaction was emphatically vocal.

Flora Hauwk spread her hands, looking like a queen perched on a cafeteria-chair throne. "I am certain this matter can be settled before we take off, Dr. Varberg. Provisions exist in the Gaea charter for commissions to recommend or drop formal charges. Let us hear, first, about the research in progress to reverse atmospheric changes. By the way—" Raising a hand before Graysha could stand up, Dr. Hauwk turned to Varberg and smiled. "Regardless of other charges, I congratulate you on developing that organism. Well done."

Et tu, Flora Hauwk? Graysha wanted to shout. Varberg rocked back and forth, toes to heels, and dipped his head to Hauwk.

Trev edged away from his father, who snatched the boron papers from Flora Hauwk and stood scanning them. As he did, Trev vanished into the crowd.

Melantha Lee stood in front of them, evidently not seeing Graysha. She peered out over the crowd. "Dr. Brady-Phillips, are you here?" she called.

Graysha pushed up from the table and made her way forward. Her legs felt like lead. *Please,* she muttered silently. *Help!*

Lee presented her to Hauwk and the elder LZalle, adding for Blase's hearing, "Dr. Brady-Phillips has been your son's supervisor. She says his work is commendable."

Blase raised his head from the boron papers. "Trev knows how to work?" His lips twisted sideways, and the expression reminded Graysha so much of Trev that it was uncanny, given their external dissimilarity. Evidently facial gestures were determined by muscles that LZalle's surgeons hadn't altered.

"He does," she said softly. "I've seen him make remarkable progress."

LZalle Senior raised an eyebrow.

Flora Hauwk hitched one arm over the back of her chair and frowned up at Graysha. Up close, she looked older, with nets of fine lines surrounding her mouth and eyes. "As Gaea understands the situation," she said, "the biosphere is about to be ruined."

"There is a chance of that, Dr. Hauwk." Graysha couldn't deny that fact. She cleared her throat. Hardly anyone in the cafeteria moved for the next several minutes as she presented her papers in a voice steadied by several terrannums of teaching experience.

"Nothing has proven effective, though," Melantha Lee interrupted before Graysha finished making her conclusions. "Dr. Brady-Phillips's report does not state this, but virtually all her samples of the mutant organism proved unviable under laboratory conditions. I entertain serious doubts as to whether any laboratory organisms would be fit specimens for antimicrobial trials."

Lee had read the proposal, Graysha realized, and forced a conclusion from the repeated sabotage. So . . . was she not responsible after all?

She had to be. Graysha could think of no other suspect. She took a deep breath, bracing herself to rebut, and as she faced forward again, she noticed a staring face—a woman standing just beyond Flora Hauwk.

Mother!

Her spine seemed to melt. All conclusions, all rebuttals vanished out of her mind. Novia was here, incognito—and her lips twitched in a slight smile of greeting.

This could mean only one thing—a Eugenics investigation was already in progress—and she knew far too much about Lindon and his people.

Had they known Novia was coming? Was that why Ari was elsewhere?

Impossible. Graysha's mind spun like a stalled track-truck. "I'm . . . planning a second sampling trip later this afternoon," she said hurriedly, stalling for time whether or not her statement made logical sense. She had to think of some way to warn Lindon without drawing attention to him. "Dr. Lee graciously offered use of a hovercopter." *Don't look at Novia. Don't look at Lindon.* "It's poss-possible," she stammered, "that the previous batch of organisms was particularly lab sensitive."

"I don't know if that is necessary." Dr. Lee spoke from the other side, and Graysha was glad for the excuse to look well away from Novia. For Goddard's sake, she had to flee Axis and escape her mother. But at the same time, for Goddard's sake, she had to stay, finishing her research. "I feel," Lee said slowly, "that at this point, closure of the Goddard experiment, for reasons of ecological failure, could be appropriate."

A wind of whispers swept the cafeteria. The idea of closure was panic seed. If they recognized Novia, there could be a stampede back toward the cafeteria's fanfold doors.

As a matter of fact, the other offworld "tech" had moved backward into the corridor. To Graysha, he looked as if he were guarding it. If that man wasn't an EB nettech, she'd never met one.

Dr. Hauwk stood up. Graysha backed a few steps away. The floor leading over to her table was so tightly packed that she decided to stand her place. She pressed her palms together to keep her hands from shaking.

Hauwk cleared her throat. "I am authorized to initiate closure if it proves necessary. Consortium finances have necessitated cutbacks during this fiscal annum, and closure of the Goddard project has been suggested all along. Dr. Brady-Phillips, would you show me that growth curve again?"

Graysha handed over the hard copy, then recollected her wits. "I have an inhibition experiment underway, Supervisor Hauwk. I should have results in less than a day. Please don't make a hasty decision." Avoiding Lee's dark stare and any hint of a glance toward Novia, she started worming her way back toward her table, then spotted Jirina—closer to Lindon—and changed direction.

"As I thought," said the system supervisor's voice behind her, and Graysha turned sideways to watch the room's front while pushing toward Jirina. "Interception of the *gaeaii* organism crosses the curve of chlorofluorocarbon destruction at such an early point that raw materials will be a limiting factor."

Before Graysha could challenge Hauwk's obviously foregone conclusion, Lindon stepped forward. Graysha paused, admiring his poise, then pushed closer to Jirina as he started to speak. "Dr. Hauwk, in the same vicinity as the boron source Vice-Chair VandenNeill mentioned, crystalline carbon sources have been discovered. Those raw materials could give us a substantial head start toward restoring the planetary greenhouse.

Admittedly they would not entirely replace depleted chlorofluorocarbons, but are we willing—"

Flora Hauwk dipped her chin and cut him off. "You must understand, sir, that I am asking neither advice nor input from Colonial Affairs. All of you have been allowed to witness this session simply to ensure that you understand precisely how and why Gaea is making its decision."

That explained why they weren't calling for Ari. Reaching the bench beside her friend, Graysha wedged into place and reached toward Jirina's arm.

Hauwk waved a sheaf of papers. "This details what we feel would be the simplest, most economical procedure for relocation of Goddard colonists. We offer you the best we possibly can. Property in Galileo Habitat."

"If this is intended as a rescue, we would prefer to remain on Goddard." Lindon's face went pale against the gray wool, but his voice remained steady. He could have no idea who stood in the doorway. "Have we no freedom, no say in the matter? Abandoning our work, our efforts, and a beautiful world we are making our home—"

"You signed a contract." Blase LZalle crossed his arms. "Your rights and freedoms are spelled out there, and your legal status, too. We investors want the best return for our money, within our own lifetimes. We want to see energy and resources that might be wasted here put to better use. Such as finishing work on Venera."

The chant at the back started again, "Blase, Blase, Blase," but other colonists shushed the youngsters—angrily, this time.

LZalle raised an arm. "Buy my vidis if you want to hear me sing. Quiet down."

"You've been promised a percentage of boron profits already, Mr. LZalle." Lindon spoke quietly, but in the silence following Blase's outburst, Graysha heard every word. "Two percent, I believe, if you'll help with off-world marketing. There's enough wealth in that strike that I think you might find it worth maintaining an investment on Goddard."

"So he said." LZalle turned around, obviously looking for Trev. "I want ten." LZalle looked Lindon up and down, as if trying to decide whether Lindon were worth noticing. "Ten at least, and custody of my son. Where did he go?"

Graysha finally managed to nudge Jirina's arm. "Please," she whispered, "you've got to do me a favor."

"Name it, Blondie." Jirina leaned close, turning her head aside. "These people are pigs."

"Get to Lindon the next time he's off center stage. Tell him that so-called tech in the green pullover is my mother, and she's got EB staff with her. But he mustn't use—"

Jirina's eyes widened to show white all around. "Your mother? The famous—"

"Yes," Graysha hissed. "But he can't use the net for messages. She's sure to have it monitored."

"Oh my. All right, Blondie. Watch this." The long-limbed virologist flowed off their bench like liquid, then edged backward between seated colonists. A woman sprang up from the floor to take Jirina's place on the bench.

"I'm going to read over these contracts," Blase LZalle was saying. "I need an hour. Alone. With Trevarre." He raised his voice. "Trev, this is your only chance, and I think you know what I mean."

"Where are you, Mr. LZalle?" called Flora Hauwk.

Blase spotted Graysha. "Where is he?" he demanded.

Graysha shrugged. Knowing Trev, he might be halfway across the colony by now. Flora Hauwk was speaking softly with Taidje FreeLand and Melantha Lee, both of whom gestured emphatically.

Finally Hauwk spread her hands. "Gentlemen, women, obviously no decision can be reached at this moment. I shall speak with colonial leadership about these alleged new resources. A further announcement will be made later this afternoon, or possibly this evening."

Graysha, eyeing Lindon, saw someone jostle him from behind. His head turned. He backed toward the standing press.

"What is it?" Lindon whispered. "How can I help you, Dr. Suleiman?"

The graceful woman bent close. "Graysha's mother," she whispered. "That tech in the green pullover. Blondie told me to warn you."

Lindon glanced at the "tech" again ... and darkness closed in at the edge of his vision. There was no mistaking that face. All thoughts of asking Flora Hauwk to prosecute Varberg and Lee fled. He had bigger worries. "The Commissioner," he muttered.

"Correct. Graysha says not to use net messages to get word out. It'll be monitored."

"Got it. Thank you." Lindon looked up over his shoulder. The tall virologist's eyes sparkled with mischief. Lindon inclined his head toward the kitchens. "Ari needs to be warned, at the D-group office. I'm going to try signaling her over a vidi link. But would you be willing to slip out the back way?"

Her voice was as rich as strong coffee. "Only because I care for the blond woman, pretty boy. And because she cares for you." Dr. Suleiman melted into the crowd.

Taking deep, slow breaths, he looked aside. Kenn and Taidje were too distant to alert them unnoticed.

Ari's D-group had wired a vidi pickup into this cafeteria weeks ago. He turned to face directly into the lens. *Novia,* he mouthed. *Novia is here.*

Novia tried not to breathe too deeply, and she hoped nasal fatigue would set in soon. She had never smelled such fetid air.

It went against her instincts to let the meeting disperse, with so many of them contained so closely—including most of the local leadership—but as Hauwk said, they must avoid all suspicion until the last possible moment for their own safety's sake.

Graysha's, too. As soon as the colonists knew she was here, the girl's situation would become precarious.

Jambling touched her arm. "Thought you'd like to know," he muttered as they backed together against a concrete wall, "that the word is out."

"That was fast," Novia whispered. "How?"

Jambling tucked a com into one of his pockets. "There's a visual monitor up under the eaves. I just saw it swivel toward you."

Graysha was already in danger, then. "Get to Graysha's room. Get it ready. Then load a copter with those missiles and head north for Port Arbor. While you're en route, I'll talk to my daughter."

As the meeting dispersed, Graysha stayed close to Thaddeus Urbansky. "Gaea station personnel," Melantha Lee called over the hubbub, "back to work, please. I'd recommend you organize your materials and record whatever loose notes you've been keeping on the net. Call it housecleaning."

That sounded to Graysha like the first step of closing up shop. She kept to the crowd's quickly moving left side, pressing forward until someone clutched her arm.

She looked into her mother's face. Her throat constricted.

"Graysha," Novia murmured, shifting her grip to squeeze Graysha's hand, "it's so good to see you. Hush, now. We're safer if you stay quiet." She pulled Graysha deeper into the Gaea housing wing, farther from the colonists. Graysha went along, unable to think of any plan beyond keeping Novia away from Lindon—and praying Ari's D-group would somehow cope. "*So* good to see you." Novia's gushing sounded false. "And it's been so long. How have you been?"

"Up and down." She longed to confront her mother, but she couldn't think of a single probing question. She hated herself for her inability to take the offense. Besides, Novia had probably stripped the med-op database en route to Goddard. She undoubtedly knew about Graysha's recent hospitalization.

"I'm glad to see you already up again," Novia said, confirming her thoughts. "Could we go to your room and talk?"

Graysha's heart thumped like an upside cultivator. Finally she made an effort to assert herself. "I'm awfully busy," she said. "Come up to my lab. It's a good place for a chat. I can show you what I've been doing." Or was that such a good idea?

Novia didn't change direction. Still clutching Graysha's hand, she walked on up the corridor.

Graysha tried feigning stupidity. "It's a shock to see you here, dressed like that. Don't you want the colonists to know you're here?"

"I'm still secret. For the moment," Novia whispered. She was practically running Graysha along, keeping close to the corridor's edge.

Making sure I don't alert anyone? Thank goodness it was too late for that. Lindon would have a chance.

Novia stopped in front of her apartment. Graysha unlocked it and gestured Novia to her single desk chair but didn't close the door. "You've been busy, then?" Graysha asked, sitting down on the bedside. "How is everyone?"

"Busy, yes. Everyone is fine. Your father is as busy as ever. Why haven't you written? Not even a quick note over Gaea net."

"Busy here, too," Graysha murmured cautiously. "I'm sorry." *All right, Mother. What is it you really want?*

"You could at least have written home. After all, I *am* the one who got you this job in the first place." Novia raised her head.

Graysha's blood changed to ice water. "You did?"

Her mother's mouth lost its firm line, and her eyebrows lifted sadly. "We've suspected the Lwuites of genefect healing for several terrannums. As I hoped things would turn out, they would have implanted infective probes in you, and then investigation would have proceeded. As things actually happened, Dr. Varberg precipitated an early move on Gaea's part by demanding passage offworld. Gaea had to send a shuttle. I couldn't delay it."

In that moment, Graysha could have strangled Varberg. Horrified, she seized her mother's hand. "I'm sure you . . . thought you . . . meant the best for me." She imagined herself cut open and displayed before the Eugenics Board. *Exhibit A: Graysha Brady-Phillips.*

Novia squeezed her fingers. "They haven't done it, I assume."

"No. I'm all right, Mother, but this is a shock."

"I'm sorry. I truly tried, Graysha. But now we must get you off Goddard." A smile, a final squeeze, and then Novia dropped her hand. "I'm still surprised you never took the time to send me a few lines."

How much was it safe to say? She hadn't dared write. Even if she'd wanted to, the colonists would've blocked any attempt at contact, seeing that as incriminating evidence that—

That the EB sent her here.

No, God! A second revelation sent her reeling: Ari MaiJidda had been right all along. The Eugenics Board sent her out as a lightning rod, hoping to draw illegal attention.

And they'd succeeded. She knew far too much. She had to get away. She tried to speak calmly. "I hope you'll have enough time to see the plantation while you're here on Goddard. What they've . . . we've accomplished in the last two terrannums is nothing short of remarkable. Do come and see my lab. It's very exciting." She started to stand up.

"No, sit down, sit down. Tell me about the colonists."

The gentle interlude was ending. Novia wanted answers.

Leaning back to stroke Emmer on the pillow, Graysha asked, "What about them?"

Novia's voice soothed, full of calm sympathy. "Whatever it is that you know but you're not reporting," she said with a shrug calculated to minimize tension.

Graysha knew those tactics. Boldly stated, the request negated all Novia's sympathy. She had to distract Novia with some new tidbit of information. She had to buy Lindon—and Ari—time to do whatever they needed to do.

If a D-squad came here for Novia, Graysha probably would go down with her. Would the Lwuites do anything that aggressive?

With Ari MaiJidda in charge? Of course!

Stall, stall. Give Ari a chance. "It appears," she said slowly, "that the work to protect their babies' callosal axons is more important to them than any kind of unified religion." She rambled for several minutes, mixing old data with harmless tidbits of new information and a few pure fabrications. "One of them even took me to a church service," she said, smoothing her hair. Her arm felt stiff. "It was very ordinary."

"CUF?"

"Something a little more antique."

Novia's mouth began to curve upward. "Which colonist?"

Graysha hesitated. Novia's eyes narrowed. "The one," Graysha said, "who brought up the new carbon find."

"Oh yes, DalLierx." Novia scooted her chair closer to Graysha's bed.

"The one who was poisoned. Former colonial chair." She rolled a hand over, indicating Graysha should keep speaking.

She simply stared over Novia's shoulder at the wall hanging. She'd said all she meant to say about Lindon.

The silence stretched thin. Finally Novia pursed her lips. "I see," she said quietly. "There has been a shift of loyalty, hasn't there?"

And how! She couldn't have hoped to outfox Novia or stall the inevitable for long. "I'm sorry, Mother. That happens."

"Particularly when the new object of loyalty is young, widowed, and attractive."

Graysha bristled. "There's far more to it than that." Even as she said it, she wondered once more: *Would* she use him if he gave her the chance?

"That creature is not human," Novia retorted. "Has he touched you?"

Incensed, Graysha curled her hands around her knees. "I am an adult, Mother. That is none of your business."

Novia shook a finger. "You're just chasing something that doesn't look like Ellard. Listen to me. Everything I did, I did for your own good. Your own good, child. I would appreciate a few words of gratitude."

Child? Gratitude? Something snapped inside Graysha, something stretched by Ellard's betrayal and tightened by the months she'd spent planetside, working in an environment she'd thought would prove hostile. "You used me," she exclaimed. "You used me without my knowledge and against my will. I did the best work for Gaea I possibly could have done, regardless of why I was sent here. *I* would appreciate an apology."

"Apology?" Novia sat upright with her hands on her thighs, feet pulled in beneath her, chin jutting forward. "I risked my position trying to get you healed, and you throw it in my face."

Furious, Graysha sprang to her feet and almost lost her balance. Her legs didn't seem to be working right. She looked over her shoulder for something to throw, not at Novia but at the wall behind her—

And spotted a black ball on her desktop's edge. A lethargy field projector!

In that instant, she realized Novia—or her nettech—had already been here, setting a trap. It made sense. Novia had walked straight to the apartment door without hesitating, without letting Graysha lead the way. She knew where to take her.

Graysha's muscles sagged, but before Novia could react, Graysha seized the ball and flung it across the room. It smashed on smooth concrete. "Leave them alone," she cried. "They haven't harmed anyone. And don't you dare use EB tactics on me!"

Novia's eyes widened, and her voice shook as she said, "You're in danger here, Graysha love. Goddard's medical facilities are antiquated. And the Lwuites will want revenge on you for the investigation, even though your part was not played deliberately. Do not trust DalLierx. He has been blocking your letters offworld. You must get offplanet quickly, and I'll see that Gaea lets you out of your contract."

Lindon blocked her letters? No. Not him. "I am no longer your child." Graysha estimated the distance to her open door. Slowed by the lethargy field, she couldn't beat Novia . . . not for another half minute. "You can't order me off Goddard. I'm a professional with work in progress."

"But Goddard's ecosystem is failing. Gaea is ready to pull out."

Abruptly, Graysha remembered Novia's bad knee. She *could* beat her to the door, maybe. And if Novia's nettech wasn't in here with them, she'd sent him elsewhere. What was he up to?

Graysha shifted her feet. "It doesn't have to fail. Melantha Lee may have given up, but I haven't."

"It is far, far too dangerous here." Novia stretched out a hand. "Sweet, you've been influenced by these people. Once you're away from here, you'll see everything more clearly."

A lifetime of waffling, of giving in to Novia's wishes, streaked across Graysha's mind. "Leave me alone. They haven't harmed anyone. Some of them are egotistical and grasping, but you'll find that anywhere. Please. Just . . . go away."

At last, the steel crept into Novia's voice. "It was Palila Lwu's geriatrics work that brought them here, wasn't it?"

Outraged, Graysha gulped for air. That was a trusted secret Novia didn't deserve to know. "The Eugenics Board is a dinosaur," she shouted, "enforcing policies that weren't fair even in 2030. It's a monster with bloody teeth, and I will not feed it one more living, breathing bite."

"Sit down. You have no right—"

Graysha lunged for the door. Before Novia could react, she was through and out, pounding up the hall as quickly as her returning coordination let her run. Her tears blurred the concrete walls as she pounded past.

Novia thought Gaea personnel looked bewildered to hear Goddard would be abandoned as a penal measure. A tall black woman wearing a pink lab coat stepped away from the wall and said, "It's evacuate, whether or not Graysha can patch the greenhouse? We have so much left to do."

Novia spread her hands. Graysha's rejection had knifed her in the heart. She should enjoy this vindication of time and Board money spent, but she could not. "I understand how sudden this must seem. If the colonists had proved innocent, we certainly would have tried to save the project." At the edge of her vision, Melantha Lee did not react to this out-and-out lie. *Good, Melantha.* Evidently this jammed mural-decorated room was her office.

Will Varberg stood glaring, ominously quiet. He really was big and smart enough to be dangerous.

Flora Hauwk cleared her throat. "Each of you will be given personal-choice status as to your next assignment, even priority over current job-holders, with a significant raise in salary, as Gaea's thanks for your efforts and support. Compared with the funds Gaea will save by withdrawing from Goddard, compensating you will be a small budgetary item."

"You're going to abandon these people?" asked a tiny man who clenched a straight-stemmed pipe. Emerson, as she recalled. "Without scientific support? That's murder."

He seemed a kindly soul. Perhaps he might understand what Novia was going through. "No, no. They will remain here only if they choose to stay.

We're simply not going to risk provoking a paramilitary confrontation. We'll make one strike only, against the clinic where their crimes are still being committed."

"So you know about this D-group of theirs." The pipe-smoking man pulled a small woman close to him and laid his arm over her shoulders.

"I am certain the majority will cooperate with evacuation. Remember the German Jews. Life in camps sounded better than death in street riots, so they climbed aboard."

"*Ja*, Frau Hitler," the little man muttered.

Tempted to slap him in a freshly stoked fury, Novia checked herself.

Flora Hauwk pushed up out of the office chair she'd appropriated. "I would suggest packing your personal belongings, plus anything irreplace-able or offworld relevant in your labs. If you must choose, be quick instead of thorough, because, my friends, if we don't get out of Axis quickly, we may find ourselves under siege. We do know about that D-group."

"May I say one thing?" A bearlike man in tweeds waved a hand. "We've got a cold front on its way down from the pole, and the wind will start picking up within an hour or so. Lander flights might be impossible after six or seven tonight."

"You heard Urbansky." Melantha Lee frowned. "It'll take two lander flights to get us all offworld. The first will take off at four-thirty, about an hour from now. Second flight will leave as soon as the lander can return, at about six-thirty. Get packing, gentlemen and women."

"Without a takeoff fast?" someone called.

"If I can survive it, you can," Lee answered. "Shut down or destroy everything on your floors before heading out. We will leave no gifts for the Lwuites. It will be kinder to them if we make it clear they, too, should evacuate."

Novia kept her seat while department heads scattered to implement Lee's orders. Maybe she ought to thank that little Emerson. He'd stopped her from wallowing in self pity. Since she had hoped Graysha would serve as a lightning rod, she couldn't be disappointed by strikes she'd collected.

Where did that girl go?

Melantha Lee remained seated, toying with a penknife, and Supervisor Hauwk shut the door. "The Gaea reward for developing the CFC-destroying organism will have to be withheld, I'm afraid," said Hauwk, "but I think no charges pertaining to that incident will be pressed."

The firm set of Lee's jaw relaxed. "Varberg needs treatment."

Novia had to agree. "He'll get it. Prepare a thorough report en route. We'll see he's helped." Helped, and put away for society's good. Novia pointed at Lee's desk. "May we use your terminal? My next job is to gather the ringleaders and pass sentence."

Lee scooted her chair aside. "Are you investigator, prosecutor, and judge, Commissioner Brady-Phillips?"

The Gaea head had no right to take that accusing tone. "With the distances involved, my judicial authorization is the only practical approach. Hauwk, call them in to the Colonial Affairs office. Lee, would you have a pair of muscular types we could take along? My nettech is headed for Port Arbor." *I should have brought at least two of them.*

Lindon pressed in through his old office door, then took up a position leaning against it. Apparently he was the last to arrive. With his books gone and Ari's abstract art hanging on the wall, the place already felt unfamiliar. Hauwk's summons claimed this would be another public conference regarding the feasibility of continuing atmospheric development.

He didn't believe it.

"Ari," Kenn was saying, "you can't stand up to EB questioning if the woman singles you out. Appoint a temporary Chair, or do something—"

Lindon felt compelled to interrupt, even though it would incriminate him in all their eyes. "Excuse me."

Kenn looked his way.

"Eric LuMori saw Commissioner Brady-Philips with her daughter," he said softly, and the secretary held her recorder toward him. "Evidently taking her into custody. I couldn't get to them." Those short sentences didn't start to cover his desperate attempts to procure a Gaea master key and free Graysha, though it might have been a foolish martyrdom—exposing himself to Commissioner Brady-Phillips when she wanted information.

Ari pressed her hands flat on the desktop. "All right, Lindon. Just how much have you told her, trying to win her over?" Her glare would have melted a wax candle.

"Everything," he said softly.

As he expected, they all drew away. Taidje's reproachful frown cut furrows in his forehead. Ari clenched her hands. "If we get out of this alive, I'm going to have you shot. In fact, I might not wait that long. Excuse me." She reached under the desktop.

Undoubtedly she kept a D-group pistol. He backed toward the door.

Taidje strode between them. "Ari, stop. Think. If Novia hadn't gotten that information from her daughter, she certainly would have had it from you in five minutes or less. You've been spared an interrogation." He glanced at Lindon, then added, "And given a scapegoat. Let's not talk about revenge, but—"

Pressure at his back shoved Lindon away from the door. Ari glared murder.

The door opened, and Dr. Lee strode through. System Supervisor Hauwk followed, with two men he didn't recognize but guessed were functioning as bodyguards. Last, hands thrust into the green tech's pullover that had disguised her—briefly—came Commissioner Novia Brady-Phillips. Her dark-blond hair was almost the same shade as Graysha's, but hard lines surrounded her mouth and crossed her forehead. Limping slightly, she carried a sheaf of papers.

Ari rose.

Yes, Lindon realized, Ari had had a good reason to try and get rid of Graysha. She'd hoped to separate her from him, protecting Henri and Palila Lwu's secrets. But Taidje was right, too. If Lindon told Graysha nothing, Novia simply would have questioned another.

Graysha. *God protect her!*

Melantha Lee stepped forward, her round face as expressionless as if she didn't feel the hostility in the room. She introduced Ari to the Commissioner. Neither woman moved nor spoke at first. The two strange men sidestepped over to stand against the shelves along the room's near side. Lindon spotted a pistol tucked into one man's belt.

"You," said Novia, "have been tampering with the human genome." She laid most of her papers on Ari's desk. "Here is my evidence against you, and Palila Lwu, and the alleged anti-aging genetic complex. You needn't study it for rebuttal. By law, I gathered enough for automatic conviction before I set foot on this planet. And lest you think waylaying me would serve your cause, I left a copy at USSC Copernicus."

"Automatic conviction? Then let's hear the verdict," Ari said through tight jaws.

Novia Brady-Phillips raised the paper she'd kept in hand. "As of fifteen hundred hours, 20 February 2134 Earth-referent, Goddard colony is hereby proscribed by the United Sovereignties and Space Colonies for the crime of mass homogenegineering."

Proscribed. Banned from all contact with USSC entities. His chest ached. Ari didn't flinch. Taidje crossed and clenched his hands. This was it—the fate they'd all dreaded.

Novia raised her chin. "Scientific support staff is withdrawn by USSC order. Colonial property of Lwuite nonhumans is forfeited to Gaea Terraforming Consortium, as partial payment for services rendered and raw materials furnished."

Nonhumans? How could she think that?

"Asteroids in tow will be diverted. Ores already mined—specifically, boron ore—are being loaded into cargo holds as I speak. Commerce with USSC entities is banned. Until you evacuate, shipping to Goddard is outlawed under strict penalties. Outlink satellites enabling offworld communication will be taken away. Legally, all Gaea satellites are Consortium property and will be confiscated as soon as time allows."

She meant to starve them out, blinded—and to make sure no one took pity. Novia flung the paper at Ari. It fluttered toward one edge of the desk, where Ari let it lie, reaching instead for her keyboard. Half a minute later, she raised her head. "She's right," she announced. "They diverted our ore trucks to the spacefield."

"No matter what you are, I would not lie to you," said Novia. "Should you choose to remain on site, we will return a shuttle to evacuate nontransgenic inhabitants of Center, mine out the rest of that ore vein, and lift all remaining light machinery."

"In that case, you'll release Goddard colony of any further monetary liability to Gaea Consortium," Ari said. "That vein probably represents half a generation's debt—reckoned by our generations, Commissioner, not yours."

Supervisor Hauwk stepped out from between her gorillas. "We're discussing an untenable option, though," she said. "I have no wish to abandon fifteen thousand people. Consider your children. Will you starve them, freeze them? Gaea Consortium will take you all, free of charge—think of that expense saved, if you will—to Galileo Habitat and relocate you there. We will save you to stand trial. You have two hours in which to accept that offer. But there will be no compromise. Either you will remain on Goddard, all of you, and die here with your children, or else colonial leadership will evacuate at six-thirty on the second lander load up. The rest of the population will follow as soon as you can institute sufficient organization. I would advise the second alternative. Chair MaiJidda, what do you say?"

Ari's smile was a narrow crescent. "Supervisor, we will take a democratic vote. We have been the first to try for immortality with any real hope of success. We will be remembered as such."

Novia's eyebrows shot up. "You," she said, "will be remembered as common criminals. Good day, Chair MaiJidda." She faced the door. Lindon held it open for her. Hauwk and Lee hurried through, and the bodyguards waited behind.

Novia paused in front of him, glaring, looking him up and down. After several seconds, she spoke over her shoulder to Hauwk's bodyguard. "See that DalLierx straps down for takeoff under guard."

Lindon had to speak. "Commissioner, God defines humanity by its spirit, not its body. Humans come in all physical types. For too many years, each type distrusted all others—"

"Abomination," she muttered, striding out. The guards followed her.

Lindon turned his mind aside from Novia's threat. It was easy to imagine himself singled out for immediate irradiation. "Ari, longevity is one thing. Humanity will never achieve physical immor—"

"Shut up," Ari shouted.

Kenn looked sick, his face pale, hands shaking. "We can't stay, not under those conditions."

Lindon thought hard. Gaea pullout would leave them all the terraforming information already on the Gaea net, a building full of equipment and materials, weathersats, for a while, and the geosynchronous mirrors—but no staff to maintain them. *Could* they take over? Even if Graysha found a solution, who would implement it? "This is a question of freedom," he said softly. "We can live free, here. We can't give up. Wherever we go, we will die eventually. If we accept her conditions—"

"If you don't want to be shot," Ari said, fairly hissing the words, "you'll close your mouth and keep it shut."

Lindon gestured toward the door. "Then let me go. To find Graysha and steal her away from them if possible."

Ari bent toward her desk drawer again. "All we need is for *you* to be questioned! You will stay here until I tell you to do otherwise."

Panting, Graysha staggered into the Gaea building. Its silence spooked her. Always before, there'd been voices, the soft whir of ventilation, and fingers on keyboards. Now she had to turn on lights to find the elevator doors. When she waved at the call panel, nothing happened.

Steady, she told herself. *There's still power. They've just shut things down.* She found a staircase she'd never used, but no stairwell lights. She climbed, groping in darkness. She felt filthy inside. This was a worse betrayal than Ellard's.

My own mother.

And Ari MaiJidda had been right. Greed—and the EB—brought her to Goddard. Her own selfish hope for gene healing, and the promise of extra pay, played into her mother's hands. Now her greed might destroy the lives of fifteen thousand people—possibly even bring about their deaths.

Reaching the fifth floor, she pushed out into a dim hall. Planetary daylight gleamed through depolarized windows.

Did they switch off—or even sabotage—her chilling water baths? She dashed up the hall, digging in her pocket for Kevan's mag key.

The switch was off, but locked down and insulated, the temperature had risen only two degrees. Thankful, she switched it back on. Surely something would survive at cloud temperature and still inhibit *S. gaeaii*'s growth.

The instant she brought her computer back online, its net alert screeched. News of the colony's proscription scrolled past, and the no-win choice Novia gave the colonists. Official notice of Gaea evacuation followed. Gaea personnel were to assemble at the colonists' food co-op, the underground facility closest to the landing field, as quickly as possible. They were not to eat or drink anything until underway. She, personally, was ordered to depart with the first shuttle-lander load, forty-five minutes from now, because of "particular risk of being taken hostage by colonists."

Furious, she seized a hard candy from the jar on her desk and sucked on it. If she could have found more food, she would have eaten it.

She looked back at her lockdown. She might be ever so close to solving the puzzle . . . or light-years away.

It was also possible there was no solution at all.

What do I do? she pleaded. She had all the resources of the Gaea building at her disposal, and no saboteurs to fight—at last!—but no assurance of success.

She couldn't imagine the colonists would submit to evacuation, irradiation, and imprisonment to save themselves and their children from starvation.

Or would they?

Goddard was their home. It had become her home, *her* world, not just her workplace. And those children, too, would be irradiated if Novia had her way.

Well? she prayed again. *Do you care? Are the Lwuites your children or Novia's inhuman abominations?*

She slid up her tailored suit's left sleeve. Tissue oxygen looked good, but it wouldn't always be.

Regardless, she knew she'd made up her mind. If the colonists stayed on, she would, too.

She yanked on her lab coat and got back to work.

Libby JenChee bent her aching knees and passed two boxes of medical equipment down four concrete stairs. The next woman in line grabbed them and passed them farther along. Libby straightened, then reached upward again, working silently in near darkness that intensified everyone's panic. This should have been a joyful occasion, her premarital trip to Port Arbor with Jaq—a homecoming, for she had worked at Port Arbor before moving over to Axis. Instead, the D-group had arrived and demanded everyone's help.

She would do her part. Jaq passed her a carton of small containers, and she sent them on.

Palila Lwu's pool of DNA-infected retroviruses lay safe already in a limestone cavern below Port Arbor Clinic. Those caverns had been chosen as a hiding place ever since landing day. This human chain stretched down four flights of laboriously hewn stairs, and everything that possibly could be saved was being passed down into the caves. On the clinic's other side, groaning elevators shuttled similar loads. Topside, an older group of heterozyg volunteers watched the sky for—

"Here it comes!" she heard. Boxes and cartons came faster. From a distance echoed an amplified bass-heavy voice. "Attention, groundside residents. You have five minutes to leave the Port Arbor Clinic. It will be destroyed in five minutes. Seek shelter. Protect your face and eyes. Five . . ."

As the voice droned on, cartons kept coming, these filled with delicate surgical equipment. Not one person abandoned his or her place.

Her arms ached, her back cramped, and her legs were ready to buckle when she heard the amplified voice again. "Thirty seconds. Take cover if you can hear my voice. Take cover." At last, people started racing downstairs. Each one clutched one last carton. "Come on," Jaq cried as he caught up with her.

Libby dashed with him around one more bend, then fell behind a massive natural wall and covered her face with both arms. Jaq set down a flask and knelt over her, shielding her body with his own.

Blase LZalle sat on Trev's bed. Trapped inside his tiny clean room, Trev perched on the toilet's lid.

"We'll be leaving in forty minutes." His father's voice came through the door, which was jammed shut with everything Trev could find, but couldn't be locked. "You don't need to pack. I have everything you'll need."

Including, Trev guessed, cooperation drugs. He wiped sweat from his forehead. He wouldn't need so much as a change of shorts for transport if Blase meant to keep him harmoniously tranked.

Homing instinct and sheer bad judgment had driven him back here to his private little hole. Blase had arrived almost immediately. Someone on staff, forever condemned in Trev's mind, had given him a master key.

How ironic that he'd hoped Blase would back him. He was taking revenge on Goddard, all right. "Love the hair, Blase. And the new chin, too. Great."

"Next time, I can see I'm going to have to ask for a four-striped nose" came the voice. "What have you been doing? Face it, Trevarre"—Blase's voice became sweet and calculated as he switched on the vocal doubler—

"you have to come out. Gaea personnel are being evacuated."

"You want to get mad at somebody?" Trev called. "Take it out on Gaea, not the colonists. You could get even richer here. They're just going to abandon the place. Think of it—a whole planet!"

"We're leaving. Now. The colonists are, too."

"No!"

"Yes. Some this trip, the rest in a few weeks, once the Eugenics Board can get a transport here."

Trev's stomach curdled.

"Exalted Ms. Novia already called for it, and three more medical teams. You want to come along now, or do you want to go when the colonists do and take a dose of full-body irradiation along the way?"

"Get out of my room." Trev pushed open the door a few centimeters. "Get out of my life. Leave me alone."

"Out of your life? I *gave* you life, boy."

"But it's mine now, mine to live."

"Come home where you belong and we'll forget it was my money you spent on shuttle fare off Earth."

"Mine," Trev cried. "You gave it to me!"

"For surgery," Blase shouted back. Trev could tell his father had reached the end of what little patience he started with.

"You never even missed it. Listen, you'll recoup that much and more from the boron ore, if you come back for it. I'll be your agent, your onsite rep. Nobody here cares what I look like. I'll be legal age in a terrannum and eight months."

Behind Blase's legs, browncloth rippled. *Dutchy*. In an instant, Trev saw a new possibility. "Dutch, wake up. Want a treat?"

The kitten sprang out of hiding and pranced toward him, short tail erect and quivering.

"Cat, huh? Nice healthy one." Blase reached down to pet Dutch.

"I wouldn't do that," Trev said. Dutchy whirled around, snarling out a hiss.

Blase's recoil was Trev's chance. Yanking open the heavy door, he scooped up the kitten and threw him into Blase's face. "Treat, Dutchy, treat," he yelled. Dutchy might bite or follow, but Trev didn't have time to reason it out. He'd spotted a trank gun on his bedcover.

He ran hard, without looking back, until he made it out of Gaea housing into the hub. The absolute-black shadow followed. Choosing a corridor at random, he ran north for it at full speed, scattering knots of Lwuites. He knew of only one door up this corry that opened to him: Ari's greenhouse, left around the first bend.

Left, then right, then two, three, four doors, and he flung himself at the fifth. He dove through and locked it from the inside, not much better off than he'd been before. Blase still had that master key.

But maybe he hadn't seen which door Trev chose. He stood panting, trying to swallow. Maybe, if he was lucky, the master key only opened Gaea housing. He dove onto the pebbled floor behind Ari's lushest ferns.

Ten minutes later, he'd heard no sign of the door opening. His heart slowed down enough to let him think.

Gaea was pulling out. It was going to happen within the hour.

After that, the EB would come for the colonists. Well . . . he wasn't a colonist, and no one was going to shine a radiation torch on him because . . .

That didn't wash, either. He had no ID. The EB would have no reason to believe him if he claimed he was no Lwuite.

They'd have to catch him first, he decided. Ari couldn't afford to turn away D-group volunteers now. She was probably his only chance to claim protection.

Pebbles kneaded his stomach as he crawled to a small com unit he'd seen on her worktable. He tried calling her office but got a busy signal, tried again with the same result, then again, then again. Everyone on site was probably trying to call her.

He rolled away from the table, pulled his knees up against his chest, and clasped his hands around them. His best chance, then, was to lie low right here.

35. SOLITAIRE

Lindon heard wind gust past Ari's window, and the building's concrete corners howled an answer. The First and Second Circles of Axis, Hannes, Center, and Port Arbor, communicating online for fifteen minutes, hadn't reached an agreement on the Brady-Phillips ultimatum nor on Ari's insistence Lindon be charged with collaboration. She still wasn't letting him leave, and some of his friends were shooting hostile looks.

"Chair MaiJidda," said the secretary, "we have another power drain in the Gaea building."

Ari turned aside, frowning at the small desktop speaker. "Then it can't be a line malfunction. What are you reading?"

"Usage on fifth floor. Five outlets active now."

Ari slid her chair aside and typed in a code, then peered at the screen. "This is an inventory of some kind being scrolled. Bacterial, I think." She cocked one eyebrow. "Lindon, it appears your Dr. Brady-Phillips is entering new data, negative reports on the inhibition of *S. gaeaii*. That's our CFC killer, isn't it?"

Kenn walked around the desk and read off the screen. "Why? Lindon..."

"Yes," said Ari, and when she looked up, it was at Lindon. "You told her 'everything,' as you so demurely put it, and we know you for a man of your word. That means the two of you have discussed marriage. Am I correct?"

Lindon felt his cheeks flush. Evidently he still was not a private person. "Yes, but only in general terms."

"Get over there. We don't dare use the net. Get a commitment—now—and then hide her."

This woman, he reminded himself, wanted to be a prophet, a speaker for God Almighty. "No one," he insisted, "has the right to force Graysha to stay here, not in her medical condition. She—"

"I think you could," she said quietly, "with a face like yours. Remember what she wants from us. She'd stay on and help us finish Gaea's work if you asked outright. We'd have a chance of survival if she could fix the CFC layer. It certainly would influence my vote."

"That kind of personal pressure is not fair. There are spiritual issues. She has barely—"

Ari slammed one fist on the desk. "Lack of hostile aggressiveness is one thing. Lack of guts is another. Do you think God wants your daughters to freeze to death or die irradiated in prison? Sarai is emotionally crippled already."

She wanted guts? He shouted, "Why do you want Graysha now? You tried to kill her. Three times. Are you going to try again after she saves us—if she can carry it off?"

"All I want," Ari said in a rising voice, "all I've ever wanted, is to see this colony survive. There was a time when she was a danger to us, through you. Now we're in the worst situation possible, thanks again to you, Judas."

Taidje extended a hand between them. "Lindon, one trained terraformer, no matter how inexperienced, willing to train others, might tip the balance in our favor. She will not be harmed. Correct, Ari?"

Ari continued to stare narrow-eyed. "While you are gone, we will take a preliminary vote on whether to evacuate."

The thought of sending Graysha away with her mother sliced through Lindon's heart—and really, his hopes had not changed. "I'll check in from the Gaea building," he said.

"Be careful," Taidje suggested. "She might not be alone."

Graysha jumped and shifted her grip on a 10-mil tube when Lindon slipped into her lab and shut the door behind him. "Did she hurt you?" he asked urgently. He still wore the elegant short coat, but long dusty smudges marked his fine slacks.

Thank God it wasn't Novia—or Paul! She'd half expected to catch a breath of citrus lab lotion. She set the tube in a rack. "Only where it doesn't show. What are you doing here?"

"I came to ask you the same thing. Graysha, Ari wants to know if you intend to stay here. But I didn't come here as her messenger. Tell me. . . ."

She wanted to hold him again. She wished she'd known him at Einstein—except there, he wouldn't even have spoken to her. "I mean to stay," she said simply, "if you do."

Lindon took a step toward her window and looked out, down toward the barns and crop fields. "To me, Goddard is the choice of hope, and evacuation is despair. I tried to convince them, but I'm not sure how the vote will go. First Circle committee members are probably voting. I'd check in, but I don't dare use the net."

"Of course not." She dropped her second tube of mingled *S. gaeaii* and another strep strain into the spectrophotometer's tube port.

Ari MaiJidda glared up at Kenn VandenNeill. "I don't believe this," she snarled.

"It is ironic." He thumbed the Acknowledge key.

She felt cold, and bitterly cheated. Of the electronically assembled CA committees, eleven First Circle members had voted to stay and eleven to evacuate, with two abstaining. She wanted to fling those numbers at Lindon and drop the weight of fifteen thousand lives like a millstone back on his shoulders, but on that issue, the others had outvoted her. He would not be told that he held the deciding vote until he cast it. Lindon—Lindon alone, after all her maneuvering—would decide the fate of Gaea colony.

"Get me a cup of coffee, someone," she demanded.

Lindon's warm hand closed around Graysha's arm. "I won't ask you to stay for my sake, because the vote could go to evacuate. I can't ask you to share prison. But—"

"Why not?" she interrupted. "I'd be responsible for putting you there. Just like the—"

"If we accept Novia's terms, that will be our decision, not yours. There are twenty-five First Circle members. That spreads out the authority—and the responsibility. It lets each one of us vote our conscience."

"So," she asked, setting down another tube, "why did Ari send you over?"

"Because I'm responsible for the automatic conviction, if anyone is."

That didn't seem to follow. Unless—"Because you were afraid Novia would find out things, from me. Because you told me everything and wanted to—"

"To convince you to marry me. Eventually."

Her breath caught before he spoke the last word. Slightly deflated, she reached for one more tube. "In a couple minutes, we'll eliminate one more possibility. I could set up the entire sequence of 192 cultures for a tech to read, but I don't have a tech anymore. I could leave with Novia now—and I could lobby against EB actions from Copernicus. But Lindon, if you people leave Goddard, that will be . . ." She imagined the hideous effects of full-body irradiation. "You mustn't," she finished weakly.

"The vote will be close, I think. We don't want to watch our children freeze or starve."

"But you don't want to watch them die of a dozen different cancers over the next ten years. That would be even crueler."

He lowered his eyes. "They might suffer one way or the other, or for some reason we don't even foresee. There are no guarantees of an easy life. Only eternity is certain."

Plainly, Lindon—a father of two—was still trying to spare her the pressure of deciding for the whole Lwuite colony. "Did you come over here only because Ari ordered you to?"

He closed his hands around her shoulders. "No! I want a good life for you, Graysha. I can't ask you to give up medical support."

She crossed her arms, laying one hand on each of his. "People do strange things for love. Ask me, not for Ari, and not to soothe your conscience. Do you want to know if I love you?"

His shoulders rose, then gradually dropped. "If the vote goes to stay," he said slowly, "and if you're willing to stay, I'd like you to stay as my wife. Help us survive. Help *me.* But if they decide to evacuate," he added, sliding his hands down to grasp her upper arms, "go away with Novia on that second lander flight and do what you can for us offworld. Please. She already knows everything about us, doesn't she?"

Graysha set down the tube she was holding, acutely aware of Lindon's warm hands on her arms, of the faintly musky smell clinging to his fine clothing and the protectiveness in his voice. "She knew before she got here, Lindon. She didn't even interrogate me."

His eyebrows rose. "What did she do?"

"She tried to save me . . . from you." And this time she strangled her compulsive honesty instead of telling him Novia had meant for her own genetic healing to condemn his people. "I won't leave you to end your life in a prison alone," she added. "Don't ask me to. Don't think so little of me."

He slipped one arm around her waist. "Here, in habitats, or on Earth, we all live in God's hands. There is no safer place."

She pressed to him, crossing her hands behind his back, and he lifted her chin with one hand. Slowly he kissed her, then he pulled back just far enough that his lips brushed hers when he spoke. "Would you marry me, then, either way? If the votes goes to evacuate, I'll probably be the first one on the irradiation table."

"Yes. I will," she said, "either way." She kissed him again, silencing his fear. His hand curled around the back of her head. She grabbed the hair tie off the nape of her neck and flung it away. "I wasn't supposed to have children anyway." She leaned her cheek against his shoulder and tried not to sound bitter. "If I can't have gene-healed children, I'll have none. Let Novia live with a little of the same anguish and emptiness she has caused other people. But you already have a family. Will Bee and Sarai accept me?"

"They already like you."

Pushing away, she glanced over her shoulder at the water bath. Nearly 190 samples remained to be run through Jirina's spectrophotometer. "Tell Chair MaiJidda I'll stay with your people. Here or . . . wherever."

"Can you leave these for a while without ruining them? She'll need to hear it from you."

She hesitated. What difference would an hour make? "Yes. I'll lock down. Since I'm staying for a while one way or the other, it won't make any difference whether we get our readings now or later."

"What if we vote to stay and there's nothing here to kill that organism?"

She didn't want to answer. "Lindon, how will you vote?"

He pulled her against him. "I've prayed over and over for the right desires. I have only one now."

"You want to stay," she guessed.

"I do."

Ari MaiJidda sat erect behind her desk, hands folded on its surface. Graysha read defiance in that posture.

"So you still claim you mean to help us," she said to Graysha. Then she glared at Lindon. "We're staying. By one vote."

Graysha thought Lindon looked a little pale. He'd said he would vote to stay. One vote—his vote, after all—established their course. Their doom, maybe.

She thrust trembling hands into her pockets. "I don't know if you care, Chair MaiJidda, but Commissioner Brady-Phillips learned nothing new from me, except the fact that Lindon and I are close. The conviction was already registered. She only needed physical confirmation. Cheek scrapings, blood samples. You'll eventually hear from the test victims."

MaiJidda did not sound impressed. "There are people who will die because of this decision, Doctor. There is no escaping that."

She felt Lindon's warmth close to her right shoulder. "I'm one of them," she said. "And it won't be long for me, compared with some of your people."

MaiJidda crossed her forearms on the desk. "That's correct."

"I can teach your young people, though. That's a legacy I would like to leave."

The others in Ari's office—Graysha recognized Taidje FreeLand by his shock of white hair—exchanged glances. Ari asked, "What if your present experiment fails?"

What could she do against an unending ice age? "I don't know," she said softly. Outside, the wind gusted again. "I can only promise my best effort, with God's help."

MaiJidda's eyes narrowed. "So, you're one of *them* now."

"Yes. I am."

The CCA scowled. "Congratulations, Lindon."

"Chair MaiJidda," Lindon said, "Graysha is leaving all hope of medical aid. She deserves our promise that we will try to heal her genes, both those she will pass on and those . . . killing her."

"There is no assurance we can do either," Kenn VandenNeill looked pale, standing close to the depolarized window, and Graysha guessed he'd voted to evacuate. "Our access to USSC net is due to shut down immediately, with no medical exceptions, because as the Commissioner put it, this is a 'medical offense.' And it will take months to rebuild Port Arbor Clinic."

Graysha turned toward him, startled.

"Yes, he said rebuild." Ari leaned away from her desk. "Your mother's assistant sent an air-to-ground missile into the facility fifty-five minutes ago. That doesn't change your mind, does it?"

"Not at all. But can your researchers really—"

"Until the Commissioner is offworld," Ari said sharply, "and you still stand here, I will tell you nothing more. I think you can understand, you better than anyone else, our need for security."

"Yes," Graysha whispered.

In the distance, a roar rumbled skyward. Graysha looked out the window and caught a glance of smoke trail.

"First load off," Taidje announced.

"Just a minute," said the secretary at Ari's terminal. "Something just came over the net: 'Alert, Axis Plantation. Dr. Graysha Brady-Phillips did not report to the evacuation station with the rest of Gaea staff. She is believed to have been kidnapped by former Axis Chair DalLierx. Commissioner Brady-Phillips authorizes full pardon and a five—'" the secretary hesitated, then read on, "'five-thousand-maxim reward, payable immediately, for information leading to the apprehension of DalLierx or restoration of Dr. Graysha Brady-Phillips to the Axis co-op within the two-hour period before second lander takeoff at approximately six-thirty. Dr. Brady-Phillips must be unharmed for the reward to be honored.'"

Graysha shook her head. Loose hair flapped against her shoulders. "She still thinks she's trying to save me."

"Lindon," Ari said, glancing at the door, "you'll notice no one's asking for *you* to be unharmed. Get her out of here and get her hidden before I decide to pick up a pardon and a little spending money."

At last, Trev got through to the CA offices. In an instant, he found himself faced with a staggering choice: throw in with the colonists, who were risking everything to stay on, or go home with Blase?

No choice at all. He wasn't afraid of risks, and hunger had never hurt him before.

Gaea was confiscating the boron ore he found. So what? There would be more, and he'd find it. Goddard would need prospectors worse than ever. Maybe Yukio would work with him.

Blase would come back, he guessed, scouting for more and better ores to invest in . . . and hunting Trev in the wild.

A terrannum and eight months, and he'd be legal age. Hiding that long was worth trying. He knew how to kludge, sneak, and pilfer. He'd find a cave. Graysha would help—that is, he assumed she was staying.

He crept back to his hiding place behind Ari's prized ferns. He simply had to lie here and wait for the Gaea lander to ferry its second load away. In two hours, Trevarre Chase-Frisson LZalle would be almost a free man.

He just hoped he'd be able to find Dutchy. That would be one mad little weasel cat.

Graysha hurried, with Lindon, back down the CA building stairs, hardly daring to hope to pass through the corridors unseen by Lwuites hungry for pardon and the proffered reward. She hated to run and hide, but short of demanding an armed escort, she could think of no other way to keep from being dragged on board that lander.

"This way," Lindon said softly when they reached the lowest landing. He opened a narrow door across from the corridor arch. To her surprise, she stepped outdoors onto an unsheltered balcony. Freezing wind whipped her loose hair and stole her breath.

Lindon stripped off his gray wool jacket and draped it over her shoulders. "We're not as likely to be spotted out here, but it won't be safe for long."

"Where are we going?"

"It's a straight shot over the hub to Wastewater."

She glanced up. Nearly at its zenith, Eps Eri shone red through the incoming clouds.

Lindon plunged down metal-grate stairs and waited at the bottom. By the time she reached him, she'd managed to thrust her arms into his jacket. Ragged clouds hurried overhead, chased by the oncoming storm. She scrambled across piles of rubble laid down to protect Axis's residents from ultraviolet radiation, and that reminded her to squint. Ankle-high dwarfalfa stems tugged her feet on the way over one edge of the hub. Lindon avoided the skylight, keeping to its southerly side, and led to a blockhouse not far away.

Once inside the blockhouse, they pounded downstairs. It was a short dash up the empty Gaea corridor to Wastewater. Graysha sank panting onto the pebbled walkway.

"You're getting better," he remarked. "There was a time when running that far would have made you very sick."

"I guess you're right." She caught a breath of fragrant air and listened to warm water trickle down raceways. Lindon fiddled with the door, wedging it shut with one foot.

"Will it lock from inside?" she asked, pulling off his jacket and then her own. Wastewater air seemed stifling after that run outdoors.

"I don't think so—"

Something hit the door from the other side. She scrambled to her feet.

"Hide," he whispered.

"You too." She splashed through the nearest raceway onto a narrow concrete dry strip, behind tall cattails along the wall. Kneeling, she strained to listen.

Low male voices drifted unintelligibly above the water's noise for a minute before Lindon's rose. "It's all right. It's Kevan."

Graysha stood up. Lindon's brawny brother carried a D-group pistol inside his belt. She worked her way cautiously up the raceway and then sat down, pulling off her soaked shoes and stockings. "Good thing it's so warm in here," she said. "I guess I panicked."

"I can understand that." Kevan grinned down at her—way down. He stood half a head taller than Lindon.

"Did someone send you here?" she asked.

"Ari." Lindon frowned. "She sent him to help us, but that worries me. If this was the first place she thought of, we'll have others here soon."

Graysha pursed her lips. "Mother will send the nettech. I know enough about those people to be afraid of them. We'd better go somewhere else. Someplace that wouldn't occur to Ari or my mother."

"Pastor's study?" Kevan suggested.

Lindon nodded. "She probably wouldn't think of that."

"Maybe not." Graysha sat down cross-legged, wishing she could think of some brilliant place of concealment. "But he'll have an infrared snoop scope, and our footprints will show up as warm spots. The less we travel, upside or down, the better."

"Yes," Lindon said reluctantly. "Is there anywhere close?"

"The Gaea building has plenty of little hiding spaces." As soon as she said it, though, she shook her head. "Too likely to be searched." She stared around the wastewater plant, biting her lip. "What time is it?"

Kevan checked his watch. "Five o'clock."

The ExPress relief pilot scurried around the co-op, distributing sickness bags and skin patches, warning Gaea people that this flight—after inadequate fasting—would be less than comfortable. Ignoring him, Novia leaned forward over her table. "Totally destroyed?" she asked.

Jambling smiled back, the satisfaction in his eyes making her nervous. He'd just checked back in. "Not one block left standing on another. It wasn't quite evacuated, either. I got warm spots on the snoop just before I fired."

"That's their worry. I need you to find Graysha."

"I saw your message on the net. Sounds like you'd just as soon have DalLierx iced."

After all Novia had done for Gray—two terrannums of waiting for that opening, careful planning, strings pulled, the risk to her own career . . . Novia hadn't known she could feel such self-righteous anger.

"Kill him if you have to, just to keep him from molesting my daughter. You have an hour and a half, maybe two or three if the weather holds."

"And if I don't find her by then?"

Novia lowered her voice and fingered a rough spot on the table. "Are you afraid of spending a few weeks here?"

"Not at all."

"Good. Then the lander can take off on schedule, ahead of the storm. They'll think you went with me and come out of hiding. Once you catch her, take a secure position—give her a quiet pill, for her own sake—and signal the shuttle. You'll have to protect yourself from them, as well as the weather."

"I can take care of myself. And them," he added. "You should have seen their so-called defenses at Port Arbor."

"You will not harm Graysha." Novia loaded her voice with threat. "Do you understand? I am sending you back out there with only one purpose. To get her safely offworld. To me." Copernicus had excellent euthanasia facilities. Graysha would not suffer.

And then Novia's conscience could rest.

36. DEEP SOUP

Graysha looked back and forth across the raceways, breathing the warm green exhalations of thousands of plants. "If only there were someplace we could hide in here," she lamented. "It's almost warm enough that he'd have trouble using the IR snoop—" Her eyes caught on the huge glass tanks along the south wall. "Wait a minute." Lindon and Kevan followed her up the pebbled raceway.

"Any one of those is big enough to hold two people, even if both of them were Kevan's size." Lindon tapped an algae tank.

"One thing concerns me," she said. "Temperature. It wouldn't take long to die of hypothermia if they were only a few degrees too cold." She examined the sampling panel.

"Well?" Kevan asked.

She turned back around. "No thermometer. Guessing from ambient air temp, they might be a little cool. But that hour and a half until the second lander takeoff is a long time in even slightly cool water."

Lindon looked dubiously at the roiling black sludge in the aeration tanks on his left.

"Yes," she said reluctantly, "they're warmer. But bacteriologically speaking, that is not a good place to be. We'd sink like stones. It's something about the chemistry in there."

Kevan raised an eyebrow. "Good thing we have you along. I would've thought they'd be perfect. Warm, dark . . ."

"Algae," Graysha said, "smells bad enough."

Lindon shook his head ruefully. "I hate to remind you two, but I lost my sense of smell when I was poisoned. This will be worse for Graysha than for me."

"You'd be harder to see in the sludge," Kevan pointed out.

Lindon tilted his chin and grinned up at Kevan. "Do you have it in for me, little brother?"

Graysha shook her head. "Don't even think about it. We've always been taught the sludge tanks are deadly, Kevan."

"I'm willing to try the corridors," Lindon said.

Kevan frowned.

Lindon straightened his gray suit coat over his arm. "Graysha, could we catch anything dangerous from the algae? Would we ruin the colony's water supply?"

"No," she murmured, "on both counts. I can readjust the microbial pops later, just like the raceways out here. The little shrimps living in there don't bite, either." She slipped behind one tall tank for a closer look. Narrow metal service ladders mounted the back of each tank. "If I'm right about tank design, there'll be rungs inside them, too."

In another minute's hurried debate, they finalized a plan. Kevan cut long breathing reeds for each, not to be used unless the nettech actually entered the wastewater plant.

Graysha led up the central ladder, wearing Lindon's wool jacket again, clutching the reeds in one hand. Perched at the top, she caught her balance. "Okay," she said, "these are simple mag clamps holding the lids shut. Don't close them on us, Kevan."

"You can keep your heads above water inside."

"Yes, enough to breathe for a while. But please don't close the clamps. Claustrophobia would finish me."

"We still haven't decided it's warm enough in there." Kevan handed up their shoes and her suit jacket, tied together and weighted with raceway stones.

She lifted the clear glass lid, took a last gulp of clean air, and swept a foot into the water. "It's warm," she said, deeply relieved. "It's actually warm." Frowning, she dropped the knotted bundle into roiling deep green water. "Novia," she groaned, "you owe me for this."

She checked her pants pocket and made sure she still had her lockdown key, then turned and started descending the interior rungs. "It's warm, all right," she said as it lapped at her calves, then her thighs. "Not bad at all," she added for Lindon's sake, then kicked off the rungs and plunged into the soupy water to her shoulders, trying not to breathe deeply. The musky smell was inescapable. She found another rung with one foot and then squeezed aside so Lindon could climb in. "One hand to hold on with, one to hold the reeds. This is going to work, Kevan."

Lindon started down stocking-footed. The water level rose as he descended until less than a quarter meter of air remained under the tank lid.

"Check this." Kevan pointed right and left. "This tank sticks out like three sore thumbs."

"It should drain down to equilibrium." Graysha eyed a thin line of scum that collected on the ladder. "Yes, look. The level's dropping."

"Don't go under unless you have to," Kevan warned. "You lose a lot of body heat through your head."

"And we won't be able to see at all once we're down." Churning water clutched at her loose hair. She shuddered at the slimy touch. "How will we know if it's safe to come up?"

"I'll pat anything I can reach underwater twice if I come for you and you're under. Good luck." Kevan dropped the lid and it thudded home.

Water-borne touches against her arms and legs had to be shrimp grazing on the algae. The smell had vaguely fishy undertones. As Kevan hurried out, the soft hiss of tiny bubbles breaking at the water's surface made Graysha laugh softly.

"What?" Lindon's head appeared to float less than a meter away. Down one of his cheeks, a thin green stripe dribbled.

"Soup." She chuckled again. "Trev would say we're in 'deep soup' now."

Smiling, he pressed her hand on the ladder rung. "Warm enough?"

"Just fine." She checked her watch. She could stand this for an hour and a half, or even a little more.

Clinging to the ladder at her right side, Lindon settled into a brace position and watched the door through the tank's clear wall.

Jambling pulled the IR snoop off his right eye. Down this deserted northerly corridor, he'd followed the lingering infrared signature of two sets of footprints leading to a single door. Only one led away. He disrupted its lock and slowly slid the door open. "Come out," he called, crouching to level his trank gun into a tangle of ferns, "and you won't be harmed."

No one answered. One-handed, he brought the snoop back down. Someone lay along the nearest wall, a clear and easy shot. He took it, counted a slow ten while echoes of the trank gun's *zing* died in his ears, then cautiously walked in to claim his prey.

Novia stroked the tight black ball she'd recognized as Graysha's pet when Jambling sent it up from her room with Paul Ilizarov. She liked that young Russian. He'd admitted a particular distaste for Lindon DalLierx, so when he offered help, she hired him.

Four tables away, across the co-op, Blase LZalle's shouting match with Flora Hauwk—over the share of boron ore he already imagined was his own—made it hard to think. It took the combined efforts of three Gaea men and that tall, strong black woman to hold them apart.

Her com emitted a soft tone. She held it to her ear. "Thought I'd found her," muttered Jambling's voice, "but it's the LZalle kid. He's tranked. Instructions?"

LZalle Senior stomped the floor to emphasize a point. Novia stifled the temptation to gloat. LZalle's money couldn't buy help from Supervisor Hauwk—or the love of his only son. Hauwk had ordered Trevarre bound over to his father, but Novia did not feel compelled to comply.

All this baffled her. Both their children had chosen isolation, hunger, and lingering death on undeveloped regolith, while habitat life was secure and tightly controlled. "Leave him," she grumbled into the com. She went back to stroking the velvety gribien. It calmed her.

Something crashed against the upside stair. The ExPress relief pilot clumped downstairs, slamming the door behind him. "It's getting wild out there," he called. "Sorry, we can't delay. When that lander gets back, we'd better take off. No more waiting."

Blase LZalle froze in position, a red-haired statue carved in black. From across the co-op, Flora Hauwk raised an eyebrow at Novia.

LZalle, Novia reflected, could afford to come back to Goddard on his own. He wouldn't need EB help. She and Hauwk had business to conclude. As the pilot said, *No more waiting*.

But this was her last chance, too. She balled one fist and struck the table. The gribien curled tighter still.

She touched the com's Alert button.

A few seconds later, it said, "Yo."

Novia held the com close to her mouth. "Go to the new Chair. MaiJidda. Find out whatever she knows about Graysha."

He started sending eight minutes later, as all around her Gaea personnel gathered up belongings and started to form a line. "MaiJidda talks very well with a minimum of persuasion," he said. "Graysha has chosen to stay here with the colonists. MaiJidda told her to hide, but there's no love there. I'm on my way to check out the locale she suspects. Take off without me if you have to."

Novia felt her facial muscles go slack. Graysha chose to stay behind, just as she'd feared. She wished DalLierx dead. No—imprisoned, helpless, emasculated.

Her conscience demanded she confess hatred as sinful. It demeaned the holy human organism, flooding her bloodstream with harmful substances.

On second thought, anger felt good.

She'd confess later.

Though the churning water had seemed warm at first, Graysha felt shivery, even sleepy. The rung kept slipping from beneath her feet, but it was her turn to watch the door. Her back ached from twisting around so far.

To pass the time, each had practiced ducking and holding the reed in place, near a rung for concealment. Lindon's dark hair now looked caked with pale green dirt, and it hung lank, dribbling green slime back into the tank. They talked, on and off, comparing their childhoods—her mother's required Sunday morning indoctrinations, set against his family's courageous step of giving all three children solid training and then full spiritual freedom. "I asked to be baptized when I turned eighteen," he said. "It was my first decision as a legal adult." He looked sleepier than she felt, and the dark circles under his eyes had a blue-green cast. He'd admitted staying up all through the previous night.

Graysha shifted her grip on the ladder rung. "Full immersion, I suppose," she said lightly.

"Oh yes."

"Could this count as mine?" She didn't really think so, but she wanted to see him smile.

He did. Beautifully, peacefully. "Probably not."

"Oh well," she whispered, then froze in place. Had the door moved?

Lindon's eyebrows sank. "Down," he whispered, slipping a reed between his lips. He must've seen it, too.

She held the other reed to her mouth, clamped her nostrils shut, and pushed off.

Blind, she groped for lower rungs with one hand and both feet. When she found them—it felt like a long way down—she blessed Kevan for plucking long stems. She breathed as slowly as possible. For some reason, she felt warmer.

Her body wanted to float, especially when she inhaled. Thrusting her arm through a rung from underneath, being careful not to touch the glass, she wedged herself down and started counting slow breaths.

Her right hip pressed against Lindon's left, a solid contact with reality.

The eerie darkness seemed green and stinking through her closed eyes and pinched nostrils.

. . . 75, 76 . . .

. . . 399, 400. The shivering returned. Later, it stopped, and she no longer cared so much about the danger. In water this warm, even she ought to be able to last for hours. Her arm slipped, and she started to float upward.

Jolted awake by terror and loss of coordination, she flailed to catch the elusive rung. If only she still had her hair tie, she might lash one arm to the ladder.

If only they'd chosen the sludge tanks, they would be warm, and there'd be no trouble staying down.

Was she thinking clearly? Weren't sludge tanks fatal?

Lindon's arm bumped her, then curled around her back to grip a rung on her left side, pressing her against the rungs. His closeness eased the clammy chill settling into her flesh and bones.

Count, she reminded herself. She started again, *1, 2, 3 . . .*

Would it do any good to pray? She wished she'd switched hands while she had the chance. Her right palm cramped from holding the reed while thumb and forefinger pinched her nostrils.

. . . 24, 25 . . .

Jambling lowered the snoop again. Several sets of faint footprints criss-crossed between walkways, making it hard to tell how many people had entered Wastewater and how many had left. The corridor was similarly overtracked.

Walking slowly, purposefully, he reexamined each waterway, forward along the concrete, back along the pebbles. His own tracks confused the search. At the back wall, he hurried past bubbling, evil-looking green and black sewage tanks, then peered behind them. Faint telltales of lingering heat ascended one ladder. Here and there were prints, and the right hand-rail barely glowed. Had the climber descended?

Gripping the trank gun left-handed, he peered inside as he mounted. No bright spot inside betrayed evidence of body heat. Perhaps it had been scaled as a vantage point. Cautiously he reached for a magnetic clamp.

Unlatched!

He let himself smile. *Found her, Novia.*

Soundlessly, he lifted all three clamps and levered the lid open.

Movement among the cattails made him freeze. Crouching up here, he was a sitting target.

But he also had a commanding view. Ventilators had kicked on, that was all.

He leaned over the tank and got one good breath.

Retching, he leaped down. The stench was horrible. Unquestionably toxic chemicals boiled away inside, purifying Axis's drinking water. That tank was plainly unsafe for human habitation, and Graysha Brady-Phillips, microbiologist, would know it.

Covering the quivering cattails with his trank gun, he walked one more circuit. MaiJidda had been dead certain they'd be here. He keyed on his com. "It appears," he said softly, "they scouted the facility for hiding places, as MaiJidda expected, but moved on."

"That doesn't feel right," Novia's voice murmured in his ear. "Duck out for a few minutes."

How dare she challenge his judgment? Still, he had to take orders. He holstered his trank gun.

Novia thumbed off the com and pounded her table once more. "That's it," she said to Supervisor Hauwk, "we can't wait. We have to go. I can't believe she did this to me."

"Do you have other children?" Hauwk asked, sympathy softening her voice. Both women pulled on long coats.

"Oh yes. Better educated, more cooperative ones, but that doesn't make up for losing one." Abandoning the black fur ball on a concrete table, she shuffled to the upside stair. Her knee throbbed in rhythm. The co-op was almost empty now.

Blase LZalle paused at the doorway, did something to the side of his throat, then cried in a bass-heavy voice that boomed toward the corry, "I'll be back with help, Trevarre!"

No one mentioned Jambling.

Lindon felt two pats on his shoulder and flung himself upward, pushing Graysha in front of him. Wide-eyed and open-mouthed, she clung to Kevan's hands.

Kevan yanked her out of the water. Balancing her over one shoulder, he descended the outer ladder two rungs at a time.

Lindon came behind. "Graysha, are you all right?"

"Of course," she began, "I . . . what. . . ?" Trying to step away before Kevan set her down on both feet, she stumbled. Lindon lunged to catch her. Her hands tightened on his arms, then relaxed.

Gently, he let her droop onto the walkway. Her ruined suit clung to her body; her hair and face were as green as his hands.

Lindon pushed up her left sleeve. His formerly gray jacket—and her t-o button—were also dark green.

Relieved, he blew out a breath. "I've seen her worse." He knelt down. "At least she's not in pain this time."

"Hypothermia," Kevan said, "bad stuff. Her internal temp could go on dropping for an hour or more. Lie down beside her. Keep her warm. I'll get help. The Gaea people are loading the lander. Final call just went out. But I gotta tell you, the lid to your tank was wide open. Duncan's been watching the co-op door, and that nettech wasn't in the group, and neither was Paul Ilizarov. They're probably still searching. Here's a pistol."

Wide open? He'd heard nothing. Chilled, he took the weapon. "It's come to this?"

"That's why you trained with them." Kevan scowled. "That stuff is disgusting. If the black tanks smell worse than this, you would've died of it." He dashed out.

Gripping the pistol while watching the door, he lay down beside Graysha. Carefully he curled her onto one side to make sure she wouldn't breathe any of the soupy water dripping off her green-gold hair. Then he pressed his knees against the back of her legs and rolled his chest against her back, warming her as well as he could.

He wished he'd slept last night. Lying down made him yawn. He must decide what he would do if the EB man—or Ilizarov—burst back in. There wouldn't be time to think if it happened.

He didn't want to kill or even wound anyone. The nettech would carry esoteric armament, though. Lindon didn't doubt he was marked for death. For Graysha, capture would mean imprisonment . . . at least. Her own people would never trust her again, after she chose to stay here.

Something rumbled in the upside distance, not the erratic gusting of wind but a planet-pounding shuttle lander taking off again. It brought him fully awake.

If there were causes worth dying for, there were causes worth killing for. He must cling to that decision and hope God approved. His next thought was a desperate prayer that he wouldn't need to shoot anyone, even defending Graysha.

Paul Ilizarov might have a rotten core, but he was no habitual killer. The nettech, though, would keep trying to kill him and seize Graysha unless Lindon stopped him. With a targeting priority settled in his mind, Lindon smiled bitterly. So he was capable of considering other men as targets, of deciding what order he would shoot them in if the people he loved were in danger. So much for Henri and Palila Lwu's efforts to protect humanity by rendering it long-lived and nonaggressive.

But could he—

The door flew open. Lindon raised the gun, hoping Kevan had returned.

A stranger's voice called, "Come out, and you won't be harmed." Someone thin and pale-faced crouched in the doorway. Something red hung over one eye.

Jambling wobbled in his firing stance, aghast. What insane overconfidence had made him holster the trank gun and draw his pistol? DalLierx lay with Graysha in front of him, using her as a body shield. He took an extra second to sight on DalLierx's forehead.

That dark eye peering down gunsights was human and alive. For the longest quarter-second of Lindon's life, he hesitated.

God forgive me! He fired before second thoughts killed him.

The pale man crumpled.

Echoes of the blast died away. Graysha groaned, twitched, and then lay still. Footsteps pounded away up the hall. Torn by the urge to chase the other attacker, probably Ilizarov, he clutched her against himself and aimed the gun again.

The nettech lay slumped in a heap, face down and bloody, arms and legs at unnatural angles. Above his body, a faint hazy splatter surrounded a small crater blown into the concrete wall.

D-group training had paid off. His marksmanship was flawless. He'd taken a life.

He started to shake.

Graysha coughed herself awake, flailing for a ladder rung. Her hand caught on something soft. Startled, she opened her eyes. Crystal DalDidier gripped her wrist, loose braids dangling down a pale brown maternity smock. "You made it," she said softly. "You're going to be all right. We'll get you some alfalfa tea with lots of honey. You lie still."

A quick perusal told Graysha she was on someone's apartment bed, under a thick blanket and a dull skylight. Her next good sniff made bile rise in her throat. The essence of Goddard—dead algae and processing chemicals—clung to her hair, clothing, and skin, and oh, her shoulders ached. "What time is it?"

"Nearly nine. Dr. GurEshel diagnosed acute exhaustion and hypothermia, then gave you the biggest hypo I ever saw and said you were free to walk out as soon as you felt up to it. Drink your tea first . . . please? And

Lindon says this is yours." Crystal handed her a tight black ball. "Someone found it at the co-op."

"Emmer!" Graysha cradled the gribien in pale green palms. The steaming cup arrived half a minute later with Crystal's husband, Duncan. "Where's Lindon?" Graysha asked him, then nestled warm little Emmer over her shoulders and sipped as quickly as she could stand the heat.

The curly-haired man frowned. "In the front room. Dr. GurEshel says he's all right, but he hasn't rested, and he's acting like he's not well. He won't tell us what's wrong, either."

Graysha drained the sweet tea and checked her tissue oxygen. If someone else was looking after Lindon, she could spend a few minutes to get warm and clean. "I'll talk to him as soon as I've had a fast bath."

As soon as she'd scoured off the stench, dressed in browncloth coveralls from Crystal's prematernity wardrobe, and settled Emmer on the coveralls' collar, she joined Lindon in the apartment's outer room. To her surprise, he wore a D-group pistol in a belt holster. "What's that for?" she asked.

He looked everywhere but into her eyes. "Paul Ilizarov is still some where downside. Ari put out a call for him to give up, and she announced we'll hold him unharmed for lander pickup, but evidently he hasn't responded yet."

"Paul?" A terrible thought occurred to her. "What about the nettech?"

Lindon looked down, splayed his fingers in his lap, and shook his head

"Did you kill him?" she whispered. She saw now that his hands trembled. She'd heard that sometimes even police officers were excused from duty after killing an assailant, even one who was armed and dangerous. Lindon, with his kind heart, must be in shock. He mustn't be left alone, mustn't be forced to shoot Paul, too. "Will . . . would Duncan walk with us, back up to the Gaea building?"

"Yes. Duncan, and Kevan, and about six others. Graysha, can you forgive me?"

"Forgive you?" She crouched beside his legs, mentally re-creating a scenario she had somehow slept through. "Lindon, he found us. Didn't he?"

Lindon nodded once.

"I *wouldn't* forgive you if you'd let him kill you. Do you understand? If I'd been the conscious one, I would've shot him. Or else I'd've spent the rest of my life despising myself for letting him murder you and drag me back to Novia."

"It did seem," he murmured, "the only thing to do. Still, maybe . . ."

His dark eyes, wide and blinking, had lost their fire. She doubted he even heard her. Suddenly she realized what he really feared. "He'll forgive you, too. I know He will. You were defending me, after all. Thank you.

"Let's get to the lab," she added, gripping his hands. "I've got to get busy."

"Dutchy," Trev called softly. "Dutchdutch, come to Pops. Want a treat? Tre-eat," he repeated. He'd been walking these corries for three hours, cackling like some idiot mother hen.

Just about to give up, he strode around a corner . . . into the clutching arms and leering face of Paul Ilizarov. One hand clamped down over his mouth as the other arm twisted him around with all the strength of the Russian's wide shoulders. Trev glanced down. *Oh chips, another trank gun.*

"They promised me safe passage off the planet," Ilizarov growled in his ear, "but I think I'd better have someone with me to make sure they keep that promise. I'm not stupid enough to trust Ari MaiJidda. Besides, you're wanted offworld. I'm going to retire on your father's reward money. Forward." He pushed Trev ahead of him. "To the CA building."

It was only a trank gun, Trev reminded himself. He'd been tranked once already today. His head felt like someone was squeezing it in an airlock door, but he'd had worse hangovers.

Dutchy bounded up the hall, apricot blond against yellow-tan concrete. "That's my cat," he said, barely turning his head. "He's really tame now. He'll make you a good hostage, too."

"Sure." Ilizarov lowered the trank gun past Trev's shoulders, aiming at the little cat.

He'd overdose Dutch! Trev grabbed for the gun, yanked Ilizarov forward with all his weight, and screamed. Up and down the corridor, metal doors popped open. He saw them as whirling objects as he tumbled with Ilizarov, first on top, then beneath. Dutchy snarled and swiped at them both.

"One . . . two . . . three," he heard. Someone pulled him free from behind and came up with the trank gun. As he struggled to his feet, a second and a third colonist seized Ilizarov. A fourth fended Dutchy off with a broom.

Stinking soup, he'd have to retrain the stupid cat.

All right, Graysha thought, *it's plain enough that you really are there. You saved us at Wastewater. Please don't leave us hanging now.*

She lifted cloudy turquoise tubes one by one from the water bath. "These still aren't ready for a visual exam, but I set the spectrophotometer to quantify certain wavelengths." At least Flora Hauwk's predators hadn't taken away all the Gaea equipment. And though a few Gaea labs looked sabotaged, Jirina had plainly turned up her nose at that order. "If I get a negative reading—any tube where chlorine isn't being liberated—I'll know our culprit died in that tube and that we found an organism that stops it from growing. I ran two specimens before you took me to speak with Ari."

"I see," he murmured, then yawned. "Can I help?"

She waited until his hand dropped from in front of his face. *Not with those shakes.* "That's right," she said, "you people practice job sharing. Would you keep records?"

He crossed his arms on the countertop and rested his chin on them. "Yes. Go ahead."

Out in the hallway, Duncan and several friends sat in pairs, two guarding each bend in the passage. Two more watched the stairs. She reached into the water bath for a random tube. "Number 186," she announced, scooting her pocket memo toward Lindon.

His head, laid sideways on crossed arms, remained still.

Finally asleep . . . and he must need it terribly. She let herself stare at his slanting eyebrows, straight nose, and relaxed lips, finally free to let herself care. She didn't love him just for what he might do for her. Finally that seemed very clear.

She recovered her pocket memo and entered the tube's number, dropping it into the reading port. *Please,* she repeated silently. *You set the standard for being unselfish. This isn't just for me.* Her hand shook, rattling the tube against the port's metal sides. Lindon, genetically predisposed toward nonaggression, had had to kill a man. Thank God he was able to do it. Time and love would heal him. She could give him plenty of the latter.

All our lives are short, compared to forever. Please heal him—heal us both. You were a healer, weren't you?

The image made her smile. How odd, feeling kinship with the very god her mother tried to chain her to for so many years.

No, not the same god. Her mother's god was someone else called by the true God's name.

She hoped it would all seem this clear in the morning.

Graysha spent the next minute resetting temperature levels on incubators and refrigerators. On her reactivated computer, a terse message described Paul's capture. After directing Axis Plantation to truck him to Center for evacuation with the nontransgenic colonists, the Gaea pilot had promptly left orbit and headed for Copernicus.

So Gaea net was still up?

Momentarily, at least! Seizing the opportunity, she typed.

+To Commissioner Brady-Phillips, Supervisor Hauwk, and other officers of Gaea Consortium and the Eugenics Board:

Despite accusations made in my absence, remaining on Goddard is my choice. There was no coercion by any colonist. I hereby resign my position with Gaea Terraforming Consortium and request that wages owed me be credited against Registered Lawsuit #0633451.+

What else, what else? Jirina! A true friend—but they hadn't even said good-bye.

+Jirina, think of me kindly. I'll miss you. Good luck, and thanks. Mother, thank you anyway. Don't worry for me.

Graysha+

She touched the Send key. To her relief, the Acknowledge panel lit.

Clutching a sickness bag in one shaking hand, Novia pressed a hard-copy handed her by ExPress crew against her fold-down tray to steady it. Her knee ached and her stomach lurched with every course correction. EB personnel would doubtless interpret that "thank you anyway" statement correctly. She could face a conspiracy hearing.

She clenched her free hand. Graysha was already dead, really—dead to family, dead to any constructive future.

Perhaps if she took early retirement the EB would not prosecute.

Perhaps she had outlived her usefulness.

Perhaps Graysha was right and the Eugenics Board was a dinosaur no longer relevant to the survival of humankind as a genetic entity.

Blasphemy! Humankind had evolved the ability to change itself into something else. She—and others dedicated to serving the Creator—must stand in the criminals' way.

Groaning, she reopened the sickness bag.

Hours of tedium crawled by. The first wave of the oncoming storm passed over, and a second wave hit. Graysha yawned, which reminded her to check her watch. It was 3:02 A.M., and her fourth to last specimen had finished. Three more cultures and hope would be gone—but she was ready. During the last few hours, she'd made peace with her fears. Whatever happened now, she would be given the strength to face it.

And she would have Lindon.

She walked back out into the lab, mentally preparing herself for the last disappointing moments of her search, and stared at the red-bar reading—then at tube 84, which she'd replaced in its tray.

Negative. Red bar. *S. gaeaii* growth had established but ended. Too sleepy to do anything but keep acting on autopilot, she wondered if she'd inoculated too sparingly. She had done that once as a grad student, years ago.

She ran the backup, tube 83. It, too, scanned negative. She couldn't have missed both tubes.

Nervous energy made her pulse surge. What about the control culture? She ran it. It, too, read negative. The other bacterium, by itself, didn't release free chlorine.

The significance of these readings filtered in through her thick aching skull. This was a solution, another bacterium that inhibited the CFC-killing organisms. This was a chance at life for Bee and Sarai.

Instinct flung her arms toward the ceiling. *Thank you!* she shouted silently. *Thank you!* Hurrying back to the computer, she identified the organism on Varberg's inventory as *Streptomyces bovii*. Geneginecred for soil enrichment, it did not cross-inhibit any of the terraforming soil streps. Rained down on soil, it would be harmless. Possibly even beneficial.

No, wait. She couldn't start inoculating clouds yet. She didn't know if *S. bovii* could survive under cloud-borne conditions. She'd need techs to start growing it in quantity, producing its natural antibiotic. *That* biochemical could be cloud-sprayed immediately—within as little as two circadays if she used all the glassware left in the Gaea building, and if the media kitchen had stock on hand to finish the work, and if Gaea Consortium left them any airworthy planes.

What would she do once the media stocks or airplane fuel ran out? The supply ships might never come again.

The consequences of their decision to stay finally seemed real. Denied tech support, could the colony survive?

Another yawn squeezed her eyes shut while pressing her mouth wide open. Actually, abstract discussions of the future would have to wait. Lindon slept on, black hair dangling over his sleeve, and she couldn't fight the urge to close her own eyes much longer. Outside her window, snow pellets swirled.

She forced herself to keep moving. After inoculating every TSY flask on hand with *S. bovii*, she sheathed her loop dropper and locked down the water bath. When she was finally satisfied she had everything prepped, she checked the time again—4:14. Gently shaking Lindon's shoulder, she murmured, "Hey, Lindon. Hey."

He blinked at her.

"It's after four, and I found a strep that will probably do the job, and you shouldn't be sleeping alone."

He pushed awkwardly off the countertop, arms wobbling. "Found it? How long was I asleep?"

"Not long enough. Lindon, what's the chance your pastor is awake at this hour of the night?"

He stretched, blinked, and stared.

Not that wide awake after all, she decided, amused. "I've got to lie down," she said, "but I don't want Gaea housing to myself. Do you think your pastor might be awake?"

A light of understanding switched on in his eyes. He slipped down off the stool and seized her shoulders. "He's a light sleeper."

"I won't be, tonight—I mean this morning. I'm about ready to fall over."

He kissed the top of her head, which probably took courage. Every time she turned her head, she smelled dead algae.

"Let's not rush things," he said. "We'll rest for now. Our time begins tomorrow."

"Yes." *How ever long that time might be.* She waved off the lights. "Duncan," she called, "let's turn in." With a solemn wink, she silently asked Lindon not to say more, not yet.

The group kept silence all the way down narrow concrete stairs.

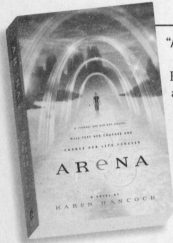